James Wright's *The Kraken Imaginary* is a dynamic, fluid, sexually enlightened romp through a Terry Pratchett-esque world slightly to the left of our own. At the intersection of mythology and fantasy, filled with arresting locations and characters you immediately fall for, the book guides you confidently through a tale of gods and goddesses and the passions of the mortals at the mercy of their whims. Wright's intelligent and heartfelt prose paints a story that is both classic fantasy and relevant to today set in an upbeat and refreshing world where kindness, love, and compassion are the hallmarks of heroes.

W. V. Fitz-Simon,
author of *The Witch of Cheyne Heath* series

The Kraken Imaginary is an immersive adventure that threads in unpredictable ways through tales enlivened by familiar and yet newly imagined myths, monsters, and gods. The story is told from the first-person perspectives of three charming characters as they make their way into and out of a series of surreal events that turns their world, and everything in it, upside down.

Ben Stapp,
musician, composer of the suite
"Imaginary Kraken" and the opera
"Myrrha's Red Book"

James Wright's *The Kraken Imaginary* is a tale of the weirdly wonderful presented in three parts set in distinct locations, delighting the reader with a highly entertaining blend of myth, folklore, and adventure. That said, *The Kraken Imaginary* takes us far beyond the confines of much fantasy literature, providing the reader with deeper considerations on stereotyped gender-based roles and the full spectrum of human sexuality. Beautifully written, erudite, informative, and yet totally accessible, *The Kraken Imaginary* is a breath of fresh air in a genre that too often wallows in obscurity and cliché. None of that here! Thoroughly recommended.

Pete Peru,
author of *The Reeking Hegs*

Wright's description of place and characters immediately captures our attention.... The author sets his thrilling tale in an archaic environment, where the issues of feminism, war, power, and religion are as pervasive as they are today. And then there is the kraken...

Anne Weber,
author of *Constabulary Tales*
and *A Pencil in His Pocket*

Gods, monsters, bacchanals, warriors, and adventure. The Kraken Imaginary stretches past all boundaries to deliver a juicy, edgy quest with unforgettable characters. Prepare to experience magic!

Charis Emanon,
author of *51 Ways To End Your World*

THE
KRAKEN
IMAGINARY

BY
JAMES M. WRIGHT

Montag Press ISBN: 978-1-957010-09-0
Design © 2022 Amit Dey
Montag Press Team:

Cover art: Matt Crane
Author Photo: Susan T. Landry
Music: Ben Stapp
Editor: Charlie Franco
Managing Director: Charlie Franco

A Montag Press Book
www.montagpress.com
Montag Press
777 Morton Street, Unit B
San Francisco CA 94129 USA

Montag Press, the burning book with the hatchet cover, the skewed word mark and the portrayal of the long-suffering fireman mascot are trademarks of Montag Press.

Printed & Digitally Originated in the United States of America
10 9 8 7 6 5 4 3 2 1

CONTENTS

ACKNOWLEDGEMENTS

Thanks to Charlie Franco and the wonderful conglomeration of authors, editors, and staff at Montag Press.

Thanks to Matt Crane for his visionary artwork, his polyrhythmic drums, and his lingo.

Thanks to the Casco Bay Writer's Group for enduring recitations of the work in progress, staying awake, and setting me on a better track.

Thanks to those brave souls who read the work in early stages and offered encouragement and direction: Colleen Chen, Peter Keaveny, Jane Treat.

A special thanks goes to Ben Stapp, a comrade in the trenches of monster love, for his reading, his consultation, his incredible music, and above all, for his enthusiasm.

And without the involvement of Susan T. Landry, an intricate part of every tentacular day, none of this would have swum out from under its rock.

I: LANGUAGE OF THE DEEP

[Corax's Story]

"Actually, he's quite right," I said. "I've heard of that painting. But the subject it illustrates was based on legend, and you know how circumspect we must be in dealing with legends involving natural history. In any case, where monsters are involved, the human imagination is only too ready to go to extremes."

Jules Verne,
Twenty Thousand Leagues Under the Sea

…Plato suggests that if the appetites, those tokens of the soul's materiality, are not successfully mastered, a soul, understood as a man's soul, risks coming back as a woman, and then as a beast.

Judith Butler,
Bodies That Matter: On the Discursive Limits of "Sex"

The discourse of reason, solar and paternal metaphor, will never oust the fantasy structure of the cave completely.

Luce Irigaray,
Speculum of the Other Woman

[1]

I arrived on the Holy Island in foul weather and fractious mood. The crossing from the mainland had taken ten hours in the four-man currach, a crude open boat fashioned from woven sticks and cow hides. For most of the passage, we undulated through deep furrows of the swollen sea, the wind-borne rain infiltrating my wool cloak, working its way under the hood while I tried to level my gut. The crew hoisted the sail and took it down many times, cursing and rowing against the fickle winds, an uncomfortable situation, but common enough for the seafaring traveler. The craft was buoyant, and the crew knew their work. No, my mood was tarnished by the usual: words. Despite the conditions, we talked to pass the time, and under my influence, the talking soon led to argument.

At the rustic dock on the mainland there had been several crews vying for passengers to the island; due to the weather, there were few takers. I picked a hearty-looking bunch and paid handsomely for the voyage, hoping that a bonus would expedite the crossing. Thus, we set off with good cheer. They put me on a small plank between the helmsman and the three men at oars and offered a collegial swig from their drinking gourd. I doubt that I made a good impression when I spewed the vile whiskey into the bottom of the boat, but I cannot tolerate such venom. I prefer to keep my wits, thank you.

I knew that the whiskey was a test of one sort or another. So what? Being an obvious foreigner, I was unlikely to fit in with the local customs anyway. My appearance was considered

3

a sensation in most places that I visited and there was no difference in this backwater. Rather than the unshorn locks and beards of the locals, or the peculiar frontal tonsure of clerics, my skull and chin were smooth as an egg. Above my nose, large like my penis, I wore a pair of goggles with leather frames and reflective lenses, pulled tight so that no part of the eyes could be seen. My cloak and robes, instead of the typical gray or brown, were black and red--bright, proud colors. Underneath lay a body built for cuisine and I yielded to none in my gustatory prowess. If all that failed to grab their attention, I pushed up my sleeves to display the clinking and clanking of copper bangles on my olive-skinned forearms. But no matter where I went, the stares followed. I used it to calibrate a response: the longer they looked, the sharper my sarcasm.

The typical initiation for newcomers to the region, as with every other region I'd visited, involved an anointment with outrageous tales and lies. This started straight away, while we were still rowing out of the harbor. With grave looks and repeated shaking of heads, I was cautioned to keep my extremities inside the gunwales or sure as Old Nick I'd be snatched overboard by the monster kraken. Being a well-worn traveler, I had heard such things before, always delivered with the same obsequious goodwill. My first response was a loud sigh.

"Surely good advice and I thank you for it. But have you, yourself, any of you, ever laid eyes directly on this kraken?"

I looked at them each in turn and saw that they were confused by my challenge. No doubt they were used to passengers who trembled at their bluster. But none would admit to seeing one, so I plunged on.

"Mind you, I have heard tales of them. No end to the tales. Giant beasts with long, snaky tentacles and a savage taste for human flesh, or so the stories tell. They dwell in the deepest ocean yet dine on land mammals; an inconsistency, wouldn't you say? Despite many miles of travel across the seas I have never seen this amazing creature nor met anyone who has. Given the distances required for the beast to commute from the watery depths to the edge of the land every time hunger compels, this seems odd, does it not? And such a massive predator must be constantly hungry. Whales I have seen, vicious sharks and octopi aplenty. But never this kraken, who seems to mimic the whale in size, the shark in appetite, and the octopus in form, a bit of a hodge-podge, wouldn't you say? And you, gentlemen, you are no novices to the sea, that's obvious. Yet you haven't seen it either, or any part washed ashore, that's what you say?"

The forward oarsman stopped his labor long enough to take a long draught from the gourd, then growled, "Bah, what manner of talk is this? The dregs from your hefty bottom, you say?"

The others laughed loudly. I forced a smile to defuse the banter, not wanting to lose any ground. "Now, now, 'tis only a manner of reasoning, following a trail of questions that, sooner or later, may lead us closer to the truth. Bear with me, my fellows. None of us has seen the kraken, so let us inquire further. Perhaps we can determine the reason for this omission."

There was grumbling and muttering until the helmsman, no doubt weighing the worth of relations with a generous customer, replied, "Pay us no mind, traveler. We live on the sea and our talk is salty. Continue to lead us down your trail of questions. But we'll not wish a kraken into being just to prove it to you; I've no desire to see one."

"Very well." I paused to regain my argument. "Would it not be safe to assume that you have seen whales and sharks and even the shy little octopi, not only once but many times?"

The nodding of heads indicated that it was a safe assumption.

"Well then, my friends, how are we to believe a beast that preys on humans yet has never been seen by one? Are we to suppose that all encounters result in instant termination?"

"Your words wind around themselves until all the sense is squeezed out," replied the oarsman nearest me. "Islanders have known the kraken for centuries and none have cause to doubt it. Why, only last week two fishermen, one of them my own cousin, nearly lost their lives in a tussle with a mighty kraken, rising from the deep. 'Twas a close call, but they saw the monster and lived. I need no other proof."

I wiped the annoying rain from my goggles and considered my words carefully. "A dire escapade, surely. And did you see any damage or markings on the boat or injuries to the bodies of these fellows after their harrowing escape?"

Damages were unknown. The lucky survivors, however, had told the story in elaborate detail, many times.

"And were these tellings performed in the public house with great relish and the company of alcohol?"

Indeed, they were.

"Let's put aside the lucky survivors for the moment. None of us were in the boat. This renders our knowledge second-hand, no matter how reliable its sources. Let's confine our inquiry to the direct experience of our own senses, shall we? So, in your years of living on the land and the sea, you must have observed many sorts of creatures, birds and fish and amphibians and mammals and so forth. You may have heard talk about these animals before you saw them, but once you laid eyes on them, you recognized them as flesh and blood inhabitants of the world, isn't that right?"

No one bothered to disagree.

"How many types of creatures, would you say, inhabit this region yet have entirely avoided your keen and experienced eyesight?"

There was a pause and glancing back and forth, perhaps some confusion, followed by mumbling. The helmsman scratched his beard before replying. "Not seen, you say, but real enough, so far as we know?"

"Exactly."

The answers came from the oarsmen, in turns, bow to stern, each answer accompanied by a pass of the whiskey gourd. "Ah, then, there would be the wee folk…"

"and fairies…"

"…and, to be sure, the kraken."

My stomach lurched as the boat rolled and my enthusiasm for the demonstration of logic slackened. Still, retreat was not in my bones. "Well then, three in number. Wee folk, fairies, and, certainly not least, the hungry kraken. I'm impressed that you've never seen these things. How so, given your sharp eyes? You've seen everything else in your world, no? If I don't see, hear, or touch a thing, no matter how insistent the talk about it, I cannot conclude that it's real based on hearsay. I must confirm it with my *own* senses. Otherwise, I remain skeptical. No doubt this is a poor way to live, but it is what I know and how I know it."

The crew leaned into the rowing and were silent. I should have left it there, but once I get going, I can't stop. I've been told it's a character flaw. Who knows, maybe it is?

"Certainly," I continued, "there are many things in the world that I haven't seen yet still seem plausible. However, if I haven't seen them then I don't really know them, either, at least not as facts or truths. And if I don't *know* them, then I don't try to convince myself that I know what I do not. Yet you gentlemen subscribe to a method of knowing things that, actually, you don't. Where is the advantage in that, do you think? I can't imagine. Yet, as always, I am eager to learn the ways of knowing. Will you explain this method?"

There was no answer to this query. It seemed that I had failed to interest them in anything other than the rowing. Finally, the lead oarsman spit into the sea and fixed me with a hard eye. "And do you not believe in God, then? Assuming that your holiness hasn't seen Him in the light of day or touched Him with your own fat finger."

I'd been waiting for this question. It always came up. "I confess that I have *not* seen this god of yours. Have you?"

The conversation deteriorated rapidly. Despite my enthusiasm for probing the foundations of their beliefs, the dialectic produced few answers and a lot of irritation. Citations from the island monks were tossed out as unassailable veracities, especially the proclamations of the abbot, a fearsome monk known as Saint Terminus. None of the crew confessed to a sighting of God himself. Instead, I received references to miracles and fabulous deeds. I proposed that these sanctified accomplishments must be distinguished from the common magic of bards and alchemists. They questioned the relevance. Pressing on, I

proclaimed that neither bardic magic nor lordly miracle proved
to me the existence of invisible beings. I elucidated the logic in
loud detail, ignoring their scowls.

The only merit of this conversation was that it provided
a distraction from the tedium and discomfort of the voyage.
The argument occupied the entire crossing, with numerous
interruptions when the sea demanded the crew's dedicated
attention. Eventually, I thought that they were on the verge
of pitching me overboard to prove the existence of the kraken
once and for all. I opened my mouth to argue against it when
we sighted the island. The crew cheered, redoubled their efforts,
and soon rowed briskly onto the beach. The bow man chucked
my bag on the sand. I barely had time to leap into the shallow
water and flail to shore before they pushed off and rowed away
to their own harbor without a farewell. The rain dripped down
my face as I stood on the beach and watched them go, wondering exactly what I had said.

The remaining daylight dissolved while I slogged up the
beach toward the glow of an inn. The small village offered
several accommodations, I had been told. Wet and peeved, I
decided on the closest shelter. I wanted food, a bed, dry clothes,
and a sound sleep. The trial was scheduled for tomorrow, and
I needed to see the abbot before it started. Thinking about the
abbot and his formidable reputation, I winced at the prospect
of more religious argument. So be it, contention is the fate of
the philosopher.

The sign for the inn swung back and forth in the wind.
"The Holy Cow," it said. A lamp fixed over the sign revealed
an intricate painting of three monks in a currach transporting
a cow across the water. I pushed through the battered door

and found myself in a loud public house, perhaps the same one that provided a forum for the tales of kraken escapades. A few people turned and looked, but most were preoccupied with shouting and singing. The thin woman behind the bar stared at me without a blink. I stepped to the counter and leaned forward, a maneuver that required standing on my toes since the bar was a bit tall for my stature. I could have rested my chin on it if I wanted to play the clown, a role to which I'm not adverse when the mood is right, a rare event. "I'd like a room if you have one, as well as food, if that's not a bother."

"Not a bother, though pardon my curiosity, would you be needing regular food or something else perhaps?" Her arched brow conveyed an unspoken query regarding the human nature of my appetites. I believed that this might be a joke, though her expression was carefully neutral.

"Regular would be best, I think."

"That accords with our offerings. Very well then, one crown per night, in advance. Name?"

"Corax."

"Ah, that's different."

"From The Academy."

"Sure, you *would* be. No matter, as long as the money is real. Call me Ita, that'll serve."

I pulled out five coins and passed them across the counter. I didn't know how long the trial would take, but certainly at least that long. She gave me a key and pointed up the stairs.

The room was small, but it had a bed, a storage trunk, and a window. Rain spattered the panes, warping the view of the darkened town. Lights were few and there was little to see. I changed into dry clothes and returned to the public room, taking the last free table in the corner. Again, I drew a few glances and a nod or two. In some regions, my gnomish appearance was considered bizarre, but I supposed that folks who believed in fairies and krakens would hardly bat an eye at a short, fat, bald scholar with silver-lensed goggles. Besides, it looked as if there were plenty of strangers already in town for the trial, judging from the oddities scattered throughout the crowd. At the far end of the bar were two men, remarkably tall, dressed in vividly colored robes that highlighted their black skin. Five women sat at the table next to me and talked in a huddle while sipping from teacups. They had various lengths of short hair and wore drab clothing--men's trousers and tunics. I liked their bold androgyny, and tried to eavesdrop on the conversation, but they spoke in low tones and whispers. When I could make out a phrase or two, it suggested that the discussion was esoteric, involving terms I had never heard before, such as "gender performativity," "interpellation," or "the body imaginary." Strain as I might, I could make little sense of their discourse.

In another corner I noticed a ruddy, hook-nosed man wearing a black felt hat with a jaunty feather. With studied elegance, he pushed back the brim of his hat and leaned into his chair while propping his feet on another. He had long black hair, a sharp goatee, and wore buckskins. Smoke rings rolled from his mouth between puffs on a long-stemmed pipe. His eyes met my stare, then moved on.

The room buzzed with talk of the trial. The innkeeper brought me a large bowl of lamb stew, setting it under my nose with a grunt. As I inhaled the savory aroma, I felt the saliva loosen. Eagerly, I shoveled in the stew and overheard the bits and pieces of many conversations.

"She's getting a raw deal, I say."

"Yes, but she brought it on herself, the harlot, with her wanton ways."

"And tell me you wouldn't roll over and bare your belly for her if she wanted!"

"She's perverting the word of God, I say! And claiming to be holy all the while!"

"She needs to be locked away before she brings brimstone to us all."

"Well, then, lock me away with her, please!"

"And would you be clamoring for punishment if she was a man? Remember Father Arky!"

"That would be Black Arky, you mean?"

"The same. Shuffled along to another parish, wasn't he? Poof and gone, somebody else's problem, eh?"

"Yes, but men have greater needs, surely you know that."

"She's not a man, she's a succubus. People are saying that she was seen in the midnight company of Old Scratch himself!"

"You can't deny that she's giving a bad name to the bardic order."

"Is that even possible?"

"But I thought she was a monk!"

I fought down the temptation to interject logical quibbles with many of these assertions. Given the amount of alcohol lubricating the proceedings, I recognized that logic would find no welcome here. This time, I held my tongue and used it to slurp the delicious stew while my ears were well educated with gossip. Then I went upstairs and collapsed on the bed, shedding only my shoes.

[2]

I woke up sweaty, in a tangle of covers. Outside the window, heavy overcast pressed the ocean into a monochromatic horizon. Groaning, I rolled out of bed and clumped down to the empty public room, where I found Ita cleaning the tables. She complained about my lateness, and only reluctantly agreed to feed me, then brought the largest breakfast I had ever seen. I grinned at her in thanks. She pursed her lips as if such marvels were commonplace, then shared an observation. "Folks say that you dispute the kraken, that there be no proof."

I studied her features closely, looking for the joke or tease that never seems far from these people, but her face was stone. "Word travels fast, I see. But yes, ma'am, I do dispute, at least until I see one for myself."

"Well, God help you that never comes to pass." She nodded and returned to her usual position behind the counter, avoiding further eye contact with someone like me, clearly a doomed soul.

After stuffing my belly, I waddled along the shore road toward the monastery of St. Terminus. Scattered clusters of people ambled in that direction, presumably early birds trying to get good seats for the trial. I hoped that I would be in time for an audience with Terminus; it was an integral part of my assignment. Perhaps I could have started sooner. However, I hated denying myself the necessary hygiene of sleep, especially after a long journey. And the breakfast had been a phenomenon that demanded full investigation. If self-care and a savory meal compromised the work, then my priorities would spark another debate with the Cynics when I returned to the Academy. So be it. As I walked, I rehearsed potential arguments. Of course, my philosophy studied all phenomena, and nothing was irrelevant, including food, a biological and aesthetic necessity. Yes, something along those lines could be worked into a persuasive rhetoric.

The monastery was less than I expected. I had heard that these monks of the Western Isles were austere, but I wasn't prepared for the humility of the architecture. Quite a contrast to their decadent brethren on the Continent who erected cavernous warehouses of the spirit. As I pulled up the hood of my cloak to ward off the infernal drizzle, I surveyed the monastery and its modest structures, judging that the whole compound might fit inside one of those grandiose continental cathedrals. No matter, large or small, the buildings of this religion always seemed a bit grim. Frankly, I preferred the courtyard of the Academy, where I could lounge all day on sheepskins under the clear light of a constant sun.

Stepping through the monastery gate, I encountered a disarray of stone buildings. A few showed precise masonry with vertical walls, high-peaked gables, and thatched roofs, but most of the buildings were tiny, windowless beehives. These were *clochans*, huts where the monks spent their time in solitary meditation, dwellings so stark that no one who saw them could fail to marvel at the commitment of the inhabitants. I had heard about them from travelers and should have been prepared, but the first sight left me in awe. Here was the rigor of contemplation, a fierce withdrawal, and retreat from the world. Personally, I believed that reason required light, and I chose to do my thinking under the sky with a full palette of the senses. The beehive cloister instead offered a praxis of darkness and interior excavation, a burrowing into the recesses of the soul. Mirthless work, it would seem.

In the middle of the compound, I found a chapel, the largest structure, though hardly bigger than a barn. Limestone gray, it blended into the rest of the monastery and, indeed, the entire island. Under the dull sky, the effect would have been continuously glum, but the ground was covered with brilliant swards of green and clusters of floral explosions. An interesting place for botany, no doubt, if you enjoyed that sort of thing. The monks, apparently uninterested in the beauty of plants, had done their best to dampen the verdant joy by using all the available soil to bury the dead. Bleak headstones were jammed into the ground at each gravesite, as if to defy the horizontal eternity of the deceased.

I walked over to a monk who was digging a hole. I noticed his broad back, the power of his movements, and the impressive size of his well-formed body. Neck-deep, he shoveled at a steady pace, tossing each blade of earth over his shoulder to land neatly on a loose pile. I watched him for a moment, idly admiring the play of his muscles and wondering how he might look lounging naked in a thermal bath.

"Brother," I called, "have you no brother to help?"

He paused and turned, pulling back the hood of his grimy robe before leaning on the shovel with a sigh. He was a young man, with large eyes and a solid jaw. We stared at each other, one oddity to another. Not only his extraordinary stature made him unusual; his tonsure, the one favored by local monks, was downright bizarre. The front of his scalp had been scraped clean in a line from ear to ear. The effect was confounding, as if the owner of the head couldn't decide whether to be bald or hairy and settled for half of each. At least he had the potential to go either way, which I did not. My hair fell out one day, many years ago, and never bothered to replace itself, the side effect of an unfortunate alchemical experiment.

"No sir, there is no help for me," the monk answered. "This is my penance."

"Surely unpleasant, but it looks as if you are nearing completion."

"Oh no, my penance is to dig this same grave from dawn to dusk every day for a fortnight. When it is empty, I must fill it up and dig it out again. Every time a cycle is complete then I am required to eat a scoop of the dirt."

"Eat the dirt, you said?"

"I did. There are worse things to eat. Occasionally I find a worm, which I have learned to welcome for the flavor."

I had heard many things in my travels, but I had not heard that. "Good grief. You have my sympathies. I suppose every scoop of dirt that you eat is one less to shovel, though that's a small boon. If you don't mind the query, what was the deed that placed you in such an early grave?"

"You may ask, but it's my shame to tell."

"I apologize. You need not answer. I'm looking for Saint Terminus."

But the monk had withdrawn in thought and was no longer paying attention. He had a curious blemish on his forehead, oval-shaped, and enhanced by the surrounding bare skin of his tonsure cut. I envied his strength and adaptability, if not his penance. It seemed the waste of a fine young man, though. I decided that the conversation was over and thought to wander off when he looked up at me and delivered a monotone statement as if reading a script: "My name is Brother Diarmuid. I had illicit congress with the *ollamh*, Lady Fedelma, may the Lord curse me for speaking that name with anything other than scorn. My vows are smirched. If I attend to the penance allotted by holy merciful justice, I will be healed. I must return to my prayers of digging. The abbot can be found in the building behind the chapel." And he resumed the digging with devoted energy.

I stroked my chin and wished to talk more, curious about the reference to Fedelma as an "*ollamh*," whatever that was, but Brother Diarmuid bent over his laborious prayers, and it seemed that this was not the time for further questions.

A meandering route around the chaos of graves, walls, and paths soon brought me to the gabled stone building behind the chapel. As I passed the entrance, I noticed that spectators were lining up at the chapel doors, gabbing and gesturing with excitement, no doubt anticipating the entertainment of holy justice.

I knocked on the wooden door of the rectory. It had stopped raining, but that looked temporary. I flipped back my hood, offering the respect and goodwill of a bare head. Of course, the goggles were weird and drew all the attention, but there was nothing I could do about that. Without them, my vision played tricks. A long moment passed before the door swung open and a monk looked through me as if I didn't exist. I waited for him to speak but he only stared. The awkwardness did not bode well. I summoned some cheer and made a countermove. "Greetings! I wish to speak to the Blessed Saint Terminus!"

I heard muttering from within and the monk slowly moved aside to allow entry. Sitting at a table with his hand on a book was a wiry, hawk-faced man in a robe the same gray color as the ubiquitous limestone of the island. If he stretched out on top of one of the numerous rock walls dividing the fields, he would be invisible. He stared coldly at me and did not shift from his seat. I stood like a schoolboy and fidgeted while he completed his inspection. If my mission wasn't so important, I would have unleashed a torrent of pre-emptive sarcasm. Instead, I twiddled my thumbs. Finally, he spoke, in a severe voice that cut open the layers of potential guilt regarding my presence in his sanctum. "From The Academy, I see. Here for the penitential proceedings, yes? Wanting to see how we deal with our own, no doubt, eager for gossip and sensation. Especially in this case, where a woman, of all things, has dared to flaunt the rules and ethics of propriety!"

I cleared my throat. "Yes, your Excellence. Corax, master logician, at your service."

Terminus' left eyebrow elevated at a steady rate until it reached an imposing zenith on his forehead. "And did you have an expectation regarding the character of your service, master logician?"

"An impartial observer, or consultant, or perhaps even judge, if such is needed. I fear to boast in front of an esteemed scholar such as yourself, but The Academy has expressed the utmost confidence in my dialectical surgery -- a proven method of extracting the truth. I would be honored to assume any relevant duty at this trial. At no cost to yourself or your church, your Worship!"

Terminus burst out laughing. "This is rich! No cost, you say? Listen, I don't know how the Academy learned of the proceedings here, but we have no need of a consulting logician, let alone a judge. And a pagan no less, who wandered in, uninvited, from a godforsaken institution a thousand miles away. God himself is the judge! This is not a trial; we already know she's guilty. What will happen here will be a rite of restitution: a review of malfeasance, an ecclesiastical winnowing of shared sins, a thorough public confession, and the assignment of a suitable penance to repair and heal the damage done within our devoted community!"

I was taken aback by Terminus' proclamation. No trial? Apparently, the information passed along to me was inaccurate. The Academy's long-distance communications were always carried by the Rapid Aeronautics Guild, the best available. Messages inscribed on durable parchment were given to a corps of experienced handlers and their network of doughty pigeons. The hallmark was efficiency and timeliness, or your fee was refunded. Rarely did any go astray or fail to deliver; the birds were exemplary. The messages, however, were only as reliable as the original transcription. Sometimes the chance to impart the news inspired more than a little creativity on the part of the scribe. "Aha," I said, fumbling for a rejoinder, "it appears there was a lack of clarity in my information."

Terminus smirked and picked wax out of his ear, casually wiping it on his robe. "There is always lack of clarity absent the Word of God. But perhaps your logic hasn't taken you that far. You know, it's never too late to see the light, philosopher. You may learn something here. Unlike your sanctimonious Academy, in the Realm of God, we don't murder our wrongdoers. You may prefer to forget the fate of your darling founder, but the world has not. Interesting, isn't it, that the charges are the same? Corrupting the public—surely a significant transgression! Yet here you will see real justice, divine justice. The goal is to heal the sinner and the community, not to extract a simplistic revenge like your draught of hemlock. Rather a final solution, wouldn't you say? Nowhere to go from there except down – straight to hell!" Terminus cackled wildly at his joke.

Filled with the momentum of his sermon, he rolled on. "Within our flock, healing is achieved through penance and, yes, punishment, but living penance that feeds the spirit and honors God. We have no reason to defame Creation through the taking of life! The Lord only has that right! But… oh yes, there will be penance, certainly, there will be penance…" He trailed off as if imagining the delights of penance.

I flushed with embarrassment. What he said about the early ways of The Academy was nearly true. The mentor of our founders, a great public intellectual, was sentenced to death for asking too many questions. However, it was the State that provided the trial; the Academy came later, established to prevent future miscarriages. The founders did attend the trial, though. They sat on the benches and wheedled and cringed, leaving a legacy that we couldn't escape, no matter how adamant our repudiation of the verdict. In fact, the underlying element of my mission, and the reason for my journey to the Holy Island, was to ensure that another scholar was not executed. In this case, that scholar might be a woman, as Terminus said, but only blindered nitwits still insisted that women could not contribute to culture. Fedelma was a rarity, a bard of distinction, an original poetic voice whose achievements were known even as far away as The Academy. A person of such merit deserved the chance to practice her craft. It seemed that her life was in no danger if I could take Terminus at his word. However, I wasn't convinced that I could. Clerics had ways of managing their idealistic principles to further mundane concerns.

I decided to press on. "I'm pleased to hear your elucidation on the goals of punishment, surely an enlightened attitude! And you are correct to point to errors in the past. However, to avoid future errors, which I believe are not entirely unknown to your own order, would it not be wise to involve other perspectives as a check on the narrowing vision that so often accompanies runaway enthusiasms?"

"Ha! You philosophers are so full of yourselves, you think you know it all. This is hardly a matter of your concern. This is work to better the soul. Even the founder of your Academy recognized the importance of such endeavor. He was wise enough to understand that the greatest impediment to the progress of the soul is the body, the flaws of the body. Always, always it comes down to this! The flesh is weak, weak! It must be scourged for the soul to fly!"

I looked at Terminus in alarm as he cranked up the shrill volume of his voice. I was getting nowhere. Might as well defend my institution. "Yes, well, what you say about the man who inspired our founders is true enough. But new ways of thinking have evolved and, for the most part, we have moved on to phenomenology."

He looked at me as if I were standing on my head. "And what in Satan's syphilitic sphere is phenomenology?"

I looked at my fingernails, which I noticed were getting long enough to store dirt. "Quite simply, it is the study of reality, your Holiness. It represents the attempt to achieve a direct and primal contact with the world, devoid of the fog of assumption and conjecture. For example, I ask you to consider how much of your knowledge is based on immediate sensory experience? And how much of this knowing is influenced by your preconceptions? Do your preconceptions dictate your perceptions? If we pursue…"

"Enough! Take your heresy elsewhere!" He stood, unbending his angular form with surprising swiftness. He waved at me to depart. "You may watch the proceedings. Learn from them and report that to your Academy."

[3]

I stalked out, irritated that I had let Terminus burrow into my bones. I would have pushed my points harder but being in his territory put me at a disadvantage. It's vexing to argue with someone who has no interest in dialectical reasoning. Of course, it had been a long shot to hope that I could have overseen the judgment itself, but worth a try; it's surprising how often weary adjudicators will defer to the potential of an uninvolved party. However, the wily Terminus understood that I was far from disinterested. And though it seemed as if the righteous Saint, or his God, had no intention of taking her life, I still fretted over the nature of the punishment. The sturdy Brother Diarmuid, shoveling his way to a clean soul, had only been the subject of Fedelma's devilish seductions, which an impartial mind might imagine qualified him for status as a victim. Yet he was sentenced to severe, humiliating labor that was truly idiotic. I couldn't pretend to understand the severity of the transgressions, anyway, because I didn't follow the reasoning behind their ethics, if there was reasoning. It was forbidden for monks to engage in sexual activities, a stricture endorsed by a few religions, and nowhere, to my understanding, practiced with compliance. How such a prohibition was supposed to work for any beast of biology puzzled me. I appreciated that austerity and contemplation were compatible, but surely the flesh must be fed and polished if the animal is to survive the heat of its holy fire.

I walked around to the front of the chapel and joined the throng of spectators seeking entry. The chapel was certainly the largest building on the island, but it wouldn't hold everyone, and it looked like everyone wanted in. I pushed through the crowd, applying pressure up to and perhaps beyond the limits of diplomacy. Most of the pews were filled and people lined the walls and crammed into every open space. The ceiling echoed with chattering, although in hushed tones, creating an odd juxtaposition of church decorum and mob chaos. I heard a hearty voice call out, "Scholar!" It was the pipe-smoking man from last night at the inn, beckoning to me. As I approached, he picked up his feathered hat and indicated a space next to him at the end of the pew.

"We took the liberty of saving you a seat in the hope that you might join us," he said in a silky tone as he clasped my hand. He sat with two women, who, one at a time, leaned over to greet me with smiles and handshakes. The far one, after releasing my hand, began to fiddle with the bangles that had slipped down my sleeve and piled up on the wrist, turning them this way and that, making soft noises in her throat as she reviewed each piece. I was astonished at how casually this was done. Not sure how to respond to such familiarity, I sat in awkward silence.

None of the three were dressed in what I understood to be customary attire for church attendance, a situation that drew attention and some disapproving expressions from the spectators. The man's eyes shone blue in a face defined by stringy hair, a waxed mustache, chiseled goatee, and an outstanding nose. He wore snug trousers with broad vertical stripes of black and purple, topped with a loose-sleeved white blouse and a black velvet jerkin. He grinned and put his arm around both women, giving them a squeeze as he addressed me. "These divine morsels of the feminine," here he paused to put two fingers to his lips and kiss the air, "are my guardian angels."

He nodded at the woman seated next to him. "This is Marianne: do not cross her or she'll knock you on your ass." Marianne was tall and lean, yet more muscular than any woman I had seen this side of myth or mountains. She stared at me impassively through narrow eyes. I didn't dare to breathe during this inspection. Finally, she looked away, dismissing me with a flip of her blond, braided tail. She wore a sleeveless green tunic of tight wool, tan leather pants, and brown stalking boots. Her right arm was decorated with a tattoo that spiraled around her limb and looked to be nothing other than the common notion of a kraken. I noted that every one of Marianne's movements demonstrated an economy of grace, efficiency, and unconcealed strength, like a wolf moved under her skin. I made a silent vow not to cross her, now or ever.

"...and this is Isabeau, the protector of my heart and truly, the heart of the world. A partisan for the cause of Love. But make no mistake, she is the responsible one." The other woman, the one who had inventoried my jewelry, was short and plump with a round face and a wide smile. She had long black hair that swung about her head with a life of its own, concealing and revealing face and neck in a fluid, ever-changing display. Her skirt featured bright horizontal colors as if made for twirling, and scarves of pastel hues were tied about her waist and wrists. Her blouse concealed little, which I tried to ignore, without success.

"And... I am François, a mere poet and vagabond, the least of souls. I trust you have no objections to our company. I'm not certain that the rest of the audience is of the same mind, but life is too short to worry about the obsessions of the dreary. In the end, only God matters, no? Some have said that I have no right to speak of God because I'm a sinner, which I don't deny, but God hasn't taken me yet—though who knows, the day is far from over."

I laughed. However, I was a little nervous sitting next to François and the angels. I have nothing against libertines on principle but in truth I was confused. My sexual curiosity rated very high, my experience low, and I couldn't sort out with any certainty whether I preferred men, women, or something else entirely. Displays of sensual confidence stirred up all my insecurities and I never knew what to do. These three left me flushed, bothered, and fascinated.

"Thank you for the seat as well as the wit. I am Corax, a logician. I represent The Academy."

François lofted an eyebrow. "What brings such a weighty thinker from so far away to this tawdry convocation?" Isabeau laughed while Marianne frowned as he carelessly waved his arm in contempt.

"I might ask the same of a poet. But I am here to help the bard Fedelma, if that's possible. Her fame has reached the halls of the Academy and we have no wish to lose her sharp work to the appetites of institutional dogma."

François scratched his nose with a forefinger, then stroked his goatee while studying my face. Isabeau shifted her hips, twisted, and stretched sideways over Marianne's lap, propping herself on François' legs so that her face was directly in front of mine. This maneuver was accomplished with animal grace and suggested an intriguing level of familiarity with her companions. As if to confirm my musing, Marianne draped her arm around the voluptuous waist of her friend. Isabeau's green eyes seemed to bore through my goggles and left me flustered. With a gulp, I eased backward to gain space. François smiled and stroked Isabeau's cheek with his free hand. "I haven't met this Fedelma," he said, "but my darling Isabeau studied with her and counts her as a friend."

I was happy to seize a topic. "Studied? Truly?"

Isabeau winked at me as if she could read through my twitches. "Oh yes. Two years ago, we spent a long session together at a bardic school on the mother island. Being the only women students, we shared quarters and got to know each other very well. Her poetic skills were keen: she could sing with the birds, alter the weather, summon the deer, that sort of thing. And, I might add, she was a remarkable lover." She flashed me a smile so lascivious that it burned.

Isabeau sat back with a laugh. I quickly changed the subject, remembering one of the questions I had taken away from the encounter with Brother Diarmuid. "Since you know these bardic ways, do you know about this title, the 'ollamh?' Can you explain it to me?"

François and Isabeau began to talk at once, then exchanged quick looks while Marianne smirked. François bowed his head and was silent.

"Yes, the ollamh," Isabeau explained, waving her hands to accompany her nouns and verbs. "A high-ranking bardic mentor. This mentor is a spiritual guide who teaches the deepest secrets of poetry. Not a priest, exactly, more like a professor, though the spirit world occupies much of the instruction. It seems that as one learns to sculpt words into lyrics then many operations of nature are revealed. Magic, for example."

Normally, I would launch a debate regarding the so-called spirit world, but I merely gazed at Isabeau, charmed, ready to believe anything she said. François, however, could contain himself no longer. He lifted his head and started talking as soon as she paused. Marianne slugged him in the shoulder, but he took no notice. "Which brings us to Fedelma, that marvelous poet, who is accused of having seduced some of the lucky few who were able to call her a mentor. Fuck me! As if such things are unknown to these hypocrites."

"Are the charges true, do you think?"

Isabeau answered, "Likely so, though not in the debased way the abbot thinks. Many times, Fedelma said that the path to spiritual enlightenment exists right here on the earth; it moves with the flesh and through the flesh. At the end of that path, one finds that the ecstasies of the body are in no different place than the ecstasies of the spirit. At the bardic school, she thought deeply on these things, and she wanted to work out what it might mean for a practice. We experimented with her ideas in many ways...." Her eyes glistened and stared into the distance; I envied her such poignant memories. She shook her head and again seemed to gaze right through the silver lenses of my goggles. "Anyway, it helped me to believe that love is a truth, perhaps the ultimate truth."

François had more. "These puffed-up God-spewers talk forever of love but in the end, they think it is something separate from the body. For their own God-given flesh, they have only contempt. Incredible!"

I thought of my tradition and its complicated history. The ancient mentor of the Academy argued on and on about the examined life and the purity of the abstract soul, all the while feeding his carnal passion for boys. Such unions were deemed pure because they existed apart from the profane involvement of women. Women were thought to be mired within their bodies, unable to rise above the flesh. Only men could indulge in pleasure and still encompass the abstract ideal -- the soul in its perfect, disembodied state. We had learned much since then, especially regarding the truths of women, but there remained little experience with the dirt and tears of life at The Academy. Our priority remained the thin air of contemplation. No doubt, we also deserved the scorn of François.

Sitting in the chapel with this vibrant, embodied trio of free spirits made me wonder what I had missed in life. As I confessed to the currach crew, there were many things I had not seen. I was just making a point, but it was true. The kraken was a minor omission. For example, I had been touched out of lust but never out of love. I could use a mentor to remedy that lack.

"As if holy sex is something new," François continued, "like a fire that must be stomped out before it spreads! Meanwhile, it's been a common practice elsewhere for thousands of years. One goes to the temple and communes with the god or goddess through a sexual act. *Hierosgamos*, the divine marriage. The rite is at the heart of the earliest religions! These monks can't stand pleasure; I swear they treat it like poison. They're insufferable! You know," and here he lowered his voice slightly, "I killed one once. A priest. I'm proud of it. One less hypocrite cluttering up the world with his fucking bullshit!"

Marianne squeezed Francois' bicep and said in a mocking voice, "Oooh, you're so brave... What a hero! Actually, I heard it was a knife in the back."

Francois' expression grew dark and pinched; he seemed ready to erupt. Instead, he exhaled a burst of laughter. "I allow such talk from very few people, my dear. Luckily, you are one of them. Besides, if I tried anything, you would thrash me." He kissed her hand with exaggerated deference. Marianne's response was a slight curl of the lip, a subtle sneer.

My new companions were a volatile threesome. Before I could query further regarding their history and philosophy, the chapel doors swung shut with a thud and the sound of chanting voices rose, reverberating against the ceiling. Absorbed in the conversation, I hadn't noticed that the chancel had filled with monks standing in rows. Slightly, they swayed back and forth as they sang. The audience scuffed feet, shifted, and fell quiet as all attention turned to the front of the church. I noticed that the first pew contained the same group of five incomprehensible women who had sat next to me in the pub. Even across the crowded church, they seemed tense. After a few minutes of solemn hymns, Saint Terminus strode in and halted at the lectern. Chin elevated, he turned his head, surveying the assembly along the length of his hawkish nose. Clad in plain white robes, he stood out from the others, even without a vestige of shining jewelry. His only adornment was a plain wooden cross hanging from a string around his neck. In one hand he carried a carved wooden staff. I couldn't see the details cut into the wood, but I suspected the complexities of braided knotwork. Terminus lifted the staff and pounded the butt into the stone under his feet, three times. Each blow resounded like a whip. His long fingers curled around the staff, and again I thought of a bird of prey scanning the fields of his domain. His eyes landed on me, and my companions, and I saw the flicker of a frown. He faced the ceiling and spoke, as if to his Lord.

"Today we gather here within the sight of God to restore Balance, to set things Right. As a community, we have humbly dedicated ourselves to the Honor of the Lord and the Eternal Struggle against Sin and Depravity. We all know that this endeavor never ends; the Temptations of Satan are under every rock and in every shadow! Weakness comes to us all, that we know, and when it does, we have a Duty to our Practice. That Duty carries the triune simplicity of Holy Truth. First: identify the Sin. Second: Confess it. Third: accept the Penance required to restore Wholeness and Balance to the community. This is how we live; this is our Mission into the future; this is our Calling. 'Tis the Way of God—blessed be His name!

"Today we convene to provide Witness for Restoration and Healing. One of us has Sinned, broken her Vows, and undermined the Sanctity of our Mission. She will be brought forth to Face the community and she will Confess her Sins before the Assembly. Thus, is the beginning of her Journey toward Forgiveness and our Journey back to Balance. Bring in Fedelma!"

We all craned to see her entrance. A door swung open, and she stepped into the church, a tiny woman in a tattered shift, escorted by a duo of monks. Marianne gasped and Isabeau cried out. "What have they done to her!"

Fedelma's hands were tied behind her back. With a crudely shaved head and a gag in her mouth, she looked wretched. She tried to walk with dignity, but the monks on either side looped their arms through hers, jerking her along until she stood in front of Terminus. He waved his hand and the monks turned her to face the audience. I saw her as porcelain, hardly vigorous enough to merit notoriety, let alone such barbaric treatment. As I studied her, I noticed a translucent quality to her skin and her eyes glowed like gemstones. She had a power in her after all, though I didn't understand it.

Terminus leaned his staff against the lectern, stepped forward, and loomed behind Fedelma. With rough tugs, he untied the gag. He spoke sharply in her ear, heard by all, "Now, now, be good. No fancy words of conjuring. You know what you must do. So do it!"

Fedelma's eyes wandered over the crowd. She appeared haggard and hardened to her plight, though her face softened when she spied Isabeau, who had stopped crying and waved her hand. Astonished, I watched as Isabeau's hand became a clenched fist. Fedelma's eyes glowed red. Was that a response?

Despite the circumstances, I found myself in admiration of this woman. Thin and pale, with delicate features, she resembled a dryad or fairy of the myths. Vulnerability rested on her skin like a flowing garment. No doubt, she provoked desire in many. I felt an unusual yearning in my loins, tempered only by the growing realization that beneath her frail exterior lay a core of energy—magic, I'm sure. Clearly, she was no trifle. No wonder Terminus had gone to such lengths to exert control. Wild thoughts sprang into my head, and I felt summoned to her rescue. Me, who had never done a single, heroic thing. Who was she? A spirit of nature, a messenger from a realm beyond logic? Whoever or whatever she was, poet or magician or goddess, her life must be spared, I was sure of it.

When Fedelma opened her mouth, birdsong accompanied her speech, although I saw no birds. "Good people, so be it," she said. "I must confess. I joined in union, physical conjunctions, with seekers both male and female, using common means of pleasure to merge in spiritual ecstasy. Moreover, I have done these things with those generous enough to call me a teacher. If any feel wronged, I humbly ask your forgiveness."

As Fedelma was talking, I watched the face of Terminus behind her. He had started with a guarded expression, but his face screwed tighter as she talked. She saw none of this and continued. It was a curious confession, devoid of contrition.

"Let us consider scripture: 'When you make the two into one, and when you make the inner as the outer, and the upper as the lower, and when you make male and female into a single one so that the male shall not be male, and the female shall not be female: . . . then you will enter the kingdom.' Many people dispute the meaning of these words, but they are clear enough. The joining of genders in bodies creates a body beyond identity, a transmutation accomplished in the alchemy of ecstasy. Flesh and mind are forged into spirit. Is that not one of the powers of love—the divine union? My intent has been to channel this power for the liberation of our potential. I forced no one. I charmed no one. All came of their own free will, and left, and came back. Together, we found union and honored the Holy Spirit in the *mysterium coniunctionis*."

She began to sing softly, and the peace of a forest grove permeated the chapel,

"Apple tree branches I bring
Where twigs of white silver do cling.
And a song of great love we'll sing…"

"SILENCE!" Terminus broke the spell that Fedelma was weaving as he leaped forward and yanked the gag up over her mouth. Her voice faded in muffled sounds. He signaled to the monks to take her away.

As they grabbed her arms, I stood up, yelling with my best impression of a commanding voice. "WAIT! What travesty is this? You call this divine justice? She's not allowed to speak! Where are the so-called victims to make their complaints? What is the definition of the sin that's charged? And who has been misused in this affair? How can there be healing and balance without a resolution, without a fair hearing of perspectives, without the work of finding the truth? Many questions must be answered first!"

Terminus fixed me with a look of daggers. "You have no place here. Begone!"

That was hardly an argument or an answer, so I carried on. "At the very least, allow me three questions!" Three questions are all that is needed, if skillfully applied, to peel the layers of the irrational.

"Remove him. And get her out of here." Terminus waved at two monks to come forward and deal with me. The cluster of women in the front pew jumped up and started chanting with a martial cadence, "HANDS OFF HER BODY! HANDS OFF HER BODY!" As the two monks ran up the aisle toward my position at the end of the pew, I felt François and Marianne slip past me to face the charge. François held a stiletto loosely, tossing it from hand to hand with expertise, while Marianne stepped in front of him and positioned herself in a peculiar stance, shifting her weight from foot to foot.

"François, no!" I yelled at him, having no desire for blood to be shed on my account. Isabeau pressed against my back, wrapping her arms around my neck and sobbing on my shoulder. Her warm body was troublesome, but I had no time to reflect. I was transfixed by the drama in front of us. The monks veered apart to take on my defenders separately, but when the monk saw the knife, he dropped to a crouch and slowed his advance. The other one ran straight at Marianne, attempting to trample her with his momentum. As the gap closed, she stepped to him, slipped to one side, grabbed his arm, and flipped him completely over. He crashed onto the stones on his back, stunned. The physics was ingenious, and I wondered where she had learned this maneuver. Before the flattened monk could regain his breath and rise, Marianne whirled around in a blur, stretching a leg to deliver a sweeping kick to the back of the knees of the other monk, falling him like a mighty tree.

"Put the fucking knife away, François, somebody could get hurt!" Marianne flashed me a grin as she turned to face the altar, anticipating reinforcements. She radiated the contained energy of combat and I understood completely why I had been warned not to cross her. By that time a dozen or more monks were running up the aisle, rendering the odds less appealing. In the direction of the altar, I still heard the women chanting, but I lost track of their voices as the melee embraced us. The clamor and echoes of clamor filled the chapel. There was scuffling, a lot of grunts and moans around Marianne, but it didn't take long for the monastic surge to bundle us along the aisle and out the front doors. We were shoved *en masse* down the steps. I heard the doors slam shut with a thunderous boom.

[4]

I sprawled across the flagstones at the base of the steps, afraid that any movement would trigger cascades of pain. I lay as still as possible, wishing I'd never come to this stupid island. Like I said, I wasn't hero material. My goggles had gone missing in the melee, and I kept my eyes squeezed shut, forestalling the psychic chaos of my unfiltered vision. I heard Marianne pacing and snarling. François strung together a creative skein of curses. Then someone leaned over me, a woman—Isabeau of course—and cradled her hands under my head.

"On no!" She cried. "Our philosopher, he is dead!" She pressed my face into her bosom and splattered kisses on top of my head. I didn't know if she truly believed that I expired or if she was pretending out of enthusiastic sympathy. Regardless, it was difficult to breathe, and I squirmed.

"Isabeau! You're suffocating the poor man!" François bent next to her, and they helped me to sit up.

I remembered when the goggles were torn from my head during the struggle because that was the point at which I'd been forced to close my eyes. Surely, they had been crushed underfoot. A serious loss, though I did have two pairs stowed at the inn. After past misfortunes, I had learned the value of carrying replacements. My dependence on the visual shield was complete, not only to protect my eyes from the world but to protect the world from my eyes. I was all too aware of the effect on others should they catch even a glimpse of my unique orbs.

Timidly, I raised an eyelid a few degrees. The result was an instant wave of dizziness amidst bursts of raw light and dancing shadows. "Oooh," I groaned and shut the eye. It was a serious disability, this problem with my eyes. What I saw through them was always too intense; images had excessive definition and color as if they were illuminated by an inner sun. Simultaneously, these crystalline outlines trailed curling, smoky auras in constant movement, creating a paradoxical vision of clarity and murk. It left me disoriented and nauseous. As a child I had lived in a kind of blindness, wearing patches to block the light. The family treated me as a helpless burden until I discovered that silver lenses negated the effects. Wearing goggles gave me a strange look, as my peers repeatedly reminded me, but it was a price worth paying to live in the world of sight. Hardly surprising, I should think, that I gravitated toward a philosophy grounded in sensory reasoning.

Groaning with self-pity, I wanted the problem to go away. Usually, this is where I railed against the gods. But even if the gods were real—a matter of dispute—they don't accept blame, nor do they offer help. What were the benefits of belief, after all? I'd yet to receive a convincing response to that question. At least I was with allies. I inhaled slowly, and on the exhalation, opened both eyes.

François and Isabeau gasped, which drew Marianne to cease her pacing and join the tableau. Isabeau's excitement was irrepressible. "Your eyes! They have the triple iris! My god, you know, it's the same with Fedelma."

"What?"

Marianne crouched down for a closer look and drew in her breath with a hiss. "I have heard of this, but never have I seen these eyes!"

François peered into one eye and then the other. "Three concentric circles! Remarkable! The outer iris is blue, the second amber, and the third is a dark brown. A pleasing palette; it's a stunning look. Isabeau, are these the same colors in Fedelma's eyes? Inside the chapel, I couldn't tell."

"Yes, that is the same. Exact."

Meanwhile, I squinted and blinked, desperate to establish visual stability—a hopeless project. "My goggles, can you find them? I can't see without them!"

Marianne trotted around the chapel threshold and returned to say no. François offered consolation. "I, too, lost my fine hat. We left quite abruptly!" He alone snickered at his irony.

As if on cue, the church door opened, and François' hat came sailing out, then my goggles were gently placed outside the entrance by a robed arm before the door closed again. I heard the chunk of a deadbolt. François snatched his hat, dusting it off while clucking his tongue. Marianne jogged to the entrance to retrieve the goggles and handed them to me with a sigh. "I'm sorry, scholar, I hope they may still be useful."

One lens had a spider web of cracks; the other was badly scratched. They would provide a fragmented and distorted view but that was better than none. I slipped them over my head, which also felt scratched and scuffed. "Thank you, Marianne. I do have replacements in my room. These are beyond repair, of course, but they will at least get me to the inn. It's hard to describe my experience without them. I can see, after a fashion, but it is painful and imprecise."

Isabeau wrapped me in her arms and landed another wet kiss on my cheek. I was so surprised that I didn't have time to flinch. "I am pleased that you live, dear philosopher. You were so brave to stand up for my darling Fedelma, I will never forget it! That abbot is a horrid creature, yet you spoke the truth straight to his face! And you, dearest Marianne, and my beautiful François, you fought with such *courage*! Could there be better companions? I think not!"

François bowed low with a sweep of his hat while Marianne put both hands together in front of her chest and tipped her head forward. Isabeau's gratitude and the ease with which she shared it were admirable. I envied those who possessed effortless social grace; they made it look so uncomplicated. "I, too, want to thank all of you for supporting my cause, each in your own way and with singular expertise! It was a proud moment for the forces of reason if all too brief. However, I'm concerned about the situation. I believe it's quite serious. If you share my goal—which is to protect Fedelma—I fear that won't be easy. A rescue is required, an exfiltration, you might call it. I do not trust that abbot."

"Nor I," spat François.

"Nor I." Marianne's voice was cold.

"And I, I love everyone, but I don't love that abbot. How can he justify torture and cruelty? Not part of the creed, not as I understand it." Isabeau shook her head.

"Philosopher, I agree with you. Absolutely. Time to plan a rescue," said François. "The choice requires no effort of thought. On the one hand, is the well-being of a poet. On the other, the pride of a priest. Bah! It is no choice at all. It is life, or it is death, and I will continue to choose life… that is until death finds me out."

Marianne smiled at the broad gestures François used to emphasize his hyperbole. Her statement was simple: "I'm in."

Isabeau helped me stand, then absently stroked my arm with her hands. With each caress, her expression showed more resolve. "Oh yes, it is time for action! And it seems that we're now a team of four. But we do need a plan, preferably one with a likelihood of success." She put her hands on her hips and cocked them to one side, adopting a look of haughty sarcasm. "Most fortunate that we've recruited a Master of Thought and I do not have to do all the thinking, eh?"

Together, we smiled and laughed at Isabeau. More than anything else, this laughter formalized the founding of our conspiracy. I tried to remember the last time that I had even so much as chuckled during a mission. Usually, I work alone and stay aloof, which is hardly conducive to social pleasures. "I'm glad you saved me a seat, then," I said. "Well met, indeed! I propose that we return to the inn and indulge in the excellent cuisine while we discuss our options. One of the benefits of representing the Academy is that I've been given a generous fund and, if I may, I should like to secure food and drink for us all." None said a word against this idea. "But before we leave this troublesome place, I'd like to consult with someone I met earlier. I think that he may have useful information."

They agreed, so I led them to Brother Diarmuid. As we threaded our meanders around the cemetery, a question for Isabeau bloomed in my head. When I stopped suddenly and turned to ask her, she followed close in my steps and we nearly collided. She grabbed my arm for balance while I blurted out the query. "But Isabeau, if Fedelma's eyes are the same as mine, how does she manage without filter lenses? I can't believe that her vision is calm if she sees what I see!"

Isabeau relinquished her grip but did not step back, teasing me with her breath as we stared face to face. I tried to shift away. She smiled at my all-too-obvious discomfort and answered the question. "I don't know how to explain that, philosopher. Fedelma didn't mention any difficulties with eyesight. Certainly, I never heard her describe the problem that you have. I imagine that you will have to ask her yourself. Let's hope that you get the chance."

As we approached, we could see the burly monk at his labors. He shoveled with the steady energy of a draft animal, scooping and flinging earth from the grave in dedicated repetition. He was only a foot down into the latest cycle of digging. Once again, I thought that he had received a punishment of perverse design—entirely diabolical, in fact. The sense of it eluded me. "Hail, Brother Diarmuid!" I called to him.

"Oh," he said, without lifting his head. "Did you find the abbot?"

"Yes, I did. Not that much came of it. He struck me as a rather sour individual, little inclined toward discourse. I then met up with these folks in the chapel, where we witnessed a bizarre public shaming of your mentor. I have no idea how it ended, as we were ejected, rather roughly, by a phalanx of your brethren."

"Oh," he repeated, as he shoveled on. "And the Lady Fedelma?"

"I'm sorry to report that she didn't look well. They've not been kind to her. She tried to address the assembly, but her speech was truncated by your Abbott, who then had her bound, gagged, and forcibly hauled out of the church. Apparently, her confession deviated from his expectations."

Diarmuid stopped digging. He slowly stood to his full height, dropping the shovel to the dirt. His hands hung limp. "What? What did you say?" His face, a mask of wood so far, sagged in despair. He gazed without focus across the sward of graves and into the distance, as if projecting his soul away from the island. We exchanged awkward looks while we tried not to gawk at his distress. Eventually, his eyes returned to the immediate surroundings and then to us, as if seeing our faces for the first time. "I don't know what you want with me. Who are you, anyway? Why do you disturb my labors?"

I blushed. I hadn't introduced myself at our first meeting, merely pestered him with questions and sarcasm, my usual approach to conversation. I apologized for my oversight and provided proper introductions. Diarmuid bowed his hands in prayer at each of us as we were named. I said we were partisans for Fedelma and narrated a full account of the events at the chapel.

By the time I finished, I thought Diarmuid was going to weep. He rubbed his grubby palms over his forehead and temples and looked at us with wild desperation, a hulk of a man in tattered robes. I could think of no consolation and his hands dropped to his sides where they opened and closed without purpose.

"Ahhh. Well. 'Tis a sad day, then, isn't it?" With that, the tears flowed, descending his cheeks like water seeping from a cliff. Isabeau leaped into the hole and grabbed him in a powerful hug, a touching image, if somewhat comic, since the top of her head barely reached his chest. He returned the hug, smudging her clothes with the dirty prints of his large hands. I saw that we were all affected by the spectacle of this open-hearted monk. François strung together a line of muttered curses. Marianne stamped her foot twice, then began picking up pebbles and hurling them across the wall into the weeds. I didn't know what to do, but it occurred to me that Diarmuid might be an ally for our plans.

"Monk," I said, "I think we share your sadness. We didn't come here to suffer in solidarity, though. Perhaps you can help us. Do you have an idea of what the abbot will do next?"

Diarmuid and Isabeau released their embrace. He grabbed her waist and lifted her out of the hole as if she were a child. "Ohhh…," she said and ran to François, who was slashing furiously at the air with an imaginary blade. She clasped him and stood on her toes to kiss his cheeks. He ceased his martial spasms and succumbed to her nuzzling.

The monk wiped his hands on his robe before answering. "Well, Master Corax, I can't say with certainty. I believe that the abbot wanted the Lady sequestered within a *clochan* for a month of fasting and prayer. But his notion of penance appears to have gone beyond that. I do not understand the shaving of her head… Those shiny red locks were the grace and glory of God, I say. The abbot is a righteous man, praise the Lord, but he does not abide defiance. And his temper is a force of nature, to be sure. As for the binding and the gagging, I am dismayed. She's a peaceful soul, and as you saw, a wee lamb, hardly big enough to hurt a fly." He paused and thought some more. "I do believe that the abbot is afraid of her. It's her skill with words. She can be very persuasive."

Isabeau nodded at this, but François fumed. "Fasting for a month? Is that not a death sentence?"

Diarmuid shook his head. "Not necessarily. Water is allowed, which does help. Such an extreme fast is done from time to time when a soul wants to ascend far into the realm of the holy spirit. Those who approach God in this way are given many visions. But the price they pay is high. Some recover, in time. Some fall into lingering sickness that ends at the cemetery and the permanent embrace of God, bless their souls. The extreme fast has always been a practice chosen by the seeker, never assigned as penance. Oh, a week of fasting and prayer is not unusual, but this…"

François extricated himself from Isabeau's hug and spit in the direction of the chapel. "Give me ten men with swords and we end this now!"

Marianne leaned up against a gravestone and picked at her fingernails. "That would be ten more swords than we have. There is also the math problem of the men. Of course, we do have two women, which some would say is at least as good."

Diarmuid watched this exchange closely. "I cannot endorse any inclinations toward violence; I am a man of God. However, … I can tell you where Lady Fedelma has been held and where it's likely she'll be placed for this sequester."

"Tell us, please!" I urged. He nodded and pointed up the hill behind the monastery. "If one follows the wall here to its corner, then turns to the left, about halfway up the hill just inside the wall there is a tiny *clochan*. I say no more. Now, I must return to my penance. There's much digging to do. I thank you for your words and you, my Lady, the kindness of your touch. God bless your work in this world, and may we meet again."

After that blessing, Diarmuid picked up the shovel and resumed his labor. We wished him well and walked away. It was hard to know what to do next, but at least we knew where to find Fedelma. A geography of escape had to start somewhere. We strolled in silence down the road, four abreast, breathing easier the further we got from the monastery. François finally broke through the ruminations. "Watching the hard work of others makes me hungry and thirsty. Scholar, I would be glad to accept your offer of sustenance. We can plot our next step as we walk, but speaking for myself, I always think best with good food and a flagon of wine!"

[5]

We sauntered four abreast along the road to the village, devising and abandoning various schemes as we walked. These ideas were more expressive than practical, often involving assets that we didn't have and couldn't get. My companions fell into a sustained hysteria that puzzled me, giggling, and encouraging each other's excesses of imagination. "Ten men with swords" became "ten women with whips" or even "ten wolves with teeth." Further absurdities included the arrival of a battalion of troops under our command, a royal decree sending Terminus into exile, a boatload of sympathetic pirates, or a squadron of griffons to fly us away to *Tír na nÓg*, the land of eternal youth. I made a fool of myself by taking these sentiments seriously, interjecting critical questions at each suggestion until they howled and slapped their knees, at which point I would realize my error and shut up, a situation I could never maintain for long.

Arriving at The Holy Cow, I halted under the sign. It hung listless, dripping rain from the latest heavenly flood. It seemed to be the same sign I'd seen in the night, yet different. The engraved drawing of the currach carrying several monks and a cow across the waves was just as I remembered, but also in the picture, directly in front of the prow of the boat, I now noticed long tentacles extending above the surface of the water and hovering, as if reaching for the cow. I didn't remember seeing tentacles. Of course, it was late, raining, and I was irritated. Still, the full image implied a great drama. How had I missed it?

The others stood with me in silence as the rain increased its tempo. Along the way, Isabeau had produced a shawl from somewhere and wrapped it ingeniously around her head and shoulders, though it was soaked through by this time. I stayed dry under the hood of my robe, and François' hat shed most of the rain above his neck, but Marianne stood sleek and unperturbed. Diversely anointed, we ignored the rainfall, a necessary strategy to avoid going mad in this region. I brought my eyes down to their faces and saw that Marianne studied me with an arched brow. "Is there something about the sign that plunges you into thought, philosopher?" I couldn't miss the trace of sarcasm.

"Yes, it does. I believe that I am seeing it, as a whole, for the first time, having missed key elements before. The image is perplexing; I cannot fathom its significance."

One side of her mouth curled. "I suppose there's a limit to everyone's knowledge, even that of a philosopher. Would you like an explanation?"

"Yes, yes, by all means. Please." It wasn't worth bristling at the condescension, which perhaps was more tease than torment. Besides, having seen Marianne in action, I had vowed to be deferential in all my dealings with her. "But shall we escape the deluge and let the innkeeper ply us with her admirable food and beverages?" François muttered agreement and dashed into the inn, closely followed by Isabeau.

Marianne assumed a blank face and gestured for me to enter first, a token gallantry that, I believe, usually works the other way with gender. As my gaze ran along her extended right arm, I noticed again the impressive kraken tattoo. Was there no escaping this tedious myth and its iconography? It seemed to be taking on a life of its own. I sighed and preceded Marianne through the door.

The public room was empty but for Ita polishing mugs. The entire town must have gone to the chapel. I wondered what had happened after our ejection and the bolting of the doors. No doubt Terminus would have spun an eloquent and fearsome harangue to capture his flock, reframing the conflict as an infiltration of violent, godless agitators from away. I was beginning to suspect that there was little room on the island for the discourse of reason. Perhaps I should have figured that out already, especially following the acrid dialogue with the currach crew, but I tend to overlook social evidence when caught in the compulsion of my own logic.

While my companions found a table and ordered food and drink, I went upstairs to replace the broken goggles. Restored to clear sight, I hurried back to the public room and dropped into the empty chair between François and Isabeau. There was a halt in conversation, which I ignored, and nodded at Marianne. "Please proceed with your explication of the sign. Will you apply an inferential semiotic analysis or some other method?"

She frowned and stretched her tattooed arm across the table, inviting my gaze. The arm was a hallmark of athletic development, taut with veins and muscles. Impressive, yet secondary to the tattoo itself, which was executed in detail and with a skill that turned the arm into a simulation of the mythic beast. From shoulder to elbow the skin ran heavy with blue ink—woad, I assumed—and depicted the body of the kraken with its huge, unblinking eyes on either side of the bicep. The open mouth could be seen in the crook of her elbow and a formidable array of tentacles crawled and curved down her forearm. The paddle-shaped extremities of the two longest tentacles ended on the back of her hand. The details were precise, even down to the suckers, and the overall draftsmanship evoked a semblance of life. It was almost good enough to make me think it had been drawn from an actual creature. No doubt modeled on a squid seen many times by the artist, I thought.

Marianne traced a finger along her forearm, following the wavy lines of the design, caressing herself with unabashed pleasure. I squirmed in my seat and rearranged my penis. "Some dispute the existence of the kraken…" and here she gave me a sharp glance, "…but there are many who do not, including the monks of this island. Every ten years they paddle into the strait with a cow, delivering it to the kraken as a sacrifice. I haven't seen this ritual; the monks don't allow witnesses, but they claim that the kraken rises to the surface and plucks the animal from the boat. The sign over the inn merely commemorates this ritual; I leave the semiotics to you."

I sat back, once again amazed at the gullibility of humans. "And do you consider that there may be other motives for the secrecy of this ritual, such as the possibility that there is no kraken, and the monks merely toss the unfortunate bovine overboard?"

Marianne retrieved her arm from its place of prominence as Ita arrived with platters of food and tankards of ale. François frowned at the ale, failing to conceal his disappointment about the lack of wine. I asked for water, as always. After a long draught of the brew, Marianne shrugged. "Who knows? Like I said, I haven't seen the ritual. I only explain the sign."

"May I ask why you display the image of this imaginary beast on your arm? It's certainly a masterpiece of tattoo art, but I confess mystification."

"The beast is not imaginary, philosopher."

"Ahh. And have you seen one?"

Marianne smiled. "Indeed, I have."

That was not the answer I expected. My mouth gaped. Unwilling to dismantle any paradigms at this point, I was forced to assume that she was mistaken or lying. I nervously picked at the fish stew, ordering my thoughts, preparing for a diplomatic foray into the dialectics. It was always best to start with the phenomenon itself. "Can you describe the circumstances of this encounter?"

"No, philosopher, I cannot. Or will not, to be precise. It happened during a ceremony the details of which I vowed to keep secret. You may believe or not believe, as you wish. Telling the story proves nothing, anyway." She was right about that. Marianne looked at François and Isabeau, who both nodded at her. "I will tell you this, however. The three of us represent a small but influential fellowship. Our profile remains discrete. The group is known, when it is known at all, as The Kraken Imaginary. Among other things, we promote intimate human relationships with the chthonic elements of the world. The kraken, of course, is one of those elements. It is a shy, strange creature beyond the comprehension of most humans. Since we sometimes share its watery realm, there is much we can learn from it. Most people consider the kraken to be a frightful monster. This kind of fear is an obstacle to our hope for human engagement with the world in its complexity. The kraken, seemingly so alien, has become the symbol for our efforts to include all beings in a family of relations."

François was preoccupied with draining his tankard, but Isabeau vibrated with excitement and jumped in. "Philosopher, what would you say if I told you that a forest is more than a collection of individual trees but is actually a continuous being with a profound collective intelligence, most of it out of sight—underground?"

"Oh, I'd have many questions. Starting with how you know this fantastic claim to be true."

François banged his empty mug onto the table. "Let's not get distracted with the infinite possibilities of debate, no matter how fascinating. I suspect this philosopher could argue us all under the table, whether right or wrong. We have a rescue to plan, you know?"

"By all means," growled Marianne. "What's your proposal?" François shrank under her glare.

"I have one!" Isabeau dropped her voice to a whisper, even though the room was still empty, except for Ita, standing behind the counter with her endless job of polishing. Isabeau looked at each of us in turn. "There can be little doubt we must escort Fedelma away from this island. Terminus' word is the law here. Whatever the extent of her penance, he'll be in no mood to humor requests from anyone on her behalf. Therefore, whatever we do must be done on the sly, under cover of darkness, and with the utmost discretion. We will need a boat and arms to pull the oars. Also, provisions to keep us afoot for a few days on the mainland as we would do well to avoid the harbor in case Terminus has agents there. That much seems clear."

I bowed my head. "Aptly reasoned, good woman."

François embellished the proposal. "Then a boat must be purchased or stolen, preferably the former as I have no wish to undermine the livelihood of these poor folk, who without fish would be hard put to scrounge any nourishment. Especially since they can think of nothing better to do with their cattle than throw them in the sea. We do have some funds, at least enough for the provisions, but I doubt it's enough for a boat. Damn! We may have to steal it after all."

I rubbed the skin on the top of my head. "I have ample funds for such a purchase, if one can be found. Given the simplicity of their construction, I should think one of our islanders would be pleased to exchange a well-worn craft for a handful of crowns. That would be more than enough to keep him in drink while he builds a new one."

Marianne laughed. "If your funds are that ample, perhaps we can obtain a boat in good condition and avoid the 'well-worn.' I have no wish to drown."

I blushed. "By all means! A turn of the phrase, merely. And here's another thought: the good Brother Diarmuid gave us an important clue this afternoon. I suggest we use it. Let's take advantage of tonight's darkness to find our way up to Fedelma's *clochan*. At the least, we can assess how well it's guarded, if at all, and we may be able to confer directly with her. She would surely have ideas about the ways and means of escape. Not to mention we should establish that she does want to escape, though I struggle to imagine otherwise." I fiddled with the bangles on my arm.

The others nodded their heads. We raised glasses and resolved on a midnight ramble to the monastery. I heard the stomping of feet on the porch, the door banged, and people streamed into the pub. Along with damp clothes, they brought in their chatter; the name of the abbot was mentioned more than once. Voices trailed off when they saw us, but quickly resumed as drinks were ordered. It seemed foolish to continue scheming amidst the public, so we sat back and watched the influx. My back was to the door, and I found myself twisting around to witness the hubbub. Within a few minutes, my joints throbbed, and I gave up, turning back to the table and massaging the stiffness in my neck. It wasn't long before Marianne's eyes narrowed, and I felt a presence behind me. Twisting again, I flinched as the five women who had been so vocal at the chapel advanced toward us with determined steps. They stopped and formed a semicircle around me. François' hand dropped to his boot where he kept the stiletto.

The woman in the middle stepped forward. "You, sir, are a credit to your gender. We honor your efforts on behalf of an oppressed woman and acknowledge you as a fellow traveler on the road to a better society. Thank you."

All five presented their outstretched hands to me, palm up. I looked at them in confusion. Isabeau nudged me from behind. "You're supposed to touch your palm to theirs, I think."

Hesitantly, I placed my right hand, palm down, on the hand of the speaker, then touched the others in the same way. Satisfied, they withdrew their hands. They stood still and looked at me. I guessed that they waited for a response, but for once, I didn't know what to say.

I cleared my throat. "Well, um… yes, glad to help. Glad to. I do wonder, since you're here, if you can tell us what happened after we left the chapel?"

Another woman stepped forward, her face tight and her voice brittle. "Goddess have mercy! They hustled the poor woman away and that misogynist pig lectured for at least an hour, as if we were fools, saying entirely nothing. The usual patriarchal nonsense we've heard from priests for hundreds of years. The entire event was inexplicable and inexcusable. The situation is a travesty. That Abbott must be made to pay. If respect is not given, then it will be taken."

I looked around at my companions, thinking that perhaps these women might become allies with our cause. François gave me a funny look and shook his head. Marianne and Isabeau were carefully neutral.

I turned back to the women. "No doubt you're correct. Thank you for your kind words. Perhaps we can exchange ideas at another time when we are all not so vexed. I admit to overhearing some of your conversation from last night and your terminology was novel and intriguing."

"Yes, we've found it necessary to develop a new vocabulary to express our ideas, a vocabulary devised by women, for women. Until next we meet, then. Good day to you." The women turned away, though not before the speaker gave Marianne a lingering glance. The group found a table on the other side of the pub.

"Who was that?" I asked.

Isabeau answered. "That, my dear philosopher, was The Calyx, a society of radicals and freethinkers. Supporting a new bloom from the husk of the old, that's the idea. Among other things, they offer refuge for mistreated women, first giving shelter, then training towards independence. Their activities confound the authorities and infuriate many men, especially those who have been abandoned by wives or mistresses. They seem harmless enough and have so far avoided serious reprisals. However, there is a rumor that they're considering more direct action and militant tactics to advance their cause."

Isabeau stared at Marianne, who stared back. Their faces were composed, but the tension between the two women was obvious. It radiated with energy that even I couldn't ignore. François studied the floor. Marianne finally replied. "There is that rumor, yes."

I wanted to ask more questions, absolutely, but even I recognized that was a bad idea.

[6]

Well after midnight, when the inn lay quiet, the four of us met in the hall to negotiate the creaky stairs. We wore hooded cloaks the hue of stone, standard issue for The Kraken Imaginary. Luckily, they had an extra one. Even though I preferred to work alone, I found myself enjoying being part of this odd and interesting team. I could always go my own way later. Halfway down the stairs, Marianne, in a tight whisper, reproached me for the tinkling of my bracelets, and reluctantly I stuck them in a pocket. Stealth is not one of my skills, but I did the best I could, and we slinked out the front door and left the village in relative silence.

Approaching the monastery, we slowed to a cautious pace. There were a few lights in the chapel, but otherwise, the grounds were dark and still. At the wall that divided the compound from the fields, we turned to follow its course like Diarmuid said, creeping along in a careful procession with Marianne in the lead. Despite the light rain, the cloud cover was thin enough to allow a diffuse light from the waxing moon. Marianne suddenly hissed and we froze, peering ahead into the night. A hooded figure sat cross-legged on the wall. I sensed Marianne and François alter their stances for combat, and I caught the gleam of a blade.

"At ease, pilgrims." From the shadowed hood came the voice of Brother Diarmuid. "I thought I might accompany you if you have no objection. I was certain that you would come this way tonight. So, I sat and waited through the darkness, and

while I waited, I prayed mightily. Thank the Lord, I was blessed.
A guiding vision was given to me. It's my calling to assist you
and ease your travails however I might. To such an end, wherever it goes, I offer you my humble services. The Lady means
much to me, and, apparently, to you as well."

"Well met, then, Brother Diarmuid," I said as I moved forward to extend a hand in friendship.

François stopped me with an arm across my chest. "That's
all very well, but why should we trust you? Why shouldn't we
assume that you're an agent of the Abbott?"

A wave of embarrassment swept through me. François had
a point. We didn't know much about this monk. I instinctively
trusted him because he reminded me of a whipped dog, and
easy sympathy evoked a simple trust, but where was the reason in that? Inexplicably, my grip on logic had slackened. True,
Diarmuid had said a few things that led me to assume he was
more faithful to Fedelma than Terminus, but he was, after all, a
man of the cloth with a presumed allegiance to his order.

Marianne moved to the far side of Diarmuid's post on the
wall, hovering close to him, hemming him between her stance
and the restless knife in François' hand. Her tone was cold and
sharp. "Speak fast, monk, or say your final prayer. And if you try
to raise an alarm, there won't be time for the prayer."

Diarmuid nodded his head, then pulled back his hood so
we could see his face. He had the raw look of someone who
has recently shed tears. "I understand. Please, let me explain
myself and perhaps you'll be reassured. If not, I've already said
my prayers…. My service has kept me on this island for five
years. I pledged vows with all my heart and soul, and I fashioned
my life to become an instrument of God. At first, I assumed that

temporal service to the Abbott would be the same as spiritual service to my Lord. Any troublesome occurrences, and there were more than a few, I attributed to my own poor understanding of the holy praxis. Then, one year ago, the Lady Fedelma came here to study and reflect, as many do. Her presence ignited feelings in me that I still do not understand. I did everything I could to be near her, to talk with her, to hear her voice in song and lyric. Even to see her at a distance, walking in lonely thought across the hilltop as the wind blew her robe and her long hair danced… why, such a sight would warm me to the bones."

As he spoke these words, the monk's face took on an exalted look. Isabeau threw her hands above her shoulders. "Oh, the poor man, he is in love!"

New tears trickled down the monk's face. He sniffled and wiped his nose. "Yes. I know little of such things, but there are no other words for it. At first, I told myself that it was only a matter of the spirit and that I thirsted for her knowledge. The Lady recognized my enthusiasm and was good enough to enlist me as her primary student. We sat together and walked together in long conversations and, as our dialogue deepened, she explained her understanding of the divinity inherent in the world, including the sacrament of physical union. In a reckless moment, I confessed my ardor and begged her for a sign of generosity. I was so desperate. When she disclosed her own affections, we touched, and I experienced heaven. Many may disapprove, but Lord help me, I regret nothing.

"And now… my original beliefs are stronger than ever, but I see God in every aspect of His creation. As the Lady taught me, the world is in our flesh and our flesh is in the world. It is all part of God."

Diarmuid ceased talking. His eyes were wet with rain and tears, but his expression radiated contentment. I was convinced of his sincerity. I looked at the others. François shrugged and put his knife away. "Monk, if you tell us anymore, I'll be in tears myself. For love, much can be forgiven."

Marianne also relaxed, reached out to caress the shaven part of the monk's head, then leaned in and kissed him softly. Even in the dim light, we could see his blush. Isabeau stepped forward and patted his arm, saying "I knew he was a good man. All I need is one hug and I feel a person's soul. Let him come. We can use another hand."

I was relieved that my first impression proved accurate. "Let me repeat myself, then, Brother Diarmuid: well met. Can you lead us to the *clochan* of Fedelma?"

"Indeed." He hopped off the wall and put his hood up against the rain. "Follow me. They send out a guard every three hours to wake her so she can't have continuous sleep. The abbot would rather that she prayed instead. He's desperate to break her, and his methods grow more torturous. The last guard was about an hour ago. He made a lot of noise and was cruel; I could hear him from here. I wanted to go to him and plead for mercy, but that would be futile. The inner circle of monks loyal to Saint Terminus have lost the thread of God, I fear. I chose to wait on the wall and hope that you would pass this way. Together we may accomplish something more useful to the Lady. She must leave this island, and soon."

Our recruit took the lead, and we continued along the wall, turning at the corner, and angling up the hill. My calves soon ached from the constant stepping up, over, and around the slabs and stones that occupied the greatest portion of the hillside.

Diarmuid pointed across the low wall to a solitary *clochan* a few yards away. It was so small that it was difficult to believe that someone could live inside it for more than an hour or two. Like other examples of its kind, a steep corbelled arch of dry-laid stones formed the walls rounding to a peak. Though it might be tall enough for a short person to stand within, only a child could lay flat across the narrow diameter. As we contemplated this claustrophobic chamber a sound of singing leaked through the *clochan* stones. We scrambled over the boundary wall and crept to the structure. Diarmuid motioned for us to crouch down at the back of the *clochan*. Marianne ignored his gesture and circled the hut, scanning the layout and, no doubt, assuring herself that we were truly alone. When she returned, she said casually, "There's a door on the other side. Unfortunately, it's locked."

The singing stopped. "Who's there?" came the thin voice from inside.

Diarmuid put his mouth to a crack between the stones. "Lady, it's Brother Diarmuid, and some people who wish to speak with you!"

"Ah. Would one of those people be comrade Isabeau?"

Isabeau imitated Diarmuid in putting her mouth to the joints in the wall. "Yes, my darling. We have come to help you leave this terrible place! Unless you wish otherwise, of course."

"Well," came the reply from inside, "it's about time!"

"Sorry, my dear, there have been… complications."

"I don't need to hear about it. Any longer and I believe this abbot would start removing my body parts to add to his collection of relics. His attentions are growing more than weary. Who else is with you? Your companions from the scrimmage in the chapel?"

"Don't be so cross. We're here now and a little gratitude wouldn't be out of place!"

"Fine. I'm grateful that my colleagues have seen fit to haul me out of another catastrophe. So, who is with you? I was impressed with that tall woman. Is she one of ours?"

"She is, indeed. One of our new intervention specialists. May I present Marianne? Or at least her voice."

Marianne did not sit but leaned against the *clochan* wall and whispered into a crack. "Very pleased to meet you, Fedelma, although I'm not sure this qualifies as meeting, tempered through stone as it is. I have looked forward to this for some time. Your safety is my prime directive, and I will do whatever needs to be done."

Fedelma's voice was enthusiastic. "Hmm, I like the sound of that."

Isabeau continued the introductions. "I also brought François, a poet. Another intervention specialist, though with a different set of skills."

François said nothing and there was a pause from inside. Then, Fedelma's voice emerged. "Not the François, the well-known rake, raconteur, and slayer of priests? Not that François?"

François spoke into the wall. "The same, my lady. At your service."

"We'll have to exchange a song or two and perhaps a flagon of wine, if not a bed. And who else? How about the little man who boldly challenged Terminus in front of his minions? Is he with you?"

I didn't wait but put my lips to the wall and spoke for myself. "That would be Corax of the Academy. I have come far to—I hope—avert a potential tragedy here."

"Corax of the Academy! Not the phenomenologist?"

"The same. You've heard of me?"

"Oh yes. I read your text: 'Dialectic of the Seen and the Unseen.' Ironically, they have a copy in the archives here at the monastery. A most interesting work, though I do have a few quibbles. I doubt that Terminus knows of it. Or if he does, perhaps he keeps it to serve as a cushion for his darts."

"And what are your quibbles, if I may ask?"

Marianne was already up and prowling. Isabeau looked at me with a mix of wonder and sarcasm. "Scholar, your ability to concentrate on matters of the mind is admirable. But perhaps this is not the best time for philosophy."

I nodded vigorously and pushed on. "Yes, yes, you have a good point. We will need to find the time for a full examination. But just one more question." I rushed to prevent objection. "Apparently we have a similar condition of the eye: the triple iris."

"Intriguing. That was why you wore the silver goggles in the chapel?"

"Yes, exactly. Why don't you need a similar apparatus to control your vision? How do you manage?" I guessed by the expressions on the others' faces that their exasperation was nearing a limit.

Fedelma responded in a serious tone, however. "This is another matter for prolonged discussion. The condition is rare—practically unknown. However, I've heard that its effects vary relative to biological sex. Details will have to wait until we have more time. Though now that you've brought it up, it gives me an idea… Yes, that might work."

Isabeau motioned to Marianne to come back and join the conversation. After a last scan of the surroundings, she crouched down next to the wall and, like the rest of us, pressed her ear to the joints between stones.

"I am eager to quit this place. I think I know how that can happen. We will need to be surreptitious. Although these monks hardly qualify as crack troops, they are capable of surprising vigilance and energy. And, for the most part, they do whatever Terminus tells them to do. Diarmuid, are you listening?"

"Aye, my Lady."

"Are you willing to abandon the Order and seek fortune elsewhere?"

"Indeed I am."

"Good, because we need you. This is what I'm thinking…"

Fedelma outlined her scheme, which, after a few comments and questions, we endorsed. I wasn't entirely clear on the purpose of every phase, but Fedelma assured us that it would address several needs at once, including a last try at completing her original mission to the island.

We mulled over the assigned roles, murmured agreement, then heard a sudden shouting from the central part of the monastery. Jumping up, we strained to see what was going on. Doors slammed in the main buildings, bare feet slapped on paving stones, metal clattered like weapons, and lanterns bounded along the paths. The chaos of noise and lights converged on the rectory.

"What the hell?" said François.

Diarmuid's face creased in anxiety. "This isn't right. I should return immediately. Meet me at the grave tomorrow! God bless you, Lady!" He ran down the hill toward the mayhem.

We informed Fedelma of what we could see, which wasn't much, and promised we would come for her tomorrow night, or as soon as possible once everything was in place. She replied that she would spend the time devising a satire on Terminus that would singe his balls. As we walked away, she resumed the chant we had heard before.

We were curious about the commotion but had no intention of getting involved in another scuffle. Slipping over the wall, we detoured across several fields to avoid the monastery grounds. During the detour, we stumbled and scuffed our shins repeatedly on the uneven folds of bare rock, staggering along like drunks in the dark. Cursing the island and its lithic fundament, we made our slow way back to the inn.

[7]

The next morning, the public room was crammed with people and animated conversation. I spied Marianne sitting at a window table, gazing out at the rain as it pounded against the glass.

"Where are the others?" I asked as I sat in the chair across from her. I'm not adept at reading facial expressions, but even to me, she looked weary.

"They decided to linger in bed... since it was raining so hard." Her smile was faint and distracted. "Meanwhile, there is news."

"Oh?" I signaled to Ita for a mug of mint tea, a house specialty.

"Yes. It seems there was an assassination attempt on our holy Saint Terminus."

"What?"

"Divergent narratives are in the air, as you might expect. From what I've pieced together, it looks like the valiant women of The Calyx snuck into the rectory last night and tried to slay the abbot. For better or worse, depending on your point of view, they were unsuccessful. It was a bloody affair, though. Two of the ladies are dead, and at least two monks, according to one account. By other accounts, the numbers are different. Regardless, the abbot has been wounded. However, he isn't dead and, as they say, he is fearsome wroth."

"Fuck me, Zeus!" I barely noticed the large, steaming mug as it was placed in front of me.

Ita stood next to the table and eyed us both for a moment before speaking. "I hope to God you were not involved in that foolishness last night, either of you. Bad enough that our idiot men have naught better to do than batter each other to death over trifles, but to see women stooping to foul violence leaves me right ashamed, it does. And I'm as devout as the next islander, but nothing surprises me about these monks anymore. I'd stay well away from that business, if I were you."

We murmured denials of involvement and with a final, hard look at Marianne, Ita trailed back to the kitchen.

"Do you know more than you've said about these Calyx women? After we met them yesterday, Isabeau implied something, I'm not sure what, but it was tense, even I could see that." Marianne's stare was sharp enough to puncture bone, and I started fiddling with the bangles on my arm, clinking them up and down under the sleeve. "Well, of course," I stammered, "none of my business, is it? There is that."

"You know, philosopher, you would do well to stow once and for all those adornments cluttering your body. I'm thoroughly tired of hearing you tinkle your way through the day, broadcasting every gesture or step. Whatever comes next, I'm sure it will require more stealth, not less."

I winced at her hostility. "Yes, yes, you're right. I hadn't considered the element of noise from mere jewelry, but I take your point, I do. I'll divest myself of them; anyway, they serve no purpose for our work." Nervously, I continued to fiddle with the bracelets until Marianne grabbed my arm to make me stop. "Oh, yes, sorry. Anyway, I agree regarding a need for discretion. Especially given these new developments. We won't escape suspicion, I suspect, if only for our public showing against Terminus in the chapel. Obviously, our innkeeper carries some doubts."

Marianne softened her voice. "Thank you. As for your question, I see no reason to provide details to satisfy your curiosity. Listen, as much as I love Isabeau, and I do, we don't always agree. She has chosen the way of the heart and wants to change the world through love. As for me, I have less faith in that power. I prefer action. We must defend ourselves against the brutes of the world. Especially women, who are fodder for subjugation. I'm sure I don't need to explain to you the widespread deployment of violence by men against women. I expect that you're familiar with the conditions of rape, having seen it or possibly even participated." I put up my hands to object. "No, no, I'm not accusing you. But you are a man, or so it seems. Men need to stop it. It shouldn't be up to women. But if that's the way it has to be, then I'll continue to do what I do."

"A new discourse of power..." I muttered.

"Hmm?"

"Power. It's administered through discourse, the net of thoughts and action that coalesce around a social pattern. It's true, the old discourses of power benefit men, for the most part. The only way to challenge these discourses is by starting a new one, which seems to be your aim. It's not really phenomenology, but... oh, never mind."

Her smile was bitter. "Right, as I said, I'm a woman of action. I don't do discourse."

At that point, François and Isabeau came through the stairwell door. Entwined, they sauntered across the room, hips rubbing, arms around torsos, ignoring the attention they drew.

They slid into the bench behind our table, giggling at each other. Marianne lifted her hand in greeting but said nothing, just stared past me toward an invisible horizon. I asked François and Isabeau if they had heard the news about Terminus. They had not, so I repeated Marianne's tale.

"Shit. It is unfortunate they didn't succeed. Now vigilance will increase, spies will circulate, and Terminus will be looking for scapegoats. I hope no one tries to link us to The Calyx cell." François stared at Marianne, who gazed out the window and ignored him.

"That is life," said Isabeau, lowering her voice. "Later we can weep for the loss of our sisters. Despite our differences, I respect their goals. But it's probably best if we implement our plans as soon as possible. I suspect there will be confusion and disorder at the monastery, which may work to our advantage if we move fast enough."

"Indeed," I bobbed my head in agreement. "Few things will motivate me to skip breakfast, especially when the cook is this good, but we should begin our tasks. Perhaps Ita can be persuaded to pack us a basket and we can take it with us to Brother Diarmuid."

Before leaving the inn, I returned to my room and stripped off the bracelets. I pulled a satchel out of my travel bag and placed the remainder of my funds in it, along with another spare pair of goggles and a journal of field notes. Changing into the gray robe from the previous night, I packed the remainder of my possessions into the travel bag, ready for departure.

I peeked into the hallway, which was deserted, then slipped out with the bag and satchel. I had overpaid for the lodging, but I left a crown on the windowsill anyway, to show my appreciation.

Aside from the interminable rain, this would be a delightful spot for sabbatical. Given the political climate, it was not unreasonable to think that my services might be required again. At any rate, there was no reason to alienate a fine innkeeper. I walked carefully down the hall, trying to avoid the squeaks in the floorboards, and knocked lightly on the door to my companions' room. Marianne opened it and yanked me inside.

The first thing I noticed was the odor, heavy with scent and sweat. I stood and gawked while the others focused on their tasks. The room, larger than mine, was filled with a cluttered array of clothes and equipment. The two beds had been pushed together and the bedding was rumpled and askew. I wondered who had been doing what to whom. If I wasn't such a goggle-eyed freak, maybe they'd want me in on it. But I'd learned long ago to seek more reliable pleasures. Humiliating others with logic satisfied me at least as much as thrashing toward a fleeting paroxysm of ecstasy.

Isabeau sorted clothes into neatly folded piles while François inspected a formidable collection of knives. He picked up one after another from an open leather roll, checked the edge with his thumb, stropped the blade a few times, then carefully returned it to its pocket. I felt like an intruder in a cultish ritual. Meanwhile, Marianne returned to the corner to wrap a rawhide case around a heavy bow and a quiver of arrows.

"So, where should I put this?" I hefted my travel bag.

"On the bed," answered Isabeau. "Have a seat, we'll be ready to go in a few minutes. We can finish this later. Did you bring coin enough for the boat?"

I nodded and trooped to the bed, dropping my bag. Seeing no other place to sit, I perched on the edge of the mattress, avoiding the stains, and watched their preparations. Fedelma's plan required us to split the group in half. Isabeau, Marianne, and François would find and purchase a boat, outfit it with supplies, then row to a small rock island about a mile offshore. They would hide on the island and wait. Meanwhile, Diarmuid and I would release Fedelma from the *clochan* and hike to the top of the hill overlooking the monastery. There we'd enter a cave system that ran beneath the island. Although the bedrock looked solid enough, it was a type of limestone easily eroded by water, and water, refreshed by the constant rain, permeated the island matrix. In time the rock yielded to the seeps and courses of drainage, developing a warren-like network of underground tubes and caverns. By following a devious but known route through these passages, we could traverse under the sea and emerge on the same rocky isle where the others waited. Fedelma knew the way, she said, although it sounded like a labyrinth to me. Reunited, we would row to the mainland. The plan itself struck me as convoluted, but Fedelma insisted on it. She said Terminus and his minions would never imagine such an escape, which seemed true, but logic preferred simplicity. Why not break out Fedelma as a team, sneak to the shore, and row away under the cover of darkness? Spelunking seemed risky. Splitting up also seemed risky. However, everyone accepted the plan without argument, just as they accepted that now Fedelma was our leader. How had that happened?

My musings were cut short when the others announced they were ready to go. Downstairs, I paid Ita for a basket of food and drink. We pretended we were heading out for a stroll to see the sights, no doubt a mad presumption. At least the rain had

stopped though it was still overcast. We walked to the monastery with few words. Marianne complimented me on the lack
of random noise generated by my outfit. Caught up in a rush
of goodwill, I stopped, went to one knee, and reached for her
hand. Amused, she extended it and I kissed the back, right on
the tip of the kraken tentacle. I have no idea why I did that. It
was remarkably undignified, but I felt a little wild. The thought
crossed my mind that I might be smitten with Marianne, but I
dismissed it as improbable; I wasn't even sure I wanted women.
Maybe what I wanted was to be one. The giddiness fled as
quickly as it had arrived, and I stood up, embarrassed.

"So, it seems our philosopher has blood in his veins after
all," Isabeau said while François smirked.

We approached the monastery indirectly, through the fields,
to avoid monks on patrol. Several times we had to duck behind
stone walls. When we got near Diarmuid's grave, we crouched
along the wall on the other side of the path. I ventured my head
above the stones and called his name. Without a word, he stuck
his shovel in the dirt pile, climbed over the monastery wall,
crossed the path, and sat on top of our wall as if he were taking
a break, looking out to sea, and holding his hands for prayer. We
crouched at his feet, trying to stay out of sight.

"At first light," said the monk, "pretending to get an early
start on my penitential duties, I hiked down to a fisherman I
know who lives alone in a small hut not far from here. If you
follow the shore from the village, his house occupies the edge
of a cliff over a cove. You cannot miss it, for there is a large
menhir directly in front of the house, a menhir carved with spirals. There's no other like it on the island. His name is Corc Ó
Dálaigh. He's a good man as well as a good friend. He has never

seen the worth of the abbot and bears him no love, which, to my mind, assures his discretion. Most important, he's willing to part with an old currach for a few crowns and no questions. Despite its age, the craft remains seaworthy. I have used it myself. For another crown, he will supply four oars. I explained to him that if anyone this day should come looking to purchase his boat, he would be well-advised not only to consummate the deal but to keep it to himself. He concurred it would be wise, indeed, in the event of such good fortune."

"Well done," I said and handed him a chunk of the bread they call scone. "I'm sorry that I have no worms to go with it, Brother Diarmuid, but there were none on the inn's menu."

He snickered and grabbed the scone eagerly, stuffing it into his mouth in one bite.

"And how fares the beleaguered abbot?" asked François.

"I wish him no ill, and it seems he may yet live," supplied Diarmuid. "That would likely be for the best, as control of the monastery has passed to a triumvirate of zealots. They are anxious to initiate a purge of those with questionable faith. Bad as Saint Terminus may be, this trio is worse."

"That's alarming," said Isabeau. "Reprisals often backfire. But it does suggest that our window for action is slender. We must proceed! Philosopher, if you provide the crowns for the boat and oars, we'll take care of the rest."

Diarmuid thrust a cupped hand below the crest of the wall, and I filled it with more scone. "I best return to my labor. So, Master Corax, we shall meet after dark at the corner of the wall? I will requisition the key to the *clochan*. Then we shall liberate our Lady! Farewell, for now. Go with God." I looked up to see him wolf down the scone in one bite.

After Diarmuid went back to his work, we crept along the wall and crossed over into another field. We climbed the slope, angling away from the monastery. After a swift, wheezing hike that took us around a hill, we arrived at an old dolmen in the middle of a rock-filled pasture. Sitting down, we leaned against the upright stones and explored the remaining options of the food basket. I retrieved a purse from my satchel to parcel out several coins, passing them to Isabeau. She thanked me and handed back a plain wool robe. "Here, take this for Fedelma. It's not so large that she'll vanish in it. She may have nothing warm for the caves." I nodded and stowed the robe in my satchel.

The megalithic structure at our backs stood in the same impassive way it had for thousands of years. I was satisfied to be in the presence of such antiquity while we munched and gazed across the waters of the strait. It soothed my edges with the promise that some legacies lasted more than a season or two. Would mine? I'd never know, of course. The clouds lifted and though the sky was far from clear, there were small patches of blue and the mountains of the mainland didn't look so far away. The others only nibbled out of the basket since it constituted the provisions for the underground crew. When we finished, I transferred the remaining contents into my satchel so they could return the basket to the inn.

Isabeau got to her feet, smiled, and extended her hand to help me stand. "Time to part, dear philosopher, so we may sooner meet."

Marianne unslung a goatskin flask from her shoulder and placed it on a rock. "Some water for your journey, to keep those vocal cords oiled." She bent over and kissed me, cheek to cheek, on each side. I blushed; I don't know why.

François stepped forward and gave me the same kiss, with the same result. He reached into his sleeve, pulled out a slim knife in a sheath, and placed it in my hand. "I know that you're a warrior of words, but sometimes, words fail. Now you have an alternative."

Lastly came Isabeau's embrace as she pressed against my girth with all the warmth and roundness of her body, finishing with more kissing of cheeks. I was on fire by the time she let go. Like a fool, I stood there, panting, while the three of them turned and walked down the hill. The wind carried their laughter back to my ears with clarity, which only stoked the flames.

[8]

Since I had no tasks before dark, I chose to spend the rest of the day at the dolmen. For the first time, I could see the island and its surroundings without the impediment of clouds, fog, haze, and downpour. On a sunny day, the island was a remarkable place and surely it would take a lifetime to catalog its marvels. We had agreed that it was better if I kept out of sight, removing from observation a known opponent of Terminus. I could think of no better place than this ancient perch where I could revel in solitude and rumination, my favorite activities.

I tested several of the dolmen stones for back rests. Although they had relatively flat faces, certain rugosities made their presence known when I lounged against them. Few stones were suitable to the task because I wanted comfort combined with the best view over the water. I settled on the one that François had used; the man had an eye for luxury.

Letting my thoughts wander, I considered my companions. An interesting assortment of personalities, each amusing yet uniquely formidable. François was dashing—a classic, volatile sensualist. Isabeau radiated both warmth and a precision of thought, not to mention a fluid engagement with space. Diarmuid intrigued me due to his size and the mystery of his monkish perspectives. Even with the outlandish haircut, there was a raw beauty of manhood about him. I wanted to know more. And then, of course, there was Marianne. The contained ferocity marked her as dangerous in the extreme. It made me weak in the knees to think about her. I tried to imagine what it might be like to share intimacies and slipped into reverie. As the fantasy unfurled, when it came to the part where she disrobed, she had a penis. Preposterous, even for a daydream. Yet I couldn't get the image out of my mind.

I stared across the strait as if insight would materialize from the blue sky and clear air, which it did not. No matter how I tried, I remained perturbed by my own renegade desires. I wasn't very good at sex, or so I'd been told by the few men and women who'd gotten close enough to qualify for conjugation. Bah—a clumsy, nasty business. Reasoning offered more reliable rewards. No doubt the Cynics were right: masturbate wherever you were, even in public; get it over with and get on with the important things. Like crafting irrefutable cascades of logic that would flow unchallenged into the mist of time, a worthy ambition for a philosopher. However, since arriving on the island, I kept finding myself tossed about on a sea of emotion. Anger, anxiety, and lust blew through my body like one squall after another. Why? This was not my first mission. Usually, when those stormy demons slipped out of the box, I shoved them right back. Perhaps it was the rain, the food, the endless gray limestone, or just the intensity of my companions. Regardless, my reason eroded in the wash of sensation; I could feel it.

After failing to resolve anything with rumination, I fell asleep in the warm sunshine, slumping against the dolmen stone. Hours later, I came to with a jolt. My heart hammered like it was trying to break out of prison. I sucked in buckets of air to flush away the lingering images of the dream, but vertigo swirled through my head, and I felt more than a little crazy. I wondered if the final lunacy had come for me at last, as it does for so many philosophers.

I pushed myself upright against the stone and wiped the sweat off my forehead with a sleeve. My heart calmed while I chewed on the rough fabric, tasting the salt of my dreams. Nothing in that realm was rational, of course, but this one flipped my shell of reason into a flailing terrapin. What I remembered was simple enough: in the dream, I sat in a featureless room and watched Marianne slowly disrobe. There was nothing erotic about the scene; it could have been an anatomy lesson. When she came to her trousers, I stirred, curious to see the penis I expected from my daytime reverie. Instead, she revealed between her legs an array of dangling tentacles, twisting and writhing like a medusa. I stared as if turned to stone, caught in a never-ending moment of fascination and repulsion. The paralysis spread through my body, stopping my breath, the beating of my heart, and any volition of movement. When suffocation clutched my lungs, I was driven back, in panic, to the waking world. .

I stood up to reactivate my body, proving that I could move after all, and freed myself from the dominion of underworld fantasy. The sun had dropped behind the island toward the western sea; it seemed that I had slept most of the afternoon. I took a few steps down the slope to empty my bladder.

When I turned back to the dolmen, I noticed a raven sitting on the capstone. It tilted its head one way, then another, looking at me for all the world as if it had something important to say. But no sound was uttered. Perhaps it had brought the dream, a message from the gods, if I could unravel the signs. Such things are best left to the mystics; my interest in augury was non-existent. Besides, it was time to stifle the imagination and do something, for a change.

Leaving the dolmen stones to their lengthening shadows, I walked uphill across the field, clambering over the walls on crude stiles, aiming for a point where I could gain the path and descend it to the rendezvous with Diarmuid. I chose the roundabout way to avoid a chance encounter. Hardly likely, though, since there were no dwellings up the hill, only the patchwork infinity of stone fields and rock walls that seemed to cover the entire island.

I arrived at the corner in the fading dusk. Diarmuid wasn't there, so I crouched down behind the wall and waited. Pulling up my hood, I sat cross-legged and withdrew into the enclosure of the robe, pretending to be another rock. I watched the moon, already at three quarters, replace the blaze of the sun with its own pallor. Under a clear sky, it would not be a dark night. Good for finding our way but harder to pass unseen.

Before long I heard the cautious tread of someone creeping up the path from the monastery. I reached into the satchel for the dagger that François had given me and withdrew it from the sheath. Gripping the well-worn handle provided surprising confidence, even though I knew that if I had to use the blade, I was more likely to hurt myself than anyone else. Still, as a weapon, it was a fierce talisman.

The steps slowed, then stopped before reaching the corner. Thinking of Marianne's admonishments, I held my breath and kept quiet. The person on the other side of the corner lowered himself to the ground with a grunt. It was amusing to consider the two of us, friends or foes, sitting in similar postures, hidden from each other yet so close.

Tightening my grip on the knife, I spoke softly. "Diarmuid?"

There was a sharp intake of breath, then a hooded head peeked around the corner. "Master Corax?"

I pushed back my hood and smiled. "Indeed. Glad to see you again! I was terrified beyond reason that I would have to use this... this toadstabber." I wiggled the dagger back and forth before stowing it back in the sheath.

"It does carry the hint of danger."

Diarmuid slid around the corner to sit next to me. When his bulk brushed against my shoulder, I sensed the strength of his body. Being next to him made me feel safer. "I have the key and I was able to filch a cheese from the storehouse," he said. "Also, I secured a portable lamp, with enough whale oil to give us light for a day or two."

Why I hadn't thought of this I didn't know. Too obvious, perhaps. Of course, we'd need some light to find our way through miles of underground passage. I felt grateful to Diarmuid, obviously a clever young man. I leaned into his muscular arm, savoring the contact.

"Excellent! And I have some provisions as well: cheese, salt cod, and more of that scone you like. I trust we have enough to get through the passage; I've no wish to expire of starvation underground. Is it too early, do you think, to release Fedelma? I've not heard any guard activity, so I have no sense of their cycle."

"Things are in chaos following the attack on Saint Terminus. Guards may be more, less, or entirely irregular. I cannot say. We might as well take our chance and go now. The sooner away, the better."

We clasped hands in agreement. His grip was firm, but far from overbearing. I detected a gentleness in his touch, and we held the clasp longer than necessary.

Diarmuid led the way along the wall to the *clochan* and I stumbled behind. Once there, we looked around and saw no activity, so we slipped over the wall. As we approached the corbeled hut, the sound of chanting seeped through the cracks. Diarmuid whispered into a crevice and the singing stopped.

"I certainly hope that you have the key," Fedelma said. "Otherwise, we'll have to deconstruct the damned thing."

We crept around to the other side of the *clochan*. Diarmuid unlocked and removed the beam that secured the door, and I pulled it open. A prolonged squeal burst out that could be heard all over the island, I was sure. Cursing myself, I spun around and peered down the slope into the monastery maze. I perceived no movement and no obvious alarm. Diarmuid stepped past me to gather up Fedelma into an embrace, her tiny frame disappearing into his massive arms. I felt a twinge of something and promptly stuffed it. She stretched up to kiss him on the lips, then pulled away and offered me her hand. She looked haggard, but there was a gleam in her eyes, and she radiated restless energy. A brief shake, and she was in charge again. "Let's go."

The *clochan* contained nothing but the bard, so we headed straight to the wall, slithered over, and set off toward the top of the hill. I was eager to question Fedelma, but she scrambled briskly up the slope and I fell behind. Diarmuid stayed with me, occasionally offering a hand when things got steep.

I arrived at the broad summit out of breath. Fedelma stood atop a pile of stones, the ruin of another dolmen, striking a proud pose as she gazed into the western sea. Shaved head, slender frame, she resembled an elf lord returned to claim her archaic domain. I don't know where that thought came from;

I didn't find elves a credible species. Perhaps it was the brilliant moonlight, the pallid reflections off ocean and stone, the slight breeze, and the daring of our venture. A giddiness floated in the air, an intoxication of silver luminescence.

The view satisfied my own requirements for magic. I could see all the island below our stance, a long and narrow mound that resembled a sea creature risen to the surface, a whale or… the body of a kraken, I suppose. Moonlight bounced off the waters of the strait like a dance of crystals and arced over the island to shine into the vast western ocean. It wouldn't take much to imagine that we might set forth on that expanse, the whole massive island plowing into the unknown night. I wondered what need there was of spiritual mystery when the ordinary patterns of nature could summon such visions.

My reverie was broken when Fedelma hopped down from the stones and announced. "Okay, gentlemen, we have some rocks to haul."

I looked at her in dismay, afraid that she meant the dolmen stones themselves had to be removed. Of course, this was exactly what she meant. Without a word, Diarmuid walked back to the last wall we'd crossed and, reaching down to its base, retrieved a stout length of wood. Hoisting the stave, he stated, "Right where we left it, my Lady."

"What? You've done this before?"

"Yes, we have, Corax. This isn't a blind gamble," replied Fedelma. "During my stay, I've made it a point to explore some of the passages and caverns below the island. The dark places within the earth call to the psyche, don't you think? And why would anyone resist the urge to delve into the matrix of the earth mother, the great womb? I've learned

more than a few things about the underworld of this magnificent ark of stone, this place they call the Holy Island. If only
they knew how holy! I admit that I haven't found the most
important thing, the thing I came for, but I hope that one last
try will change that."

"Dare I even ask what it is that you hope to find?"

"Far be it from me to stymie the questions of the great
Corax. Besides, you should know, because it is pertinent to your
understanding of the world, and, in fact, to your sight. Beneath
our feet, I seek the kraken."

[9]

Diarmuid wasted no time in putting the stave to work, using it as a lever to lift and slide the biggest stones away from the pile. The smaller ones he tossed aside like pebbles. I looked at Fedelma, trying to swallow her wild claim about an underground kraken and wondering why we'd given ourselves over to her self-absorbed leadership. Poets were not famous for the stability of their temperament, and so far, Fedelma conformed to the type. Meanwhile, she stared at me with a look of triumph, as if daring me to quibble with her conceit.

"What say you, Master Phenomenologist? Are you ready to meet the kraken?"

"I don't know what to say. I appear to be in a minority hereabouts, but I have long believed the creature to be imaginary."

"Well, the form and notion do proliferate in images, and the sum of those signs and their meanings composes an imaginary, so in that sense you're correct."

"That's not what I meant. Your terminology is perverse."

"Or fluid, as you may come to see."

I looked to Diarmuid, who was no help. He ignored us and continued to labor over the stones. I felt guilty to let him work alone, but in truth, there was little I could do with my soft body.

"Perhaps we can argue vocabulary and neologisms another time. I'd like to know what you meant by saying there's a kraken 'down there.'"

Fedelma grinned. Maybe her smile carried an enchantment, because her skin glowed with a golden hue and the soles of my feet grew warm as if I had stepped onto hot sand. A conviction formed in my mind that I would follow her any-where, despite my reservations; whatever they were, I forgot. She spoke with a musical lilt. "Dear Corax, you're a thinker. Well trained in the ways of your profession, well trained in an orderly world. You've assembled the tools of your method and you apply them in the mastery of your craft. I honor the con-sistency of your structure, the reliability of your procedure. I, myself, ramble and carouse down a different path. Not a plod but a line of flight. I seek the crossroads of difference, the mat-rimony of chaos and flesh. We know so much, yet we know so little. I explore the little and dance beyond the boundaries. I aspire to everything."

The wash of words nudged me toward a dreamy state until reason forced a return to my wits. "Your words are lyrical, indeed, but I have scant patience for riddles."

"Sometimes things cannot be explained in linear fashion. Sometimes it all comes out a jumble, yet for all that is closer to the truth."

"Hmm. And the kraken?"

She gave me a blank look and I watched the glamour drain from her face. "You'd prefer the mundane version, then? Of course, you would. Well, under the island there's an enormous grotto. Within that cavern is a lake of saltwater, accessible, so it's said, through an undersea passage. It can be reached from above through a network of old channels in the rock. I know because I've been there several times, as has Diarmuid. We've ventured to the grotto and explored it in the attempt to verify an old story, which claims that it's the sanctuary of a rare kraken, one that I dearly wish to meet."

"Meet? A strange way to put it. And what's so compelling about this beast?"

"Compelling to me, if not others, because it exemplifies a particular interest of mine. The kraken is a hermaphrodite."

I stared at her, dumbfounded. The woman was exasperating.

"How can you know this? Or even imagine that it's true? A hermaphrodite? What does that even mean? The union of two gods collapsed into the body of an unfortunate offspring? And what does it possibly have to do with getting to our rendezvous with the others?"

"Your reputation for questions is apt, Corax. Let me burrow through your barrage. I only know the story; the truth of it's more than I can say. There's certainly an old kraken presence around the island; the proliferation of sightings, tales, beliefs, and tradition is a bit much for coincidence. As for the hermaphrodite, *that* is what's so intriguing. The divine marriage contained within a single form, such a rare treasure! Unfortunate, you think? Or simply misunderstood? You must be aware of the existence of such creatures: they can be found in all types, even humans. As such, they challenge all our petty distinctions and notions of gender and sexuality, do they not? Or have such phenomena not risen above the horizon of phenomenology?"

"To be honest, I'm still trying to work out the rudiments of sensory perception, how it operates, what it means. I look for denominators of the normal, not elaborations of the arcane. Your questions are more suited for a mythologist or a poet, I should think."

"Exactly, but hardly irrelevant for an understanding of perception, no? Consider gender, for example – are we not all mixtures of attributes both male and female, stirred together in random stews, fluid, fitting into the form of the container but conveying a singular flavor with every preparation? And does not our experience of gender filter our perceptions? For example, when you see me, do you see man or woman? If the former, would I not appeal to your Academicians as a wayward boy in need of a stern guiding hand, yet indulged shamelessly anyway? And if the latter, would I perhaps be seen as a dainty thing with unaccountable ambitions who needs to learn her place at the feet of a mighty protector? What do *you* see, Corax?"

"Hmm. Well... interesting questions."

There was a resounding *thunk* from the rock pile and Diarmuid announced, without a pause for breath, "The entrance is free."

Fedelma bounced on her toes and dashed to the open space in the middle of the pile. I followed, curious to see the product of Diarmuid's herculean labor. I had watched, but still had little comprehension of how one man moved these lithic giants. Although I shouldn't be surprised; I assumed that they were brought here and set up with similar labor. My own countryman had boasted that he could move the earth itself with a lever, but I always dismissed it as mere rhetoric. I'm rarely wrong, but maybe this once.

Fedelma beamed at Diarmuid and the two of them stood over the hole. Inauspicious, it looked like nothing more than a small, crude well.

"This is it? The passage to the kraken grotto and our route to freedom? This?"

Diarmuid smiled. Fedelma put her hands on her hips as if poised for another lecture. "It *is* rather unassuming, isn't it? Which is precisely why it remains unknown. And it'd be better for us if it stays that way, no? But don't worry, Corax. It's a short drop through this hole to a lateral passage large enough for even Diarmuid to walk erect. From there we'll connect to other passages that meander toward the grotto."

"And after that?"

"After that, there are further passages, one of which will take us under the sea to the island where we meet our comrades. I admit that the route beyond the grotto is unfamiliar..."

"What?!"

"...but I found within the archives of the monastery an ancient map that shows the way."

"And do you have this map?"

She tapped her skull. "Yes. In here."

"Oh, dear."

"Stop worrying, fretful man! Part of the bardic training requires honing the memory to prodigious feats. I'm quite skilled."

"I suppose we'll find out soon enough just how skilled," I grumbled.

Diarmuid pulled the lamp out of his bag and filled it from a flask. As soon as he uncorked the flask I recoiled from the pungent aroma—whale oil, no doubt. The lamp was a simple affair, a fist-sized metal reservoir topped with a wick, the whole suspended within a frame that allowed it to be dangled from the hand like a censer. He struck a flint to make a spark. He repeated this operation. In my experience, many sparks would be required before we had a flame. Meanwhile, I offered Fedelma a drink from the water skin, which she gladly accepted. I rummaged through my satchel and produced the extra robe.

"A gift for you from Isabeau."

Fedelma took the robe, immediately slipping it over her ragged shift, apparently all she'd been allowed in the *clochan*. Another layer of clothing obscured further contemplation of her androgynous body, which was just as well. I couldn't tell whether my fascination was curiosity or attraction and given the peril of our circumstances, I didn't need the distraction.

"Thank you, Corax. Isabeau is a most thoughtful woman, don't you think? I do love her so."

I nodded and left it at that.

Diarmuid finally ignited the lamp and handed it to Fedelma. Slinging his bag over the shoulder, he slid into the hole. Fedelma passed the lamp down to him. Within seconds, his hands emerged from the depths, and Fedelma, sitting on the edge, eased into his grasp and was lowered from my sight. The hands popped back out. "Come, Corax, I'll help."

I peered uncertainly into the hole and saw Diarmuid's face looking up at me. "Are you sure you can handle this? I carry no shortage of mass."

"And did you fail to account for the movement of the stones, good sir? They didn't wander off on their own. Come."

Like Fedelma, I sat on the edge and felt Diarmuid's firm grasp on my hips. Sliding forward, I let myself go. For a moment, I had the curious sensation of being suspended in the air. Diarmuid's amazing hands lowered me to a gentle rest on the floor of the passage as if I were no heavier than a child. His touch lingered at my waist, and I felt a swoon rush to my head. Rather than make a complete fool of myself, I pinched my cheek, hard. The sting sobered me up and I stepped away from the monk, pretending that everything was normal.

"Thanks," I squeaked.

Looking up through the hole, I saw the pale moonlit sky and hoped that it would not be my final glimpse of the earth's exterior. With a sigh, I turned to face the underworld. We stood in a tube-shaped passage about as high as it was wide. As promised, Diarmuid's head just cleared the ceiling. Fedelma took the lamp and walked ahead a short distance, then came back. The passage went both directions from the access hole but the way she pointed had a mild downhill slant. I looked around and felt my orientation to the cardinal points of the upper world slip away. As if to reinforce the phantasmagoric character of the setting, the heavy shadows cast by the lamp exaggerated our faces into theatrical masks. Another time this might have been amusing. Fedelma handed the lamp to Diarmuid, who moved past her to take the lead. She indicated that I should go next, and she came last. Diarmuid moved slowly, which I appreciated, for if he got too far ahead, I knew that I'd be stumbling along in the flickering light.

The floor of the passage had been polished by endless runnels of seepage. At times, floods might have roared through, sweeping it clean of debris. Now it was dry, and we could walk unimpeded, rather than scramble. Once before I'd been in a cave, with a theatrical group from the Academy. We trooped into the underworld to re-enact one of the founder's famous scenarios, the one about shadows, light, and some nonsense about seeing the truth. The descent and return had been difficult—over boulders, gravel, and minor cliffs—and I ended up with battered shinbones and a variety of lesions. Plus, the play had been stupid. Of course, I had been younger then, considerably lighter, and readily swayed. In the interim, I'd acquired some extra volume and a lot more skeptical inertia. But the heft had its uses.

It wasn't long before I had more questions. "What if they pursue us underground? Would we not be trapped?"

Fedelma laughed. "They're too superstitious to venture here, even if they knew about it. Besides, it's hardly a trap since there is a way out, as I said."

"The abbot didn't strike me as an overly superstitious man. Quite the opposite, in fact."

"True. However, I heard that he was quite indisposed and likely to remain so for a while."

"Then you know about the assassination attempt."

"Yes. Some of my guardian monks have been quite talkative. What happened is tragic. I feel badly for those women. I appreciate their energy, but they were rash. If they want to improve the general lot of women, they'll have to exercise more cunning and less precipitous tactics."

"I agree. They paid a high price to prod the wasp's nest."

"But I don't think the abbot's minions will follow us here if they can even trace us to the entrance. They're overwrought and uncertain how to proceed without their guiding light. Why, earlier today a small contingent of monks surrounded the *clochan* and cursed me for some time, wildly and to no purpose that I could see. They blame *me* for everything, it seems. I was told that if the abbot should die of his wounds, they would see to it that I was pitched off the tallest cliff into the western ocean."

"All the more reason to flee."

Diarmuid stopped and turned. "My Lady, I cannot believe what I just heard. That my brethren would act with such venality... it's contrary to the vows! What has come over them?"

"Only grief, my sweet Diarmuid, only grief. It beggars us all." She motioned for him to continue, and we resumed our pilgrimage into the bowels of the island.

However, I had no intention of ending my queries. "So, Fedelma, what about the eyes? You said there was a sex factor to the triple iris?"

"Yes, though any explanation will sound convoluted. Generalizations are, as a rule, anathema to understanding, so forgive me if I use them now to outline the problem. Regarding eyesight, especially as it's influenced by the mind, and it always is, men are keen to see things in sharp definition, distinctive and discrete, each form identifiable as itself. Keep in mind these are general tendencies, rough outlines, no more. Definitely not truths or essences. Anyway, women have an ability to perceive the permeable boundaries of things, maintaining awareness of the auras of potential that surround these boundaries. Sharpness is not as important as seeing the whole. Of course, nobody is all one or the other. Consider that these extremes of perception mark a spectrum of possibility. We each have a different position within the blending."

"I do prefer things to be precise, or at least as precise as allowed by reason."

"And so, you employ your dialectic. But the binary scheme of the dialectic is undermined by the third point that stands apart, expanding the realm outside the domain of one dimension. In this case, the third point is the hermaphrodite: not exactly a combination of male and female, more like an assembly of the same components into something completely different. A third sex, if you will. Or fourth and fifth, depending on how much detail you want to encompass."

"This seems rather fantastical and requires rather more examination."

"You're welcome to examine as closely as you wish." I could feel her grin behind my back and was glad she couldn't see the blood in my face. Her offer was intriguing, but I knew she wasn't serious. I walked on, following Diarmuid, listening to Fedelma's weird ideas.

"Bear with me for now, Corax. We approach the threshold of relevance. It seems that the triple iris is a phenomenon coincident with hermaphroditism. Not all hermaphrodites have this condition, but as far as my research shows, all humans with the triple iris are hermaphrodites. Now, the array of possible combinations of sex characteristics means that hermaphrodites occupy a domain of diversity within their condition. I wouldn't call it a spectrum because it can't be mapped on a line. It would be more productive to imagine a field of wild blooms, scattered in no obvious order."

"And what are your sources for this compendium of far-fetched assertions?"

"I do know the language of the birds."

"Well, okay then. Difficult to argue with that." The language of the birds was an esoteric discipline that allowed an adept to tap into avian lore, reportedly a well of endless wisdom. It had a formidable reputation in some circles and was so difficult to learn that there were few practitioners. I'd never met anyone who claimed to know it; thus, I had no experience in gauging its value. As usual, I was dubious. Impressed, but dubious.

"Birds see all and remember all. Nothing escapes them. Much can be learned in communion with the winged ones."

"If you say so. But what are you saying about my eyes? That I'm not a man?"

"Evidently, you're not, Corax. At least not completely, according to the usual definitions. If you don't carry observable body evidence of female features, then it may be that your blood does. But because you're man enough to embody a majority of the characteristics of that sex, it suggests that your vision overemphasizes the hard clarity of sight associated with the masculine. Feminine perceptions, which coexist in your vision, are not working in conjunction with your masculine perceptions, thus creating cognitive dissonance and rendering your mind unable to process what you see. Since you are a hermaphrodite, your eyes see both ways, but your masculine and feminine body chemistry battle over the integration of sensory information. The silver lenses filter out most of the female perceptions, which is why they help."

"Staggering! I... have to think about this!" I felt sweat dripping off my forehead and under my arms. "I... I must confess that my body isn't entirely normal. I have breasts, sort of. I mean, I have a penis, too."

Fedelma's voice was gentle. "Anomalies are difficult to admit, I know. Don't be ashamed."

Salt stung my eyes. "Yes, well... But, if what you say is true, it doesn't explain why *your* sight isn't affected. Are you not also a mixture? Wouldn't the masculine aspect of your sex provide perceptual dissonance?"

"A logical question. However, it seems that masculine visual debilities aren't equivalent for the female. A shortcoming of the sex, I'm afraid. In other words, female eyes can see through the perceptions of men without distortion. Not so the other way.

And though I, too, am a hermaphrodite, the greater portion of my sexual allotment is female. Thus, my vision functions without adaptive equipment. I'm sorry that yours does not."

I felt uncomfortable with this discussion. Once again, it occurred to me that I was losing my edge. Why wasn't I pounding at her absurdities with relentless queries, fracturing those bizarre assertions with the light of reason? Being underground was a disadvantage. I worked better in the sun and air. The possibility that I didn't have a substantial rejoinder lurked in the back of my mind, which is where I wanted it to stay. I was also tired of hearing about my so-called deficiencies. Lacking anything else, I retreated to sarcasm. "So, what are you saying, that in order to see better I need to enhance my femininity?" I waved my arms and minced like a silly fool.

Fedelma chuckled. "Ah, my queenly Corax, that would only involve gender, which wouldn't help you much. You could dress and act as a woman, like many specialized performers, but it wouldn't change your sight or your sex. You may enjoy it, though."

I stopped my prancing before I tripped over something. "Wait -- didn't you imply that there was a possible benefit for me in skulking through these endless underworld chambers? Perhaps I was mistaken, but I thought it was related to my sight."

"You weren't mistaken. Improving your sight requires a chemical intervention, not a behavioral change. If we can find this kraken, then we will ask for its help."

[10]

Fedelma's answers were troublesome. Luckily, the angle of the passage steepened, and I had to focus on my steps. Diarmuid advanced cautiously, holding the lamp to his side so that it illuminated behind as well as front. The cross-section of the tunnel was no longer circular, but oval-shaped and canted about forty-five degrees. Diarmuid tilted his body to avoid scrapes. The floor of the tunnel grew irregular, and we had to walk slowly. I moved without rhythm, shaking a little and wishing for an oaken staff to lean on. I didn't dare turn to look at Fedelma for fear of losing my balance, but I could tell from the movement of air that she stayed close. I imagined her flowing in perfect grace, unlike the lumbering, grunting bovine that I surely resembled.

Despite my care, the flickering light deceived me, and I missed a step. With mass uncentered, there was a twinge of vertigo as I flailed in panic. Suddenly, a small thin hand, feeling like a claw, gripped my upper arm and pulled me back to vertical. Automatically, I steadied myself by putting a hand on Fedelma's shoulder, feeling the hard muscles under her robe.

She could have said many things, none of them flattering, but instead, she smiled and stretched her neck to give me a kiss on the lips. What was with these women of the western lands? My own mother had never kissed me this much. A fire coursed through my veins, and I stood up as straight as I could, feeling a rush of strength. How did Fedelma do these things? A most surprising woman—or whatever she was.

Diarmuid, unaware, had gone ahead and I hastened to catch up. I ransacked my mind for a category in which I could place Fedelma. Dryad, nymph, daimon, gorgon, shapeshifter, or what? None of them fulfilled the requirements for classification. Perhaps I should just accept her own label—bard—though surely, she was more than that.

The angle eased and Diarmuid stopped. He held up the lamp and peered into the dark.

"Crossroads," he announced.

Fedelma joined him and looked around. She took the lamp and held it above her head while pointing out the three possible continuations. "The right-hand passage winds around like the canal of your ear, narrowing as it goes, shrinking until you'd have to be a mouse. To the left, we find the descent to the grotto. Straight ahead, that's our escape. I've explored only a short section, but the map is clear that it'll lead us to the rocky isle and our rendezvous."

"Lead on," I muttered in resignation.

Fedelma gave the lamp back to Diarmuid and stepped aside. I marveled at her fluidity. She shifted from place to place without effort or even the perception of movement. No wonder people thought she wielded magic. I figured it was nothing more than well-trained muscles.

The left-hand passage was narrow and Diarmuid turned sideways to negotiate the constriction. He managed to do so while holding the lamp above his head. We shuffled along behind him. Due to my girth, it wasn't easier to go sideways than frontwards. I took an oblique approach and used my hands to push along the wall for additional propulsion. I heard Fedelma chuckle; I thought about a sharp rejoinder but decided to save my breath.

The passage remained narrow past the point of reason, winding and twisting through the limestone matrix. It was laborious going and several times I had to fight off the urge to panic. Fedelma anticipated these attacks and as soon as I started to feel the inner tension, she placed a hand on my neck and with a few gentle strokes, calm was restored. I don't know how long we pushed through the narrows; time seemed to be a relative concept, divorced from the usual chronology of a changing sky. After a claustrophobic eternity, the passage grew wider, and we were able to walk at a faster pace.

Diarmuid stopped and pointed to the right. We were at another junction. An oval opening in the wall carried a scent of the ocean.

"We must be close to the grotto, then," I said.

"Shhh!" whispered Fedelma. "If the kraken is present, we do not want to scare her away!"

Fedelma stepped into the oval and stared down the dark passage. Without a word, she motioned to Diarmuid to leave the lamp in the main corridor. She grabbed my hand and pulled me after her as she crept forward. I had no intention to resist, but I thought that if I had, she would have dragged me anyway. It seemed daft to venture into the blackness, but as we plunged into the void, a dim blue light filtered up the passage from below. As we moved down the incline, the aroma of the sea and the strength of the light grew more pronounced.

Fedelma made us stop before we left the tunnel and we crowded against her back, peering into the grotto. It was a vast space, cloaked in shadows and difficult to gauge, but clearly larger than anything constructed by the hands of man, even the imperial coliseums. Before us was a sandy beach that arced partway around a reservoir of glassy water. The lake was the source of the light, filled with bioluminescent creatures, from jellyfish to plankton, glowing blue and green, pulsing with languid motion as they danced slowly about the pool. Looking into the water was like gazing upon the great Imaginarium of the gods, a simulacrum of the cosmos itself.

The vaulted ceiling of the grotto rose far above us. Around the periphery were columns of stalagmites joined with their stalactite progenitors, coated in a marble polish of delicate hues. All the stone looked as if shaped from melted wax: surfaces gleamed in a sinuous harmony. Recesses along the walls hinted at cabinets of the arcane, repositories of secrets unknown to the upper world.

As we contemplated the wonder of the place, I realized that we had our arms around each other, as if the overpowering beauty required an affirmation of touch. We huddled in awe and insignificance.

Fedelma slowly raised her hand and pointed, indicating a spot along the shore, past the end of the beach. There the stone formed a broad platform between the cavern walls and the lake. She trembled and kept her finger fixed. As I stared, trying to see what she saw, I perceived a dark silhouette on the water, then a slight movement. The realization came over me that I saw a living shape floating on the surface. A snake-like tentacle lifted out of the water and casually draped itself over the rock. A cephalopod, no doubt about it. The tentacle was at least a hundred cubits long. No longer could I deny the existence of the kraken.

Even a social dullard like myself could see the excitement on Fedelma's face. She motioned for us to stay put as she eased out of the tunnel and onto the floor of the grotto. Next, she did something unexpected: she slipped off her clothes. I experienced a twinge of disappointment to notice that she looked like a conventional woman. There were no astonishing anomalies of genitalia or other body features that might reveal an ambiguous sex, at least none that I could see. I realized that my disappointment stemmed from wanting to find someone as odd as myself, another freak.

She glided forward like the passing of a subtle breeze. As her form receded, I gauged the true size of the grotto and understood that it was even bigger than I thought. The tentacle of the kraken, still draped over the side of the basin, dwarfed Fedelma as she approached. She slowed her pace and began to sing. I couldn't understand the words, if they were words; the melody rose from her throat like the chirping of a wren before gradually expanding into a chorus of birds, layering notes in orchestral complexity. The sound echoed and shifted around the grotto, shaping itself into delaying rounds of music. If anything could bring stone to life, this would be it, I thought. But outside of Fedelma, nothing moved, and it felt like time itself came to rest.

Fedelma reached the great tentacle. She extended a hand, still singing, and stroked the smooth upper surface of the appendage. The kraken abided her touch. Fedelma's height matched the tentacle's thickness; it could have crushed her with a flick. She sprung up, mounting the tentacle as if it were a horse. Sitting for a moment, facing toward the head of the beast, she stopped singing and stretched out prone along the top of the tentacle. I held my breath and watched in horror. She looked like a youth relaxing in bed. Her arms and legs embraced the limb and she resumed singing. The new melody featured throat rumbles and unusual polyrhythms so that it was hardly a melody at all, but a wild assemblage of primal sound. The kraken slipped its other feeder tentacle out of the water and held it in the air, waving it in cadence with Fedelma's music, then lowered the paddle-shaped end to rest gently on her back. Diarmuid and I stood without a rustle of movement, afraid to breathe, watching the scene play out like a dream.

I don't know how long Fedelma lay sandwiched between the beast's limbs, but it seemed forever before the kraken lifted its extremity and she slid off to stand calmly next to it. She looked back at us and waved her arms. "It's good. Come on over!"

Diarmuid and I glanced at each other and started to advance. She called a warning. "Leave the clothes. Bare skin only!"

We halted and looked at each other again. It made as much sense as anything else. I watched Diarmuid shuck off his robe, admiring his muscled shoulders and tight abdomen. His penis, I noted, was well-formed, even if smaller than my own. As we walked together toward Fedelma, I hoped he didn't register the incongruities of my body, though it was hard to imagine otherwise. It's not like I could hide them. As far as I could tell, he paid no attention, which I found curiously disappointing. I gasped and forgot about all that when the beast suddenly rolled in the water, lifting and re-arranging its tentacles. Fedelma stood unfazed as the giant limbs shifted over her. The kraken appeared identical to a squid, magnified to colossal proportions. The body rode higher in the water, revealing an eye on the side, just behind the beak. It was the largest eye I'd ever seen, the size of a cartwheel. Around the enormous pupil in concentric rings,

I saw three irises of contrasting color. A point of commonality between us. It was shocking to consider that we were all freaks here, all except for the statuesque Diarmuid.

Fedelma smiled at us. She glowed with a bioluminescence like the other creatures in the grotto. So, this was the glow I'd seen in her before, which caused me to even consider a magical explanation. Maybe it was, after all. Or maybe she wasn't entirely human. I put my speculations aside when she pointed at two parallel grooves worn in the rock.

"Lay down on your backs, you two, heads toward the wall. Corax, you should remove your goggles. I know you have questions, but this isn't the time for them. The Great One will soon leave, but they have agreed to mingle before departure. Trust me here."

As she pronounced this statement, it occurred to me that we had done nothing but trust her every step along the way. Oh well, I thought, logically there was no reason to stop now. I lay down in the trough and removed my goggles, glancing at Diarmuid, who was already tucked in. The limestone was smooth and cool on my back. Premonitions of unspeakable acts flashed through my head, reflecting the anxiety tumbling in my gut. Fedelma began another song, and I found some calm in its melody. I closed my eyes to reduce the visual incoherence and let the sound of her voice work its charm. The situation was strange, no doubt, but it wasn't so bad, was it, in the scheme of things? Surely no more outlandish than the Founding Master's delusion of the shadowy cave and its parade of silhouettes going nowhere and doing nothing. Why did these things always take place in caves? Underground, the underworld, the antithesis of clarity and definition, where substances merge and are crushed into a matrix, the womb, the mother, the source. I felt giddy with my own surrender.

Diarmuid's hand touched my own and I clasped it eagerly. Lost in ruminations, I had forgotten he was there, but he was, perhaps going through his own confusions, yet he hadn't forgotten about me. I tightened the grip on his hand and felt a surge of heat in my loins. Unbelievably, my member thickened in defiance of any wishes to the contrary. I was embarrassed and tried to think of other things, but I did not let go of his hand.

I knew it for what it was as soon as the tentacle touched my foot. Cool and moist, with a delicacy astonishing for its size, the paddle-shaped extremity caressed and pulled at my toes. If it wanted to, the tentacle could grab my ankle and yank me back toward the eight, shorter arms where I'd be stuffed into the maw of the beak. Should the kraken desire, I would become its food. But the rough pad didn't clamp down, instead creeping up my leg to settle on my chest. The heel of the pad sunk into my abdomen, letting its full weight sit on my torso. It was heavy, but I could still breathe. I felt the rough outline of its numerous suckers, not soft at all, but sharp as stone. In the area of my heart, they dug into the skin, cutting the flesh, and I wanted to scream from the pain of a thousand gouging needles. The agony dissipated in a rush of analgesia. I felt transported to a placid realm, floating on air or sea or a thousand feathers. After that, I lost consciousness.

I woke to Fedelma's voice, singing in low tones yet still reverberating in the acoustics of the cavern. Her hand rested on my forehead. Opening my eyes, I saw that she sat cross-legged between us, her other hand on Diarmuid. She sang with eyes shut. I lifted my head to scan the water for the kraken. The surface of the lake was placid, though underneath the carnival of bioluminescent creatures swam in arcs.

The singing stopped. "So, Corax, you have returned to your senses."

I twisted my head to look at her. A delicate smile formed on her lips, and it occurred to me that I *saw* her, clearly and without distortion. "By the gods! I can see!" And it was true, all the fragmentations and confusions of sight, the curse of the triple iris, were gone. I saw the world as it was, directly, at last.

I squeaked in delight and tried to sit up, but the attempt revealed a grogginess that forced me back to the rock slab. Like a seal, I wriggled onto my side to get a better look at my companions. Diarmuid's eyelids fluttered, and I watched him regain consciousness, thinking what a beautiful man he was, even with the hideous tonsure. Fedelma leaned over to kiss the birthmark on his bald forehead. I thought how nice it would be to do the same; instead, I fidgeted.

"My dear fellows, how do you feel now that you've been initiated by the Great One?"

Diarmuid struggled to hoist himself upright, while I remained on my side and unleashed an avalanche of questions. "What do you mean initiated? What makes the beast great, other than its considerable size? And what's happened to my vision? I assume there's a connection."

"Of course, there is. Let me explain. All kraken are great, in a sense, but as I'm sure you noticed by the triple iris, this one is hermaphroditic. Like many other nonhuman examples, such as trees and corals, the Great One is functional in at least two sexual capacities. Not only can she/he mate with male and female kraken, but he/she can also mate with herself. If one were looking for a god, it would be hard to imagine a better candidate. But we have no need of mystification – the reality of the being is awesome enough. What truly makes this kraken the Great One, though, is that they have achieved a biochemical balance across the diversity of their sexual potential. Essentially, they can be what they want when they want. We human hermaphrodites, as you know all too well, often struggle to maintain equanimity amidst a jumble of emotions and internal essences. The Great One holds the secret of balance for us. The original goal of my mission to this island was to find this being and to ask if they would share their knowledge. Finally given the chance, you can believe that I asked very nicely.

"The results are even better than I expected! Corax, your body chemistry has been adjusted and now you can see unhindered. Diarmuid, caught up for years with indecisive longings, may now find himself able to set aside doubts and explore what it means to be a man. As for myself, I gained another language, the tongue of the deep, allowing me to sing to the creatures of the sea. There may be other effects—for all of us—to be revealed over time."

She broke off her explanation and started vocalizing a strange series of clicks, squeals, and staccato rhythms. There was something musical about it, if your idea of music was free of the usual conventions. As these sounds echoed around the cavern, many of the creatures in the lake swam or drifted in our direction, pulsing in colors that replicated the rhythms of her voice. The alien ensemble resembled nothing more than a performance of synchronized dance and music.

"But Fedelma," I interrupted, "how did all this happen?"

She stopped the vocal flow and grinned. "When the Great One put their tentacles on our skins, you felt the sharpness of their grip. We've been marked." She pointed to my abdomen, to Diarmuid's, then spun around to show us her back. We all bore the same circular red welts the diameter of a palm, dozens of them. Blood still oozed from a few but most were already scabbing over.

"Blessed moly! Look at these bites! We could have been ripped to shreds!"

"Could have been but were not. They're not bites, but the points of contact where the tentacle cups penetrated your flesh. The wounds became portals for the kraken to mingle their chemistry with ours. Given the disproportionate sizes, I think their touch was most delicate. Besides, you're not harmed, though there may be a scar. Between us, I find them rather attractive." She bent to one knee and kissed a mark on Diarmuid's belly. His hand stroked the back of her head as she licked his wound. I'd never felt ghoulish, but I wanted to do that.

"I feel full of spirit," he said. "A little dizzy, but with keen awareness of the layers of meaning that surround us. What an amazing world this is!" He gently pushed Fedelma away and stood up to gaze at the grotto as if he was seeing it for the first time. "Look at this place. Have you ever seen anything like it, philosopher?"

I agreed that I had not. With little grace and a lot of grunting, I labored to a standing posture. Fedelma bounced to her feet as if sprung. Her lithe body and the energy that hovered around it sparkled in my new vision. She was really quite attractive. I looked at Diarmuid, looking around the cavern in dumb wonder, and I thought he was attractive, too. It wasn't long before these sensations migrated to my loins. What had come over me? Was this part of the kraken's "chemical balancing?" Was I now embarking, despite my dedication to a life of reason, on a voyage of sexual discovery? Oddly, I could conjure no resistance to such an idea.

Fedelma grinned at the two of us and rocked from foot to foot. "The Great One returned to its rounds of the deep. Shall we continue our own journey? We wouldn't want to keep our companions waiting. Is anyone else hungry? I wouldn't mind some food before we set off."

We were all hungry. A short walk around the lake and we reclaimed our clothes at the tunnel entrance. As I reached for my robes, Fedelma spoke again. "I love your shape, Corax. It's unique and marvelous and reminds me of those old goddesses carved in mammoth ivory. Only with a penis, of course."

Diarmuid looked at me and grinned. I didn't know whether to blush or strut but settled for getting dressed as quickly as possible. I arranged my face into a careful blank and said nothing. After a final scan of the shimmering grotto, we turned to the tunnel and climbed back into the stony maze.

[11]

At the last junction, we paused and ate a quick meal of scone, salt cod, and cheese. Even in the meager light of the lamp, I savored the novelty of unfiltered sight. The kraken infusion had done more than just replicate the adaptations of the goggles, it surpassed them, enhancing every aspect of vision. I could see further into the shadows, delineating shapes instead of a blurred mass. The mineralized colors and polished surfaces of the limestone provided a sensual pleasure to behold. Yet it was the sight of my companions that held my attention. I not only perceived their three-dimensional occupation of space, the lines and limits of their figures, but I saw these images surrounded by auras of life-warmth. Irrational, perhaps—I didn't care. It was love, wasn't it, and when is that rational?

Soon we were on our feet and hiking through the passage back to the four-way intersection. We fell into the same procession, with Diarmuid and the lamp in the lead and Fedelma padding along in the rear. We stayed close together and walked in a rhythm of bobbing light and careful steps.

At the junction, we gathered in a huddle. Fedelma asked for silence, saying that she needed to gather her memories about the map. Without waiting for a response, she closed her eyes and slipped into a trance, swaying back and forth like a sapling in the breeze. Diarmuid and I exchanged raised eyebrows and watched her. I worried that she might lose her balance; however, it was obvious that she knew exactly what she was doing. Her thoughts played across her face like weather over the sea.

This performance of memory entertained me and I was sorry when she came to rest, opened her eyes, and nodded at us, pointing down the middle passage.

"Perhaps a mile of walking until we get to the exit. The map is vague about some sections but there are no deviations: the way is straight. Shall we?" She gestured for Diarmuid to take the lead and we entered the new tunnel in single file.

The passage sloped downward along a rough surface. Every step over the uneven floor had to be taken with deliberation. The jaunty mood that we carried out of the grotto shifted into a single-minded concentration necessary to avoid tumbling onto jagged edges. I imagined the abrupt contact between my skull and a rock, the thought of which motivated the full measure of my attention. Diarmuid picked his way with similar caution. Fedelma, however, hummed and danced behind us.

I lost track of time. We could have been underground for hours or even days. Divorced from the sun and sky, there was nothing to measure. A curious vertigo accompanied this realization, a sense that being lost in time generates a need to locate stable space. In the gloom of the tunnels, this remained an unmet need because the light of the lamp offered the only promise of stability, and it bobbed along with its porter, a constantly receding target. My ruminations, or distractions, or whatever they were, rather than honing themselves toward brilliance, sloshed around in pointless iterations, and I was glad to abandon them when Diarmuid put his hand up and came to a halt.

"There's a gap," he said.

Fedelma slipped past and stood beside him, peering ahead. The way had leveled after a lengthy descent, but it hadn't made the going much easier. I waited patiently for the two of them to assess the obstacle in front of us. I didn't like the sound of "gap," and I had no wish to see it until necessary.

"We'll have to jump," she said.

"What are you talking about?" I whined.

Fedelma turned her head to look at me. Her face lay shrouded in Diarmuid's shadow, and I couldn't see the expression. "There's a cleft in the passage, perhaps from an old earthquake. It cuts straight across and there's no way around. It isn't insurmountable, but it'll take more than a step, even a long one. How are your leaping skills?"

I thought the question was cruel. Obviously, I had no leaping skills. I sighed and shuffled forward, putting my hand on Diarmuid's back and leaning around him to see the problem. Despite being prepared for a daunting sight, I gasped anyway. The situation was exactly as described, a clean break across the passage, maybe three cubits wide. It didn't take a close inspection to know that the gap was deep. Falling in would convey a quick descent to Hades. I couldn't imagine leaping over it, but I easily imagined plunging to my death, screaming the whole way.

"That... seems too far for me."

Fedelma rubbed the bristles on her head with the palm of a hand and nodded. "I thought you'd say that. We need another solution."

Diarmuid handed me the lamp and put his arms around us, pulling us into a tight cluster. He cleared his throat. "I'm taller than the gap is wide. Let me be a bridge for both of you."

"No," I protested, "surely I'm too heavy for you."

"Doubtful," he muttered as he squeezed my shoulder. I recalled again how he'd muscled away the massive stones that covered the cave entrance and how effortlessly he'd lifted me down through the hole. Though I often disparaged my own bulk with comparisons to boulders, I was hardly in the same category as a dolmen stone. Without waiting for further debate, he stepped out of the embrace and advanced to the edge of the cleft. He took one deep breath, rocked up on his toes, and dropped forward, keeping his body board straight. Arms out, his hands slapped down on the brink of the far side. He checked his fall with those powerful shoulders, well-toned from perpetual grave digging, and flexed slightly as he landed. He made some minor adjustments, then settled into place. With his full weight supported by his hands and the balls of his feet, he formed a plank across the void.

"Best get on with it," he said.

Fedelma took the lamp from me and skipped across his back, barely touching him. I didn't move. The thought crossed my mind that it might make more sense for me to go back the way we had come, leaving them to go on without me.

"Corax," Diarmuid grunted. "Just slide across on your butt, like crossing a log over a stream. But be merciful and do it quickly."

At this point, I had no real choice but to indulge in the scheme. Otherwise, I could anticipate nothing more than a life of humiliation and lingering shame. With Fedelma holding the lamp high, I sat on the back of Diarmuid's ankles and scooted forward, bending slightly to keep my hands in front and balanced on his legs.

"Is this okay?" I asked.

"It'll be less okay the longer you take," was the response.

I advanced, sliding my hands up over his bottom, a gesture that might have been interesting in another context. What drove my heart into my mouth was the glance I took over the side. I looked straight down into an unholy blackness; a place crafted out of the worst nightmares. This convinced me to clamber across the plank of Diarmuid and reach the other side as quickly as possible. Fedelma's free hand grabbed my own and she pulled me to standing on the far side. Diarmuid sighed in relief. He extended his arms and elevated his rear, forming a triangle across the gap, then kicked off with his feet, launching the lower part of his body across the void and into a somersault, rolling up next to us.

Before he could stand, Fedelma pushed the lamp into my hand and threw herself on him, kissing his face and head and squirming over him like a gleeful child. I had no intention of dropping the precious lamp, but it seemed rude not to show gratitude, so when I saw my chance, I leaned in to plant a swift kiss on Diarmuid's forehead, right on the birthmark as I wanted. He laughed and when I pulled back, our eyes locked for a moment, and I felt a warmth in his gaze.

We sat down for water and a bite of food to celebrate the triumph. The bowels of the Holy Island beckoned, however, and we soon returned to our task of finding the way out.

"How much farther? Do you have a sense?" I asked as we scrambled through the rough tunnel.

"Not far, I should think. We're ascending, and I believe a return to the surface is in the offing. We've certainly covered enough lateral distance to be near the isle."

I failed to understand how she knew this. Perhaps part of her memory bank included a pedometer function that traced the distance on the mental map. A prodigious feat of data collection and storage, but not impossible, I supposed. Trying to estimate the breadth of my own memory, I forgot the here and now. My right foot wedged in a groove, and I fell face down, turning slightly to take the blow on the shoulder and protect my head. That worked, but it also wrenched the jammed foot. Pain speared my ankle and I screamed. My companions rushed over and gently extricated my foot. Unfortunately, this didn't negate the pain. Fedelma held my leg and palpated the ankle and extremity, measuring the intensity of my groans and winces as she probed.

"Nothing is broken, I would say. A sprain, perhaps," she announced.

I sat up and held my throbbing ankle. Self-pity took over when I recognized that I wouldn't be able to walk. Now I was even more of a liability. "Just leave me," I moaned.

"Don't be ridiculous," admonished Fedelma. "Just consider it another existential problematic, mister philosopher. Now would be a good time for a dose of stoicism."

Diarmuid looked at me with concern. "I'll carry you."

"No, no, no, that's out of the question."

"It's not a question, sir." He handed the lamp to Fedelma, reached down to spread my legs, then turned his back and crouched in front of me. "Wrap your arms around my neck."

"You can't be serious."

"Do it." His tone allowed no opportunity for argument, so I did it, glancing at Fedelma, who crossed her arms and smirked. Diarmuid scooped his massive paws under my thighs, leaned forward, and stood up, barely staggering under the lift. We shifted around to discover the best arrangement but settled for something less than comfortable for either of us. We were quite a sight, I was sure, a theatrical combination suitable for automatic audience hilarity.

"All aboard, Corax?" Diarmuid asked.

"Yes, yes. Thank you, friend. And if it becomes too much, please leave me along the way."

"You say that, and I hear you say that, but I will not."

With Fedelma in the lead, we continued to hike along the passage as it angled up through the rock. Fortunately for Diarmuid, it wasn't steep. However, gravity kept trying to drag me off his back and persistent readjustments were required. I clung hard, trying to avoid throttling him. While I rode, my mind wandered, as usual. I ticked off the geography of our venture: after the grotto, we followed a tunnel that descended under the Holy Island, ran laterally beneath the floor of the ocean, and now returned to the surface on the isle where our collaborators waited. I was eager to see them, to be sure, but would welcome the sky even more. Despite the high probability of rain.

Fedelma stopped and sniffed the air. "Can you smell it? Brine of the sea? We're almost there."

Soon I saw light filtering down the tunnel, at first dim and diffuse, but getting brighter with each step. Fedelma doused the lamp. We heard the shouting long before we arrived at the end of the passage. Other noises echoed down the tunnel: metal, rocks, and the crunching of things breaking apart. Fedelma put her finger to her lips, and we crept forward. Isabeau stood in the entrance, facing away from us and toward something we couldn't see. She had a sling in her hand that she twirled in a furious circle. She dropped an end, and a rock went flying. Immediately we heard a scream.

Fedelma called softly to Isabeau, who spun around in fear. She saw that it was us, and a broad smile lit her face. Her hair was tangled, and her clothes were in disarray. She did not run to hug us, as I expected, but bent down to reload her sling with another rock, then motioned for us to stay in the tunnel. She turned her head and spoke over her shoulder. "They're here," she said.

We stood at the threshold, unsure of what to do. The passage emerged high on the island, and I saw the sea a hundred cubits below. In front of the tunnel were the signs of struggle. Draped over a short rock wall was the motionless form of a monk, an arrow jutting from his chest. Diarmuid nodded at the corpse. "Brother Cillian," he said. "Always an ass."

I craned my head and saw Marianne, tall and magnificent, standing on the same wall with her longbow cocked. She released the arrow, and we heard another scream. Past her, François grappled in hand-to-hand combat with a monk wielding a table leg. The monk raised the cudgel for a blow and François tossed a stiletto into his ribs. The furniture remnant and the monk dropped to the ground.

Marianne yanked repeatedly at the arrow, trying to pull it out of Brother Cillian. I noticed her quiver was empty. Two monks crawled over a large rock and charged forward. She heard the pounding steps and turned to face the attackers, dropping her bow and leaving the arrow to its victim. The monks charged side by side, swinging staves over their heads like they were going after a mad dog. Marianne feinted to the left, then leaped at the monk on her right. The blow from the left-hand attacker swooshed through empty air and clattered against the stone wall. She drove her fist into the groin of the other monk and removed his staff as he collapsed. Spinning, she twirled the stout wood in a dazzling series of moves, delivering strikes to the head and torso of the monk who had missed, followed by another cluster of blows to the one still doubled over. Within seconds they lay in crumpled, unmoving heaps.

Marianne turned and beckoned to us. "Let's go!" She looked at François, who had just stopped an oncoming monk with another knife thrown to the belly. She ran to the tunnel, gleaming with sweat and excitement. Her proud face turned to dismay when she saw me clutched on Diarmuid's back.

"Shit, what's wrong? No, tell me later. There's no time to lose. The abbot's men have connected the dots. They set upon us an hour ago. They're more cautious now that a few lie horizontal, but there are more—too many more. We can't hold them off forever. The boat's down the slope, off to the right. Let's be away before they discover it."

Fedelma nodded. "Agreed. And there's no future in retreat to the caves. I've no desire to become a cornered rat. Plus, let's just say there are things down there best left unknown to the Saint and his minions."

We scrambled out of the tunnel without a word and plunged down the steep grade toward the currach. My reunion with daylight was far from celebratory, but I was pleased to note that at least it wasn't raining.

Marianne urged us on. "Go! I'll hold them back until you get to the boat." She waved and disappeared behind the slope, presumably to gather as many arrows as she could before the next onslaught. Isabeau led us down the hill, leaping through the rocks with surprising grace. If I lost a few pounds, maybe I could do that. We followed her in a line: Fedelma, prancing like a deer, François, grumbling the whole way about only having one blade left, and Diarmuid, steady as an ox with me loaded on his back. There were no corpses or combat debris on the descent, so I reasoned that the monks had yet to study the merits of flanking tactics, perhaps the only reason they hadn't cut off this line of retreat. I offered a silent prayer to the gods for discouraging the study of wars and means at the monastery.

Isabeau and the others steadied the bouncy currach while Diarmuid stepped in and deposited me gently in the bow. I scooted up and leaned my back against the curve, shoulders hitched over the gunwales while Diarmuid untied the bow-line. He stepped over the two thwarts and sat down in the one closest to the stern, facing backward. Using an oar to push the bow away from the rocks so that it pointed out to sea, he then lifted and fitted an oar into a lock on each side. Previously, I had only seen one person per oar, but I understood that he meant to double the effort. Having been the beneficiary of his tremendous strength, I saw no reason to coax him otherwise. Isabeau and François clambered around him and took the next bench, side-by-side, fixing their oars. Fedelma untied the second mooring and jumped into the stern, holding us into the rocks with the tiller, a loose oar with a broader blade.

Marianne emerged on the rise above us. She fired an arrow, then dropped the bow to grab something on the ground, a staff or rock, I couldn't see. A monk leaped on her before she could get the staff and the two of them fell to the ground. The scuffle was intense but brief, ending with a sickening crack that we heard all the way down the slope. Marianne jumped up, threw the bow over her shoulder, and started running. She took giant strides and leaps, all the while gripping her left forearm with her right hand. As she got closer, I could see a knife impaled in her bloody arm.

Isabeau was distraught. "Fuck! You're wounded! Get in! Get in!"

Marianne jumped into the boat, shedding bow and quiver, and stumbled over the thwarts and rowers to collapse in my lap. "It's nothing. Go! Quickly! The monks have retreated for the moment. Row! I can take care of this bee stinger myself."

There was no time to assess options and there was only one, anyway. Fedelma pushed off and Diarmuid, François, and Isabeau dug in with the oars. It took a few strokes to get up a rhythm, but with Diarmuid's power and experience setting the pace, the other two caught on quickly and we started to speed across the water. Fedelma steered us on a beeline for the mainland coast, visible if I craned my head, and the island quickly fell astern.

Marianne groaned a long, guttural cry of pain. Something about that sound, coming from her, made me ache inside. I put my hands under her armpits, dragging her up on my chest. "How can I help?" I asked.

"I need a length of cloth, preferably clean but whatever you have."

Isabeau dropped one hand from her oar and fished into a bag, emerging with a roll of cloth that she tossed over her shoulder. "It's clean," she called as she put both hands back to the rowing.

I unwound the cloth and held it ready. Marianne gritted her teeth and took hold of the knife. It was a pathetic combat weapon, a table utensil for slicing off morsels of roast, but sharp enough to penetrate human meat. It was driven vertically into the forearm and parallel to the bones. Although Marianne was bleeding, it wasn't profuse, suggesting that no major vessels had been severed. I thought that the knife may have only separated the grain of the muscles since she still had some function in the hand. She gave me a look, I nodded, and she pulled the knife straight out with a chilling yell. There was a surge of blood, but I quickly wrapped the cloth around her arm and with pressure, the bleeding subsided. As soon as I tied off the bandage, she sighed and slumped against the softness of my belly. Nothing seemed more useful at that moment than putting my arms around her. I cradled her like a child.

Meanwhile, the crew pulled hard, rowing like our lives depended on it, a more than likely assumption. We gained distance from the island and with every additional boat length, I felt better. Hope grew a little but fizzled entirely when I saw two large *curraghs* crammed with monks appear around the last promontory of the island. We had many lengths on them, but they had twice the oars and more than twice the crew. They would overtake us, it was certain.

I heard Diarmuid say one word: "Lord." He made a curious gesture, a kind of shrug as if donning the skin of a beast, stretched his neck, and with a shudder unveiled a new level of power, rowing like a swan taking flight. François and Isabeau struggled to keep pace with the giant, and it was all they could do to maintain a helpful cadence. Despite these efforts, the monks advanced, cheering themselves on with rhythmic exuberance.

The two pursuing boats, having discovered the maneuver of flanking, fanned out to take us from either side. We cruised over the water at a tremendous rate, helped by the lighter load in our craft, but the gap closed inexorably. A monk standing in the bow of the starboard boat had been gesturing wildly and yelling since we saw them. He was now close enough to be heard.

"Serpents of Satan!" He spewed. "The Lord's wrath is upon thee! Make haste, make haste, 'twill do thee no good! Vengeance, vengeance!" There was plenty more of the same raging gibberish, most of which I didn't bother to remember. His face swelled and twisted into a mask of such exaggerated fury that it would have been comic if our situation were not so dire. I detected not a trace of reason or spiritual doctrine left in either monastic boat. No doubt these monks, once men of God, would tear us to ribbons with bare hands if they got hold of us.

The ranting monk egged on his fellows, and they were soon within a boat length. Marianne tensed and sat up, readying herself for a last stand. I tightened my embrace, keeping her close like a charm. "What the fuck?" I said when Fedelma removed the rudder from the water and calmly placed it in the bilge. She stepped onto the stern gunwale, somehow balancing on the narrow perch despite the swells and rolling of the boat. Ignoring the oncoming pursuit, she launched a chant in a piercing voice, expelling a syncopated string of clicking noises and whines, mixed with solid, drawn-out notes: the language of the Deep, as she had called it. It carved out a moment of silence before the monks exploded with new curses and threats, with the loudest shrieks coming from the raging figurehead. François stopped rowing, pulled out his last knife, kissed the blade, murmured "*au revoir, cherie,*" and hurled it with astonishing accuracy into the throat of the fuming orator. The monk gurgled, clasped his neck, and fell into the sea, blood gushing from his mouth. The brethren promptly ran over him, caught up in the inertia of their strokes. This only seemed to excite them further, and rather than stopping for their mate, they redoubled their efforts to close the gap.

It occurred to me that I should reflect on my life during these last moments before death, especially the unexamined parts. I thought of sharing this notion with Marianne but figured she would scoff and reach for a weapon. In any case, such reflection merely offered a benefit if I survived, in which case it was also unnecessary. I wondered what I might do to help our cause. If only I knew how to fight! I was truly a disability in the physical realm, as had been demonstrated many times over on this mission. I vowed that if I got out of this, I would embark on a campaign of conditioning and martial discipline.

Fedelma stopped singing and said, "She's here." It didn't occur to me what she meant by that until I saw two enormous feeder tentacles rise out of the water behind the boat of the now-deceased haranguer. Before any of the unfortunate crew realized what was happening, the kraken crushed them between the two powerful limbs, swept them off the deck in a mass, and thrust the writhing clump of monks back into the eight shorter arms, where they were seized and shoved, one by one, into the maw of the beak.

The monks in the other boat stopped rowing and began to howl, beseeching their god and blaming the devil, none of which did their fellows any good. On our boat everyone froze and stared, all except for Diarmuid, who kept rowing. The feeder tentacles of the kraken again shot forward and grabbed the empty boat, lifting it into the air and waving it around like a toy. In a demonstration of raw power, it swung the boat in a wide arc and brought it crashing down, edge-first like an axe, across the other monastic boat, cleaving it in two amidst an explosion of spray, wood fragments, sections of cowhide, and screams. The several monks that were not crushed by the impact jumped into the sea and paddled frantically, calling out to us for mercy and succor. Their cries trailed away to silence as, one by one, they were pulled under the surface.

We sat in limp shock. Even Fedelma looked stunned. Stepping down from the gunwale, she retrieved the tiller, lowering it into the water. She surveyed the aftermath of bloody flotsam with a grim expression. Indeed, there were no words for it. Yet Diarmuid continued to pull steadily at the oars, expanding the distance between us and the debris left in the kraken's wake. "Amen," he said.

The concentrated violence of that moment was like nothing I had ever seen or imagined. My body still shook from the terror, yet I couldn't deny a satisfaction at the outcome. It was mythic! And who could dream up such an ally? To think that I started this journey in total disbelief! Clearly, I needed to reassess my paradigms.

Diarmuid interrupted the trance that had settled over the rest of us as we tried to digest the event. "I hesitate to follow the visitation of a god with mundane concerns," he said, "but I surely could use some help with the rowing."

[12]

It was dark when we landed on a remote beach several miles south of the port. There was no sign of habitation or traffic but given that we had directly or indirectly caused the deaths of a number of monks from the Order of St. Terminus, we elected not to reveal our presence with a fire. I dearly wanted the warmth and distraction. Instead, we found a sandy nook beneath a small limestone outcrop, huddled close together, and shared what we had of food and warmth.

We sat in the stillness of the night without chatter. No one had the energy for it. During the long afternoon of rowing across the strait, we had taken turns to tell our stories, marveling at the exploits and close calls. Marianne grew feverish from her wound, but Isabeau applied herbs, and the fever dropped. Diarmuid, after he had carried me from the boat to our nook, sank into the sand next to me, flinging a tree-like arm across my waist. Exhaustion reigned in our pile of flesh. My hip touched Isabeau's, and she and François wrapped themselves around Marianne, cuddling her like loyal comrades. Only Fedelma seemed distracted. She paced along the edge of the water for a long while. The breeze caught her soft voice and I listened as she alternated between human melodies and the language of the Deep. Her coda lingered with me for weeks, haunting my memories of that day.

I fell asleep at some point, waking slightly when Fedelma squeezed in between Isabeau and me, kissing us both as she slid into the meld.

The next morning dawned fair. As we consumed more rations, we made our plans. It was agreed that lingering in the area was foolish and we should make haste to increase our distance from the Holy Island. I urged Fedelma to return with me to the Academy where I was sure that she could teach us many things and secure additional renown if she desired. She declined, although not without regret. She, François, Isabeau, and Marianne felt obliged to head directly inland, traversing the Emerald Isle and making their way across the sea to the continent where their fellowship was based. There, in their sanctuary, they would report to their colleagues the myster-ies of the great hermaphrodite kraken and seek to understand what it meant for their mission in the world. I felt the pull of their connection to this group and each other, and I longed to be a part of that, though I had my own commitments. Still, I felt a tenderness toward each of these people, even the prickly Fedelma, and a sadness grew as I contemplated our parting. I also wondered how I was going to get home. Perhaps I would have to sit here on the beach until my ankle healed enough to hobble off on my own. The irony of this self-indulgent bathos irritated me, as it always did when I became aware of it. I thought to interrupt the logistics and ask for help when Diar-muid clasped my hand.

"Corax," he said, "there is much I wish to learn about the world beyond the monastery and I can think of no better place to study than the Academy. If you take me with you, maybe they'll take me as a student. If you don't mind the company, to be sure."

"Of course, they would, you dear man! I'll insist! And there's nothing I'd like more!"

And so, it was settled. The four companions of The Kraken Imaginary set off into the rocky barrens, heading east, while Diarmuid and I took the trusty currach and rowed south along the coast, making for the port where we could book passage for the sunny skies of my homeland. I already envisioned the expression on those Academy faces when I walked through the portal arm-in-arm with a giant, handsome monk.

II: THE DIONYSOS DISORDER

[Diarmuid's Story]

Dionysus presents us with borderline phenomena, so that we cannot tell whether he is mad or sane, wild or somber, sexual or psychic, male or female, conscious or unconscious.

James Hillman,
The Myth of Analysis: Three Essays in Archetypal Psychology

Who is he, this Dionysus? Not a proper god, is he?

Euripides,
Cyclops

[1]

The supply boat from the mainland, a former imperial vessel, arrived twice a week. I'd met it at the pier for the last month, ever since sending the message for help. Despite my years of training as a monk (praying and fasting for days in a cold stone hut), anxiety made me restless. Instead of sleeping, I spent half the night clawing at my skin, digging satisfaction out of the bloody scabs. I needed help, my partner needed help, and I hoped the team at The Kraken Imaginary would come through for us. Two weeks ago, I'd received an unsigned reply via pigeon courier. "COMING," it read. Who or what was coming? And when? Meanwhile, Corax—the man I loved—drank himself to dissolution.

I prowled the wharf, ignoring the stares of fishermen and idlers. They watched but said nothing. I've been told I'm a big man, naturally intimidating. I would be lying if I didn't admit to using that to my advantage—mostly to avoid fights rather than win them. I considered myself a peaceful soul, or at least I aimed for that. The boat was due to arrive soon, but tired of being a target for the steely-eyed attentions of the locals, I scrambled up the rocks and walked the length of the breakwater that sheltered the harbor. The wind whipped my hair and robe with the usual island bluster. I wondered if the weather would prevent the boat from its journey but decided that it probably made no difference. As in all seas, the winds blew, and sailors sailed.

The breakwater linked the town to a small island, a mound of rock that I climbed to get an unimpeded view of the western horizon. On top, I sat under a giant marble portal, all that remained of an ancient temple. Some folks claimed that it had been a shrine for Apollo, but whisperers gave it to Dionysos, hinting at dark sacrifices and unrestrained orgies. Having met the god myself, I didn't discount the rumors. Most of the islanders claimed to worship the new religion out of the East with its solitary paternal god, yet they argued about the multiplicity of old gods with unconcealed zest. I puzzled over this ambiguity until I decided that it was another example of the fluidity of human faith.

Parked on the sun-warmed stone, I tugged at the hairs of my beard until one pulled free. I inspected its bulbous root and savored the lingering soreness of the follicle. I wasn't proud of my new habits of tearing away at my body, but there was no one to care, and I didn't give a damn. These sins helped distract me from the emotional pain of watching Corax swill booze and wallow in vomit—a daily occurrence if I let him. I released the hair to the wind and studied the mesmerizing chaos of the sea. Its random activities reminded me of ruminations in the night and I dropped my gaze to the barren ground. A lizard darted from a crack between stones, froze, and zipped out of sight. I noticed a white cyclamen blooming in the rubble and reached to pick the delicate flower. Twirling it by the stem, I realized I had taken the only one. Ashamed of the waste, I stuffed it in my mouth and chewed, tasting bitterness.

Finally, sails cleared the head of the nearest island. It would be at least an hour before making port, but it had to be the supply ship. To purge the flower's aftertaste, I took a sesame and honey cracker from an inner pocket. Like all the food in these islands, the simple ingredients contained the flavor and life of the sun, a welcome relief from my damp home in the West, where overcooked fish and potatoes passed for the daily staples. I didn't miss the food or the dampness, no matter how much comfort lived on in childhood memories. Well, sometimes I did miss it, a little, even the rain. After all, it was the place where Corax and I had met and fallen in love. Circumstances had required us to leave quickly, and I accompanied him back to his homeland—a paradise of sunshine and reason, or so he boasted. At first, Corax delighted in sharing the ways of his people and I reveled in his joy. We grew close, as I knew we would. But in time, he over-reached—inevitable because of who he was— and now our life was a ruin. Even his colleagues at the Academy had given up on him.

Tired of chasing the tail of my thoughts, I uncapped the waterskin I carried on a sling and poured a few drops into my hand. Dipping a finger, I anointed my forehead, tracing a cross followed by a spiral. I said a prayer to God, whom I had once seen in the form of a kraken. As always, the ritual cleared my head and I saw, as if for the first time, the azure sky as it merged into the cyan sea, broken only by the jutting islands of stone. The marble of the portal shimmered under the midday sun, a living doorway into this ancient landscape. My hopes escaped as a sigh, and I headed back to the wharf.

Once the ship was tied to the pier, the crew secured a cleated plank for passengers. Only one appeared at the gunwale, a tall woman I knew as Marianne, the warrior adept and champion of the mysterious group known as The Kraken Imaginary. Were there no others, I wondered? She scanned the pier from the top of the plank and seeing me, she smiled and nodded. Clad in a thin, knee-length chiton instead of her usual deerskins, archery tackle over one shoulder and duffle on the other, she looked ready for sculpture. Our greatest need probably wasn't a warrior, but I knew Corax would welcome her presence. She was genuine hero material and he liked heroes. Which doesn't explain why he liked me; I did save his life once or twice, but that was more a product of my size and strength rather than any notable courage. Still, despite my inexperience in such things, I recognized that love wasn't rational.

She descended the plank with casual grace as the crew lined the gunwale rail to watch. At the bottom, a brash youth, the kind that lurked around the wharf hoping to scam a copper or two, rushed forward to offer his services as a porter. He miscalculated the passivity of his mark and as he reached for her duffle with one hand, he slipped the other toward her bottom. With a shrug of the shoulders as if adjusting her baggage, Marianne cuffed the boy with her elbow, knocking him off balance. He tumbled into the gap between the hull and the pier and hit the water with a splash, causing the spectators to raise a cheer. I wondered if they had expected something like that to happen. No doubt Marianne had persuaded them of her boundaries early in the voyage.

She walked over and we embraced, a gesture that brought groans from the watchful crew. I clung to her beyond propriety and may have even shed a tear of relief. At this point, any ally was a godsend.

"Diarmuid," she said, pulling away and looking me up and down. I saw a flash of concern, but she concealed it behind a measured smile. "Well, then. I'm sure there's much to discuss." She paused. "My dear man, you look like you're carrying the weight of Atlas."

I wiped my cheek with a sleeve. "Feels that way sometimes. But it does my heart good to see you. Thank you for coming. It's a long journey, to be sure."

"True, but you know me: I go where I'm needed." She stroked my hair, sending chills down my spine. "This is nice. I'm glad you abandoned that silly tonsure. I never did understand the purpose."

"In theory, a mark of devotion," I explained. "But also, a stigma. I've moved on from much since last we saw each other."

"Me too. I've decided to improve my scholarship, for example, and I've been trying to learn the Language of the Deep. The journey offered ample time for practice."

"Can you, like our bardic friend, summon the tentacular god?"

She shook her head. "No, not yet. Dolphins, mostly." My eyes dropped from her face to the intricate kraken tattoo that covered the length of her right arm. It writhed as her muscles flexed, creating a fascinating display. She followed my glance and elevated her arm to show off the prized body art. Tattoos were common across the world, but nothing else I'd seen radiated such mystery and menace.

"And Corax?" she asked. "He's well?"

"No," I answered, "he is not. Corax is a problem for me, for himself, and now, unfortunately, for you as well. But you must be tired from traveling," I suggested, even though she looked fresh and ready for action. "I propose that we head to the inn where we can get out of the sun, have a drink and a meal, and I'll relate the whole sad story."

"I'm not the most patient person," she objected.

"I remember," I said. "Humor me, please. The story is epic in complexity, and I'll need the focus to tell it."

She hesitated but finally nodded.

"May I help with your luggage?"

She frowned. "No, thanks. No one touches my stuff."

I wasn't sure if that was a reprimand or a warning. Marianne was a stalwart companion, though bristly at times. "No problem," I said, realizing that she might have pushed the boy off the pier as much to guard her things as her body.

"Lead on," she said. "I wouldn't mind a good meal."

As we walked away from the ship, the ill-mannered boy pulled himself over the top of the wharf ladder. Water clung to his curly hair and his clothes were drenched. He glowered at Marianne, who ignored him, and I wondered if she had already made an enemy, not necessarily the most promising overture to the island and its insular culture. But she demanded respect from everyone, and I couldn't quibble with that.

Once past the dripping boy, she frowned and pulled at the edge of her cotton tunic. "This material is so immaterial that I feel nearly naked. Flayed, even. Yet in this heat, I cannot imagine wearing anything more. How do you survive in that robe?"

"In truth, with little underneath. And the robe is a lighter cloth than it looks. I've been told that east of here is a vast desert country where the inhabitants cover themselves with such robes as protection from the incessant sun. The scheme has merit, I think."

"Interesting. I may give it a try to discourage eager suitors. The men of this ocean have no manners with women, as far as I can tell."

"I'm afraid that's true. Women here are either worshipped or enslaved; there seems to be little middle ground."

"Bah. It's the same everywhere."

At the end of the wharf, we crossed a small plaza and passed through the arched entrance to the town. Like many seaside communities in the archipelago, the core of the town occupied a conical hill ringed with fortress walls. For a thousand years, wars, raids, slave traders, and pirates had washed back and forth across the sea, reliable as the tides. To establish a sanctuary from pillage, the city grew inward, cramming structure within structure until every protected space within the walls was utilized. Passages through this anthill were narrow, steep, and easy to defend. I apologized to Marianne as we started up the shady steps. "Bit of a climb," I said.

"Least it's nice and cool," she grunted, hefting her bags.

We toiled up the stairs and ramps, winding this way and that between whitewashed walls, passing doors painted in bright colors and overhearing, through the occasional open window, a phrase of a woman's song. After a steep section, I paused for breath at a landing. Marianne came up behind and put an arm around my shoulder, speaking softly in my ear. "You climb under a great burden, Diarmuid. It's painful to see you so distressed. Where is that great dancing bear of a man? Not lost, I hope."

I stifled a sob and shook my head, soaking up her compassion but wary of seeming weak. I knew that I had to be a leader, no matter how tempting it was to collapse. Sure, I was tired. Yet Corax needed me, and if Marianne was going to help us, she would need me, too. I patted her arm, said nothing, and turned to resume the ascent.

On the top of the hill, we emerged into an open square and blinked in the light of the unrestrained sun. Marianne adjusted her load and looked at me. I pointed across the square to an arched entry under a sign that read, "THE INN OF PURE REASON." The arch opened into a courtyard overgrown with cactus and shrubs and paved with marble worn from the passage of feet. A wooden door opened to the dining hall, empty now that lunch was over. I waved at Aristotle, the stout innkeeper, as we crossed the hall and stepped up to a terrace overlooking the harbor. Sheltered by a cloth awning, we stretched out in chairs to catch the full measure of shade and breeze. The inn perched atop the complex of walls below, the peak of a ziggurat built without a single plan but constructed over a thousand years of addition. The terrace overlooked the surrounding structures and the wall at the edge dropped thirty yards vertically into a shadowy passage. The view reached beyond the townscape to encompass the living sea, gleaming islands of rock, and fishing boats swaying at their moorings. The supply boat that brought Marianne had pulled away from the dock and was hoisting sail to clear the harbor. She watched it for a few minutes, then leaned back in her chair and turned to me with a smile.

"A remarkable place," she said. "So, feed me and tell me a story."

[2]

"I recommend the savory pie filled with spinach," I said.

"I'll bite," replied Marianne. "I'm also looking forward to a tankard of ale."

"Wine is the standard here. Wine and a distilled grape nectar. Of course, you may drink as you wish," I said, "yet I must warn you that alcohol has brought Corax to the brink of ruin. I've lost my taste for it and have given it up altogether. I keep hoping he will follow my lead, but he hasn't even noticed."

She frowned. "Fine, order our drinks as well." Slumping into the chair, she brushed the tip of her long blond braid back and forth along her cheek before tucking it in her mouth. As she chewed her hair, I watched, allowing the image that it could be my fingertips instead. In a rush of shame, I stifled the disloyal notion. But I'd gained little satisfaction or tenderness from Corax of late, and my desires had always been complicated.

"Okay, what's going on?" She demanded. "Why are you on an island in the middle of nowhere? I expected you to be at the Academy. And what's the story with Corax? Gather your focus, man, and fill me in!"

Drinks and food arrived, and without waiting for an answer, Marianne scooped up a hefty piece of spinach pie. I took a sip of tea. "Where I come from, there's a formal process for telling stories. It's been passed down through many generations until it's a bedrock of the culture itself. Bear with me, I don't know any other way to do it."

"Yes, yes," Marianne mumbled while chewing. "Of course: the bardic tradition."

"Exactly. Turns out they have something similar here, possibly even older. The archetype of this practice is a character known as The Poet. I've also heard him, or her, called The Singer of Tales. Anyway, you won't be long in this region before encountering the ubiquitous scions of that clan. Literally, everyone is a storyteller."

"Is this preamble necessary?" Marianne asked, frowning.

"Maybe not," I admitted. "I guess I'm trying to explain myself before you bite my head off. Anyway, within the tradition, a story is the essential vehicle for conveying information, instruction, wisdom, and whatnot. The better it's told, the more complete the delivery. I'll try to tell the tale as best I can, invoking the spirit of inspiration to shape it and thus enhance your understanding. I want you to truly comprehend what's going on and why you're here."

Marianne stopped eating and stared at me. "Look, I'd be happy to hear your theories of narrative—later. Is that clear? Or do I need to make a little story about it?"

I rubbed the top of my head. "No, that's clear. Sorry to ramble."

"It's okay, I guess. Do I have a choice? No, don't answer, just get on with it."

I put my palms together in the fashion of prayer and closed my eyes. "Sing through me, Muse," I intoned, "this story of a troubled man." I opened my eyes and caught Marianne rolling hers. Since I had clearly exhausted her patience, I plunged into the tale.

"After I last saw you, dear Marianne, when the team parted in the Western Isles, Corax and I journeyed over land and sea and eventually made our way to the Academy, the institution that employed Corax and where I hoped to study. A secular monastery of sorts, it occupies a large house on the outskirts of the ancient City of Philosophers. From the way Corax always spoke of it, I'd expected a country estate—an idyllic lyceum amidst stately olive trees where one could bask in views over-looking the great City while absorbing the disquisitions of thinkers. However, it turns out that the original Academy and its grove were destroyed a few centuries back by the Empire. In a demonstration of political power and a rejection of philosophy, the Imperial Army smashed the compound and harvested the trees to make engines of war. The philosophers relocated into more modest accommodations within the City. Hundreds of years have passed, and they still talk about the loss of their estate like it happened yesterday. Regardless of the changes, they've added to their archives and carried on with their studies.

"At first, I was intoxicated by the atmosphere of the Acad-emy. We had a corner room on the second level, and we spent hours entangled on the bed, exploring the capacity of our bod-ies for invention. Otherwise, we sprawled and cuddled, reading and discussing one or another of the numerous texts scattered about the room. I know people thought he looked like a toad and some snickered at our relationship, but that never bothered me. He's a brilliant, fascinating companion, and a skilled lover. And, in his own way, he glows with beauty."

Marianne looked at me with a wry smile. "Even the snail has its admirers."

"Yes, well, for me it was paradise. Dialectical discourse could be heard in every corner from dawn well into the night. The level of rhetoric was subtle, sinuous, and challenging. I learned much about the applications of sarcasm. Still, the idyll never seemed to entirely satisfy Corax and sometimes he took me on walks to the old Academy site, where he would sit in melancholic silence and stare into space. I disliked these excursions because they anticipated bouts of depression that gripped him for weeks at a time."

Marianne paused her consumption of the pie and took a sip of the tea. Her lip curled. "What is this?"

"Mountain tea, they call it. An herb that is harvested at the higher elevations. Rather lackluster on its own. Goes down well with dollops of honey. However, it's reputed to be an extraordinary tonic against disease."

"Fine wine it's not. But please, continue."

I ran my fingers through the beard that had grown into a cascade of tangles. Marianne watched with an arched brow.

"Our lives should have been a scholar's dream: research, meditation, dialogue, and plenty of extracurricular sex. The success of Corax's mission to the Western Isles was judged a triumph by his peers, and though he carefully expanded credit to include me as well as the rest of the team, he accepted the accolades and strutted proudly about the halls when he wasn't in one of his funks. He even wrote a text he called *Insights of a Hermaphrodite* that conveyed some of the vision absorbed from the bard and her kraken. Copies were made under the imprint of the Academy, signed by Corax, and sent to the great libraries of the West. I didn't begrudge him the limelight; it made him happy and that made me happy.

"It all changed when he unearthed the barbarian scroll. I'm sorry, I shouldn't say barbarian because they're not, at least in the sense of being uncivilized, but that's what the callous folk here call them, showing that prejudice can be found even in the birthplace of enlightenment. Personally, I believe that all cultures, no matter how impoverished, have their scholars and sages. Anyway, folded within a scroll of accounts in a dusty corner of the archives, Corax retrieved a forgotten document of Northern origin. How it made its way here we'll never know. But his excitement at finding it was extreme. In the following days, as he pored over its contents, his enthusiasm increased. Eventually, he would talk and think of nothing else."

Marianne, having finished the pie, picked her teeth and pushed away the cup of tea. "What was so interesting about the scroll?"

"Well, I read it. I can't say that I understood it, exactly. Full of neologisms and sentences constructed chock-a-block like brute architecture, dense as stone. I'd summarize it for you, but I'd only embarrass myself, I'm afraid. Perhaps you can get a useful response out of Corax—if he ever sobers up. Anyway, he began to expound in the Academy on one of the primary points of this scroll: that the *eidos*, or essence of things, did not reside in the archetypal Forms conjectured by everyone else, including the founder of the Academy. According to the scroll, the essence was not always already present but was entirely constituted in the intention of phenomenological engagement between subject and object. Normal perceptions and beliefs had to be reduced or contained by the subject to see through to the *eidos* of the object."

"What in the name of the gods are you talking about?"

"Exactly. Let's just say that the way he preached, and it quickly became that, suggested that not only the Forms but the gods themselves had no meaning independent of human intention. Or something like that. I thought both Corax and the scroll talked in circles of contradictions and clarified nothing. Supposedly this method of reducing the world leads to engagement with pure consciousness. Sounds more like mysticism to me than philosophy, but Corax is enamored with the notion of seeing the world as it is, no matter what. Unfortunately, in pursuing that notion, he ignored a few pertinent realities and offended a lot of people. As you might imagine, it was heresy, not only to the Academy thinkers, who had elevated the Forms into a kind of holy dogma, but also to the theologians, whether poly or monotheists, who considered it blasphemy. As Corax encountered resistance, he promoted his ideas with greater fervor. You know how he is."

"Yes. A bit willful, one could say."

"And one wouldn't be wrong. Then, as if ranting constantly about the *eidetic reduction* wasn't enough, he fell in with a group of Orphics—homeless fanatics who dedicate their lives to the teachings of Orpheus, a poet who may or may not have even existed. You hear different things. The boundary between the imaginary and the concrete is vague in these parts. Anyway, these Orphics spend their days on street corners in the City, burning incense, strumming lyres, dancing, and babbling obscure aphorisms. They claim to understand the true nature of spiritual and physical health, which includes abstinence from sex, alcohol, meat, and taxes. These lunatics had been tolerated by the authorities, despite their sedition, because they were thought to be emotionally disturbed and too pathetic to matter. Their street diatribes were low-volume rants delivered in monotones—mere background noise amongst the bustle of the City. People found their odd costumes and behaviors amusing.

For tourists, this was local color and they were a popular attraction. You know, eccentrics of the decadent city and such.

"Unfortunately, Corax incorporated their silly dogma and cranked it up another level. By that point, I must admit, I had lost my patience with him, no matter how strong my affections were. He was impossible to talk to. Even saying a word, any word, would set him off on furious, frenzied rants that went on for hours and made no sense, at least to me. He stopped bathing and was so disgusting I didn't want to touch him. Not that I could, anyway, because he was proclaiming celibacy as enlightenment. These proscriptions toward our love life struck me as especially cruel after he convinced me to leave my home and follow him across the world."

I felt a tear slide down my cheek and quickly wiped it away. Marianne noticed and reached across the table to squeeze my hand. It reminded me that despite her ferocity, she had a kind heart. I took a breath and continued my tale. "Well, this went on and people started to talk about Corax—important people. Finally, representatives of the Imperial State came to the Academy and delivered a warning that his promotion of rebellion would not be tolerated. His heresies against religion were harsh, but it was the heresy against taxes that had caught their attention. The Academy, having heard enough, kicked him out rather than once again fall under the heel of the State. Of course, I went with him. We moved to an olive grove outside the City where I worked on the farm in exchange for camping privileges. Meanwhile, the unstoppable Corax hiked into the City to preach, sometimes staying there for days at a stretch. I followed him once. He marched straight to the central plaza, where he paced in circles and broadcast grandiose doctrines to anyone present, night and day without ceasing. It was painful to see how people detoured away from him, but I couldn't blame them. The intensity of his preaching was scary, even to me. I feared that he would end up in prison or assassinated."

I drank more tea, taking the opportunity to tamp down the rising feelings. "Anyway, they have a custom in this culture, maybe you've heard of it, where they put on theatrical contests. No? Well, authors of tragedies and comedies compete for money and honor; it's a prestigious festival that happens several times a year. Everyone in the City attends, even the women. Corax, in the throes of sustained mania, decided that he would take his message to the amphitheater. He claimed that his rhetoric would silence the playwrights by putting them to shame and that his ideas would change the course of history. I tried to dissuade him in every way that I could short of chaining him to a rock, but he listened to no one, least of all me. By this point, his hygiene was so bad that he resembled a wild man after ten years in the bush."

"Oh Diarmuid, that must have been so hard for you! I, too, have seen this condition. François sometimes got like that. Isabeau and I had to lock him in a room, tending to him day and night, and wait for it to pass. Afterward, he was so morose that we continued watching him for fear that he would take his life. Eventually, he would emerge with hundreds of new poems, some of which were quite good but most of which were not."

"I didn't realize that. He seemed so composed when we were together."

"The condition is capricious and impossible to predict. Mostly he does well. But go on with your story, though it's breaking my heart."

"Indeed. I have little to hearten you, I'm afraid. It only gets worse." I closed my eyes for a moment, ordering my words in the darkness. "So, it happens that the theatrical festival is sacred to the old god Dionysos. Among the host of strange gods that attend these people, this one defies category, at least according to the tales I've heard. He dresses like a woman yet grows a beard like a man, which isn't that unusual among mortals, I suppose. Women fall at his feet, but he is faithful in marriage—unlikely for either mortals or gods, I'm sorry to say. He was born from the thigh of his father, the divine patriarch, after being transplanted from the womb of his dead mother, surely a first. Although known as the god of everlasting life and renewal, his deeds are often murderous, and his demeanor defines madness. He's a shape shifter and a plant magician, conjuring floral growth from unliving substrate just by thinking about it. It's said that he invented wine as a gift to mortals—the gift of release from sorrow. His most devoted followers are women who run wild in the mountains in a state of ecstasy, eating animals alive and doing violence to any who oppose them."

Marianne nodded. "I've heard of these women. What are they called?"

"Maenads," I said. "Or Bacchantes, from Bacchus, another name of the god."

"That's it. Maenads. Hunters, too, no?"

"Reportedly. I've heard they only hunt with nets, though, to capture live animals for their orgiastic feasts."

"Hm. No doubt nutritious, though a bit ghoulish for my taste. This god sounds improbable, though I think that's true of most gods. But do continue, please."

I drained my cup of tea and signaled to Aristotle through the open wall for a refill. Smiling, he scurried out with a pot, filled my cup, and lingered for a moment. I noticed that he kept looking at Marianne, who ignored him. I didn't invite him to join us because he would be a distraction and, if I was honest, I wanted Marianne's attention all to myself. Besides, Aristotle had already heard most of the story and would certainly try to hijack the conversation with his tales. When he reluctantly drifted inside to the counter, I resumed the narrative.

"The first day of the festival Corax marched to the amphitheater while I kept pace, clutching at him, and hounding him to turn back. He tried to ignore me, but finally erupted in rage and slapped me and spit at me until I slowed down and followed, fearing the worst. At the entrance, he took a stance and commenced ranting at the top of his lungs. It was nonsense, but filled with invective, heresy, and sedition. Again, I tried to stop him, pulling at his sleeves, begging, and pleading. He paused his rant and punched me in the face. It was nothing, maybe a little bloody nose, but it shocked me. I couldn't believe it had come to this. Like a fool, I walked away in a sulk, leaving him to his pulpit of madness. With nothing else to do, I plodded in the direction of our camp. Before long, though, I regained my wits, spun around, and hurried back to the theater.

"By that time, a volatile crowd surrounded Corax, grumbling and pressing against the stone block he had mounted as a podium. His voice bellowed over the throng. He ignored crafted rhetoric and merely shouted slogans condemning wine, meat, and drama as transgressions against the purity of reason—ironic given that he exhibited no reason himself, pure or impure. It was excruciating to hear, and every phrase stoked the anger of the crowd. Finally, he cursed Dionysos himself, damning his name, and I saw the first tomato sail over the assembled heads and splatter against Corax's ear. This was followed by more over-ripe fruit. Corax paused, but I could see that he only gathered breath to redouble the rant. I abandoned timidity and pushed through the mob, grabbed Corax, threw him over my shoulder, and ran off with him like a sack of grain. He screamed and pummeled my back while the crowd applauded."

"You're probably the only person I know strong enough to do that," Marianne said.

"He's no featherweight, that's for sure."

"I think you saved his life."

"That was my intention. I didn't want to put him down for fear that he'd go straight back to the festival, but I couldn't carry him all the way to our camp, either. I'm not that strong. After a respectable distance, I sloughed him off my shoulder, put him in an armlock, and marched him like an uncooperative prisoner. Eventually, we managed to get back to the olive grove.

"As we approached our camp, I saw an elegant-looking young man sitting on a block of marble next to our fire ring. He hummed and twitched a foot in rhythm with a kind of detached amusement. His night-black eyes bored into mine, belying his casual air. Tingles ran down my spine and I knew this was no ordinary man. Draped in a fancy woman's chiton, one leg crossed over the other, he stroked the curls of his beard with a dainty touch. On his head perched an ivy wreath adorning his long, lustrous black hair. He grinned, flashing the whitest teeth I've ever seen. A subtle aura shimmered about him, a disturbance of atmosphere, nothing too dramatic. But there could be no mistake: this was Dionysos, the god made manifest."

"I don't like where this is going," said Marianne, distressed enough to gulp the mountain tea.

"Nor did I. Corax fell to the ground and curled up, whimpering. The god paid no attention, leering at me with a gaze that could ignite stone. I hated myself for it, but I couldn't help but respond, melting under his attention. 'My oh my,' he said, 'I could certainly find a use for a stud like you! Let me know when you want a fresh start, hmm?' At that point I forgot about Corax and wanted to fall at the feet of the god, begging him to take me then and there. It's shameful to admit how easily I fell under his spell.

"I got a break when his focus shifted to Corax. 'As for fatso,' he waved at my groveling partner, 'he stepped over the line. And you know that, don't you, Master Lard Ass Logician?' A twig appeared in the god's hands, though one had not been there before, growing until it reached the length of a fishing pole. Dionysos whipped the pole against the air, demonstrating its suppleness, then used it to beat Corax across the back with light blows, drumming out a dancing rhythm. 'You must have known you wouldn't get away with this shit. Really, I'm surprised at you. Ah well, tough titties, as they say. Consider yourself cursed for now and ever, so forth, and so on. You know the drill. Have a nice life.' The god sneered at Corax, then flashed me a lascivious grin. 'Do look me up, dear.' And he disappeared, not with a flash or boom, just dissolving into the air."

"You were hit on by a god? Impressive," said Marianne. "Not a wonder—you are gorgeous." I blushed at her words, but she continued as if her assessment was nothing out of the ordinary. "I wouldn't give much time to shame, though. Gods have their way with mortals, don't they? As I understand it, resistance is futile. But what about the curse? Dare I ask?"

"I'm coming to that. After Dionysos vanished, Corax crawled under the tarp at our camp and slept for two days. When he awoke, he was profoundly gloomy, hardly talking or eating. At first, I thought it was an improvement because no longer did I hear the fixations, the ranting, and the grandiosity. I didn't have to chase him around or worry about trouble. On the other hand, he still didn't take care of himself and his misery was contagious.

"Then I made a terrible mistake. I couldn't get him to leave the bed, so I decided to bring in a bit of a feast, thinking that food and drink might lift his mood. I spent a whole day stoking the fire and braising a lamb shank while he lay in bed like a corpse. I finally dragged him out and propped him against a stone, thrusting a bottle of wine into his hands—*Assyrtiko*, his favorite. The wine might lubricate his interest in the food, I thought. He drank a bit and nibbled at the lamb. I hoped that this signaled a reversal of the downward spiral and he would soon return to normal. He finished the wine and asked for more, so I gave it to him. He drank another bottle and fell asleep. The next day, when he came to, he immediately asked for wine. I said there was none left. He said that he would kill himself if he didn't get more, so I went to town and got what he asked for. At first, it seemed that the wine brought him back into the world a bit, but it wasn't long before it became the center of his world. He drank himself to a stupor every day, whining if we ran out. When I ignored him and went to work on the farm instead of catering to his craving, he walked to the city and begged in the street for enough to buy more. .

"True, the mania had evaporated, taking with it his energy and will. In a short time, he achieved complete dereliction, behaving like an addict who'd never seen a day sober. I took to sleeping on the other side of the camp, unable to tolerate the odors of vomit and piss that lingered in his clothes. I didn't understand what had happened, but clearly, the appearance of Dionysos had catalyzed a change. Then it occurred to me that the ironical god had cursed him with his iconic gift. I figured that to beat the curse, I'd have to stop the drinking, so I tried cutting him off, holding our money, shaming him—everything I could think of. None of it made a difference. I didn't want to leave him alone, but I had to work, or we would lose even our meager sustenance. When I went off, he staggered back to the city streets. Always there seemed to be someone who took pity on him."

Marianne looked at me with such compassion that I almost started to cry again. "This is an awful story, Diarmuid," she said. "I mean, I get it. But good grief. I'm sure it's even harder to tell than it is to hear."

I nodded and drank more tea, determined to maintain composure. "After months of this desperate purgatory, I decided to do what other folk do in times of distress: consult the famous Oracle. Well, it's famous here. A thousand years old, they say. However, it's about forty leagues from the City and I had little confidence in our ability—or rather Corax's ability—to walk such a distance. I traded extra labor to the olive farmer in exchange for a small cart and loaded the intoxicated Corax on top. Like the beast I had become, I harnessed myself to the shaft, determined to haul him to the Oracle. And yes, along the road I endured ample derision and suffered much for the ingrate. Corax remained drunk the whole time. Dispiriting, of course, but I encouraged it because he was easier to manage."

The attentive Aristotle, bowing and grinning at Marianne, brought a plate of fruit and chunks of honey-saturated cake to replace the consumed spinach pie. She smiled back with a feral enthusiasm that caused him to retreat to the safety of his counter. Amused at the exchange, which helped me forget my sorrow for a moment, I engulfed a piece of cake in a single bite, thinking that sweets were a suitable reward for painful recollections.

I ate a second piece and resumed my tale. "The Oracle is a powerful institution in this part of the world. There are many oracles really, each dedicated to a specific god. Some gods have several. The most important one—central to three key cities, including the City of Philosophers—belongs to Apollo. Since divination is one of his primary attributes, his oracle has a reputation for accuracy, relevance, and whatever other criteria you want to apply to visionary pronouncements. Being completely out of ideas, myself, I figured there was little to lose by invoking a higher power. I also thought it might offer a benefit because, in the cosmology, Apollo and Dionysos are often at odds. Maybe we'd get a break from the other side. By this time, especially after meeting Dionysos, any faith I had in the lofty consciousness of divinities was in shambles. I'm not sure why I thought Apollo would offer any improvement. I guess that's how desperate I was. I suppose it all sounds ridiculous, but I was looking for any kind of edge."

Marianne selected an orange and peeled it. "I thought the One God was the official religion. Didn't the Empire standardize that a while ago, stomping out old rituals wherever they could?"

"Well, yes," I said, stuffing in another cake. "Wherever they could. Taxes, conscription—people expect rulers to make their own demands about that, but thousands of years of beliefs— those things are hard to change. I think most rulers know when to look the other way. People here go to church and worship the One God without dropping a stitch in honoring the Old Ones, too. It's like religion by addition instead of replacement. Not unlike my homeland, to be sure. As for the oracles, they may not have official standing, but they still draw crowds.

"Of course, it's not free. A goat is required as a sacrifice to the god. As you said, animal sacrifice was banned by the emperor, but you walk in with the goat on a leash, hand it over, they slit the throat on the altar, and as soon as the blood drains away, they hustle off the carcass to supply the butcher shop out back. Maybe they call it a commercial enterprise and pay taxes, which is probably enough to keep the State happy.

"Anyway, I traded the cart for a goat on the outskirts of town. I should have put the leash on Corax; I practically had to carry him as well as the unfortunate beast. Staggering along, we made it the last bit and presented ourselves at the temple of the Oracle. It sits on a hillside with a panoramic view of mountains and valleys—quite lovely if you're in the mood for that sort of thing, which I was not. My mood couldn't have been worse and the whole venture seemed complete folly. But what was I going to do at that point? Go on, of course.

"The temple should be enough to sober anyone—it's a vast and humbling enclosure with marble pillars and paving stones—not a dwelling for mortals. Shortly after entering, the goat met its end by the skillful attendants, and we were taken to the rear of the temple. There we queued up to wait for our opportunity to talk with a woman, a sibyl, who sat on a tripod spanning the lips of a chasm. Vapors emerged from the depths below the tripod, mystical vapors that revealed the secrets of the earth. Or so they say. We approached the sibyl and offered our question. I had been instructed by the attendants to make the question short. There was a ten-word limit. I mulled it over as we stood in line and when it was our turn, I barked out: 'How do I cure my friend Corax, cursed by Dionysos?'"

"Ten words, on the money," said Marianne. "So, what did she say?"

"There was moaning and writhing and then she screeched a reply: 'Seek the blind prophet on the stone island of Ariadne!'"

"Hmm," Marianne noted, "also ten words."

"Yes, it's an efficient operation. Needless to say, the reply was more than a little cryptic to me. But I guess they always are. Probably why they have a reputation for accuracy because they certainly aren't inaccurate."

Marianne chuckled and I noticed that she now drank the mountain tea without hesitation.

"The market in the town below the temple is thick with stalls and shops where a variety of experts sell interpretations of these prophecies—a reliable source of income for the locals. I had little faith that our prophecy was worth anything at all and I resisted the notion that further expense would provide greater value. Still, the market was an inviting place, lively with distraction, which I desperately needed. I purchased a small amphora of watered wine and propped Corax in a corner of the plaza, dangling the jar in his face to extract a promise that he wouldn't move. He agreed, eager for the wine, and I wandered off to inspect the interpreters. Most were readily dismissed as charlatans, hawking oracular clarifications along with cheap tourist wares such as erotic figurines of the sibyl, suitable for attaching to the wall over your hearth or home altar. Everywhere I turned, there was no end to this kind of thing. In the confusion of vendors, farm goods, and food, I found myself overwhelmed.

"The aroma of fresh and cooked food excited my hunger and drew me through the market. I caught the scent of roasting potatoes and was reminded of home. Most of the time I repressed any nostalgia for that faraway place, deeming it foolish, but despair had made me weak. I sniffed and meandered through the crowd until I found a brazier of glowing charcoal where a wrinkled crone turned sections of potato with the studiousness of a monk. A signboard advertised one free interpretation for every ten-piece purchase. Spirals in ancient labyrinth patterns were painted around the words on her sign, suggesting in its artfulness that the woman, unnoticed like many of her age, might offer unseen depth. Besides, I was hungry enough to want the potatoes whether they were mantic or not, so I emptied my purse and paid for ten.

"I relayed the question and the prophecy word for word. Saying nothing, she lit a pipe and puffed in silence while I munched potatoes. Deciding to save none of the food for Corax, I ate all the slices and licked the oil from my fingers. He would waste it in vomit, anyway. When I was done, the woman gave a toothless smile and nodded in satisfaction at my enjoyment of her cuisine. In a crackly voice, she explained that Ariadne's island was the largest of many in the eastern archipelago, so famous for its quarried stone that people called it the Island of Marble. She said that the blind prophet could mean a number of people, but most likely referred to Tiresias, a character in old legends.

"I thought he's been dead for over a thousand years," I said.

"Could be," she shrugged. "But with these mythical prophet types, you never know."

Marianne interrupted. "Tiresias? That name sounds familiar...."

"Tales abound," I continued, "but I always thought they were myths. And I guess they are. But the old woman's interpretation seemed useful. There was a real place to focus on, anyway. When I got back to the plaza, Corax was where I'd left him. His jug was empty, and he'd pissed himself. I lost my temper, I'm sorry to say. Maybe it was the cooking, reminiscent of home, that reminded me of what I'd lost in following him. I grabbed his tunic and yanked him upright, slamming him against the wall. I said awful things. I hated myself, but once the gate was open, it all came flooding out. Resentments, anger, frustration, disappointment. He'd been a real bastard to me with his narcissistic woe; I was sick of it and I told him so. And more, much more that I'm not going to repeat."

I dropped my head at the shame of the recollections, not wanting Marianne to see how vile I had become. I wanted her to see the person I thought I was—loyal, loving, a gentle soul. She leaned across the table and stroked my cheek. I looked up in surprise. "Go easy on yourself, Diarmuid. I would have killed the son of a bitch."

Something about the way she said it made me cough up a harsh laugh. With it came some relief. I patted her arm, letting my eyes fall into the details of her kraken tattoo while I gathered my thoughts to continue the tale.

"Corax's head lolled back and forth as I berated him. It was pointless to continue, so I supported him with one arm, and we made our way down to the port. Of course, our money was depleted, and we couldn't afford to book passage across the sea to the Island of Marble. Plenty of ships were headed east but none were willing to let us earn our way. I'm sure that one look at Corax told them more than they wanted to know. By the end of the day, our studies of the wharf and its shipping offered little hope. The sky grew dark and we took shelter in an abandoned warehouse. Huddling together for warmth, I ignored both the rumbling in my belly and Corax's whining about the drink. In the morning, I decided that I would leave him in the warehouse and comb the docks for stevedore work. Surely someone could find a use for my strength. I didn't want to leave Corax—we'd been down this path before—but I saw no other choice. If he came to harm, that was on him.

"By morning, Corax had sobered up, more or less. What this meant was a return of depression. He lay in my arms like a bag of rocks, staring into space, and occasionally begging in a weak voice for wine. I knew that it would get worse as his body tried to cope without his drink. He was a pathetic mess, but at that point I simply hated him. I suppose I could have walked away and done alright for myself. I considered that. Yet no matter how sick I was of him and his suffering, I just couldn't. So, I told him to stay there and left him with his shivers while I looked for work.

"I persuaded a ship's captain to let me stack barrels and amphorae in the hold, a couple of hours work that earned a few coppers. As I labored in the dank hold, I understood that it would take days or even weeks of this to earn enough for passage across the sea. It occurred to me that there might be a quicker way, though devious and even criminal. I was beyond the fineries of ethical discourse, however. When the ship was loaded and I had my money, I bought a little food, a few jars of the weakest wine, and went back to the warehouse to announce the plan to my helpless mate.

"It was simple enough. I would pretend to be Corax's owner and sell him at the local slave market. Money in hand, I'd book passage for two on the first ship. Just before it sailed, I'd kidnap Corax from the slave pen, and off we'd go. Of course, there were more than a few ways things could go wrong. But I figured that, at worst, I'd go to prison while he would become the chattel of someone wealthy enough to own a refined, literate man. Presumably, he'd be taken care of and could eventually earn his freedom. He listened to my proposal without complaint, merely shrugged his assent. Of course, it broke my heart to see him give up so easily and agree with this ridiculous scheme. Looking back at it, no doubt I found a savage delight in the meanness of the plan, switching our roles so that he would be the slave instead of myself, for truly I often felt that I had given up all agency in our relationship. Anyway, he didn't seem to care one way or the other."

"Unbelievable!" said Marianne, sitting back in her chair and appraising me with a cool look. "What's the matter with you? Sell a man? Even in pretense? And not just any man, but your friend and lover? I don't believe you're telling me this!"

I saw that she was appalled, and I didn't blame her. Rather than stumble through lame justifications for my actions, I hastened on with the story. "I'm not proud of what I did, I assure you. But as I suspected, Corax was worth a lot on the slave market because he could read and write. I pocketed a decent sum and Corax was led off to a compound where he meekly awaited shipment to the Imperial capital. As he left, I thrust another amphora of wine at him so he wouldn't get sick for lack of the god's cursed vintage. There was no time for a tender farewell; I took the money and he was gone. If I allowed even one tear, I knew that I would fall apart. I crammed it all down in my heart and scoured the port, looking for the earliest transport going east. It didn't take long to find a ship hauling amber and common wares to the desert kings. I had enough money to persuade them to expand their cargo and drop us at the Island of Marble.

"In the middle of the night, I snuck back to the slave compound and extricated Corax from his servitude. Slavery is commonplace and the indentured rarely resist, so they are thinly guarded. In this case, the night watchman was passed out drunk, for which I offered a silent prayer to Dionysos and his blessed beverage. We slipped out of the compound, down to the docks, and left the port before dawn. And that's how we got here."

"*Incroyable!*" said Marianne. "What luck! The gods must have been with you. I guess it paid off, but if we run out of money, don't be getting any ideas about me!" She snarled, but the façade turned into a smile. I was relieved to see that she was kidding.

"Don't worry," I agreed. "I wouldn't dare. The complications are persistent. For example, we can't go back to that port and I can only hope we weren't reported to Imperial agents, though maybe it's too petty a crime for them to hunt us down. However, you never know…." I ate the last cake while Marianne started on another orange. "Anyway, this is Ariadne's isle, that's certain. But of Tiresias, I've learned nothing."

[3]

"Where is Corax now?" asked Marianne.

"Here," I said, "at the inn. We have a room upstairs, thanks to the good heart of the innkeeper."

She leaned toward me and lowered her voice. "I assume you require funds?"

"Painfully so," I said.

"There were too many pressing obligations for the others," she whispered, "but I was free. Sorry if you expected a whole squad. At least they burdened me with coin." She reached into her duffle and handed over a pouch that dropped into my palm with welcome weight. "There's more," she added.

"Well, let's get you a room and we can peek in on Corax. With any luck, he'll be sober enough to recognize you."

In the dining room, Aristotle polished drinking glasses, setting them in neat rows on a shelf behind the counter. I fished a gold coin from the pouch and set it before him. He nodded. "I knew you were a safe bet," he reasoned.

I placed a second coin next to the first. "And lodging for my friend, if you don't mind."

He stopped polishing long enough to scoop up the coins. "Any friend of yours is welcome here," he said, grinning at Marianne. "Here for the festival?"

"A festival?" I asked. After the disaster at the theatrical fest, I had no desire for another.

"In a week—the *Epidemia*."

Marianne leaned on the counter and inspected Aristotle, who blushed. After I introduced the two, she asked, "*Epidemia*—what a curious name."

I could tell by his widening smile that Aristotle liked what he saw in Marianne. "It means *arrival of the god*. In this case, it honors Dionysos and the time he sailed here to marry the scorned princess Ariadne."

Marianne and I exchanged glances. Great, I thought, another festival for Dionysos. "What happens at the festival?" she asked.

Aristotle handed her a small glass of *raki*, which she tossed down like water, earning an appreciative laugh from the innkeeper. "Lots of things happen. A parade, costumes, dancing, music, buckets of wine, goat roasts on every corner—don't miss it! Lots of folks come down from the hills just to take part. The whole island turns out." He nodded at me and winked. "If you were searching for someone, that'd be a good place to look."

We walked up the long flight of stairs at the back of the dining room and emerged onto a flat roof with battlements along one side overlooking a fifty-foot drop. This was the high point of the fortress compound and served as a platform for archers in the event of an attack, though such military encounters were rare under the Imperial peace. For now, the terrace offered the pleasure of a commanding view over town and sea. Aristotle had converted the old sentry station into two rooms for lodgers. He used them as overflow during tourist season, which he believed to be always just around the corner.

I pointed at the room that would be Marianne's. "Thanks for the coin, by the way. Aristotle has let us stay here on good faith, providing food as well as shelter. I was finally glad to pay

him. You know, he had heard about Corax. He follows developments in philosophy—not surprising given the name of the
inn—and he had actually read one of Corax's texts. He told
me that he thought it was 'of significance.' He seemed pleased
to have him under the roof, not that he got much out of him
in the way of meaningful discourse. He's a good man, the kind
you sometimes meet when you need them the most."

"I got that impression, that he's a good man. Yet for all that,
he's still a man like any other."

It took a moment to register that she referred to his leering,
and I blushed because I, too, was a man. Marianne smirked as if
she read my mind and entered her room. I swallowed, standing
dumbfounded for a minute, never knowing how to behave after
such exchanges. Corax handled them much better, I thought,
but ever since discovering that his body contained elements of
female chemistry, making him a hermaphrodite, he could claim
to stand apart from the usual gender wars. I was merely a man,
for better or worse. At least I wasn't a drunk.

Sighing, I knocked briefly on the other door before peeking in. "Corax? Are you decent? We have a visitor."

Without waiting, I pushed into the room. The window
shade was closed, and a brown murk pervaded the space, pierced
only by sunlight streaming in behind me. I saw the lump on the
bed; it groaned and rolled over.

"By the blistering gods of Hades, banish the glare!"

Hung over, I knew. I marched to the bed, yanked off the
covers, and hoisted Corax to a seated position. Glancing back,
I saw that Marianne leaned against the door jamb, watching
without comment. Corax hadn't noticed her, and with no
decorum, he belched and scratched his balls. He was naked and

smelled of sweat and booze. "Diarmuid," he whined, "you're killing me! Be kind and fetch a drop to start the day, eh? You'd do that much for me, wouldn't you?"

I turned to Marianne and shrugged. "When you met him, he was a Master Logician. Lately, this is the extent of his reasoning."

"What? Who're you talking to, Diarmuid? And what nonsense! I can still shred rhetoric with a scalpel! Oww!" As he became animated, the headache found him with its own sharp edge and he moaned, dropping his head between his hands.

I moved aside so he could see Marianne. She stepped forward. "Hello, old friend," she said.

Corax lifted his head slowly, squinting, trying to make out who occupied the silhouette. "What? Marianne? You?" When he realized it was her, he thrashed weakly, then fell over on the bed, whimpering. "Go away, go away! Not seemly like this, not at all!"

Marianne looked at me. "He reasoned that well enough."

"We'll be outside, you slob. Get dressed and you can greet your friend properly." I steered Marianne through the door, shutting it behind us.

"I see what you mean," she said.

We sat at a small table on the terrace and waited.

The door banged open and Corax staggered out, wearing a dirty chiton and cloak. Something about the way it hung on him made me realize how much weight he'd lost. His amusing little breasts had disappeared, and the skin looked more like parchment than flesh. He only wore rags anymore; the fine red and black robes having been sold long ago.

Marianne went straight to the point. "Damn, you look like shit."

Corax fell at her feet and embraced her knees. "Forgive me, my dear, forgive me."

Marianne stroked the top of his bald head. I admired how well she controlled her revulsion—if she had any. I know that I did. My reserves were depleted from months of false hope and disappointment, but Marianne was fresh. "Now, now, friend. We'll get you out of this. Whatever it takes. Come, sit with us and make a plan."

Corax sniffled and nodded his head, then crawled over to the empty chair and hoisted himself into it. It was painful to watch. "I could use a drop of something," he said.

I slipped off my pouch and handed it to him. He eagerly lifted it to his lips, stopping in mid-guzzle when he realized that it wasn't alcohol, and let the liquid dribble through his lips. "What the blazes?" he said.

"Water, darling. The most precious fluid on earth, short of blood. Drink up; you need it."

Reluctantly, he took a sip. "What's happened to us?" he muttered.

"Well, Marianne's heard the whole story, but a recap gives us a point to work from. Not that you need it; I'm sure you remember the gist. For some reason, at the Academy, you got carried away with the obscurities of eidetic reduction, ignored my advice as well as that of your colleagues, cursed a god, and the god cursed back. Now you're the most lost of lost souls: an addict."

"Oh yes, the god. I should have cursed them all while I was at it," he said.

"I think one is quite enough."

Marianne interrupted. "Diarmuid tells me that the seer Tiresias might know something about your predicament.

Apparently, he's on this island. Makes sense to look him up, don't you think? However, you will need to sober up."

Corax waved his hand dismissively. "Tiresias, that old fake? Bah, what could he know?"

"You know him?" I asked, wondering why he'd never mentioned this before. Perhaps Marianne's mere presence helped to reactivate his wine-logged brain.

"I've read the books and seen the pictures. He's the classic, alright: waist-length beard, long hair, gnarly staff, blind as a bat. Talks in riddles. Bah, they all do—it's part of the racket."

Corax groaned as another headache lanced his brain. Marianne glared. "What's your plan to stay sober?"

"Plan… why should I need a plan? If I have to, I'll just stop drinking—not so complicated."

"See what I'm up against?" I sighed.

Marianne's reply was low and sharp. "Okay, Corax, you do that. Just stop drinking. That'll make our jobs easier because one of us is going to be with you every minute of the day as a little extra insurance. And there'll be no more mercy dollops. You're going to dry out, completely."

A look of panic came over Corax's face. His eyes narrowed. "True friendship, indeed! Inseparable companions! I'll stop drinking and you'll keep an eye on me for a little while, just to make sure, and we can put all this behind us. Excellent! I propose we celebrate. One last drink to seal the deal and get things off on the right foot. No more after that, I promise."

"I'm not in the mood for celebrating," I said.

"Nor I," said Marianne.

Corax looked back and forth at our resolute expressions and finally shrugged. "Whatever. The god made me say that."

[4]

We nursed Corax through a week of withdrawal. With a daily bath and a constant feed of mountain tea and squash soup, he showed some improvements. I could tell that Marianne's presence cheered him, though he wouldn't admit it. He whined at her shamelessly, begging for a wet cloth on his forehead or a bucket to catch the contents of his stomach. She wasn't gentle with him, but she attended to his needs without scolding, which was more than I could do. Sometimes she looked at me and rolled her eyes or grimaced in disgust. Truly, the work was revolting, and I'd wish it on no one, so I thanked her repeatedly for sharing the burden. At the end of the week, Corax was still ragged, but as the toxins leeched from his brain, vocabulary and reasoning filled the vacancies.

As promised, one of us stayed with Corax at all times. We took turns going out for air and exercise. Aristotle's suggestion to attend the festival and search for Tiresias or someone who knew him seemed like a good one, so we purchased new clothes to stimulate a festive mood, not only for ourselves but for our patient. I went to a small emporium and selected the first thing I saw: a desert robe of black cotton. The next day Marianne went out for several hours. She was gone longer than I expected, and I began to fret, a tedious habit of mine. When she returned, she wore a purple chiton of rare silk; it clung to her body accurately, undermining her previous sentiment about escaping notice. Perhaps she accepted that her height, fair hair, and poise made such a thing impossible.

On the day of the fest, Corax surprised us by cheerfully modeling the simple white tunic and cloak I got for him. He seemed especially pleased with a bracelet of hammered copper. Recently, hair had started to grow on his face, and even though it resembled lichen clinging to a branch, he'd combed and waxed it like our old friend François.

"Corax, my dear," I said, "you haven't looked this good in ages! The loss of a couple of stones hasn't hurt at all." I looked him up and down, feeling some of the old desire. "If you can stay off the drink, you'll be a new man."

Marianne walked around him in appraisal, adjusting his posture by pulling his shoulders back and lifting his chin. "Your nature is stout, but with some training, I could transform this flesh into pure steel."

"Bah," he said, "you pander and patronize, both of you. Stick to logic; it will take you farther. I am who I am, neither more nor less. And that will have to do."

"True," I replied. "You are who you are—indisputable. However, you are assuredly less than who you used to be, if mass is of matter in this case."

Marianne laughed and even Corax allowed a thin smile. "Who was your teacher, boy? A true master, I'll wager."

"Oh yes," I pandered, "the greatest."

I followed the compliment with a kiss on his forehead. "I do have a concern about the festival," I said. "Dionysos *is* the wine god and Aristotle made it sound like wine would be running in the streets. This is going to be like walking straight into the maw of the beast. Are you ready for that?"

Corax looked away and twitched. "Don't worry about me; I'm in control. Besides, what choice do we have? Tracking down the key to the curse requires navigating through the world of Dionysos. Couldn't be otherwise."

"There is that. Still, you must stay with us. No wandering off, please."

I felt Marianne press her body against my back, wrapping an arm around my chest and leaning into me with so much warmth that I thought my knees would buckle. She spoke to Corax over my shoulder as her lips brushed my ear. "If you can't stay sober, my friend, I'll be stealing your man."

Corax looked simultaneously startled, offended, and afraid. "What?"

She kissed my neck and pushed herself away. "I'm teasing, you old fart. But watch your step. If you don't appreciate your man, someone will." She turned away, leaving Corax and me staring at each other. My cheeks burned and I couldn't think of anything to say. For once, neither could Corax. As we walked out of the inn, Marianne caught my eye and winked. I glanced to see if Corax observed, but he walked by my side, head down. When I looked back, her grin was deadly.

Celebrants waiting for the parade lined the main road connecting the harbor and the fortress. It was another day of sunshine and a fair salty breeze off the water, just enough to ease the heat. Food dealers and pickpockets circulated through the crowd, removing spectator funds front and back. I waved to Aristotle's wife and children, standing on the other side of the road; the youngest three wiggled and bounced in anticipation of the parade. I knew that Aristotle himself remained at the inn, anticipating the rush of customers after the festivities.

The rhythm of drums echoed between the walls as the parade emerged from the fortress and started down the last stretch of road before the plaza. A contingent of women led the way, skipping and dancing in time as they beat on small hand drums. At the front a woman played the double flute known as the *aulos*; its ethereal buzzing drone filled the spaces between the marching percussion with sustained, plaintive sounds.

Marianne perked up when she heard the flute, exclaiming, "Practically like the Language of the Deep! I can almost understand it!"

Behind the group of women appeared a cart decorated to resemble a ship, pulled by a mule covered in garlands of red poppies and yellow daisies. On top of the ship sat a man dressed as a woman, the god himself, or at least his representative for the day.

Corax pointed to the mock god. "There rides the simulacrum of my nemesis. I'll forego mentioning his name lest he be invoked. Before him, frolic his maenads and behind the mischievous satyrs."

Marianne peered at the parade. "Maenads? So, there they are!"

"Well," said Corax, "not exactly. As you'll see when they get closer, no one is who they seem. The profane pretense of the ritual embodies the sacred, here as everywhere. The archetype is honored through the adornment of its signifier. But pretense it remains. Besides, true maenads would prove far too unruly for this event."

I basked in his rhetoric; it was good to have him back in sound mind. Maybe he wasn't the best-looking man in the world, but his wit, at its sharpest, gave me shivers. I smiled in appreciation as he lectured on to explain how the ritual celebrated Dionysos' arrival on the island to marry Ariadne, daughter of Minos, abandoned on the shore by the scoundrel Theseus.

"So, dear Corax," I said, "in that light, Dionysos could be viewed as the noble rescuer of a damsel in distress. Of course, we know him as an unforgiving bully."

"As with all gods, there are two sides, sometimes more. There is no ethical consistency, and the metaphysics are chaos. Hence the need for philosophy."

Enraptured, I hugged him, squeezing so hard the air rushed out of his lungs with an, "oof!"

The spectators offered the god a warm welcome to the island. Many were singing and waving fresh-cut branches heavy with apple and apricot blossoms, throwing the petals into the air like aromatic confetti. People smiled at each other, children laughed with excitement, and the crowd shared freely of holy delight. Not so pleased were two men with enormous beards and black, tent-like robes. I recognized them immediately as priests of the One God. In my heart, I had not abandoned that god, not at all, simply expanded my pantheon to make space for other valuable deities. The kraken had changed my perspective; once met, I don't see how anyone could forget. I wouldn't— ever. And of course, some deities plummet from the heavens and land square in the path of your life where there's no avoiding them. But they get their due, just the same.

The priests stood behind the spectators, frowning, and muttering to each other. Their attitude seemed ungrateful to me. This same crowd would turn out just as enthusiastically for the festivals and services of the One God. There was enough spirit on the island to encompass the breadth of heaven and I said so to Corax.

"Yes, a surly lot. There seems little room for joy in their dour cosmos."

Marianne elbowed me in the ribs. "Those women aren't exactly women, are they?"

Corax smiled. "Depends on your point of view. They say the clothes make the man, and in this case, the clothes make the man... a woman."

As the procession neared, it became obvious that the women were men dressed in women's clothes and trying to move and act as they imagined women would move and act. Some were skilled at this theatric, others verged on the grotesque. As the ship cart drew closer, we could see that Dionysos was portrayed by a woman.

Corax put a finger in the air and said, "And here we have a woman dressed as a man dressed as a woman."

A mob burst out of a passage at the top of the hill, yelling and leaping in chaotic pursuit of the mule cart. These must be the satyrs, I thought. Over the upper half of their faces, they wore masks with donkey ears. Torsos were covered with men's clothes and strapped to the hips of each one was a leather harness hung with an oversized phallus like a projecting flagpole. Despite the disguise, as they stormed down the cobblestones there was no doubt that the satyrs were women within the costumes. They cavorted with a maximum of provocation, brushing their dildoes against the bystanders, stroking themselves suggestively, leering at everyone—an outrageous mimesis that upstaged the cross-dressed men at the front of the parade.

As the maenads streamed onto the plaza, the satyrs overtook them and created a transgressive melée, rubbing bodies against bodies while gesturing a range of sexual possibilities. Corax patted my behind and giggled. I hardly noticed, transfixed by the astonishing display of liberal behaviors—something impossible in my own country where astringent morals were a given. I snuck a glance at Marianne, who I assumed was an old hand at licentiousness, but her eyes were wide and her mouth open. I was glad to share my naïveté with someone. Cheered by the spectators—children, parents, everyone—the imitation orgy continued until Dionysos stood on the cart, lifted a flagon of wine to the sky, loosed a soaring ululation, and drained the flagon in a series of prodigious gulps. The frolicking chaos ceased, and the maenad musicians regrouped, swinging into a stirring tune, capturing the feet of the satyrs in a dance. The satyrs pranced in groups and separately, skipping in time or whirling free, the embodiment of ecstasy. Spectators joined in and before long the plaza was filled with a pulsating mass of humanity at worship.

I tapped my feet; it was impossible to ignore the rhythm of the music. It filtered into the bones like a magic potion, animating young and old alike. Corax had his arm around my waist, and we bounced together, standing in place. Marianne undulated like a charmed snake in a display of lethal beauty; Corax and I stared at her, awestruck at the energy unleashed. We weren't her only admirers, though. One of the satyrs slipped out of the crowd, dancing forward until she stood in front of Marianne, matching her movements. Their eyes locked and the satyr writhed closer. Decisively, Marianne grabbed the satyr's phallus and pulled her in for a kiss on the lips. Corax cackled and leered, which would have bothered me except that his lusty hand caressed my flank, giving me shivers.

The kiss was prolonged, and when they separated, the satyr jigged away from Marianne and disappeared into the crowd.

Marianne's body twitched like she wanted to follow, but she smiled and stood in place, hand on a cocked hip.

I heard a commotion behind us and spun around. From a side street emerged three Imperial soldiers clad in chain mail and wielding spears. I wondered why they were here. Soldiers always made me uneasy; technically we were on the run after the slave scam and even though I doubted anyone was looking hard for us, discretion remained my preference. Then I saw the boy that Marianne pushed in the water peeking between the soldiers, scanning the crowd. When he saw us, he pointed eagerly and faded away. The soldiers advanced with determination. Marianne saw them, too, and her body stiffened.

"Let's not do anything rash," I said. "I'm sure you could take them out. And then what? There's a whole garrison."

She grumbled but relaxed slightly. I looked around for Corax, but he had disappeared. Another cause for worry, I thought. As the soldiers surrounded us the immediate crowd grew quiet and shrank back. A circle of somber faces watched intently, waiting to see what would happen, while beyond them the music and dancing continued at full tilt.

A soldier with a long plume on his helmet faced us while the others stepped to our flanks. The one in front was succinct. "Come with us," he said in a voice that sounded like he gargled with gravel.

"Why?" I asked the obvious question.

"Now!" the leader barked.

Marianne looked at me with a raised eyebrow, but I shook my head. The soldiers pushed us into the nearest side street, and we were escorted roughly from the festivities. I tried again to ask what this was about and got an elbow in the ribs. They herded us a short distance to the garrison and shoved us into an empty cell. The door slammed with a solid clang and the soldiers walked off, leaving us alone.

"Shit," said Marianne, "I have to pee."

"There's a clay pot in the corner," I pointed out. "You could try that. I won't look."

"Better not. Damn! I could've had those three on their knees in seconds. I don't like this docility thing."

"I know; I don't either. But we don't even know what this is about. Maybe it's nothing. At first, I thought it might have to do with me and Corax and the slave deal, but I'm pretty sure that's not it. Where is Corax, for one thing, and why are you involved? Has to be something else. I did spy that creep you pushed in the water when you first got here; he pointed us out to the soldiers. Seems more like the local boy gets revenge. Even given the byzantine laws of the Empire, I don't see how they can hold us for long. If nothing else, a few coins can work wonders. However, if you'd had your way and demonstrated the superiority of a woman in combat over three soldiers of the realm—there'd be no forgiving that."

"I suppose you're right," she said.

For the next hour or two, I sat on the bench while Marianne paced back and forth. Two steps, spin, two steps, and repeat, it was exhausting to watch. When she stopped pacing, though, she snarled insults and complaints about my courage, blaming me for holding her back. It was all my fault, that much was clear. I knew better than to argue these points, which I assumed would only fuel her wrath. Then she would apologize and say that I was probably right, after all. The pacing would resume. Now and then, she'd yell for the guard. I joined this activity, hoping to learn something. No one responded, no matter what we said or how we said it. After an eternity of tedium, anxiety, and rancor, a guard sauntered in, unlocked the cell door, and ushered us to the entrance. We stepped out of the garrison and found Aristotle, twisting in his hands the towel he used for wiping glasses. When he saw us, he rushed forward and gave us each a hug.

"I'm so glad to see you! As soon as you were taken, Corax ran to the inn and told me what happened! I'm so sorry! These idiots, they have nothing in their heads but wood!"

"We have no idea why we were arrested," I said.

"Oh, that—ridiculous! Someone reported that you were running an unauthorized prostitution business. Not that they care about prostitution—but the prospect of missing out on their tax cut—now that's a crime against the State! I understand they took the word of a child about this. Unbelievable! Anyway, I vouched for you and made them see reason."

"Yes, we've met the child…" I muttered.

"That harbor brat! What scum," said Marianne.

"By the way," I asked, "where is Corax?"

Aristotle pulled his earlobe. "The inn, I presume. I ran straight here thinking he was right behind. Apparently not."

I felt a chill in my spine. A few scenarios raced through my head—none of them good. "We need to find him. Let's start at the festival."

"I'll leave you to it; I must get back to the inn. If he's there, I'll send you a message—if I can find a runner that isn't already too drunk to walk."

Our time in jail seemed to last forever, but it had only taken a couple of hours for Aristotle to get us released. Still, that was more time than he had to spare, so we thanked him profusely. With a last look at Marianne, he hurried up the hill and we returned to the plaza.

The music, louder than ever, charged boldly onward and the crowd pranced in abandonment to the god. A giant amphora sat on a cart outside the zone of frenzy, tended by satyrs who appeared to be dispensing overflowing cups in exchange for kisses. The smell of spilled wine rose from the plaza, redolent as an orchard of over-ripe fruit. Debris littered the paving stones: scraps of food, single shoes, the odd costume part, flowers, and crumpled wreaths. I signaled to Marianne and we split up to cover more ground. There were also a few bodies lying here and there, too drunk to crawl out from underfoot. Somehow people danced over them. It hadn't taken long for the festival to spawn widespread incapacitation, I thought, though when I saw how people poured down the wine, I was surprised that anyone was upright.

I found Corax reclining against a pile of rotten potatoes and a young woman crouched over him offering a cup of wine. I stood dumbfounded, wondering about the pile of potatoes. Fertilizer for the fields? An over-turned cart? There was no time to reason it through. Marianne swept in, leaping onto the young woman, and knocking the cup out of her hand as Corax reached for it. Too late, though—I saw that he was already intoxicated.

The young woman, surprisingly agile, rolled from under Marianne and popped to her feet, unperturbed. Marianne rounded on her and stopped. "I know you," she said.

The young woman nodded and extended her hand. "Yes, we met earlier. You can call me Manto."

It took me a moment to realize that this was the satyr that Marianne had kissed, minus the costume. I understood the attraction; clad in a light green chiton, Manto was thin and supple and radiated vitality like a willow branch in bud.

"This man cannot have alcohol," I interrupted, pointing at Corax, who swayed on his hands and knees but was unable to rise. Instead, he vomited onto the potatoes. "He's cursed and addicted. We've worked hard to clean him up, now look. What happened?"

I saw that Marianne was torn between embracing Manto and chastising her. I ignored her ambivalence and plunged ahead, hoping to make up for my initial hesitation.

"I certainly hope you're not responsible for this," I said to Manto.

She refused to cringe. "Depends on what you mean by *this*," she replied. "Yes, he's quite drunk, and I'm sorry if that undermines your endeavors. In my view, though, he has a bigger problem."

"Oh?" I snapped. "What would that be?"

"He suffers from mania."

"What? How did you know that?"

"I spotted him running into the plaza a while ago and recognized him. He was with the two of you when I had the luck to kiss and be kissed by this remarkable creature." She bowed to Marianne.

"Remarkable or not, I'd prefer to be called by my name: Marianne," she said.

"Marianne... delighted," said Manto. "Anyway, your friend acted like a lunatic: waving his arms, raging, crying, swearing, and pushing people. I was certain that he'd be thrashed by someone he offended, because he was offending everyone, not all of whom were on even keels themselves. I grabbed his arm and pulled him out of the crowd. It didn't take long to figure out that he was in the throes of mania and required a sedative. For better or worse, wine was the only remedy at hand. Hardly ideal, I'll grant you that, but it does have a sedating quality. He snatched it and drained it and I gave him more. After several cups, he collapsed right here. I've tended to him, offering occasional sips to restrain the ferocious beast in his soul."

"She's an angel," slurred Corax, now sitting in a slump. "A god-blessed angel." He belched loudly.

"Well… thanks. I guess." I looked down at the drunken blob that was my mate and felt a surge of hopelessness.

"Has he had other episodes like this? Manic, I mean?" asked Manto.

"Yes," I rubbed the back of my neck, anticipating the soreness coming my way when I carried Corax up the hill. "Several, to my knowledge."

"Hmm. When you say he has a problem with alcohol, you might consider that the mania could be the real problem, and the drinking is merely a secondary effect."

I nodded. "That thought had crossed my mind, but I didn't know what to do with it."

"Yes, few people do. Despite the florid presentation, it's a subtle disease and difficult to treat. If you wish," she flashed a look at Marianne, "I might be able to help. For instance, I have some medicine you could try—medicine that specifically targets the extremes of this condition. I'd have to make a short detour for my belongings, but I could meet with you later, wherever you're taking him."

I glanced at Marianne who smiled in agreement. "Okay, thank you. I, we, appreciate that. How do you know so much about this?"

"I've studied herbs and medicine since I was a little girl, most of which I learned from my father. He's a seer—quite famous actually—but his vision is psychic. Unfortunately, he's blind to the physical world and needs assistance, which I was happy to provide even as a child, so he took me everywhere, sharing his knowledge and encouraging me to study the bounties of nature. Under his tutelage, I became adept at foraging and preparing potions, especially the medicine that treats mania because my father has it, too. When we discovered that this island is a good source of the medicine, we settled here."

I had one of those moments when the hairs march up your spine. "May I ask the name of your father?"

"Perhaps you've heard of him, though he's long retired from the chores of prophecy. People call him Tiresias."

"The Tiresias? He's not a myth? Nor dead? And you're his daughter?" Marianne stifled a laugh at the absurd attack of my questions.

"Yes, all true." Manto grinned. The sparkle in her eyes rushed into me like a cleansing breeze. Surely there was magic about her.

Marianne took over. "Looks like we have a plan. You, sweet Manto, can fetch your items and bring them to the Inn of Pure Reason. Unless you need help with them?" Manto smiled shyly and shook her head. "No?" Marianne continued, "Well, then, Diarmuid and I will herd the remnants of Corax to the inn and we can rendezvous there."

"Yes, excellent, perfect," I added, excited to have located Tiresias. "And I'd like to talk more about your father!" Manto smiled at me, squeezed Marianne's forearm, and slipped into the crowd.

"Angel! She's getting away! Stop her!" Corax looked distraught, then vomited again. I used the hem of his already stained cloak to wipe his mouth, then Marianne and I each hooked an arm under his shoulders and hoisted him upright.

"Okay, Master Philosopher, let's go home."

"Angel, angel…" he trailed off into muttered incoherence.

As we headed up a passage leading away from the raucous plaza, I spoke to Marianne over Corax's limp head. "Tiresias! We found him! What incredible luck! I guess the Oracle had something right."

"Seems so," Marianne agreed. "And this Manto may be a useful ally."

"Yes, and a lovely young shoot, is she not?" I teased.

Marianne puckered her lips and blew me a kiss.

When we got to the inn, the dining room was half-full of festival goers, mostly families, who had escaped the party before it lost any remaining decorum. All eyes followed us as we dragged the torpid Corax across the room toward the stairs. Aristotle was relieved to see him but dismayed at his condition. "I'll make some tea," he offered.

We hauled him up the stairs and dropped him on the bed. He moaned once, then rolled over on his back and stopped moving. I stared at the flecks of vomit still clinging to his wispy goatee, wondering if I should clean him up. No, I was too angry for that. I wanted to hit him or cry, I couldn't decide. The hope of the morning had vanished and all I could feel was exhaustion. Yes, we'd found Tiresias, but was it too late?

Marianne patted my shoulder and went downstairs to wait for Manto. I turned away from the drunken beast and parked a chair in the open doorway. The sound of music and revelry drifted up from the plaza, marching through the passages and over the walls of the city, thrumming along like the relentless southern wind. I had to wrestle down my despair once again or I would become useless. I tried to focus on the next thing, not easy for me with my obsessions over context and meaning. But this was no time for a crisis of existence. It was time to think about what we'd learned from Manto. If Tiresias' daughter knew what she was talking about, and she seemed to know plenty, maybe there was an answer for Corax's problem. Not just the curse of the drink, but the underlying mania, which could be at the root of it all. I felt an inkling of hope and stuffed it down immediately. It seemed too easy. Not that I wasn't ready for a resolution, but meeting Manto offered too many solutions all at once. I wondered if meeting her had been a coincidence or something else. What, I didn't know. But doubts nagged at me; I felt like a player on a larger stage waiting for my lines one scene at a time. I preferred to exercise control over the direction of my life even if that meant plodding progress. Fortuitous blessings always made me a bit nervous. Or maybe I'd just been disappointed too many times, had watched too many hopes dissolve in another flask of wine. I sat on the chair and picked scabs off my legs, lost in a fretful domain.

Marianne, toting a small duffle, led Manto onto the terrace. The young herbalist leaned on my shoulder and looked at Corax. Her hip grazed against my arm and I couldn't help but inhale the strong scent of her body, intense with the aromas of thyme and roses. I had a vision of lounging in a warm bath covered with petals, soft hands washing my hair. I stopped my hand as it automatically lifted to stroke the small of her back and shoved it safely under my thigh. I glanced up to see Marianne watching with a pensive expression.

Manto stepped away, dispelling the enchantment. "Let him rest for now," she said. "But we should talk."

I carried my chair over to the table and we all sat down. Manto removed a large, decorated bag from her shoulder. Opening the bag, she rummaged through the contents, finally handing me a small leather pouch. "Here's your magic," she said.

Cautiously, I poured a few grains of powder onto the table. White crystals gleamed against the dark wood. "What sort of magic?" I asked.

"Lithium salts," Manto replied. "Go on, both of you, taste it, there's no harm."

We each wetted a finger and dabbed at the crystals. Tentatively, I touched the finger to the tip of my tongue. "Okay," I said. "It tastes salty. What does it do?"

Manto ran both hands through her long hair, drawing it behind her head while peering through narrowed lids. "Imagine you're on a boat in the ocean. The seas roll under you, pushing you to the height of the swell before pulling you down into the next trough. When the difference is great, the extremes can be terrifying. That is the predicament of the manic, though the highs and lows are more prolonged than the movement of the ocean. Ingesting the lithium salts reduces the sea roil in the brain of the patient, calming the waters without entirely flattening them. Overall, the effect is one of improved stability."

"And how does one ingest these salts?" I asked.

"The lithium is a mineral embedded in rock. It leaches into water as rainfall percolates through layers of stone and earth. Like other kinds of potable mineral water, the filtered liquid can be used for daily drinking, offering a variety of therapeutic benefits, although the quantity of lithium is too low for alleviating active mania. It is a good tonic, however. It even helps to bathe in it, allowing the skin to absorb the minerals. My father and I live in a hut in the mountains where a mineral-rich hot spring seeps from the earth. I built a stone basin to capture the water and we soak in the bliss daily."

"That sounds divine," said Marianne, absently stroking the tattoo on her arm.

"Yes. It is. However, like I said, drinking the water and bathing don't do much for a manic episode. It does help delay such crises, as near as I can tell. When the mania comes over my father, as seems inevitable, I give him a measure of the dried salts, twice a day, dissolved in water. Within several days or a week, he returns to normal. Or as normal as he ever is. But you have to be careful with the application of the salts. More is not better and can quickly become too much. I've heard from experienced healers that it is even possible to die from an overdose. The medicine is a *pharmakon* that walks the narrow path between remedy and poison."

"*Pharmakon?*" I asked.

"Medicine that heals or kills—depending. Most of the stronger medicines work like that. Your celebrated philosopher of the City recognized the hemlock as a *pharmakon*. On one level it was the poison that killed him, but on the other, it was the welcome substance that initiated him into the immortality of the soul. Or so he said before he died—with much rhetorical posturing, of course."

"Interesting," I said. "Do you have more of these salts, or can you show us how to acquire them?"

"Yes, certainly. Tomorrow I must return to my father; I fear I've been gone long enough. You will come with me, yes? We can prepare the salts. And, of course, you could try the bath." Her lips curled back in a grin, revealing a sparkle of teeth. I felt immediate heat in my loins and when I glanced at Marianne, she stroked her thigh in a sensual trance. Manto radiated carnal energy in all directions, that much was obvious.

"Thank you! A generous offer," I replied, shaking off the effects of Manto's invasive aura. Marianne winked at me, which didn't help. "Okay, sure, we accept. We'll cajole, carry or drag our charge into the mountains and hope for the best. I do have one request. You mentioned that your father is no longer in the prophecy business. Yet the Oracle advised us to seek his wisdom. Impetuous Corax labors under a curse and the Oracle suggested that Tiresias might see a solution. We would value an opportunity to consult with him if that's not too much to ask."

"You can always ask," replied Manto. "He favors requests that are accompanied with a donation of wild honey. He has a profound weakness for the elixir of the bees. That would be the best approach." She played idly with her hair for a moment, lost in thought. "Might I ask the source of this curse?"

"A local god," I said. "Dionysos."

The smile evaporated from her face. "Oh dear," she said. "A rather fickle master, once crossed."

"So we have learned."

Manto puckered her lips in a child-like gesture. "Although the lithium is useful for managing wild moods, it isn't likely to lift a curse. No doubt the problem will twist into another shape and continue to vex. I think you will have to find a way to appease this god."

"Any ideas, my dear, on how to manage that?" asked Marianne.

"I count myself a follower of Dionysos," announced Manto. I held my breath, wondering if she were friend or foe. "And so is my father. But that doesn't mean we are his lackeys. I'd like to help you." I released my breath and tried to relax. Manto continued, "As you suggest, let us consult with my father; he may know what to do. In the morning, I can give your friend a dose of lithium, which should bolster him for the trip. It's a hike of several hours to our mountain home. Plan to stay with us for a few days; there is much to do."

"Perhaps Aristotle has some honey we can offer to your father," I said.

"Better than nothing," Manto said. "But if you want to win his heart, he prefers it fresh in the comb, harvested from a wild hive."

"Good grief." Coming up with wild honey on short notice seemed improbable and I felt another spike of anxiety. Maybe I needed the lithium, too, just to slow down the flux of my emotions. Suddenly I felt a bare foot touch the top of mine. A gentle stroke, seductive. Thinking it was Marianne, I looked under the table and was surprised to see the foot connected to Manto's long leg. She stared at me with a wooden expression, as if daring me to say anything. I kept silent and squirmed within.

"Maybe not so daunting," Manto continued in a supportive tone—as if she wasn't tormenting me on the sly. "We'll walk through olive groves on the way, some untended, with many cracked and aging trees perfect for nesting. Keen eyes, keen eyes will do."

"Probably wouldn't hurt to take some from the inn, if he has it to spare," said Marianne. "We can hunt on the way, but, as you say, offering cultivated honey is better than nothing."

"Yes, indeed," Manto added. "And now, I'll seek out the innkeeper myself and secure a room for the night, if he has an empty."

Marianne waved her hand. "No need for that. I'm happy to share."

[6]

After Marianne closed the door to her room, I crawled into bed next to Corax, who snored like a knot of croaking toads. I ignored the stink and the cacophony, but didn't even want to try for sleep, afraid that if I nodded off, then he would wake and sneak out for more wine. Of course, once I opened the door to my obsessions, the whole array lumbered into view and sleep became impossible, anyway. Thought variants chased each other in ponderous cycles, pounding my head into a slop of disappointment, despair, and rage. The latter I directed straight at Corax, who I blamed for seducing me with a sweet promise of the world and leaving me with bitterness. Ultimately, though, I could only sustain so much rancor. My bones ached from holding the tension; something had to give. I'd been waiting for a change to take place in Corax but maybe I should change. Whatever I was doing wasn't working. I still believed in freedom and autonomy and the wisdom of reason, but Corax's condition undermined those principles, fixing a bottomless anxiety as the price for freedom. And why evoke reason, anyway? It wasn't like I was a shining example. Instead of trying to rationally convince him of the error of his ways, I wheedled and whined or got downright nasty. Hard to be proud of myself these days. And yet I loved him. What madness! If only there was a medicine for that.

Exhausted with rumination, I grabbed a short length of rope from my pack. I wound one end around Corax's wrist with a complicated knot, left a couple of feet for slack, and tied the other end to my wrist. Let him get past that, I thought, and finally fell asleep.

I woke to the sound of Corax yelling and tugging on the rope. "Damn you! Who d'you think you are?"

He thrashed like a child in a tantrum, trying to crawl around me and off the bed. Tired of his agitation, I yanked my arm back, pulling him down on top of me. I wrapped my arms around him and tried not to gag on his odor. He struggled for a moment, but soon recognized the futility and started to wail.

"Shut up," I said. "Now listen to me. I've danced along with you for several months now, watching you drown yourself in booze and waste every talent that you own. No more. You're going to get up and we're going to drink some tea, have breakfast, and take a nice long walk into the mountains. For fun, we'll have the company of two genial women. Doesn't sound so bad, eh?" He nodded, subdued. "Just one more thing. Don't ask me to untie you. Not going to happen."

"What did I do to deserve this?" he complained.

"I'm not playing that game with you. You can't be trusted, you goddamned son of a bitch!" I yelled. I felt bad about what I was doing. But not bad enough to let him loose.

"I'm sorry, Diarmuid," he whispered.

It was awkward arranging our toilet and packing, but I didn't waver. Having drowned his conscience in the drink, he was now the slave of mine.

When we emerged, Marianne and Manto sat at the table, eating pastries and fruit. They looked sleek and self-assured, while Corax and I shuffled forward like the undead.

Marianne laughed. "Oh, that's rich," she said, pointing at the rope bracelet. "But probably necessary. Good for you,

Diarmuid. If you need a break, I can take over the ball and chain."

"Thanks. I'm okay for now." I pushed Corax into an empty chair and dragged another one next to him. Corax looked at the platter of food and frowned. I selected an apple and crunched into it, taunting him with exaggerated sounds of pleasure. His frown deepened. Manto had been stirring a small cup; she stopped and placed it in front of him.

"Drink that."

He squinted at her. "Who are you, again?"

She laughed. "And yesterday you called me your angel! Have you forgotten your heavenly vision so soon?"

"Really, Corax," I said. "This is Manto, the daughter of Tiresias. She's going to lead us to her father. Then we will beg for insight into your cursed predicament. Now drink the damn cup."

"What's in it?" he asked suspiciously.

Manto smiled. "Mountain tea, a lot of honey, and a sprinkle of lithium salts. Best to down it at one go."

"Lithium? White metal? You're making me drink metal?"

"Shut up," I emphasized. "Drink. Don't make me pour it down your throat."

He acquiesced and swallowed the contents of the cup, groaning afterward. As much as I hated to act the tyrant, the approach was working. At least for now.

Marianne and Manto were ready to go, so we filed down the stairs. I told Aristotle we would return, though I wasn't sure when, and gave him enough coin to keep our rooms. I asked him if he could spare a pot of honey, but Marianne said that she'd already taken care of that. As Aristotle grinned, she confessed that she'd also secured bread, cheese, olives, and a few other edibles for the trip. I guessed that she could have gotten that and more from the innkeeper just by leaning against the counter so he could look at her.

We descended through the passages of the walled city and took the eastern road toward the mountains. I carried a bag over my shoulder with belongings for Corax and myself. He looked green and weak in the knees. I didn't want to slow us down any more than necessary, so I didn't ask him to carry anything, just himself—if he could do that much. Leashed together as we were, our progress was clumsy and forced us to walk side by side at a matched pace. Manto took the lead, positioning her duffle on top of her head and holding it in place with both hands, or one hand, or sometimes no hand at all. Slung around her shoulder, over her chiton, she wore a dappled fawnskin like a shawl. Marianne had reverted to her standard deerskin pants and vest, perhaps in anticipation of adventure. She insisted on bringing her archery tackle as well as a pack. Strapped to her thigh was a sheath holding a large knife, so large that I would have called it a sword. Manto laughed and teased her about the armaments, naming her "mistress of the hunt" and "wonder woman." I thought Marianne would enjoy the teasing, but as the heckling went on, she finally removed the knife, flipped it high in the air, and spun her body in a circle, catching the knife neatly by the handle as it returned to her grip. We stopped to stare at this feat, then resumed our journey. Nothing more was said about the weapons.

The route snaked upward through low hills of granite. Between the outcrops grew thickets of low brush laden with scent. Without taking the time to stop and study the flora, I identified thyme, rosemary, sage, rock rose, laurel, and lavender. The wild herbs delivered a tonic effect, like aromatic nourishment. Sometimes we had a lovely view over the town, harbor, and sea before the road dipped into vales thick with tangled growth. On the sunnier slopes, we often crossed through groves of ancient olive trees set in rows or scattered in forgotten patterns. Goats rummaged beneath the arbors, chewing the new weeds of spring while lizards patrolled the stone walls. We waved to the occasional shepherd—some waved back, some just stared until we moved out of sight.

Corax complained periodically, and each time I offered him a handful of roasted almonds. The first time, he took a few. After that, he glared. "What, am I a child to be bribed with treats?"

"I don't know. Are you?" I replied, popping a nut into my mouth. Sensing the tension, Marianne and Manto turned their heads to watch. Corax and I stood face to face as I crunched almonds in the most obnoxious manner I could summon, smacking my lips and making as much noise as possible. He looked like he wanted to hit me. I knew he wouldn't because he wasn't like that, and if he did, I'd hammer him into the ground. Or I would if I was like that, but I wasn't, either. Still, we both wanted it.

"Come on, lovebirds, kiss and make up," Marianne mocked. "I mean it."

Finally, I shrugged and turned to walk, jerking Corax into motion. We didn't say anything for a while.

An hour out of town, Manto paused. "There's your hive," she said, pointing at a holm oak overlooking a grove of olive trees. It was old and cracked, mostly dead, but several branches stubbornly renewed their commitment to greenery. A haze of bees hovered around a fissure in the trunk about halfway up.

We walked to the tree, stopping about twenty yards away, admiring the buzzing industry of the bees as they collected pollen from the wildflowers in the grove. Marianne slipped off the sealskin bag that contained her bow and quiver, setting it gently on the ground. From her pack, she retrieved a narrow, wide-mouthed amphora about the size of her forearm. She threaded cord through the handles of the vessel and draped it around her neck. Pulling out a long desert scarf that I hadn't seen before, she wrapped it around her head, leaving only an opening for the eyes.

"Wish me luck," she said as she strode to the oak and hoisted herself to the lowest branch. The three of us watched her progress with nervous excitement.

"This woman—she's quite formidable, is she not?" observed Manto.

I nodded and looked at Corax, also nodding. There wasn't much to say. We both owed our lives to her. I watched Manto stroll to the tree. A bee landed on her arm and she brought it to her face, smiling and cooing at it. Although the bees were already reacting nervously to Marianne's ascent, Manto seemed unperturbed. With a flick of her hand, she boosted the bee back into flight as she craned her neck to watch the robbery.

Corax surprised me by putting his arm around my waist and leaning against my arm. "Do you still love me, even a little?"

"What?" I asked. "What do you mean?"

"I see the way you look at her. Marianne's a remarkable creature... and quite desirable, don't you think?"

I heard the insecurity in his voice and it aroused stings of guilt as well as anger. It was too delicate a moment to waste on impulse. I let him squirm for a bit. When I answered, the truth seemed best. "There's a man I love very much, and I believe he loves me, and nothing could be better. Unfortunately, that man has a twin who shows no love for me at all and, I have to say, I don't much care for him, either. Lately, as the twin has taken over, I've had to ask myself if the man I love will ever come back. Do I move on? The attention of others gives me hope that my life can contain something other than misery. I think too much, as you well know, and if I entertain other possibilities, it's not because I'm abandoning you. It's because you already left."

I heard him sob and moan. "What have I done to you? To us?"

My heart melted and I tried to think of something reassuring, but I heard a yell from the oak and looked up to see Marianne sucking at the back of her hand where she'd been stung. Instead of giving up, she climbed faster, swinging hands and feet from branch to branch in a powerful rhythm. As she neared the hive, the buzzing of the bees grew louder. It sounded like the *aulos* we had heard at the festival and I wondered if the bees also sang of the frenzies of Dionysos. The honey guardians were not pleased with Marianne, and I winced to see the offended insects swarm around her, crawling over her body, and I felt sure that they would stab her to death. At the level of the hive, Marianne quickly pulled her knife and reached into the opening. While gripping the trunk between her knees, she used her hands to carve a slice from the comb, holding the trophy aloft for us to see before quickly shoving it into the amphora, followed by two more segments. Slipping the knife back in its sheath, she scrambled down the tree much faster than she went up. Hitting the ground, she ran off in the opposite direction, pursued by a squadron of bees.

"A hard-won prize," said Manto. I looked at her and saw that she grinned as she watched Marianne fleeing through the grove.

The open cruelty of her expression surprised me, and I glanced away, not wanting to confront this disturbing discrepancy.

"If you ask me, and I know you didn't," Corax complained, "it's a high price to pay for admission to the conjectured wisdom of prophecy." He waved at Manto. "No offense to you, of course."

"None taken. As of yet. You'll thrive or perish by your outspoken opinions, Logician."

"As do we all," I added, hoping to derail the anticipated argument.

Marianne loped around the periphery of the grove and returned to our group at a walk, free of winged pursuit. When she got close, I saw that her bare arms were covered with blisters. Manto inspected her, clucking in sympathy, and forced Marianne to sit down while she applied salve from her medicine kit. The cruelty I saw before had vanished completely, replaced by the ministrations of a diligent nurse.

"What's in the salve?" I asked.

"A common weed known as plantain—excellent for drawing out the toxins." Manto spread the salve with a light touch and I could see from Marianne's expression that there was balm in both the medicine and the contact.

"Would this medicine also be a *pharmakon*?"

"Certainly," Manto replied. Her touch grew more sensual as she worked the salve into Marianne's flesh. "Plantain is generally harmless and difficult to abuse for most folks. On the other hand, it's not recommended for pregnant women. It also tends to cancel the effects of lithium."

"I'll have some, too, then," said Corax.

"No," I admonished. "No, you won't. Have you already forgotten our words?"

Corax dropped his eyes to the ground. Marianne looked at us with curiosity but said nothing. While Manto continued to massage the salve, Marianne untied the amphora from its sling. "Worth a taste, friends, even if we must save most of it for the prophet. No wonder he's so fond of this stuff." She uncapped the vessel, and a bee flew out, buzzed around in confusion, then zoomed off. We passed the pot of honey and agreed that it contained a godlike elixir. The amber sludge dissolved in my mouth in perfect sweetness, strong with the flavor of the neighboring flowers. Bits of wax lingered on my tongue and I chewed them in contentment.

Marianne endured her wounds like a true stoic. She brushed off the fussing Manto and we resumed our journey. The road meandered through groves and fields, around hills, steadily ascending into steeper terrain. Behind us, we saw the harbor fortress as a gleaming white cone, a sentinel over the sea. Ahead, the groves thinned out as the farmland gave way to rocky outcrops and cliffs. Marble predominated, reflecting the sun with a luster that revealed the gemstone foundation of the island. Our pace slowed as we climbed.

I considered untying Corax. Even though we'd gotten used to the leash, now and then we'd fall out of synch, resulting in a yanking of arms, followed by a growl and an insincere apology. However, despite the humiliation and inconvenience, I realized that I still didn't trust him, so I let it be.

As we marched along in irritation, Manto fell back to walk with us. She matched her steps to Corax, peering at him from angled head, intent as a heron on the hunt.

"Do you want something, woman?"

"Just monitoring the effects of my medicine. How do you feel?"

"Blah. I am neither happily drunk nor cognitively inspired. A mediocre state. And my mouth tastes of metal."

"An effect of the medicine. At least we know that it's in your system."

"And what if I decide that the cure is worse than the disease? How do I get it out of my system?"

"Let's hope you don't. You have a madness that rides you like a demon. If the lithium drains away, the demon will jump back in the saddle."

"You call it a demon; I call it a muse."

"Call it what you will; it does you no credit."

Manto darted around to my side of our leashed tandem and casually placed her hand on my bottom as we walked. "So very firm," she said.

I flinched. "What?"

"Nothing," she said, flashing a coy smile before skipping ahead to rejoin Marianne.

[7]

"You don't own me, you know," complained Corax, flapping the arm tied to mine.

"True. Technically, you're owned by Stelios Slave Services back on the mainland. By this time, I'm guessing you're filed in the *stolen property* category of their assets."

"When did you get so cruel?"

"Probably about the time I accepted that you can't be trusted and either I serve as your ego or suffer the consequences. You know, if we don't figure this out, it will be the end of us—at least as an *us*."

"Your logic and your presumptions overreach," he grumbled.

The road switched back and forth as it climbed between outcrops and terraces. At one point we skirted under a cliff and I had that uncanny sensation of being watched. Lifting my head, I saw three goats standing on the edge of a precipice, staring down with golden eyes. Two of them had formidable horns, reminiscent of the One God's demonized outcast.

Corax lowered his voice. "She's a maenad, you know."

"Who? You mean Manto?"

"Shh. Not so loud. I don't trust her. She wears the fawn skin."

"The fawn skin?"

"They all do; it's an emblem."

"Well, she did say that she was a follower of Dionysos. Yet she seems to want to help."

"Exactly. But things are not always as they seem, now, are they? Why is she so eager to help—if it's really help? I'm not convinced."

"Marianne trusts her; she has good judgment."

"Bah," said Corax, "she is smitten and has no judgment at all."

It occurred to me that Corax's paranoia might not be unwarranted. Manto appeared out of nowhere—very conveniently. She had taken charge and became our leader. How did that happen? We followed her—with few questions—based on the assumption that the Oracle's guidance would resolve the god's curse. Yet perhaps we only waded deeper into the chaos that surrounded all the gods.

"What are you afraid of?" I asked.

"There are old tales and tragedies about the maenads of Dionysos. In the throes of their ritual ecstasies, they've been known to tear animals and humans apart, limb from limb. Even kings have fallen to their frenzies. Their haunts are the mountains, which, I might note, is exactly where we're headed. Like lambs to the slaughter."

Corax peered at me from the side of his eyes and though he spoke with reason, I felt a sudden chill. He, too, could be accused of sly intent. Could he be trying to manipulate me into abandoning our quest and returning to town, where, of course, alcohol was abundant? I felt a surge of dizziness, wondering who I could trust. It pained me to admit, but I had little choice but to trust Manto over Corax, at least for now. I offered a silent prayer to the One God and the Many, asking for guidance.

"Shut up and walk," I growled.

It was mid-afternoon when we reached the hut of Tiresias and Manto. Corax shuffled in slow motion the whole way, head down, resigned to his fate. The hut was a rustic stone structure of one level, nestled against a cliff and, from a distance, well-blended into the natural formation. Like other dwellings on the island, most of the living happened outside. In the center of the patio grew a plane tree of magnificent arbors, sheltering a dining table. An old man sat in a wicker chair under the tree, soaking up the low sunlight streaming from the west. He raised a staff in greeting. Manto ran to him, hugging him and kissing the top of his bald head with an ardor I thought excessive. But, in truth, I knew nothing of such love, or any other, apparently.

"Welcome home, my dear," said the old man. "And who are your three companions?"

I stared at his face with its blackened, hollow concavities of eye sockets and their cloudy orbs. His ability to number us despite the obvious lack of sight struck me as eerie. Was the blindness a sham? Or did doubt now color all my perspectives? He certainly looked the part of a seer, almost a parody, even, as Corax had implied. The silver beard was stupendous, reaching to his waist. His craggy face might have seen a hundred or a thousand years, it seemed timeless. Enormous ears burst out of thin locks as if ready-made to gather sound from over the entire island and perhaps beyond. He wore a simple gray robe, the hem of which was hiked up to his waist to air out and sunbathe the lower part of his body. I tried not to fixate on his shriveled clump of genitals, wondering if that forecast my own decline.

"Father, this is my friend Marianne and her two companions, Diarmuid and Corax. They arrive with the hope that you might share some wisdom."

Tiresias turned his head to face Corax. "I've been expecting you," he said.

Corax, still staring at the ground in exhaustion, cranked his head upright in slow motion, like winching a megalith into place. He stared at Tiresias. "I bet you say that to everyone."

I fought down the urge to smack Corax. What was wrong with him? He knew better than to insult a host; hospitality was the true religion of people everywhere, but nowhere more than here. I inspected Tiresias, anticipating offense, but he sat quietly while my nerves stretched taut. Suddenly he exploded in laughter, slapping his knee, and bending over, gasping between peals. He rocked back and forth, then leaned forward, elbows on knees and chin in hand.

"You're right," he said. "I do. A trick I learned from the theater. Gets the upper hand right away." He cackled, pleased with himself.

Marianne crouched down and opened her pack. She produced the container of wild honey, a timely change of subject. I silently thanked her for her good sense. With reverence, she placed the pot in his hands.

"*Grandpère*," she said, "please accept this humble offering."

Tiresias turned his head to face Marianne. "No need, my dear, no need. You are guests. Offerings are unnecessary."

"Thank you, sir," she continued, "but your daughter suggested this would please you. And we do have a request."

Tiresias, nose trembling, hovered over the amphora as he brought it closer. A low hum buzzed in his throat as he sniffed around the vessel, turning it in his hands like a squirrel with a pinecone. He removed the stopper and carefully set it on a stone beside the chair. With delicacy, he dipped a forefinger into the opening, then swiftly placed it in his mouth. In silence, he sucked his finger as if it were his mother's teat. When he finished, he smacked his lips.

"I accept your offering," he said. "It is, as Sappho sang, *nectar poured from gold*."

"Father," Manto stood behind him and stroked his bald spot. "Let our guests sit and relax, take refreshment, and as the day spins down perhaps you will give them a consultation."

"Isn't she delightful? How lucky I am to have such a daughter." Though the eyes of Tiresias were dead, his whole face beamed with life. He jabbed a finger back into the honey pot and sucked it clean. Manto took the pot and lid and slipped into the hut. "Old men require young spirits to temper their irritations," Tiresias continued. "These days practically everything pisses me off. But not her—never. You people would be at the top of the shit list but for the exquisite offering. For that, I thank you and resolve to exercise at least a little temperance while you're here. Let's just hope that's not too long, eh?" He broke into another cackling laugh.

I found Tiresias amusing. A true character, the kind that will provide you stories for years to come. Corax frowned, less than charmed. Be that way, I thought, you old goat. Marianne started after Manto but paused at the entrance to the hut and returned to sit next to the seer. Figuring this was as good a time as any, I untied the rope linking me to Corax, then shifted two more chairs to fill the arc around Tiresias, steering Corax into the farther chair so I could present a buffer. While we arranged ourselves, Tiresias combed his fingers through his beard and said nothing. By the time we settled down, Manto reappeared with a tray of cups, a flask, a block of cheese, and a round loaf of seed-filled bread.

"I recommend the water," she said. "It flows from the spring behind the hut, straight out of the rock. Rich in minerals, including lithium, it will quench your thirst and soothe your stomach. Some claim that it prolongs life. That I don't know, but it certainly offers a lively refreshment."

We helped ourselves to food and drink and settled back in our chairs. "Master Tiresias," said Marianne, "I've heard tales of you, even in distant lands. My poet friend François liked to recite an epic poem from long ago, one that spoke of you as dead. Yet you seem entirely alive. Or was that another Tiresias?"

Tiresias pulled at his beard. "You have a lovely voice, dear. Would that I could see you! But I wonder—do you believe everything you hear in ancient poems?"

"That depends on whether I wish to believe."

"Ha! Good answer!"

Marianne fiddled with her braid and thought for a moment. "Let me rephrase my query. How old are you? And if older than most of our kind, are you *the* Tiresias, the one of fable?"

Tiresias chuckled. "Nice try. But the questions are irrelevant. We live in the dreamtime, where distortions of space and time, as well as life and death, are commonplace. Here, the mortal coil is unwound and flexes like a snake."

I felt the restless tension in Corax and turned to squelch the coming response, but I moved too slowly. "Bah," he snarled, "there is no dreamtime. We're born to a line, we live on it, then it buries us in the dirt like the path of an arrow. If you have evidence to the contrary, I'd like to see it."

"Evidence is beyond our science. Believe it or don't, the dreamtime is unperturbed."

Corax wasn't going to be dismissed. "No thank you, flaccid metaphysics gives me heartburn. Despite your tonic waters."

"Corax…" I warned, but he slapped my arm and pressed on.

"Oh, I've heard the tales," Corax said. "Never mind that they contradict each other. Never mind that. How did you lose your sight, anyway? Was it goddess A or goddess B?"

Manto handed Tiresias a cup of water and he downed it. "Both."

"Both?" Corax and I spoke simultaneously. I didn't know the stories, but I could spot a paradox.

"Yes. When I was a boy, I wandered in the woods and ranged far from home. One day, I'd been gone for hours and grew thirsty. When I came upon a trickle from a spring somewhere up the slope, I eagerly climbed to the source. It turned out to be a pool, as inviting a sight as you might imagine. Unfortunately, it was one of Athena's favorite bathing spots. Not knowing that, in my eagerness for a drink, I scrambled over the edge of the basin and saw her emerging from the water. Of course, she sensed my presence and spun around. For a second, I saw her head to toe, more naked than the day she was born. Her eyes flashed and dug into mine; within minutes my sight dimmed, and blackness took over. The last thing I saw was the goddess— her image carved into my mind's eye. They don't like to be seen out of garb, you know. Not that she was much to look at, but violation is all the same, I suppose. Regardless, I was blind and had to crawl all the way home, a long, terrifying journey of torn flesh, bruised knees, and head banging. My family was mortified, but what could they do? It was a matter of the gods. In time, Zeus took pity on me, I think because he had a thing for my mother, so he restored my sight on the condition that I be quietly removed far to the eastern mountains where he expected me to lay low for the rest of my life. My mother agreed, of course, and I was fostered there by distant relatives."

I listened closely; the story intrigued me. "And that was goddess A?" I asked.

"Yes," he continued. "Happy to have my sight back, I grew into an active young man, skilled in the art of herbs and medicines, which I learned from the aunt who sheltered me. I stayed away from the nearest cities and roamed across the mountains, gathering wild plants and extracting their essences. Best of all I loved to soak up the world in its visual beauty, from the delicacy of a wildflower swaying in the breeze to the rolling grace of a young woman's gait. Dutifully, I never left the hills or the scattered villages and avoided the gods like the plague."

"So, even the gods are a *pharmakon*," I mused.

Everyone stared at me, perhaps annoyed that I interrupted the story. Manto grinned. "You're a clever one, aren't you?"

"I'm sorry," I stammered. "Please continue your tale, Master Tiresias."

He nodded. "Anyway, one day as I walked high on an exposed ridge of my favorite mountain, I stumbled on another rare sight, the second of my life: two snakes copulating. They writhed entwined, a sinuous enactment of the hermetic endeavor. Entranced, I watched until they consummated their union and slithered away into a crevice. When I turned to go, I naturally glanced down to check for secure footing and noticed that my chest bulged like a woman's. I hurriedly felt up and down my body: the breasts were real, and my penis was gone, replaced by the folds and lips that had provided so much pleasure when I lay with one or another country girl. I had not noticed the change come over me when I spied on the snakes, but I could hardly deny the reality of my flesh. Incredulous, I disrobed for a full inspection."

"Don't tell us: you were gorgeous," Corax sneered.

I glared at him. Marianne waved her hands in frustration and said, "Let's just hear the story, okay?"

Tiresias continued, "I was shocked with the transformation but not entirely averse. Being a curious sort, I had wondered what it was like to be a woman. Of course, such adolescent fantasies were about sex and clothes and had little to do with the realities of a woman's lot. Soon enough, I would learn all that. My first concern was how my aunt and her family would react. But what could I do? I found my way back home to start a new life. Everyone had questions, of course, but I was surprised that no one seemed to mind. Despite their reputation, the hill folk are a tolerant lot. It turns out that compared to the whims of the gods and the endless wars of the noble class, a mere sex change is of little consequence to your common man. Soon enough I was married off to a local farmer, brought forth a son, and learned my place. I was lucky compared to many wives, though: my husband was a kind man and allowed me to continue my herbal practices. People respected my work and, as a result, they respected me whether I was a man or woman. Then, seven years later, wandering in the same hills as before, as I hunted for a rare variety of ironwort, I saw two more copulating snakes. I watched the complete act and when they were done, I was a man once again.

"I knew that my husband and son would not favor this change. It would render our marriage into a shameful union.

I vowed to spare them the embarrassment and did not return home but hiked in the opposite direction, down to the shore, and took passage across the sea to that mainland city where some say that Dionysos was born. Taking advantage of my breadth of gender experience, I offered consultations to men and women struggling with their marriages, helping them to see each other's perspectives. This venture kept me busy and I gained a reputation for wisdom, though in truth I had little original to offer. Mostly I mediated arguments.

"I changed my name in the hope that I could remain unseen by you know who, but trivial disguises offer no concealment from the gods. One day Zeus plucked me out of the street, reminding me that I had been warned about keeping a low profile. Being a god, he was well aware of my strange history and whisked me to Olympos to settle an argument he was having with his wife. They disagreed about who has more pleasure from intercourse: the man or the woman? Hera, believing that for most women intercourse primarily serves the lust of the man, claimed that men do. Zeus, the ultimate contrarian, especially where his wife was concerned, asserted that women had the greater measure. Since I had lived as both, I was designated to resolve the matter. Plopped between them as they glowered at each other, I landed in a hot seat I had never wanted. I knew that if I sided with Hera, she would be pleased and inclined to grant me favor. Zeus, though, would be furious. Likely, I wouldn't survive. If I sided with Zeus, Hera, being the vindictive type, would punish me royally. But I might survive. Regardless, there was no way out. So, I sided with Zeus. When I delivered my response, he exploded with laughter loud enough to generate a thunderstorm. Annoyed, Hera poked out my eyes with knitting needles. I was blind again.

"Eventually the fit of hilarity left Zeus and he contemplated my predicament. 'I am sorry it's come to this again,' he said. 'I cannot undo what Hera has done lest she geld me in my sleep. I'm sure you understand. But you'll get a consolation prize, anyway.' And he gave me powerful insight to see through the veil of things, even into the future. Being an adaptable fellow, I went on and made a long and successful career as a prophet. But, you know, I'd rather have my eyesight."

"I understand you answered Zeus to save your skin, but I'd like to hear what you really think about that question: who has more pleasure?" asked Marianne.

"Pleasure in intercourse derives from the energy generated between bodies; it has nothing to do with the sex of the participants. But you knew that."

"Yes. I just wanted to hear you say it."

"So, you've been blinded twice by different goddesses," I observed, "stamping it as your fate, I'm sorry to say. I hesitate to bring it up again, but this notion of the *pharmakon* aptly describes the extremes of divine intervention, don't you think? Remedy or toxin: you never know what you're getting. It's enough to make you swear off religion altogether. Which leads me to another query: why is the attention of the gods so problematic?"

"Because that is their purpose," said Tiresias, "to create problems."

I wanted to follow that line of thought, but Marianne revived her original question. "I know you dodged it earlier, but I still wonder how old you are? I'm not sure that I comprehend this notion of a dreamtime."

Tiresias pulled a tuft of his beard between two fingers and worked the fibers as though he were contemplating weaving a small garment—a skull cap, perhaps. "Honestly, I've lost count of years, my dear. As you can see, I'm very old." He straightened the hank of beard and patted it back into place. "And the dreamtime doesn't yield its secrets to analysis or logic; it just *is*. Ultimately, *what* it is can only be described as a perfect mystery."

I thought Corax was going to vibrate out of his chair. I sighed and reached for the flask to refill my cup with calming lithium water and wondered if I should be dosing him instead.

"Dreamtime, screamtime—I won't stand for it! There is no mystery, there's only the world. Are there things we don't understand? Sure, we're only human. Does that mean we have to call them *mysteries* as if it's all beyond us, a matter just for the gods? It's our world! We live in it, we die in it, and sometimes we do understand it. But that understanding comes from cleaning the claptrap out of our heads; then we can see things as they are!" By the time he finished, Corax was standing in front of his chair and wagging his finger. I clamped his arm and pulled him down.

Tiresias frowned. "I don't think the founder of your Academy considered contemplation of the mysteries as *claptrap*—if that's what you mean. Did he not proclaim that when man approaches a full vision of the perfect mysteries then he himself becomes perfect?"

"Balderdash. We've moved on, or at least some of us have. Your perfect mysteries are nothing more than imperfect science. The goal is a phenomenologically purified consciousness wherein one can see things—including your so-called mysteries—for what they are: constructs of individual perception."

Tiresias again stroked his beard and, as much as can be said about an eyeless man, turned his perspective inward for a moment. "Isn't that the line that got you in trouble?"

Corax looked surprised. "What do you know of that?"

"Just something I picked up delving into the mystery."

Corax seemed to be at a loss for words, a rare occasion. The sun approached the western horizon and the shadows stretched across the valleys below. Manto stood up. "Father, we need to prepare for bed. You've tired yourself out with dialectics."

"Yes, my darling," he sighed. He shook his head. "What would I do without you? Jabber through the night, no doubt."

Marianne stretched her arms and legs. "I do have one more quick question, if you don't mind. Master Tiresias, if you're as old as the gods, how old is Manto? Or perhaps I should ask her?"

"Oh, she's older than I am," and the seer cackled until he started coughing.

Manto shook her finger at Marianne, who looked embarrassed. "If you're so interested, you need to ask me. Really!"

"Sorry," she muttered, sheepish and out of character. Something about this father and daughter team threw even Marianne off-balance. I couldn't figure out what it was, though, so I dismissed it as my usual nerves.

[8]

Placing a mat and blanket on the patio, Corax and I curled together under the tree. Marianne ignored us, sat in a chair for a while, and later slipped into the hut, silent as a cat. The lithium must have taken the edge off Corax's mania because he fell asleep even without wine. Not me, though, I watched my thoughts march around in restless disarray. An understanding of events eluded me. Marianne traveled a great distance to help us, which she seemed to be doing, but her focus wavered. I could appreciate that she was drawn to Manto, but she seemed more beguiled than enflamed. And why was Manto flirting with me on the sly? Perhaps she liked both men and women; I had no problems with that, but her overtures had a random quality that puzzled me. At times she appeared to be a pleasant, helpful herbalist, then at other times a sadist or a tease. She controlled Tiresias like a puppet. Although a willing subject, he seemed drained of agency in the relationship. And what was I to think of this seer, his claims of mythic longevity, and the jumbled metaphysics of his dreamtime? Were his stories true or just the fantasies of an articulate tale-spinner? Force-feeding these thoughts into the machinery of reason only produced a grinding of gears; no conclusions emerged. Perhaps understanding was irrelevant at this stage. We'd followed the Oracle this far and discovered a powerful medicine, reportedly a remedy for Corax's ailment. Comprehension of the whole, if even possible, would arrive in its course—apparently not before. Exhausted by the rotations of my head, I finally stumbled into sleep.

The air became chilly during the night and dawn found me huddled close to Corax. I roused to the feel of someone massaging my bottom with a bare foot. It was Manto standing next to our mat, smirking as she tried to wedge her big toe between my cheeks. I was thankful for the thickness of our blanket. I looked at her with a frown, wondering at what point did I put my hands on her. As if she could read my thoughts, her smile broadened. "Time to rise, sleepyheads," she ordered. "It's bath time!"

Corax stirred, coughed, and hacked out a glob of spit. "What the fuck?" he said.

"Oh yes," Manto continued unperturbed, "it's springtime! Thermal spring, that is. We'll soak and make plans for the day. I have some ideas.… No need to get dressed, darlings, we'll all just tumble in like children of the rosy dawn."

Marianne stood behind Manto, watching carefully and venturing no expression. Both women were naked, and Marianne's hair hung unbraided down her back; somehow there seemed to be more of it than usual. Humming a vague tune, Tiresias limped out of the hut, also without clothes. I wasn't exactly shy of my body, but the lack of inhibitions in this part of the world astonished me. At this point, of course, insisting on any covering would have been more embarrassing than just going along with the norm. I pulled off the covers and stood while Manto leered. Corax, still grumpy, grabbed my hand and let me pull him upright.

"Lead on and we shall be purified of our sins," he said, sarcasm so thick you could lean on it.

Manto, holding her father's hand, led us to the far side of the house where we found a rocky trail. Tiresias' steps were practiced, and I thought he could have managed by himself despite the rough tread. He slid each foot forward as if in slow motion, placing it surely and never faltering. Whereas I, blessed with sight, was distracted by the view down the mountain, the yellow daisies jutting from cracks in the stone, and the antics of goats scampering from crag to crag across the scarp. I stumbled along behind.

We arrived at a basin carved from the marble bedrock by spring water as it plunged over the crest of an outcrop. Mortared stone dammed the lower end and encircled the concavity, making a giant tub. A haze of steam and the powerful smell of sulfur guaranteed that the water had been freshly delivered from the innards of the earth.

Manto and Marianne helped Tiresias into the bath and settled in next to each other with splashing and giggles. When they were out of the way, Corax and I followed—after testing the water with our toes. It was almost too hot to bear, but as I sank in, leaning back and letting it rise to my chin, I thought I'd never felt such total relaxation. Arrayed in a circle around the tub, we contemplated each other through the steam.

"I would sooner worship this than any god," stated Corax.

Tiresias stopped cleaning an ear with a finger. "Not much difference, really. Water embodies a first principle, which makes it a precursor to the divine, a matrix for the emergence of the pantheon, as the myths tell us. Truly, it is the origin of life. You would be remiss not to worship it."

"Hnnh," grunted Corax, unwilling to argue.

"As lovely as it is to contemplate dreamtime origins, let's take a look at our activities for the day," Manto said with authority. "First up is an outing for the women. Marianne confessed curiosity about the maenad rites, so we will ascend high onto the mountain to gather with a few others and celebrate Dionysos in the true spirit. Before you ask, these rites are strictly for women, who, as you may know, are favored by the gods. Men simply aren't allowed. They wouldn't understand, anyway."

Oh no, I thought, we were losing Marianne altogether. How could she run off to join the mad women in thrall to our nemesis? And what were these rites that needed to be kept from the knowledge of men? My imagination ran amok. Dismay must have shown on my face because Marianne caught my eye and winked. I didn't know how to interpret that and slid lower into the water.

"...meanwhile," Manto continued, "my father has agreed to delve into this matter of the curse. However, he needs your participation in a ritual of insight. For that, the three men shall retire to the dream chamber."

Corax groaned.

"Dream chamber?" I asked.

"Not quite a majestic *Telesterion* but at least it's a working *temenos*," answered Tiresias.

"Jettison the mumbo jumbo," snarled Corax. "My friend is from away."

"What my father means to say," explained Manto, "is that the dream chamber is a suitable *temenos*—a sacred space—even if it isn't the great and famous *Telesterion,* where folk are initiated into the rites of Demeter. Our version is a simple cave—a short walk from here. Within the chamber, you can reach into the mystery and, with father's guidance, extract the truth."

"You go," Corax waved at me. "I'll stay here and nap."

"If I'm going, so are you."

Corax looked at me like a surly child. "Whatever," he said, leaning back and closing his eyes. I did agree on one point: I had little motivation to leave the soothing waters.

"So, what happens in this dream chamber?" I asked

Manto opened her mouth to answer but Tiresias spoke first. "Everything, anything, and nothing—in a nutshell."

"Well, that's cryptic," I replied.

"What did you want? A recipe? Believe me, once you've gone through the basic training to be a prophet, you learn quickly that people don't want plain-spoken answers. It has to be cryptic or they think you're a fake. And I have a reputation to uphold!" Tiresias cackled and splashed his hands in the water, spraying droplets in all directions.

Manto patted her father on the head. "Now now, father, don't get overexcited. It's not good for your nerves." She turned to me. "The chamber is quiet and dark, but comfortable. You will imbibe the *kykeon* and sit on ram's fleece. The answers you seek will come to you."

"*Kykeon?*" I asked, feeling another sting of ignorance.

"A psychoactive substance, I believe," answered Corax, without stirring or opening his eyes. "Supposed to be a secret, but everyone in the City troops off to partake of the rites of Demeter. Then they can't stop talking about it for weeks. Especially to those of us who never went, like we missed out on the high point of existence. But, you know, a few of us had better things to do, like trying to get a grip on, oh, reality, for example. Undoubtedly another one of these damn *pharmakons*. Take a little bit and you'll see visions of the beyond; take too much and you may never come back."

"I am interested," I confessed. "As a monk, we spent long hours sequestered in the *clochan*. Visions were common. I wouldn't say I achieved enlightenment, exactly, but no doubt it was good for the soul."

"Good man," barked Tiresias. "Tally ho!"

Manto stood up from the bath and I noticed that her skin was sleek and taut like living marble. I lifted my arm to see the skin shriveled to the texture of old grapes and wondered how she avoided that.

"Time to get started," she announced. "Both our tasks require fasting, so no need for breakfast. Remember to drink plenty of water."

"Can we have more of the lithium salts before you leave?"

"Best not to mix lithium with the *kykeon*. He'll be fine," said Manto.

We hoisted ourselves from the idyllic pool and returned to the hut, Manto leading her father by the hand. On the way, Marianne fell back and whispered in my ear. "There's something funny about these two. I'm hoping to find out more. Don't worry so much."

"Easy for you to say," I complained, but was glad for the reassurance.

[9]

Marianne emerged from the hut wearing her leather hunting garb and followed Manto up a steep path through the outcrops. As usual, my friend was well-armed, which gave me some relief. I reminded myself that there was no reason to think she was in danger, yet I felt better seeing her in full warrior mode. Marianne stopped after a few switchbacks and yelled down, "See you tomorrow!" I waved and watched the two women recede into the bright contrasts of highland rock and shadow. The mountain tops soared far above, as if the island stone, bored with the runny hues of the sea, stretched for the sky's hard blue. If there was mystery in the world, I thought, surely it was in the land itself.

Tiresias, wrapped in his gray robe, hobbled around the patio, thumping the stones with his staff, as sure-footed as any sighted person. He barked orders that I tried to fill while Corax sat slumped in a chair and watched. "Fill the water amphora; we're going to need every drop! In the kitchen there, just left of the basin, up on the shelf about ear high, grab a couple of candles. Next to it should be the flint and steel pouch. Dry tinder in the other bag; take both. Then, in the far corner from the basin, on the floor under the shelf, there's a capped flask. Don't forget that. And be careful with it! All set?"

I dropped the full water jug into Corax's lap. Some of it splashed onto his chest and he gave me a pained expression. I shrugged and tried to look exasperated, which wasn't difficult.

"Okay, Master Tiresias," I said, "I've gathered the items you mentioned. Shall we go? I can lead if you describe the way."

"No need. Know it like the back of my hand, sure thing. Follow me."

We lined up behind Tiresias and embarked on our slow parade. By tapping the staff on the ground ahead of him, he read the landscape. He'd take two steps, stop, and tap again. With this method, I found plenty of time to gape and daydream. Spring had crept up the slopes into the hills and everything from weeds to trees bloomed with new life. A few goats foraged in earnest, their bells clanking with each step. Behind the mountain, the rising sun outlined the flanks of the looming peak with a glowing aura as we walked in the morning shadow. The trail angled uphill gradually, winding through rock ledges, and skirting steep drops. Corax complained about the weight of the water jug, but I ignored him. I asked myself if he'd always been such a whiner, and I honestly couldn't recall. Did I still love him? That's what I told myself, but maybe it wasn't true. What does it mean to love someone who's a pain in the ass? I didn't know that, either. I knew that I was tired of carrying so many doubts, though. After half an hour of start-and-stop progress, which felt like an eternity, we walked around an exposed corner and came to an opening in the cliff face.

The entrance was low and narrow, space enough for one at a time. Tiresias said, "I'll go ahead while you light a candle. You'll need it—not me." He chuckled at his joke and slipped into the cave.

While I fumbled with the fire tools, Corax spoke in my ear, "You really want to go through with this?"

"What can it hurt?" I replied. "We've come this far, and we have no other leads on lifting your curse. What's your problem, anyway? Would you rather keep it?"

Corax dismissed my questions with a wave of the hand. "It's a curse of the gods. Who escapes that? Besides, I'm getting used to it."

"Well, I'm not willing to live with a drunk. Nor am I willing to watch you waste your talents. Maybe it's a foolish hope, but I'm not giving up. If you do, then we're finished, aren't we?"

I thought I saw a tear in Corax's eye before he turned his head away. It took me a few minutes of fumbling and muttering to get a spark in the tinder and enough flame for the candle. Corax applauded by slapping the side of the amphora and said, "You're better at that than I am." A small thing, the compliment, but it helped my spirits. Light in hand, I ducked under the arch, glancing back to make sure that Corax followed. The passage immediately shrunk to a slot where my shoulders scraped the rock walls and caused a rush of claustrophobia. None too soon, the passage opened into a small domed chamber. Holding the candle over my head, I saw Tiresias seated on a fleece in the center, legs crossed, humming softly.

"Welcome to the chamber of our *temenos*," he said. "Hand me the small flask, take a fleece, and have a seat. Plenty of room!"

According to the candlelight, there was little room, barely enough for the three of us and a stack of sheep skins. Tiresias resumed the humming and took several cups from a small box, setting them in a row at his feet. I found a niche in the chamber wall for the candle, then arranged fleeces for us to sit facing Tiresias.

"Put the water between us," said Tiresias. "Don't forget to drink freely; the rite pulls the moisture out of your flesh like the desert sun at noon. The more water you drink, the less your headache later."

Tiresias uncorked the small flask and passed it back and forth under his nose. "Ahh," he intoned, "the *kykeon*, one of the great blessings of the gods! Thanks be to Our Lady of the Earth, Demeter. I cannot disclose to the uninitiated how it is made, but I can tell you that it contains fermented barley and a seasoning of honey. It is, as you said, psychoactive. However, unlike alcohol or opium, it does not dull the senses. No, it blows them wide open to regard the mystery itself. But enough of that. First, you must each pose a question for the dream work."

"A question?" I asked.

"Well, what do you seek? We all want many things from life, but what do you wish to gain here and now? Keep it simple."

While we mulled over another challenge for brevity, Tiersias carefully poured a thimbleful of liquid from the flask into each cup. There was no uncertainty in his movements, and he didn't spill a drop. Raising the flask in both hands, he prayed, "O Dionysos, please accept this libation." He poured a small amount onto the floor of the cave. An odor filled the chamber: pungent, earthy, radiating the scent of rot and alkaloids. I didn't relish putting my lips to a cup of that brew.

"Diarmuid?" Tiresias asked. "What do you seek?"

His tone of voice informed me that we had embarked on a ritual progression. This was step one; if I took it, I left the profane world and entered sacred space.

Don't overthink it, I told myself and opted for the simple truth. "I seek to lift the curse of Dionysos from my friend, not only for his sake, but because it bears the both of us down to infernal depths." The formality of my phrasing gave me pause; it was like I'd never left the monastery, where we'd held forth without restraint from dawn to dusk.

Tiresias handed me a cup and I drained it. Even the honey failed to gloss over the intense bitterness. I couldn't compare it to anything else I'd had, because I'd never had anything like it. It made me want to heave. I quickly filled the cup with water and chased the *kykeon*, knocking it back like a shot of whiskey. Unfortunately, it only clarified the aftertaste. Suddenly cramps seized my body. I rocked back and forth, hoping that I could dissolve the astringent effect with movement.

"It will never replace wine at the table," said Tiresias. "But you'll forget about the taste soon enough." He raised the next cup. "Corax, what do you seek?"

I expected a wisecrack, but Corax's head sank onto his chest and he spoke in a whisper. "I seek the love and admiration of my friend, for his sake, for my sake, for our sake." He took the cup and drank.

His testament surprised me. A rush of joy took hold and I stopped fretting about the bitter alkaloids charging through my blood. I felt tenderness flow from my heart and spill across the space between us, caressing the aura around Corax. I even cried, just a little. After a few tears, I realized that Corax did not usually have an aura. I checked and saw it again, pulsing faintly around his body like an envelope of light.

"I seek to guide these supplicants into the primal mystery and back again," stated Tiresias before downing his dose. "Fill your cups with water and we will wait for what comes."

Like a dutiful acolyte, I poured water into all three cups and replaced the amphora. Longingly, I looked at Corax and he rewarded me with a tentative smile. His aura was beautiful. I clutched at his hand and he gripped hard in return. Tiresias began chanting. It was in no language I'd ever heard, but it rolled around the chamber dome like sonorous reverberations in a cathedral. The hackles on my neck bristled and fresh tears fell from nowhere. Was this what Tiresias meant when he said that the rite drew water from the flesh?

While the chanting continued, the light grew dimmer or my vision clouded, I wasn't sure which. I clung to Corax, but I soon lost sight of him and everything else in the chamber as veils of swirling color dropped from the ceiling, flowing around us like rainbow cloaks, and overriding all other sensory input. I assumed that my hand remained in Corax's, but I didn't know for certain because normal proprioception dissolved, and all sensation funneled into the fields of crystal light. Somewhere in my thoughts, it occurred to me that I really should panic. However, that struck me as an uninteresting reaction. It would only serve to distract me from the tapestry of swirling colors; the arcane geometry was simply more compelling than the tired old spasms of anxiety. Alchemy unfolded and I became the alembic; how could I want anything else? Somewhere I heard Marianne's voice: "Don't worry." There was nothing I could do anyway; the *kykeon* had mounted my body and was going to ride.

I had no idea how long the carnival of pattern and color whirled around my head. Both time and ego ceased to mean much. I must have been sitting on the fleece holding hands with Corax, but I felt none of that; instead, it seemed that I floated free within a magical universe. I had experienced visions before, fasting in the dark little huts of my sect, but never anything like this. I didn't fight it; I couldn't if I'd wanted to. After a long while, the colors faded, and I fell away from the realm of geometric fantasy, plunging into a black void. I stretched my arms and legs wide, thinking it would slow the descent. Abruptly, as in a dream, I walked onto a blank stage. My skin prickled in sudden fear; turning, I saw a red-eyed hound trot out of the mist. It growled and clacked its jaws, teeth dripping foamy saliva, and I recognized it as the thing that had chased me from childhood—a Dog of Hell. The stench of death wafted my way and I spun around in terror, running for my life. Without thinking, I took the form of a hare so I could run faster. I leaped with all my might, barely staying ahead of the hound. I came to a river and sprang to the middle, splashing into a new form, a salmon, thrashing my tail back and forth in a desperate bid to escape. Undaunted, the hound became an otter and swam after me. I ran fast with the current, but the otter closed the gap. Just as I felt its teeth on my tail, I charged to the surface, broke free of the water, and took the shape of a sparrow, darting into the trees. The otter followed, becoming a hawk, pumping its wings like a bullroarer. There could be no escape; I knew it. Exhausted, I fell to the ground as a seed, lost in the litter of the forest floor. The hawk landed and shifted into a hen, pecking patiently through the debris. When she came to my seed, she swallowed me into darkness.

Within that space appeared a bearded woman, or perhaps it was a female man. They claimed my limp body, picking it up as if it weighed nothing and laying it on a broad, flat stone surrounded by an old grove of oaks. I watched, a disembodied observer. Using the sharpest of blades, they sliced me in pieces, flinging the bits among the trees. I felt no pain. Nor did I raise any objections—it seemed as valid as any conclusion. Dissection complete, dawn infused the air with rosy light. As the sun grew brighter, my consciousness fell into the ground and the roots of the trees. No longer a soul scattered in the forest, I *was* the forest. Contentment infused my being and the psyche I had once called my own now belonged to the world.

I basked in the dissolution. Nothing happened, there was only the breath of being. Who I had been was forgotten, cast aside like a husk. But after a long while, I started to remember things about my body, like the hand that held Corax's. I felt a slight squeeze, a strange sensation until I realized that it was the actual Corax applying pressure. Slowly, I ascended from the underworld, returning to the flesh.

A faint light filtered in from the entrance passage to the chamber, enough to see the others. I noticed the puddle of wax where the candle had been. Corax smiled at me like a goofy child, but my attention was fixed on his pupils, blown wide into obsidian mirrors. His face fascinated me with its relaxed wonder. I saw a beauty of subtlety and innocence. I imagined I could gaze through the skin into the delicate fire of his mind, and I felt a spur of desire. If Tiresias had not been there, I would have thrown Corax down and taken him on his sheepskin. I was surprised at the intensity of this erotic eruption, but there was little time to savor it. My knees screamed with discomfort from lack of movement and I abandoned lust for the slow straightening of my legs.

"Welcome back," said Tiresias, who looked unaffected.

"What *was* that?" I asked.

"A real trip, to be sure," said Corax, shaking his head. We stared at each other. I saw the tenderness in his eyes as we unclasped our sweaty hands.

"Tut tut," said Tiresias. "We did what we set out to do. We beseeched the god and if I'm not mistaken, the god delivered… something, anyway. Our task is to interpret what was delivered before we leave the chamber. Drink water, as much as you can. Then, Diarmuid, tell us what you saw and felt. Tell us the story and hold nothing back."

I refilled our cups and Tiresias followed his advice, draining his cup and motioning for more. We sat in silence for a few moments as we guzzled water; I couldn't seem to get enough.

"Whether dream or vision, I do not know. Maybe it doesn't matter." I told my story in a straight line from start to finish, covering everything I could remember, even the stone knife used by the bearded woman to cut me in pieces. Parts of the story were beyond words and I kept pausing, searching for a way to describe the strange elements of the experience. It tested the limits of my narrative abilities. Some sections, like the animal transformations, took me back to my childhood sitting around the hearth and the glowing peat fire, listening to the adults tell one preposterous shape-shifting tale after another. I might have abandoned a little restraint when I got to those parts of the story and laid it on a bit thick. Anyway, I got through it, though I couldn't tell if it made any sense. When I finished, I was thirsty again.

Tiresias scratched at his beard, all the while saying "Hmm, hmm." I waited for his revelation, but he only shifted his hand to scratch behind his ear, saying, "Very interesting. Corax, tell us your story."

I felt cheated. I'd assumed that the old seer was going to spell out my experience with the insight of his craft, explaining each detail. I opened my mouth to protest, but it occurred to me that he was following a ritual pattern and perhaps it wasn't time for interpretation yet.

Corax stretched his arms over his head and squirmed, either to work out the stiffness or delay his response. Settling down, he stared at Tiresias and launched his account. "I had a similar entry to the *kykeon* effects as Diarmuid: colors, patterns, sensory isolation, and so forth. I see no reason to stumble through my poor version of what he already described with eloquence. Eventually, I too had the sensation of falling out of color flux into a more recognizable imaginary state. Interesting, my dear," and here he turned to me, "that after the dreadful chase and dismemberment you ended up in a forest. I started in one. Not a forest, mostly olive trees—a grove gone wild. Anyway, I fell through nothingness until I was no longer falling at all but laying on my back under the trees, unable to move, as if held down by shackles or ferocious gravity. I felt no fear about the situation—rather it seemed like an invitation to merge with the dirt.

"As I lay there, pinioned, I heard faint music from off in the trees. The source moved and the music grew louder, but I couldn't turn my head to see anything. Finally, three satyrs pranced out of the grove. Shifting the tune, they began a stately dance, circling me. First clockwise, then counterclockwise, they kept switching direction in precise synchronization. One played an *aulos*, one a tympanum, and one a lyre. With heads tossed back and spines arched, they thrust their hips, gigantic erections bobbing in time to the rhythm of the music. This went on for several revolutions, one way, then the other, before they came to a sudden stop. The one with the lyre sang a brief song, then they resumed the circling."

"What did the satyr sing?" interrupted Tiresias.

"Something like this:

> *All that in his heart he wants to be*
> *make it be.*
> *And all the wrong he did before, loose it.*

There was more, but that's all that I remember."

"Sappho... one never tires of her lyric grace," muttered Tiresias. "Sorry, please continue."

Corax rubbed the top of his head with a palm, a gesture that always made me think he was checking to see if any hair had returned to the pate. "After the song, the music increased in tempo and the satyrs danced faster and harder, stomping the ground with their hooves. They looked quite proud of their bouncing penises, and though I confess that such a thing might seem desirable at times, it also must be quite awkward to lug around. As the music drove on, I felt a twitch in my finger, then all the fingers of my right hand stirred and began to tap the ground in rhythm. The same happened with the other hand. The fingers tapped hard, working into such a frenzy that they finally detached themselves from the hands and danced off into the woods. Then the toes did the same, fleeing my feet as if they never belonged. My rebellious arms flexed and pounded the ground until they, too, separated from the shoulders and ran off, cavorting, apparently thrilled to be free of the demands of the body. This process continued, piece by piece: one leg then the other, followed by my penis and balls, leaving merely a head and torso. But the twitching went on, and sections of abdomen separated as if sliced, rolling away into the trees.

"The music stopped. A satyr placed his tympanum on the ground, picked up my head, the only remaining body part, and set it on the drum as if it were a plinth for a bust. The satyr with the *aulos* pulled the two sections of the flute apart and thrust them deep into both of my ears. I expected pain but felt only the strangeness of these absurd procedures. The third satyr stood the lyre directly in front of my face and said, 'Use your tongue; we hear you're quite free with it.' They scampered off into the grove, jumping over the various parts of my body which lay scattered here and there. Oddly, I could sense each part, no matter where it was or how far away, as if they were all still connected.

"I didn't know what else to do, so I followed the satyr's instructions and used my tongue to pluck a note on the lyre. I created one faint sound, then the entire scene dissolved as the influence of the *kykeon* slipped away. And so, I returned to the hard floor of this chamber and the cramps in my legs. Good luck with explaining all that, Master Prophet."

"Wonderful!" Tiresias clapped his hands with delight. "You both received a message from Dionysos the Loosener. It couldn't have gone better if I'd scripted it myself!"

[10]

"Wait," I said. "Aren't you going to tell your story, too?"

"Not much to report, I'm afraid. I should have brought my knitting." Tireseias again broke into that cackling laugh that first amused me and now was starting to get on my nerves.

"But did you see things under the influence of the *kykeon*—patterns, visions, whatever you want to call them—as we did?" I wasn't ready to let him off the hook after we'd turned ourselves inside out.

"Remember that I wasn't born blind. The memories of sight live on in my mind, perhaps more vigorously than in yours. So, yes, I also see the colors and patterns that cascade from the gods. All who imbibe of the *kykeon* are gifted with these images. Beyond that, specific visions come at the whim of Hermes, who handles the commerce between gods and mortals. Being the only messenger, you can imagine that his services are overtaxed and not everything gets through. Consider yourselves blessed, that you received such prompt replies."

Corax drummed his fingers on his knees and I wondered if this new behavior was left over from his *kykeon* vision. Finally, he spoke. "Fine, fine. We're blessed, we're gifted, life is wonderful. Can you make sense out of our visions or not? I can see the obvious mythological parallels, of course—the sacrificial dismemberment and all that. Great, our experiences resemble the myths. Big surprise there—everything resembles the myths, that's why they're the myths. If this prophecy thing is your job, the calling for which you have become legendary, I'm hoping that you can suggest something a little more profound than we all live in the echo of the gods. Know what I mean?"

Tiresias chuckled. "You do have a sharp tongue, philosopher. I'm sure it will be the death of you, yet." He fell silent and resumed combing his beard with long, bony fingers.

"I, too, would be interested in your thoughts on our visions, Master Tiresias," I offered in a placating voice.

"Certainly, certainly. It's part of the rite, anyway—can't do without it. So," and here he puckered his lips and pulled at an ear before continuing, "it is my role to offer a map of the experience, but not a destination. Ultimately, you must find your way to where you want to go. Remember your intention and see where it fits. For you, Diarmuid, Dionysos offered a vision of the world as it is, beyond the gods, their curses, and concerns. We often think of ourselves as singularities of ego, but in truth, we are linked to the world through filaments of the psyche. Like Ariadne's thread, we can follow these filaments into and out of the complexities of experience. We can pluck them gently and bring forth a harmony that benefits all, or we can try to ignore them, and stagger forward ensnared by the webs of connection. To find harmony, we must let go of our boundaries and disassemble into the world, not as an extinction of the self but as an expansion.

"Dionysos the Loosener is a master of this expansive process; it is the method of his madness. His message for you, good Diarmuid, is to follow the threads. Your role in lifting the curse will reside in tending to the existing web of relationships rather than designing new patterns. I might add, on a personal note, that striving to control situations and people will bring you no satisfaction. If you have doubts about that, remember in the vision your failure to escape Fate, even by trying to change your nature. You are who you are—more of a navigator than a commander."

I felt a burning sensation in my gut. I wasn't sure what he meant by "follow the threads" but his last comment carried enough uncomfortable truth to make me squirm. Glancing at Corax, I saw his face relaxed and gentle; I took some solace from that. I couldn't have handled resentment or the usual caustic sarcasm.

"As for you, Corax the daring philosopher," continued Tiresias, "your vision is tricky. You're correct to note the dual themes of dismemberment. However, Diarmuid's procedure was imposed from above in a surgery of the gods, whereas your disassembly resulted from a rebellion of the body itself. Once you were introduced to the harmony of the filaments, which is in the essence of all music, by the way, your own body eagerly rendered itself into fragments and danced away. Away from what? One might ask. Well, what was left? Your head, the ego, the willful conscious of the human soul. This head, I understand, has labored at length, using all the tools of logic and reason to elaborate the analytics of being. Yes, your fame precedes you. Despite the achievements of this venerable head in its attempts to circumscribe reality, it has run afoul of another reality: that of the gods. Your cutting logic has sliced and diced but failed to grapple with the relational nature of deconstruction. Taking things apart is not the same as understanding how they work. You have, in sum, failed to hear the music that ties it all together. Dionysos showed you a way to avoid unnecessary division and earn the love and respect of others. Pay attention to the music. It will pull you apart yet hold you together, depending on the tune. My guess is that to appease the god, you must offer him a musical affirmation."

Tiresias paused and scratched his beard. Corax looked at me with a mixed expression, conveying frustration and an alarming tinge of mania. "What shall I do then," he said, "sing him a little song?"

Tiresias frowned. "No, you'll not get off so easy. I think something more profound is required. For example, you might give him a musical instrument, one of rare beauty and power— there's an affirmation. I know that he dearly loves to hear the serenades of his followers, and, for a god, the sounds from the best instruments are always preferred. No, I'd suggest you give him… oh, perhaps the lyre of Apollo."

"What?" I sputtered in disbelief.

Corax, fuming, as usual, cut into the astonishing pronouncement of Tiresias. "*For example*? This is just off the top of your head? A whim or what?"

Tiresias stroked his legs with the palms of his hands. "Yes, the lyre of Apollo, that would be perfect. You want the favor of Dionysos, correct? I know for a fact that he's lusted after that lyre for some time, but, of course, Apollo has little interest in parting with it. He's quite vain about it."

Corax looked ready to explode. "How in fifty levels of Hades are we supposed to get Apollo's lyre? Will he trade it for an old goat?"

"No, no, nothing like that," mused Tiresias. "I suppose you'll have to steal it."

I was dismayed. Even if stealing the prized possession of a god was possible, would we not be making an enemy of one just to pacify another? Was there a future in that?

Corax was more to the point. "This is bullshit."

Tiresias stretched and yawned. Using his staff for leverage, he stood, grunting with the effort. It crossed my mind that this display was feigned, but I couldn't imagine why, unless it was an attempt to deflect further criticism by arousing sympathy. "Well, gentlemen," he said, "We should return to the hut. It will be dark soon and you'll want to negotiate the path when there's still light. The girls won't be back till tomorrow, I predict, so we'll have to fend for ourselves. Assuming that you're hungry. I am—famished. Ah, and don't forget to bring the *kykeon* flask and the water jug."

Corax groaned and I feared that he might assault the old man, so I quickly shoved the amphora in his hands. As soon as I did that, I realized that I acted out of a desire to control the situation, especially Corax and his unpredictable energy. Wasn't I just told that I needed to stop doing such things? How soon the revelations dissipate into dust, I thought. Picking up the small flask and the fire tools, I shrugged at Corax and turned to follow the seer out of the dream chamber.

Corax spent the evening sulking on the patio, staring into the valley with a dour face. I retrieved some cheese and olives from the pantry and ate with Tiresias. Corax refused to join. I left him to his ill-temper, and there he sat in his gnarly thoughts. My earlier tenderness for him evaporated into a cloud of depression. Our new mission seemed impossible. However, I saw that there was little to do about it, as daunting as it appeared. Trying to apply the wisdom from my vision, I decided to address myself to something I could change—filling my stomach. I took a massive bite of cheese and followed it with olives, one by one, spitting the pits into my palm and making a tidy pile on the table. Might as well take advantage of a free audience with the old prophet and his considerable store of knowledge, I thought, so I asked questions. I learned that the next island to the north contained a temple sacred to Apollo. It was one of his favorite haunts, far from the mortal throngs on the mainland. The only people who journeyed to this island were worshippers and fervid acolytes. That is, aside from the obligatory pirates and slave traders that lurked everywhere these days. But even they handed over a portion of their earnings to support the god and his temple. This form of adoration pleased him no end. It was there, in this compound of the faithful, that we could expect to find the lyre.

It grew dark and Tiresias announced that he was tired and shuffled off to bed. I cleaned up the scraps of remaining food while Corax watched the sky turn black. He offered no resistance when I kissed the top of his bare head and lead him to our blankets. We curled together, adjusting for the maximum closeness. I still felt the lingering effects of the kykeon, but I was too tired to follow the fading patterns that scrolled through my head. Sleep brought welcome relief.

[11]

When I awoke the next morning, Tiresias sat without a twitch of life in his chair under the tree. I wasn't eager to start the day, so I pulled the blanket to my chin and watched the dawn transform through gray and rose into yellow. Corax snored now and then, a gentle rumbling that anchored my reveries. Otherwise, I drifted, free of intent.

The sun had yet to reach the patio when I noticed movement on the hillside. It was Marianne and Manto, slipping down from the crags like cats. With hair disheveled and full of twigs, they looked like they'd been rolling around in the mountain meadows all night. Which, as far as I knew, might have been exactly what they were doing. Marianne gave me a tired smile and walked directly to our mat. She threw herself down next to me, wriggling under the blanket and into my arms. Manto kissed her silent father and disappeared into the house. I wanted to grill Marianne about her experience, but she fell asleep within seconds. I relished the sense of her body, the warmth, the tangles of hair brushed against my lips, even the odor of her old sweat. Slumber gave her innocence and vulnerability; it was hard not to feel aroused. My hands wanted to explore her skin, but it seemed a disgraceful violation of trust, so I lay still, relaxed, and soon drifted back to sleep.

I woke for the second time to hear Corax and Tiresias arguing. "Bah," came the familiar dismissal, "you claim that the god sent us a message. But isn't it just as valid to say that our potion-jumbled brains spit out that archetypal circus you're calling a message? It's no more god-sent than a dream cobbled out of the detritus of the day."

"We do not chop logic when speaking of divinity," Tiresias growled.

"Why speak of divinity at all? It's chemistry!"

"And was it not a god who gave us fire so that we might transmute the elements one to another? There's your chemistry—a gift from the gods! And is not the earth itself with all its riches of minerals, its Vulcan procedures, and its pressured metamorphoses merely the embodiment of the goddess Gaia?"

"Debatable—why give it a personality at all?"

"Do you dispute that Dionysos himself gave us the chemistry of wine?"

"So they say. I've seen no proof. I like stories as much as anyone, but when it comes to explaining the world, I'll take atoms and matter, thank you."

I untangled from Marianne, who sleepily tried to hold me back, and stood up. "Working on another dialogue, Master Corax?"

"Hardly," he replied. "Just trying to get to the bottom of the hokum."

I saw that he was in fine form, overflowing with sharp retorts, and maybe a little manic. The relentless skepticism alienated many, I understood as much, yet it thrilled me. His quest for truth and understanding was courageous, even to the point of defying the gods. I admired that about him. It penetrated to a place within my soul that lay too dormant, a hidden place that sought release. Often, his dialectical critiques fueled my desire, spurring a passionate lust for his body, perhaps as a way to saddle his mind and prove my worth. All conjecture, of course; I claim no objectivity in such things. .

Manto emerged from the hut with a tray of food and drink, putting an end to the argument. We applied ourselves with enthusiasm to the spinach pie, bread, fruit, olives, and cheese. The apples were from last year, I assumed, but still juicy.

As Marianne joined us, I took the chance to satisfy my curiosity. "What did you two do on the mountain? I'm interested."

Manto didn't give Marianne a chance to speak. "Of course, you're interested. All men are obsessed with knowing what women do when we're together. Not knowing, their imaginations devolve to sex. Am I right?" Without waiting for an answer, she continued. "I can tell you this much: we met with a half-dozen other women and honored the god. More than that is not your privilege to know."

I looked at Marianne, who shrugged.

"Okay," I said. "I'll leave it to my imagination, misguided or no. Lacking similar scruples, I'm happy to relate our experiences if you care to hear them."

"Yes, please do," said Marianne, mouth full of spinach pie.

I told the story of our time in the dream chamber, including a detailed account of my vision. When I finished, I looked to Corax and he waved for me to continue, so I told about his experience as well, along with a summary of Tiresias' interpretations.

Manto's eyes gleamed. "The lyre of Apollo! A worthy gift, I'd say."

"I suppose. We have to get it before we can give it. We have no skill at thieving from the gods," I said.

"Are you sure about that?" She answered, a little testy. "Did not he," she pointed at Corax, who was shoveling bread and cheese into his mouth like a starving man, "steal the respect of the god and earn a curse?"

"Doesn't seem like quite the same thing."

"Well, the gods don't suffer loss glibly, even if it's something that you fail to value."

I was surprised at the depth of her animation on the subject. I couldn't make sense of it and continued my objections. "If a god can be offended by a mortal slur, what risks accompany the theft of a prized possession? My imagination goes to thunder-born incineration as a possibility. Or eternal torments."

"Always a possibility," mused Manto, smirking as she pulled back her hair and combed it with her fingers, the edgy mood having given way to ironic detachment. I found her baffling; she seemed to contain a host of personalities. She continued, now in lecture mode. "It's not hard to get to Apollo's temple from here. A couple of days' walking brings you to the northern tip of our island. There you'll find a village where you can hire a boat to make the crossing to the famous Temple Island. Depending on conditions, a few hours over the waves, and there you are. Can't miss it; there are enough varied temples and sacred structures to celebrate the whole pantheon. Apollo's is the biggest and, I daresay, the hardest to miss. Parked in front is the largest statue you'll ever see. Of the god himself, of course, in all his adolescent glory. Should you care to pay your respects or grovel for mercy, Dionysos also has a temple, tucked back from the harbor fray. You'll recognize *it* by the stone phallus." Her grin stretched across her face and achieved a feral leer.

Marianne paused braiding her hair. "And where is the lyre? Do you know?"

"That I don't, my dear. But it's in the temple compound somewhere. Once you get it, bring it back to us."

"To you?" Corax sputtered.

"Yes. We can arrange to present it to the god along with a statement in your defense."

"Why am I suddenly suspicious?" Corax rubbed the top of his head.

"When are you not suspicious?" pointed out Tiresias.

"Look," Manto wagged her finger at Corax, "the Oracle told you to consult my father. You did. He guided you to the threshold of the god. You received a vision and my father helped you understand it. This isn't smoke and mirrors, you know. Clearly, you're supposed to take the lyre. Let's assume that's a good idea. Then what? Do you have a plan for how to get it to Dionysos yourself? Yes? No?"

Corax muttered, "We could jam it on the phallus at his temple and he can pick it up when he makes his rounds."

Manto looked at Corax with a combination of weariness and frustration. "You don't know when to quit, do you? How about this? You go get the lyre and if you can figure out what to do with it, go right ahead. Otherwise, you can bring it here."

Marianne asked, "You won't be coming with us, then?"

"No dear, I have to take care of my father. I know someone in the village at the north of the island that can help you, though. Mother Nyx. She's well connected and not without skills. She harbors no fondness for Apollo, whom she considers a tiresome upstart. She may want to tag along, just for the lark of it. If she offers, I'd advise you to say yes."

Contemplating logistics made the venture seem more daunting. It all seemed impossibly overwhelming, like something out of a fable or myth. I'd rather deal with the return of irritability and paranoia in Corax's demeanor. If we couldn't keep him stable, nothing else would matter. "Manto, could you please teach us how to make the lithium salts? I expect we'll need more, and soon."

"Let it go, will you?" said Corax.

Manto surveyed Corax with narrowed eyes. "Yes, Diarmuid, I'll tell you how to do it. It's easy. I use an evaporation method to desalinate the lithium from the spring water. However, it takes a few days to dry and collect enough salt for storage. I expect you'll want to depart on your quest sooner than that. I can give you some salts already prepared, enough to last for a week or two. When you return with the lyre, as I anticipate, we can make more."

With enough lithium to keep Corax stable, I saw that there was little reason to delay. When I said as much, Marianne agreed, and since we'd finished with breakfast, we decided to leave right away. Manto offered food for the road, and we stuffed as much as we could into the crannies of our packs. As we said our goodbyes, Manto handed me a small bag of lithium salts, followed by a deep kiss that caught me by surprise. I tried to slip from her embrace, but she held on like a bramble vine. Suddenly, she released me and acted as if nothing happened. Both Corax and Marianne stood frozen with shocked looks that echoed my own. Manto provided a graceful embrace for Marianne, who returned it, though she looked at me over Manto's shoulder and rolled her eyes. Next, Manto went to Corax, lifted his head, and announced, "I'm counting on you.

You can do better, you know." I had no idea what she meant, and I could tell by Corax's puzzled expression that he didn't, either.

Tiresias lifted his hand. "Farewell, and good fortune. Hope to see you soon," and he exploded into another cackling fit.

Armed with a sketch map from Manto, Marianne led us away from the hut and across the rocky slope of the mountain, headed north.

[12]

We followed goat trails and cart paths through the rugged interior of the island. It was a beautiful landscape, raw and sensuous. Everywhere the exposed marble gleamed like crystal, dazzling when it caught the light. In between the scarps and ledges of stone grew olives, holm oaks, and gnarly pines; underneath these arbors, a carpet of herbs and grasses erupted with spring flowers. It was a dry and bright land revealed by the rays of its overlord, Helios, who rode across the sky each day wielding the hammer of the sun. Or so Corax proclaimed as he loudly recited the myths of his people.

His energy had returned, and he bounced along the trail, talking rapidly. At one point, he scrambled up onto a boulder, swung his arms wide, and yelled, "For I am the god of reason and this is my domain!"

Marianne and I exchanged looks. If we didn't arrest the mania soon, he would spin out of control. We grabbed his arms and dragged him into the shade of an oak tree, where we forced him to drink a cup of water laced with lithium. He thrashed and gagged, spitting out the liquid. Finally, Marianne put him in an arm lock while I held his nose with one hand and poured a fresh cup down his throat. Mission accomplished, we sat and enjoyed some refreshing fruit while he whined and cursed. We ignored him and waited for the potion to take effect.

By the time Marianne and I finished eating, Corax showed signs of calming down. He still complained, though. "At least you could have given me wine. It's better therapy than this damn poison. Wine pleases the palate and makes you feel good. Isn't that the point? This shit tastes bad and gives you nothing but a gray hell of life-sucking fog."

"We've seen how much better the wine is," I countered. "Now we're doing this. Sorry, but I don't know how else to deal with you. It's not like you'll answer to reason when you get that way."

"Yeah yeah, right. Whatever you say. I don't know who appointed you the medic. When I find out, I'll be picking a few bones."

Marianne raised her hand and we stopped talking. Like a leopard, she uncoiled from the ground to a wary crouch. Then I heard it—a rustling in the bushes. Slowly, she stalked toward the noise. What an astonishing creature, I thought, admiring her precision of movement. Suddenly, she launched herself into the thicket, causing an explosion of thrashing followed by frantic bleats. I heard her cooing in a gentle tone and saying "There, there, dear. I won't hurt you." She emerged from the bushes a few minutes later with a fawn cradled in her arms.

"She's lost, poor thing. I heard the whimpering." Corax, mouth open, looked at Marianne in wonder, an expression of his that always melted my heart. But I was still mad at him and gave my tenderness to the irresistible fawn, instead. I stroked the soft fur between the baby's ears while Marianne looked on like a proud mother. The fawn relaxed in her arms as Marianne murmured reassurances.

"Such a beauty," I said, thinking: the fawn, Marianne, the whole tableau. "And now what?"

"We should feed her; I'm sure she's hungry. Maybe she smelled the fruit we were eating," said Marianne.

"Knowing you, I suppose you've got some deer's milk in your teats just for emergencies, hmm?" said Corax, shedding wonder for sarcasm. Could he sense my admiration for Marianne and be jealous? People always told me I couldn't hide my feelings.

"I can do better," she said, handing me the fawn. It accepted the transfer without struggle, and I cradled it as I had done with many lambs in the green pastures of home. I felt the beat of its heart against my chest and a glow spread through my body. A brief vision of having my own child softened me to the bones.

Marianne knelt on the ground and extended her arms, digging her fingers into the dirt and clawing the surface as she raked her hands together. Where they met, a small geyser of white liquid burst from the earth, splashing her face and hands. She looked at me with a grin and licked her lips.

"What the hell?" I said.

"Looks like maenad shit to me," said Corax.

"Indeed," Marianne agreed. "I learned this last night. Milk of the earth." She emptied a small water pouch and filled it with the white liquid before the gush ran dry. Retrieving a swatch of leather from her pack, she shaped it into a tapered bag and poured it full of the milk, then tied off the top. She used her knife to prick a few holes in the tip and I saw that she'd crafted a serviceable udder.

"Clever," I said.

She smiled and stood to offer the bladder to the fawn, who sniffed it, licked it, then latched on with a grunt.

"And you learned this last night?" I asked. "I'd love to hear how that happened."

Marianne nodded. "I'll tell you. They have a pact of secrecy, especially regarding men, but I don't think that applies to you two, do you?"

"No, of course not. We're not normal," observed Corax.

She laughed. "You certainly aren't. One of the things I love about you both."

I blushed and sat next to Corax while still cuddling the fawn. Marianne continued to nurse it while she told her story. "We hiked a long way up the mountain, meeting other women as we climbed until we formed a group of ten. High on the peak, we came to a meadow tucked into a small basin—so idyllic! Evidently, this was a regular meeting place because there was a well-used firepit and a stack of firewood. One of the women had brought several large hunting nets. We divided into twos, one net for each dyad, and roamed across the mountain, looking for baby animals. We used the nets to capture them, taking care to avoid harming the creatures. Manto and I got lucky and netted three wolf pups in one throw of the net. By the time we returned to the camp, the others were already there. The round-up secured two fawns, a wild goat kid, and a hedgehog, as well as our pups. It was the strangest hunt I've been on. You'd think that the mother animals would have fought us tooth and nail, or that the babies would have done their best to flee. But the beasts were compliant, and our captures were easy. It was like a dream.

"I asked Manto what would happen to these animals, but her replies were vague. I feared that we would enact the bloody rites attributed to maenads: tearing the hapless creatures limb from limb and eating them raw. I had my doubts about whether I was willing to do that, despite my fondness for Manto. The little animals were adorable, especially the wolf pups. I had no heart to slaughter them; I wanted to be one. However, that was never on the agenda. I was eventually informed that such rumors were part of a smear campaign waged against the followers of Dionysos for ages. Several of the women were angry about these lies and grew quite animated in their arguments. True enough, the animals were needed for a rite, but the proceedings were far from sanguine.

"Two of the women had recently given birth and were in full milk. We brought the animals to them one by one, and they suckled them from their breasts. If I thought the hunt was strange, this seemed even more so. The infants took the milk with gusto, and the women gave it gladly. However, it could hardly have been about the nourishment, because after a few minutes of nursing, the women would detach the animal and send it scampering off. When the first one ran to the rocks at the edge of the meadow, I saw that the mother stood silently, watching us. As each baby or brood reunited with its parent, they slipped back into the wild. After the last one left, we formed a circle, held hands, and danced around, first in one direction, then the other, all the while chanting a song I couldn't understand. Then we fell to the ground and scratched in the dirt, causing geysers of the earth's milk to fill our mouths. I imitated the others, scratching, and guzzling; there was no technique that I could see. It just… happened. Though I'm sure there was more to it than that."

"Curious, but with its own tender logic," I acknowledged.

"Yes, I thought so, too," she replied.

"According to the old literature, the flesh-rending was reserved for the enemies of Dionysos or those who opposed the maenads," Corax stated. "King Pentheus comes to mind when he tried to chase the god out of his city. Torn to shreds by his own mother, that's what he got. Or so it was enacted on the stage."

"I can't imagine any of the women from last night tearing anything asunder," said Marianne. "They were overflowing with love and life; hardly the merchants of death I've encountered. And I've met enough to know them when I see them."

"I don't doubt that," I said.

"All true," admitted Corax, who reached over to pat the fawn, "but when consciousness is altered, be it by wine or other spirits, then the demons can take over and all bets are off."

"Demons?" I asked. "Surely, you're not propounding demons now, are you?"

"You know what I mean," he said. "That dark side of the personality that lurks in all of us. Nothing supernatural is required."

"Yes," I sighed. "I know exactly what you mean. And I'm glad to hear you acknowledge that you have demons along with the rest of us."

Corax frowned and stared at Marianne. "So that's it? No feverish orgies? You looked like you'd been thrashing all night when you came in this morning."

"No, I'm afraid not. Of course, if we had *thrashed* all night, why would I tell you? Some of the women had musical instruments, mostly those hand drums as we saw in the parade, and someone brought a flute. We sang and danced like crazy women, all over the meadow, for hours and hours, it seemed. I don't think I've ever danced so much. We danced until dark and lit a fire. Then we danced around the fire until it burned out.

After that, we lay on the ground in a circle, like the spokes of a wheel, with our heads in the center. We watched the stars grow brighter and brighter. There were times when I thought I was going to fall off the face of the earth into the infinity of space. And we talked until dawn. That was it."

"What did you talk about? If you don't mind me asking," I said.

"Lots of stuff. Woman talk. You wouldn't be interested, or I won't tell you—take your pick. However, there was one thing of relevance. The subject of Apollo came up and I was surprised at the venom and hostility directed at that god. He's notorious for preaching that women are inferior to men. At one time he even claimed that a mother is not a parent to the child, because she plays no role in its conception—she is but an empty vessel mounted and planted with the male seed, from whence springs all life."

"He did say that," interrupted Corax. "According to the theatrical version, anyway."

"Really?" I said. "Who writes these scripts, anyway?"

"The usual: cranks, crackpots, anyone with an ax to grind. There's nothing rational about any part of it. I admit that it makes for lively theater, though."

"These plays sound interesting," said Marianne. "Maybe we'll get to see one at some point. Anyway, Manto said that women follow Dionysos because woman-hating is not part of that scene. I can relate." She stopped feeding the fawn and stood. "We should probably get going."

"What do we do with our baby?" I asked.

"Her mother can't be far, but I don't want to just leave her here. Let's try something." She scraped the ground again and started another jet of milk, refilled the makeshift udder, and tied it to her waist so it dangled against her hip. She signaled for me to put the fawn on the ground next to her. It immediately went for the pouch and resumed nursing at Marianne's side. Marianne took two steps and the fawn let go, then walked after her and again latched on to the bag of milk. Marianne shouldered her pack and continued down the trail with the fawn trotting behind. After ten steps, Marianne stopped, and the fawn sucked a little more milk. Corax and I laughed at this sight. Without looking back, Marianne waved her hand at us and sashayed off, swinging her hips as the fawn kept pace.

We hadn't gone far when the fawn stopped and stared up the slope. We followed her gaze and saw a doe peering from behind a large oak. As if sprung from a catapult, the fawn leaped from the trail and galloped through the weeds to rejoin its mother.

Corax snickered. "It's almost enough to make you want a child of your own, eh, Marianne?"

"Not really. I have you two, which is quite enough."

[13]

We hiked on through the heat of the afternoon, taking a lunch break under an oak where we sated our hunger with the bounty from Manto's kitchen. Some of the paths and trails we used for our route were rarely traveled by humans, but there were signs of abundant goat traffic everywhere. Occasionally, we passed a peasant hut and waved if anyone was present, but we never stopped to talk. Marianne drove us hard, stalking ahead and daring us to keep up with her long legs. I brought up the end, herding Corax in front of me, offering encouragement or sarcasm, depending on my mood. He welcomed neither.

At dusk, we made camp off the trail, hidden behind boulders. In town, we'd heard rumors of bandits in every nook and cranny of the island, though we'd seen no evidence of them. Still, it was wise to allow for the possibility. We gathered a few sticks for a fire but were too tired to stoke it beyond a brief meal. Curled together between blankets, we quickly fell asleep.

After two days of uneventful marching, we climbed through juniper scrub to attain an exposed ridge. Marble outcrops pushed through the thin soil, gleaming in the sun where they weren't colonized by crusts of black lichen. Amidst the stonescape, every crevice and small patch of soil vibrated with blooms of red anemone and white crocus. Lifting my eyes, I spied a griffon vulture, wing tips spread like fingers, soaring and scanning the hillside below. At the bottom of the slope, my eyes fixed on our destination: a village of white-washed cubes overlooking a sandy cove. We had arrived at the northern shore of the Island of Marble. The view provided a chance to meditate on the vastness of water, spanning the world from the cove to the horizon. The hazy mound of our objective, Apollo's Temple Island, could be seen many leagues away. Beyond that, sea and sky merged into a seamless hue. Despite its beauty, we didn't linger over this spectacle, driven on by the prospect of a hot meal and a bed at the inn.

Striding along the path leading to the village, still an hour's walk away, I passed a junction with a spur trail. Glancing down the track not taken, always a habit of mine, a sheen of white stone caught my eye.

"Wait!" I called. "What's that?"

Corax and Marianne looked at each other, then slowly returned to see where I pointed.

"Looks like a quarry," Corax said. "They've mined the marble on this island for over a thousand years. In the City, you walked up and down a lot of stairs cut from this rock."

"Do you mind if we take a peek? Quarries fascinate me. I built some walls in the Western Isles, but we used the rough, natural limestone, which was shaped fair enough to stack on a wall—as long as you didn't mind restacking the tumble downs every few years or so. Hardly suitable for elegant temples and such. Marble is something else, though. Like building with gemstones."

"We're almost to the village," objected Marianne.

Corax came to my defense, which surprised and pleased me. "Oh, let the boy have his peek. I wouldn't mind a rest, anyway."

Outvoted, Marianne nodded, and we strolled down the trail to the quarry. I expected to see an industrial site with the remnants of old machinery and tools necessary for extracting massive blocks but there was none of that. The white gleam that caught my eye was the cut face of a mined outcrop, but little evidence remained of what was taken and how it was moved. Instead, weeds and shrubs occupied the abandoned site, while swift lizards patrolled the broken debris. I imagined that when the quarry was in operation, the workers must have lowered blocks down skids or rails to the sea where barges could take the heavy cargo to the mainland. I fell into the usual reverie that occupies my mind at ancient sites, reflecting on the deeds of our forebears.

"Hey Diarmuid, come look at this!" The excitement in Corax's voice yanked me out of my reverie.

I found him staring into a small hollow where lay a man of stone, slightly larger than life. The carving lacked detail and was covered with lichens, but the overall shape was clear, forming a slender man of athletic proportions. Vigor imbued the modeling, one knee cocked, as if he prepared to roll up to standing and chastise us for leaving him by himself for such a long time. Skin details and facial features had yet to be carved, but even in its unfinished condition, or because of it, the sculpture conveyed an expression of universal humanity. However, if he had something to say, he never got the chance to evolve any further from his matrix; one leg was broken in two and his makers had abandoned him.

"Behold an unborn *kouros*, unfavored of the gods, and left to its fate," said Corax.

"*Kouros*?" I asked.

"Yes, they were all the rage a thousand years ago: adornments for the wealthy, especially in the temples of Apollo. We must have seen some at the Oracle's sanctuary, though I don't remember that experience too well."

"Ah, yes. I didn't look at them closely."

"Do they have a meaning?" inquired Marianne.

"Sure, everything has a meaning. Depends on which meaning you want. For the most part, the *kouroi* depicted the beauty of young men, a popular topic for many of us. The devotees of Apollo were right at the front of that queue, putting up *kouros* statues everywhere. Looks like this one broke when they tried to move it. Fragile, in its way—stone. You can sit on it for a thousand years and it won't give, but drop it, even a few feet, and it shatters."

"So, Apollo is fond of boys?" asked Marianne.

"Yes," replied Corax. "But then he's a bit of a boy himself. Depictions show him as a buff, full-grown man, but clean-shaven and pretty. And, as the legendary Singer of Tales labeled him, 'haughty.' Like the world needs another vain princess. Yet he's not one-dimensional. He's also the god of healers, a crack-shot archer, and a wizard with the lyre. He chased women, too. Omnisexual, I guess you'd say. There's an old story that he pursued Daphne the nymph until she transformed into a laurel tree to escape his rapacious obsession. Of course, he's hardly the only one with contradictions. Whatever else can be said about them, the gods of my people exhibit an undeniable diversity of appetites."

"Nothing wrong with that," observed Marianne.

"True," replied Corax. "Might be more to our credit as a culture if the indiscriminate lust didn't lead to so much rape and incest, though."

"That's not different from anywhere I've been," said Marianne.

"Also true. Oddly enough, the only male god that never raped anyone was Dionysos. Murder seems to be more his racket if you believe the myths," added Corax.

I scrambled up a ledge of exposed rock to get a better view down the slope, hoping to discover remains of the old quarrying system. That's when I saw the giant.

"You gotta see this!" I yelled.

Swayed by my excitement, they trotted over, and we looked at a deep trough cut into the bedrock. Laying in the hollow was a *kouros* of stunning size—at least a dozen yards from head to toe. Unlike the one with the broken leg, its proportions were stout and chunky, resembling the bole of a large tree.

"See the beard?" said Corax, pointing. It was hard to miss: a prominent goatee. "Means this isn't a *kouros* at all, but some other kind of statue. Dionysos, I bet—he's usually shown with a long beard. Perhaps a monument destined for one of his temples or even to advertise his theater in the City. This carving has been here for a long time, judging from the lichen. I wonder why they left it? Maybe ran out of money; it would have cost a fortune to move this monster down the mountain, ship it over the sea, and complete the details before installation."

"Ran out of money?" I asked.

"Oh yes, a common situation. People assume the partial structures around here are the result of decay and ruin, but half the time they never got finished in the first place. Wealth has a way of going to the head—that's when you want your grandiose monuments—temples, statues, whatever. Later, when you run out of money, it turns out that nobody else cares quite as much about your pet projects."

"It's kind of sad," said Marianne. "I think the poor thing is frustrated to have to lay there like a frozen brute. It would have been something to see, you know, a true wonder, refined and polished to a splendor."

"The god that didn't get born. I, for one, wouldn't miss him," said Corax. He jumped into the gully and climbed up on the forehead of the statue where he struck a pose as if ready to make a proclamation. Instead, he lifted his hem and loosed a yellow arc of urine that splashed over the nose and lips of the statue.

Marianne frowned and I snickered at this exhibit of wanton immaturity. It seemed funny to me—the kind of high-spirited prank for which I could never muster the courage. The laughter, however, choked in my throat when the marble giant opened one eye, then the other.

"Corax!" Marianne shouted, pointing at the eyes, but Corax had already seen them. I don't know what he thought, but I can imagine the disbelief, then the terror. He staggered backward, fell off the head, and scrambled out of the trough with more agility than I'd thought possible.

As Corax retreated, the giant opened its lips and smacked them together so hard that chips of rock went flying from the impact of stone on stone. It opened its mouth again and with a voice of volcanic proportions, said "THAT'S NOT RIGHT. REALLY NOT RIGHT."

"Good god," I said, edging away.

"Something's not right, I'll agree with that," commented Marianne, also in motion.

"NO PROBLEM. WE MAKE IT RIGHT!" The statue slowly lifted its shoulders, wrenching its frame upward with a terrible grinding noise. When it sat up, it raised a fist and smashed the ground, pulverizing rock into dust and an explosion of shards. "SOMEBODY'S GOTTA PAY!"

I had no doubt who was intended to pay, and his fate would likely include us. As the giant moved, the friction of rock against rock created a deafening racket and atomized sulfuric dust. It was like being in the belly of an earthquake—I reeled with nausea and it was all I could do to fight down the urge to retch. Corax backpedaled, mesmerized by the apparition while trying to maximize his distance from it. I thought that if we scattered in different directions, the giant might be too confused to decide who to follow. Its grammar suggested that it wasn't very bright. The panic left me frozen, though, and I did nothing. While I vibrated with indecision, Marianne threw off her pack and pulled out a hunting net. Where it came from, I had no idea. Then I remembered the maenads and their live capture of animals.

"Corax!" She yelled. "Stop running! Just keep it distracted. Taunt it!" She turned to me and crammed into my hands one end of the net. "Stay calm. Maybe we can bring it down."

I was surprised that Corax stopped and obeyed Marianne. Lack of a plan does that to you. He began to jump up and down in place, screaming and shrieking. "Nah nah, blockhead! Did not like his golden shower! Nahhh!"

The giant finally attained a standing position, shedding bits and pieces of itself as it worked loose the joints, flexing, and flailing its limbs. When it stomped the ground, the earth shook, and I had to fight to stay on my feet. "CRUUUSH!" it yelled with the sound of rolling thunder.

The giant laboriously turned around and saw Corax, leaping and yelling like a maniac. For some reason, it never looked down where it would have seen Marianne and me at its ankles. Stiff neck, perhaps. "CRUSH!" it reiterated and took a step. Corax's voice faltered, but he continued with the antics, and the giant took another earth-punishing step. Marianne signaled for me to stand firm while she darted in front of the giant's legs. When the goliath paused, sensing movement below, she ran around behind it with the remainder of the net, grabbing my end and quickly tying them together. Corax perceived the plan and reignited his vocal cords, which caused the giant to look at him and growl, a sound like the ocean dragging rocks in the surf.

The giant lunged forward but the net caught it around the ankles, abruptly halting the step. The slender fibers stretched, and I thought they would surely break, but the maenads who crafted the net did their work well. It held long enough to delay the legs of the giant from keeping pace with the forward movement of its torso. With the slow pull of inevitable gravity, the stone monster tilted and pitched to the ground. It hit exposed bedrock like a meteor blast, churning up fragments and dust as if Zeus himself had struck. The statue cracked into pieces, but the head broke off at the neck and tumbled along the ground to stop at the feet of Corax, pelting him with a shower of dirt and shards. I heard one last word from the giant's mouth, faintly: "Crush."

As the dust settled, I grabbed Marianne in a hug and swung her around, kissing her cheeks until she put a hand on my chest and pushed away. Corax yelled "Hooray!" and fell to the ground in a slump. We ran to him, and I saw that blood streamed from the top of his skull. Alarmed, I wiped the wound with my robe, noticing a shallow incision, probably caused by a sharp fragment of rock. He moaned in mortal agony.

"Now, now," said Marianne. "It's a surface cut, is all. I'd say if that was the god's bedrock best shot, you'll live to blaspheme again." I cleaned the cut with drinking water and a fresh cloth from my pack. Marianne offered one of Manto's herbal salves, and as I applied it with a fingertip, Corax relaxed.

"What the hell just happened?" I asked the obvious question. "Please don't tell me that your piss carries the principle of life."

"I was wondering about that, myself," said Marianne.

"How should I know?" Corax, now sitting up, applied himself to brushing dirt from his clothes. "We could just pretend it never happened; then we wouldn't have to explain it."

"This is the philosopher who leaves no stone unturned, pardon the pun, in search of the meaning of existence?" I teased.

"What can I say? Rocks, in my experience, don't get offended that easily. Let alone move around, talk, or threaten revenge. I'm baffled. But thank you, Marianne, for coming to the rescue. Once again, we are in your debt."

"You're welcome," she replied. "I don't want to be an alarmist, but I can think of one force that could have animated that statue."

"Yes," I said. "The god. Dionysos. Which means he might be watching us."

She nodded. Corax opened his mouth and I waited for the caustic remark, but he closed it again without a word. What were we up against, really? I don't think any of us knew. And speculation promised more questions, but no answers.

[14]

The fishing village provided a single, weather-beaten inn, with the ominous name of The Trojan Horse. We trooped in, drawing stares from the scattered patrons, locals I guessed from their worn and patched clothes and reek of the sea. I was certain that most of these people had spent the day fixed at their stations in the inn because I had observed the same scene in every public house in every fishing village I'd entered, and I'd seen more than a few. Fishermen fished or repaired their gear and when they weren't doing that, they complained about the vocation and washed down the words with whatever they could afford to drink. It was a hard life. For me, it would have been either that or the monastery and I never regretted my choice.

The innkeeper introduced himself as Diomedes and appeared pleased to have paying customers. He assigned us his "finest" rooms for the night. After depositing our baggage in the rooms—which were at least clean—we headed to the beach for a swim, washing off the rock dust and sweat. Refreshed, we returned to the inn and ordered generous helpings of a savory pie. Diomedes identified the contents as minced lamb, eggplant, potatoes, and secret spices, with olive oil sluiced through every cranny. My thoughts again flew back to the homeland at the first bite—it conveyed a familiar load of calories and grease— but never at home had I tasted anything so complex. There, it had been a matter of whether you wanted your mush salty or sweet; this was a symphony of flavor and texture. With groans of satisfaction, we applied ourselves to the pie. By the end of the meal, I felt as if I'd eaten a whale. I thumped the solid mass of my belly and ordered a pot of mountain tea to aid digestion.

"We're looking for someone named Mother Nyx; you wouldn't happen to know her whereabouts, would you?" I asked as Diomedes delivered the tea. The dining room had filled during our meal and at the sound of the name, the nearby customers stopped talking and many faces turned our way. I looked around in confusion, worried that I had said something out of place. Both Marianne and Corax had expressions of pretend neutrality.

"Now, what in God's name would you want with her?" replied the innkeeper.

"We heard that she lived nearby. Curiosity, that's all, nothing particular." My dissembling sounded lame even to myself.

"Hmm," Diomedes said as his eyes burrowed into mine. "Regardless, I don't recommend it. Unpredictable, that one is. You'd do well to stay away."

"And if we don't do well…?" interjected Corax.

The innkeeper turned to Corax and inspected his face. Corax tried to feign innocence, though the impression was marred, in my opinion, by the gouged flesh on top of his bald skull. "Your funeral," answered Diomedes. "But if you're in a hurry to get to Hades, there are caves in the cliffs, high above the shore west of town. She's got a thing for caves." He picked up our dinner dishes and left. By that time, people had resumed their meals and conversations.

"Sounds like we know where to start. However, this hero is up past her bedtime. See you in the morning." Marianne got up, kissed each of us on the cheek, and went to her room.

I saw that Corax couldn't keep his eyes off the bottles of wine and liquor arrayed on a shelf behind the bar counter. I suddenly felt tired.

"Let's call it a day as well," I suggested.

"You go ahead, I'm not quite ready."

"Yes," I insisted. "You are. You're coming with me." Remembering what Tiresias told me about not trying to control things as much, I switched tactics. "Look, I'm sorry. You can do what you want. I'm tired of trying to hold you accountable. But you know and I know that if I leave you here, you'll be insufferably drunk within the hour. Since we're doing this whole crazy mission for you, risking our lives and whatnot, I think the least you could do would be to show some respect. You know, we both love you. I love you."

Corax looked at me, then dropped his gaze. He nodded and stood, took my hand, and led me to our room.

In the morning, I asked Diomedes if he knew a boat and crew that could take us across the channel to Temple Island. He looked skeptical but said he would ask around. I thanked him and complimented the inn on its lodgings and food, doing my best to make a favorable impression, and thus encourage his inquiries on our behalf. I also purchased bread and cheese for the day's outing to find Mother Nyx. The sun was barely over the ridge above the cove when the three of us set off westward along the shore. At first, it was easy walking on the beach, but that soon ended, forcing us to scramble up onto rocky scarps and natural terraces. The sea churned below; the higher we climbed, the more intimidating its appearance. It surged against the rocks, whitecaps, and swells in procession, a liquid muscle flexing against the limits of the coast.

Ascending, we traversed around a headland and lost sight of the village. Along the uninhabited coastline ahead of us, the conjunction of sea and stone expressed only wildness. Marianne led us through ledges of granite accented with rock rose, gesturing at us to keep up. She seemed entirely in her element and moved over the terrain with uninterrupted grace. Finally, she stopped and pointed.

"A path, of sorts," she said.

Faint, but there it was. The path traversed the slope, well above the sea. I assumed that it started in the village, but we had missed where it connected and only now came across it from below. We turned west along the trail and I noticed that even though it wasn't much used, it had a look of artifice to it; stones had been set in specific positions to provide a tread where otherwise there would be none. It continued uphill, into an area of cliffs and buttresses, the gray granite faces streaked with the black and purple mineral stains of time.

Further on, the path turned into stairs of flat rocks and switchbacks to negotiate the steepening terrain. At one corner, I could look a hundred yards straight down into the sea as it pounded the rocks below. I noticed that Corax hugged the inside of the corner and refused to look at all. Understandable—one glance was enough.

Above us, cliffs dominated the slope, interrupted by grassy ledges and stout, overhanging trees. I spotted a goat feeding on wild greenery atop a rock pillar. How it got there I couldn't tell, but that was often my experience with goats. Surprising creatures—I admired their agile curiosity.

We turned a switchback, climbed a few more steps, and emerged on a broad terrace. Half a dozen goats stared at us from where they rested under an olive tree. Beyond that, I saw the high arch of a cave entrance. The opening had been walled off with stone, neatly laid around a door and several windows, fashioning the cave into a home. In front of the entry, a young woman sat on a stool shucking mussels. She stopped to watch us as we approached. I studied her with interest: she had an enormous head of hair so frizzy that it framed her head with a spherical shadow as dark as her onyx-colored skin. Glistening and wet, her brown robe shimmered, gesturing as if it had a life of its own. As I looked closer, it seemed to be made from strands of kelp.

"Guests! It's been ages! Welcome!" She angled her head and called into the open door of the cave. "Oizys! Refreshments for three!"

Marianne stopped in front of the woman and promptly fell to one knee, bowing her head. Figuring it wouldn't hurt, I followed her lead, pulling the reluctant Corax down next to me.

"We seek Mother Nyx. Do you know her?" asked Marianne.

The woman clapped her hands, pleased with the question or the kneeling, I couldn't tell. "Oizys!" She repeated. "We have guests! Hurry, dear! One of them bears the mark of the tentacular god!" She stroked Marianne's tattooed arm and lifted her head to smile at us with confident beneficence. "That girl… She usually needs a poke in the butt. She's depression, you know."

It seemed an odd confession to strangers and the three of us exchanged looks. "I'm sorry to hear that she's depressed," I ventured.

"No, no, you misunderstand," replied the woman. "She doesn't have depression, she *is* depression. She embodies it." The woman nodded as if we understood what she meant.

Another young woman—thin and pale with stringy brown hair—emerged from the cave carrying a heaping platter of food, which she placed on the ground in front of us. This pallid creature was in truth a classic personification of depression, from the dark circles under her eyes to the reluctant movements of her limbs. As soon as she deposited the platter, she returned to the cave and brought out an amphora and four cups. All the while, the black woman smiled at us in a prolonged frozen moment as if waiting for Oizys to accomplish her task before resuming the flow of life.

After setting down the drinks, Oizys glided back into the cave and did not return. Bobbing her globe of hair in apparent satisfaction, our hostess gestured for us to sit on the ground. "Eat, eat! And drink," she urged. "We rarely have guests and I dearly love company. What was your question again?"

"We're looking for Mother Nyx," Corax said. "Assuming she's real. We've taken some questionable advice to get here."

Unperturbed, the woman smiled at Corax and waved at the beverage flask. "You really must have a drink of this. It's our brew, made from honey we get in trade with the local bees."

"Uhh…," I tried to intervene when I heard the word *brew*, but Corax had already lunged for the flask, pouring a cup and downing it as if his life depended on it. He smacked his lips and refilled his cup, shaking off the hand I put on his arm.

"Wait," said Marianne, also pouring a cup for herself. "You said you traded with the local bees. You mean, directly?"

"Certainly, dear. Why go through middlemen? The bees are so much nicer to deal with." Her broad smile engulfed me, providing its own radiance. "And you, don't worry so much," she said, pointing at me. "Our mead is entirely therapeutic."

I sagged in acquiescence. Resistance seemed futile. "And regarding Mother Nyx?" I asked.

"Oh, that," she replied. "That would be me."

I should have been prepared for the answer, but I wasn't. I looked closely at the woman, who had the skin of an adolescent. She couldn't have mothered anything, I thought.

Corax beamed in the blissful rush of the mead. "Glad to meet you. This is an excellent concoction and I'm absolutely in your debt for the measure of it. But aside from that, let me get this straight: if you're Nyx, as you say, then according to the stories that makes you the first-born daughter of Chaos?"

"Oh yes, that was my progenitor."

"Progenitor? You mean father? Mother? None of the above?"

"Absurd question. Not relevant to the matter, not then, not now."

"I don't want to seem rude," Corax continued, "but I come from a skeptical school. Can you show some token that demonstrates this primeval affiliation? If not, no problem, perhaps we could purchase a jug of this elixir and we'll be on our way."

I didn't like where he was going with the conversation, but Mother Nyx, if that's who it was, didn't seem offended; instead, she smiled and giggled. I looked at Marianne, who rolled her eyes. As with Tiresias and pretty much everyone else, we never seemed to get in front of Corax's impetuous refusal to accept the world as a possibility outside of his relentless logic.

Mother Nyx extended her left hand, palm up. As she moved, the strands of kelp undulated, and I wondered if the costume was something she wore or if it was an extension of her body. We looked down at her palm, paler than the dark skin of her arms. The hand, ordinary at first, grew dimmer under our gaze until it disappeared altogether. Except that it hadn't disappeared; it had become transparent, like glass. I expected to see the ground through this hand-shaped window, but what I saw seemed to offer a view into another realm altogether, something akin to the visions of the *kykeon*. Within the hand, indigo forms swirled in a constant movement against a gray backdrop, forming cloud-like abstractions without a pattern. Unlike the ordered geometry of the *kykeon* hallucinations, these images conveyed the terrible implication of infinity—an infinity without structure, harmony, or coherence. Surely, we beheld chaos.

I tore my eyes away from the vortex and saw that Corax and Marianne were entranced. Captured, might be a better term. I looked at the face of Mother Nyx, who smiled and slowly closed her hand.

"I'm convinced," I said and glanced at Corax for his reaction. Subdued, he had none.

"It is an honor to meet you," acknowledged Marianne. "But why do they call you *Mother*? You look so young."

"Oh, that's far too long a tale, I'm afraid. We'd be here a fortnight to do it justice, and I bet you have more pressing engagements. Let's just say that Oizys is my child, along with over two thousand others, many of whom you may have met at one time or another. As far as the youthful appearance," she paused to fluff her ball of hair, "I keep my beauty secrets to myself. Anyway, I do know a few things about being a mother—enough to deserve the title, wouldn't you say?"

How could anyone respond to a claim of two thousand children? It defied comprehension. I grasped at a detail. "We've met them?"

She grinned another vast smile that tossed a bright shroud over us. "Certainly—most people have! For example, there are the thousand Oneiroi, those precious boys who deliver dreams each night—nobody gets by them. Not to mention my sons, Sleep, Doom, Death, and Blame—surely, you've heard of them—along with my daughters, the Keres, that attend the deaths of the sick and murdered. And let's not forget the three Fates, ditto Deceit, Nemesis, etc., etc. You know them all, do you not?"

"Wait a minute," Corax interrupted. "These so-called children of yours are what—archetypes? An embodiment of Essential Form, *eidos*? Yet you refer to them as if they are flesh and blood. Sure, I see how they could be real children with symbolic names, but they can't be the Thing Itself as an *eidos* and simultaneously a manifested object. The essence isn't a thing, not in the material sense."

Mother Nyx laughed and clapped her hands together as if indulging a child, which perhaps she was, I thought. "You are a clever thing! Oizys! Come here, please!"

A few minutes later, Oizys plodded out of the cave, head down, moving as if the gravity were twice normal. Nyx held out her hand and Oizys stood next to her mother—assuming, of course, Nyx's story was true, and she was the mother of this grown woman. Nyx used her foot to scrape aside the pile of mussel shells and motioned for Oizys to move the food platter. With sloth-like deliberation, she put the platter to the side and knelt facing us, staring at the ground. Her submissiveness made me anxious, and I worried that something awkward was going to happen.

"Place a hand on her skin and tell me what you feel," instructed Nyx.

I took one of her limp hands while Marianne took the other. Corax, in the middle and perhaps emboldened by the honey wine, leaned forward and placed his palm on her chest. I thought she felt solid enough, though her skin was cool and slightly clammy. Oizys lifted her chin and looked at us with the palest blue eyes I had ever seen, eyes like crystal celestite. Sadness poured from those eyes as if they were bottomless reservoirs of inertia. I stared into her terrible beauty until I couldn't stand anymore and dropped my gaze to the ground, feeling the tears dripping down my nose and cheeks. I glanced at the other two and they were in the same condition, slumped and awash in grief.

I looked up again to see Nyx stroking her daughter's hair, who shrugged off the gesture, rose, and returned to the cave. I was willing to concede the point. Oizys had a real, material presence, but she also embodied depression, and not just in a metaphorical way. If anyone could *be* depression, they would look like this, I was convinced. Maybe this kind of duty was required of the gods—that they serve a function for the multitudes as the price of their existence. Suddenly, it didn't seem so bad to be mortal. At least you could be a person, free of the burden of embodying universal principles.

Corax, of course, saw it differently. He wiped away his tears, and despite the intensity of my glare, launched into a debate. "Very moving. I know something of this condition, myself. I feel sorry for her, I really do. But my condition is internal, belongs to me and no one else. Though Oizys may represent *a* depression, she can't be *the* depression—the agent of everyone's despair. It simply defies the laws of physics."

"Ah yes, the laws of physics. By the way, who decreed those laws?" Nyx asked the question but didn't wait for an answer. Her body turned glossy black and lost all surface definition. She retained her basic shape, but no details or features could be distinguished within the opaque sheen of obsidian color. She stood and spun around and then there were three, identical at first, then shifting into elastic forms moving at different speeds, without rhythm or synchronization, three expressions of a presence beyond understanding. The three stretched into columns, flowed into spheres, or pulsated in globules, constantly shifting beyond any pattern or prediction I could discern.

"Alright, alright! I get it. Stop, please!" begged Corax. I didn't blame him. The sight was awesome but profoundly disturbing. We take so much for granted about how things behave in the world, I thought, that when confronted with something far outside those expectations, we can hardly tolerate it.

Nyx merged back into one body and lost the sheen, resuming her kelp robe, her smile, and her position on the stool. "Oh, how I love to show off! But you didn't come here for the spectacle, did you? Or even to debate metaphysics, I bet. Let's talk about your mission and how old Mother Nyx can help you."

"I've seen a lot of things, Mother Nyx, but I've never seen anyone like you," said Marianne. "I'm sure you can help us! We come from the seer Tiresias and his daughter Manto. They encouraged us to find you. We need advice, especially from someone with your... ah... depth of experience with divinities. See, Corax has been cursed by a god: Dionysos."

"Oh my," said Nyx.

"Yes, we do need help," I said. Nyx was strange, but I liked her, and I thought we should trust her. We didn't have much choice, anyway, if we wanted real guidance. "Here's our problem: Corax can be a bit argumentative, as I'm sure you've noticed, and over in the City he managed to go public with loud skepticism where Dionysos was bound to hear it: at the theatrical festival in his honor. Barely an hour passed before Dionysos found us and cursed my friend face-to-face. I was there and saw it all. When we realized how bad it was, we left the City and consulted the Great Oracle. We worked through the riddle and followed its recommendations to come to the Island of Marble and speak with Tiresias. It took a while to find him, and when we did, he offered some encouragement about lifting the curse—but it was daunting. Our best chance, he thought, would be to visit Temple Island and, believe it or not, steal Apollo's lyre, which we could offer to Dionysos as a sort of apology."

"I love it!" squealed Nyx, clapping her hands like a little girl. "I love it, I love it!"

"You do? So, can you help us?" I asked.

"I should think so," she answered. "We don't get along, me and Apollo, not at all. He's one of those new-fangled upstart gods, strutting around like a peacock—a self-righteous prick if you ask me. Those Olympians are insufferable. They can't stop meddling, can't keep their hands off, and can't stay out of trouble. They act like they own the world. But they don't, oh no. My children dog them around like they dog you mortals—no way they get a pass for being holier than thou. Always happy to take one down a notch. Especially Apollo—he's the worst of the lot."

Encouraged by her response, I asked a question that had been gnawing at me. "Do you think Tiresias' plan will work—offering the lyre to Dionysos? Will that lift the curse?"

Nyx looked at us with a wry smile. "That's a complicated question. Can you explain to me what you think the curse is?"

I turned to Corax, who shrugged. "Sure. Right after the god pronounced his curse, Corax fell into a depression and started drinking wine like it was water. He can't, or won't control it, so I'd say he's cursed with addiction."

"And Corax, do you agree with this interpretation?"

Corax shrugged without speaking.

Nyx shucked a mussel and popped it in her mouth, swallowing it whole. "We'll get back to the curse in a bit. First, let's talk more about Dionysos. You know, he's not one of *them*."

"You mean he's not an Olympian?" asked Corax. "That goes against the tales I've heard."

"You can't believe everything you hear, my dear. He's one of us—an elder god. I'm not sure where he came from originally—some say the Distant South. He travels so much it's hard to nail him down. He's not one of my offspring—not that I wouldn't be proud to claim him. But he's been around a long time, certainly long before the Olympians. Kind of a trickster. No question but he's got interesting abilities. The Olympians, drunk on power, tried to recruit him into their gang, thinking he would make a nice asset. Dionysos played along, like he always does, because he's mad for theatrics, but he's not keen on playing second fiddle, especially to younger gods. Ignore the fables you hear about Zeus being his father; I knew him before that narcissistic windbag even came on the scene. Not sure what Dionysos would want with the lyre, but since Apollo loves it so much, I imagine he'd be tickled to get his hands on it, if only to spite Mr. Sunshine. Or maybe he just wants it as a prop for a new play."

"New play?" I asked.

"He's always writing plays, trying out ideas, seeking new themes, new plots. As I said, he's crazy for theater. Sometimes I think he's more interested in being an author and actor than a god. Offending him at the festival would have seriously hurt his feelings. Not so good for you! He doesn't hold a grudge, though. Usually." Nyx twirled a finger in her hair, lost in thought.

Corax hurriedly quaffed another cup of mead. His expression mixed anger, sadness, and vulnerability, but anger won out. He stared at me with defiance. "I'm only drinking this to ward off the inevitable headache. All this talk of gods and chaos and tricksters and prophets... ordinarily, I'd call bullshit on the whole mess and go back to my scrolls where things either add up or not." Suddenly, his shoulders slumped, and I could tell that the anger rushed out of him, leaving a deflated man. "I tell you, if you want to talk about depression, this talk makes me depressed. Where's the order in the madness? I've spent my whole life delving for the structure of reality. I know I haven't found it, but I thought I was getting pretty close, you know? Do you understand what I'm saying?"

I picked up Corax's free hand and brought it to my lips. As I kissed his knuckles one by one, he looked at me with astonishment. I saw that underneath all the bluster, the man I knew huddled within, wanting to be loved.

"Aww…" admired Nyx, and Corax blushed.

"Yes, Corax, my love, I understand. I've wanted that structure, too, and I've followed you and studied with you and read many of the same texts. A lot of it makes sense, at least when you're reading it. But now… maybe we're reaching the limits of that kind of knowledge. Too many things have happened that challenge those reasonable structures, whether it's meeting a hermaphrodite kraken that transforms your body chemistry or a sixteen-year-old goddess who has given birth to two thousand children. The structures we've learned can't explain those things; it's easier to deny their existence and insist on the integrity of your system. Yet we've seen, and continue to see, just how real these improbabilities are. At the monastery, I came across the writings of a sage, an investigator of profound mysteries. Much of what he said seemed to be written for another era, but one line stuck with me. He said that if you want to penetrate a mystery, when you have eliminated the impossible, whatever remains, however improbable, must be the truth. You can touch Mother Nyx; she's real. And if she's real, and the kraken is real, then all those logical structures are the bullshit, pardon my language. It's time to face facts—however improbable."

Corax looked at me with admiration. "You've done well, boy." He leaned over and kissed me on the mouth, taking me by surprise. Over his shoulder, I saw Marianne grin.

Nyx clapped. "It's so sweet! I love it!" Corax and I separated and squirmed, but I held on to his hand. Nyx continued, "Diarmuid is correct. Structures of universal knowledge don't work. Sure, they work for limited applications, but that hardly qualifies them as *universal*, now does it? There is so much that can't be readily explained, even by the gods, though most of them would never let on. Like the Olympian project: they want to establish rule and structure over the universe but it's a joke. They can't even rule themselves. And if the gods can't create a universal structure, where does that leave mortals? Think about it. Where did the world, gods and all, come from in the first place? Chaos! There's your *structure!*"

"Wait—what are you saying? Because everything grew out of Chaos, there's no point in order?" asked Marianne. "Just do whatever and take what comes, like tossing dice?"

"Well, dear," replied Nyx with a sly smile, "that's always a choice. But choice doesn't have to be random." She reached into the bucket of mussels and resumed shucking, popping the clean flesh into her mouth. The next one she offered to Marianne, who accepted it and chewed slowly. "Perhaps I should explain a few things. I always forget how much mortals don't understand, no offense. Try to pay attention; this is basic stuff. Chaos is not nihilism—quite the opposite. Far from nothing, it is everything. Accepting Chaos doesn't prevent us from trying to make sense of things. Chaos is the progenitor of the universe and as such, contains the potential for patterns and structures. But these patterns are a subset of the whole. The true nature

of the world is messy; understanding it is more about acknowl-
edging possibilities, relationships, and fluidity than trying to
find the overarching key to the puzzle. No reason to panic or
pull rabbits from hats. Go with the flow! Toss the dice—or not!
Do you get it? I haven't given a lecture in a long time! I'm a
little rusty!"

"More or less," said Marianne, noncommittal. Corax
savored a mussel and stared at Nyx. I couldn't tell whether he
was crushed or enlightened by this metaphysical revelation
straight from the mouth of a goddess—one who was present at
the creation of the world, no less. Or so she claimed; I struggled
to wrangle these majestic time frames into the person of the
young woman sitting in front of us. It reminded me of Tiresias'
dreamtime, a useful concept if you're trying to collapse all time
and space into the moment.

"Interesting," I said. "And what does that have to do with
the curse again?"

"Ha ha! Good question! Shall I blather on, then?" Without waiting for an answer, she continued. "Maybe you know
this, but if not, Dionysos is called the Loosener. He pulls things
apart—deconstructs them. Hence all the talk about his maenads
dismembering animals. But it's not like that, not at all. Honestly,
for all the metaphors floating around this godly queendom, it's
astonishing what gets taken literally. Of course, it's a symbolic
process! Because when you pull things apart, you can see how
they work, you can appreciate the weave of relationships, and
you can find where you fit in. All from going to pieces! But
don't we cling to our rigid little mindsets, holding our breath
to hold it together! Silly, really. Why, there's nothing I like better
than an old-fashioned coming apart at the seams."

"I'm not sure I understand," Marianne said. "Are you implying that Dionysos' "curse" may not be a curse?"

"You are a sharp one, aren't you, dear? Yes, that's exactly what I'm implying. It might be a gift."

The three of us sat in front of the youthful old goddess, stunned. This perspective had never crossed my mind. Remembering the sad nights watching Corax drink himself into a stupor, it seemed impossible to put a positive spin on such self-destruction. Although I found Nyx charming and courteous, this claim was too much.

"Please explain how what you call a "gift" can be found in drunken oblivion and the dereliction that accompanies it," I demanded.

"Not entirely obvious, is it?" she replied. "Let's ask the expert. Corax, love, why do you drink so much?"

With a jerk, he pulled the cup away from his lips. "What?" I watched his face slide from sudden guilt to cunning. Looking at the ground, he said, "Everyone knows it promotes good humor and digestion."

"You'll have to do better than that to satisfy your friends, I think," Nyx insisted. "We're not here to play word games. Give us a little respect. Assume I'm making a phenomenological inquiry and I need to know what you're thinking, feeling, experiencing in your body—everything. Tell us what it's like to be in your skin before you take that first drink. I'm not interested in passing judgment."

Corax looked at Nyx like a boy caught in the cookie jar. "Not much to tell. Same old stuff."

"Details are helpful. What do you mean by *stuff*?"

Given the amount of mead he had consumed, Corax didn't act as drunk as I would have expected. Perhaps the brew contained a minimum of alcohol. Yet it did something—he was relaxed enough to allow these questions without blasting back from the trenches. He paused, then spoke in a faint voice. "Spun up, mostly."

"Spun up?"

"Wound up tight. Flying high, right into the sun. Like Icarus, maybe."

"Oh yes, the trajectory of Apollo. If I understand you correctly, before burning up, you reach for a drink. And what does the alcohol do?"

"Pulls me back to the ground—when I get enough. In the ground, really: buried to my neck. Safer, I guess. Better than crashing out of the sky in flames. At least when I'm drunk, I don't do anything too crazy—just pass out, mostly." He shot me a glance and I nodded for encouragement. This was new to me; he'd never confided as much. Perhaps I should have asked these questions.

Nyx smiled at Corax and I noticed that he straightened his back. "Mania, that's it," she said. "An affliction of the disembodied head. It shoots skyward, speeding away from the body, reaching for the perspective of the gods. A rushing exaltation full of the crackle and spark of solar energy. It's like eating pure light, eh? And the alcohol—it dampens the head and drags you back to earth. With a thud, maybe, but it brings you down out of the burning sky."

"Yes," Corax admitted. "That's it."

"I never looked at it like that!" I said. "Explains a lot."

"Doesn't it?" Nyx agreed. She turned back to Corax and gazed at him for a moment. "Funny that you didn't mention being cursed by Apollo."

"What?" The three of us reacted at the same time.

"The mania. It's from Apollo; I thought you knew that. One of his special touches, the soaring madness."

"But I never said anything against Apollo!" protested Corax.

"You didn't have to," Nyx said. "Apollo has a thing about philosophers: he hates them. Especially those that throw a torch into the dim crannies of dogma. No doubt you recall that the hero of your Academy was endorsed by Apollo many years ago as the wisest man on earth. Unfortunately for him, that philosopher took the endorsement and used it as a tool of sarcastic deconstruction against all and sundry, even the god himself. You can imagine the reaction. Fury is too mild a word. Ever since Apollo has a dedicated hole in Hades for sarcastic philosophers. Which is pretty much all of them, as far as I can tell. You don't even need to gain his specific attention. He blankets the land with a curse on your kind."

"Good grief," said Corax, shaking his head.

Marianne patted his back. "Strengths are also weaknesses, no doubt about it," she said.

"Corax has been cursed by two gods?" I objected. "What kind of bad luck is that?"

"Honey, I hate to break it to you," said Nyx, "but you mortals are cursed with the whole damn pantheon."

"Hah," said Corax, "There's a point of view. And a factor that led to the development of philosophy in the first place. If the gods won't be reasonable, then it's up to us to find our own reason."

"Sad to say," Nyx responded, "you haven't bettered your-selves with this tool of reason. A shame, really. Some of us in the divinity racket are quite fond of mortals. And we honor our responsibilities. At the end of each day, when I bring Night down to embrace the land, I love to see all those little human lights glowing like fireflies across the earth. What a beautiful sight! Makes me feel warm and cozy inside."

For a moment it was difficult to decide if Nyx was a god-dess from the origin of the world or a giddy ingenue. Perhaps she was both, and more besides. Given enough time with our hostess, we could learn a few things, no doubt, but my thoughts returned to our mission. "I'm not sure where we stand any-more. If the curse isn't a curse, but a gift—I mean the curse from Dionysos—should we continue with the plan to steal the lyre? If the underlying problem is a separate curse from Apollo, why would we risk his further wrath? And if the drinking is supposed to be an antidote to the mania, well, it's a long way from health, in my opinion. I'm confused."

"Of course, you're confused! You're mortal!" Nyx bobbed her head vigorously, bouncing the halo of hair along with it. "And you haven't even considered the possibility that your adventure is some kind of an audition or rehearsal being staged by Dionysos!"

"Say that again?" said Marianne, her lips tight. She no lon-ger looked relaxed.

"Oh dear, have I upset you? Well, just trying to help, like you asked! I wouldn't be doing you any favors by avoiding pos-sibilities, would I?"

I felt the onset of intense weariness. "Maybe you could explain that, Mother Nyx? About the audition thing? What does that mean? You did mention something earlier."

Nyx handed each of us a debearded mussel. We gladly ate them. "Sometimes Dionysos auditions his theatrical ideas in the world. He likes to see how they play out; helps him evaluate plots and characters and all that thespian stuff. So, yes, maybe he didn't curse you as you think and he's playing with ideas. Or maybe it's not a curse from Apollo, but a plot device of Dionysos. Or it could all be true, or only a fragment, or some mixture, including things we haven't even considered. You really can't know; that's the sad part."

"In that case, we might as well go home and forget about all this bullshit," said Corax. For once, I agreed with him.

"Land sakes, I wouldn't do that!" said Nyx. "Break it down: the Apollo curse, if it is a curse, isn't personal. The Dionysos curse, whether it's a curse or a passing fancy or some other notion of the god, *is* personal. You've been selected, so to speak. That should be your priority. Get it done and get that off your plate. Maybe it'll all work out for the best. If you give up or push back, hard to say what comes next. Probably nothing good."

"I guess," I said. "Makes as much sense as anything else these days. We're in too deep to back out."

"I think so," said Nyx.

"Mother Nyx, you've been very helpful," said Marianne, using a voice of unusual sweetness. "We know a lot more than we did before we came. Perhaps you'd want to come with us? We would welcome your excellent company." I stared at Marianne, aware that she was trying to curry the goddess's favor. Bold, I thought.

Nyx scrunched her face before replying, which I took to be an answer of sorts. "So, you'd like me to get the lyre for you?"

Marianne looked mortified. "No, no, I didn't mean that. I mean… I'm sorry, I didn't mean to presume. Tiresias thought you might want to come along; I don't know why he thought that. If not, of course, we appreciate what you've given us and if we can do anything to repay you or show our gratitude, we will."

Nyx looked at each one of us with a solemn face, then burst out laughing. "Oh goodness, I forget how much fun it is to have company! No dear, I'm just messing with you. I don't need anything…" She paused in thought and chewed another mussel. "Well, there is one thing you could do. It would benefit both of us, I think. See, I can't go with you—though it does sound like a blast! It may not look like it when I sit and blab away the day, but I have many responsibilities. But Oizys, now… She could go in my place. And, if I do say so myself, the girl needs to get out. It would do her a world of good. I think you'll find she's quite handy. She's an excellent cook!"

My heart fell and I struggled to keep any sign of dismay out of my expression. Did we need the embodiment of depression on our team? Corax stared at the ground while Marianne and I exchanged glances.

"Yes, Mother Nyx, we'd be delighted to bring your daughter." What else could I say?

[16]

"Well, I must confess," enthused Mother Nyx, "this has been a lovely visit! And now I'm sure you'll want to get going. Oizys!"

Oizys shuffled out of the cave and Nyx told her to pack a bag since she was going to show us the way to Temple Island. Her daughter sulked for a moment, then went inside.

"This will be so much fun for her! Do bring her back in one piece now, won't you? Oh, she's sturdy enough—nothing to worry about. Depression has deep roots; you can't move her if she doesn't want to move. But when she gets going, watch out!"

The three of us stood and stretched after our long conversation, aware that we had been dismissed. From the terrace in front of Mother Nyx's cave, I looked north across the sea and saw the distant hump of Temple Island. It would be a long haul, the best part of a day's sailing. I hoped the innkeeper had found a boat for us, a thought that prompted me to gauge the shadows and realize there remained barely enough time in the day to get back to the inn before dark. Our time with Nyx had gone by much faster than I perceived, perhaps an effect of her chaos wrangling. Who knows? The gods lived outside of time, anyway, and socializing with them promised no end of dream-time distortion. The sooner this affair was resolved, the better. Getting in this deep with gods and goddesses seemed fraught with uncertainties, not to mention risk. No wonder humans had devised philosophy as an antidote to this religion—the deities needed ethics even more than the mortals.

Oizys emerged from the cave wearing a long gray pep-los with a black sash tied under her breasts. A matching black headband held her hair behind her ears and she carried a small leather pack. She moved in slow motion, which managed to appear both graceful and labored, as though she walked under-water. Despite her haunted eyes and lethargy, or because of them, I saw a vulnerable charm in her.

Stopping in front of Nyx, she bent to kiss her mother, who responded by placing her hands on Oizys' temples and star-ing into her eyes. "Help them as best you can, my dear. Don't worry; they're quite nice, for the most part. I think you'll have a lovely time. And you can tell me all about it as soon as you get back!"

Oizys shuffled over to join our group, clearly reluctant. Nyx resumed cleaning the bottomless bucket of mussels and ignored us as if we were long gone. A tiny, spotted gecko squeezed out from under the bucket and made a dash for the cave. The eerie magic of this place suddenly seemed less welcoming, but awk-wardness and indecision left me paralyzed. I looked at Mari-anne and Corax while Oizys scrutinized the ground. Finally, she raised her face to reveal a nervous expression that car-ried the hint of a plea. Marianne, the consummate diplomat, kneeled in front of a startled Oizys and kissed the back of her hand. "Mistress, we're honored to have your company. Tell us what you need, and we'll do our best."

Oizys signaled for Marianne to rise by lifting her palm. I was locked in indecision about whether to plunge to my knees and vow fealty or some such deference when Oizys laid her hand on my forearm. "Be at ease," she said, and her voice trickled into my ears with the sound of water flowing under rocks. The tension in my body drained away. She turned and gazed intently at Corax, who stared back until he squirmed and shifted his weight from foot to foot. "I am ready," Oizys said. "Lead on."

It was dark when we walked into The Trojan Horse. Diomedes greeted us with an eager smile that informed me we were still his only lodgers. Marianne volunteered to share her room with Oizys and we paid for another night. Pulling me aside, the innkeeper mentioned that he had found two fishermen willing to give us passage to Temple Island. Their boat was small but seaworthy and they had made the journey many times, he confided. We were to meet them on the dock at sunrise and ask for Isus. I shared this news with the others, and we celebrated with bowls of pungent fish soup.

Oizys stirred up a small whirlpool in her bowl, gazing into the liquid as if she could penetrate a hidden reservoir of wisdom. On the walk down from the cave, we had briefed her on our quest, and she had listened without comment. I wondered if she thought we had any chance of success. Finally, she lifted the spoon to her lips and took a cautious sip. Expressionless, she set the spoon back on the table and looked at us in turn. I paused with my spoon halfway to my mouth. "What?" I asked.

"Swill," she pronounced, with a tone of final judgment.

Marianne nodded. "It is, however, sustenance. Another weakness of mortals, but there you have it."

"I will cook for you," pronounced Oizys in a flat voice.

"I look forward to it," Marianne said carefully.

Retrieving the pouch of lithium salts from an inner pocket of my robe, I reached for Corax's glass of water. "Time for a dose, I believe."

Oizys surprised me by placing her hand over the top of the glass, preventing the addition. "No," she said.

"No?" I had already grown used to the passive nature of the goddess and couldn't understand this assertive move.

"No. At this time, it does not serve him."

"Pardon me, your highness, but do you even know what this is? He needs it if he is to remain stable, surely not a minor consideration, given the demands of our mission."

"I know what it is. At this time, it does not serve him."

"Because…?" I invited her response, but she ignored me. I looked at Corax, who offered no objection, of course, and at Marianne, who shrugged. I had no leverage. I returned the pouch to my robe.

Even without the calming effects of lithium, Corax snored into the night. While he rumbled, I rolled back and forth on my side of the bed in helpless rumination. I tried to sort the information of the day, but it kept curling into confused knots. Even though it was too late to do anything about it, getting mixed up with the gods made me anxious, and I couldn't stop obsessing about it. The amount of control that had to be ceded to them was chilling. Not that I ever assumed I had full agency in the world, but at least I could pretend. With a god around, that was impossible. And what were we doing, anyway? Were we atoning for an insult or were we trying out for a play? I didn't see how Corax's damned eidetic reduction was helping us plumb the essence of reality.

I woke up with Marianne shaking my arm. Behind her, I saw Oizys watching from the doorway. They were dressed and ready to go. I pounded on Corax's back and pushed him out of the bed, which earned me the philosopher's curse.

The inn was silent in the gray dawn as we slipped out. At the town wharf, we found two fishermen fussing with their boat, a white, single-masted caique with blue trim. The boat had seen better days, as was perhaps also true of the fishermen. Ragged and unkempt, they went about their preparations with practice, pausing only to swear or spit over the side. They completely ignored us, even though we stood at the edge of the pier, awkwardly staring.

"We're looking for Isus," I announced.

"Look no further," said one without looking up.

"The innkeeper said you would be willing to take us across to Temple Island." I was undaunted by these grizzly fishing types. I'd grown up with the like in the Western Isles and they were always this way: gruff and suspicious.

The one who spoke before, who I assumed was Isus, stopped what he was doing and straightened up, eyeing us with insolence. His gaze lingered on the women, especially Marianne. "Have you the coin?"

"We do."

"Climb down, then, and park yourselves out of the way. If that's possible." His partner snickered and hawked more phlegm, this time into the shallow slop in the bilge.

Marianne and Corax scrambled down the dock ladder while I assisted Oizys, who allowed me to spot her descent, though I have no doubt she could have made it on her own by floating or teleporting or some other divine skill.

Isus extended a calloused hand, palm up. I placed two pieces of gold in the palm, but he didn't budge until I added another. The money disappeared under his tunic and he waved for us to move to the fore of the boat. The caique was only slightly bigger than the fishing *currachs* of my home. It looked seaworthy, though the amount of water in the bilge suggested we might be enlisted for bailing. Isus' unnamed partner sat amidships and used an oar to push off from the dock piling. Once clear, he launched into an expert demonstration of rowing while Isus manned the tiller.

The village had never seemed large, but as we rowed away, it shrank rapidly into a conglomeration of white boxes on the hillside above the beach. As soon as we could catch a breeze, the nameless one shipped the oars and hauled the sail into place. The swells were mild, and we rolled through them in a mesmerizing rhythm. A cluster of dolphins cruised and leaped alongside for a while but disappeared as swiftly as they had arrived.

"How long for the crossing, do you think?" I ventured to Isus.

"Depends," he said, and that was the end of it.

Marianne leaned back against the bow and studied the fishermen through narrow eyes. Her casual manner failed to conceal the underlying tension. "What?" I asked.

She shook her head. Corax, sitting in the middle of the bench, struggled with nausea. On the other side of him, Oizys sat in a trance, staring out to sea as if she were entirely alone. I looked back at Marianne, who arched an eyebrow. Trying to be subtle, I slowly turned to see the back of the boat. Isus sat at the tiller, his partner next to him. They gazed off to starboard with unconcealed intensity. I looked back to Marianne.

"Something's up," she said.

The village was a distant smear of white as we cleared the final headland and moved into the open sea. The swells increased their amplitude and Corax moaned. Muttering to each other in low voices, the fishermen continued their inspection of the eastern horizon. When Isus stopped talking and stretched his neck up for a better view, I followed the direction of his gaze. From behind the headland emerged a ship bearing in our direction. It looked to be a warship, judging by the banks of oars and the speed it made. I turned to point it out to Marianne, but she'd already seen it. No longer pretending to lounge, she sat upright and had her long knife in hand, tucked out of sight behind her ankle. Her eyes drilled into the two fishermen, who paid her no attention and openly pointed at the approaching ship.

I reached out my hand to stay her, but she pushed it aside. "Not this time," she said.

Isus glanced in our direction with a brazen smirk. I felt a chill in my guts and understood that we had been betrayed. The appearance of the war galley was not an accident. Anger boiled up my spine, countering the cold fear, and I turned to Marianne. Before I said a word, she slipped past me, ducked around the sail, and leaped on the two fishermen. They were unprepared for her ferocity, especially from a woman they had ravished repeatedly with their eyes. I saw Marianne's blade glint twice in motion and both fishermen slumped to the bottom of the boat, bleeding their lives into the bilge. She cleaned her blade on Isus' tunic, re-sheathed it, and then motioned for me to join her.

I clambered aft and we tumbled the bodies overboard. "Was that really necessary?" I implored.

"I don't like being set up," she said. "No doubt that warship bearing down is full of pirates. No doubt we were supposed to be fodder for the slave trade. Do what you will, but I'll be dead first. My grandmother didn't raise me to be a slave."

"Your grandmother?" I'd never heard her mention her family.

"Later. Take down the sail and work your magic with the oars," said Marianne. She took the tiller and swung us around while I lowered the canvas, more trouble than it was worth against the prevailing wind. Corax lay curled up on the bench. I couldn't tell whether he was that sick or withdrawn in fear. Oizys stared into space, apparently uninterested in the murders or the peril of our situation. We were an odd lot, and the thought crossed my mind that we would make obstinate slaves, anyway, so we might as well fight. I set the oars in the locks and leaned into the work.

Instead of making straight for the village, which would have been my choice, Marianne set a course for the rocks of the headland. It didn't take long to understand the wisdom of her strategy. We'd never outrun them straight to the village, but the galley wouldn't be able to close in near the rocks. Our smaller and more nimble craft could dodge and weave its way along the cliffs and possibly escape. However, a long stretch of open water lay between us and the headland and the warship advanced with terrifying precision and speed.

I quickly found the rhythm of the oars and pulled with every muscle in my body. Marianne smiled at me, a brief encouragement that offered hope, and I dug deeper into the task. I remembered our flight from the pursuing monks in the Western Isles where my rowing skills were also put to the test. Despite my best effort, that would not have ended well without the intervention of the kraken. I wished that Marianne could truly sing the Language of the Deep and summon another salvation from a creature of the sea. Surely, if she could, she would have done it already. No, we were on our own.

I rowed hard, but it didn't take long to see that we weren't going to make it. The galley anticipated our scheme and altered course to cut between us and the rocks. The speed of the craft was astonishing, no doubt driven by the insatiable human lust for wealth and booty. I wondered if they knew anything about their targets. Did they know that two of us were women? Did that excite them? A sense of irony crawled through my thoughts as I pulled the oars like an automaton. Was this compensation for enslaving Corax? A joke of the gods? Another twist to the plot? Then I remembered Oizys. How would she respond to this abduction? Surely, she wouldn't accept it. Of course, even the divine hero Herakles had been sold into slavery at one time. As the blood pounded in my chest, I picked up the pace.

[17]

The galley dwarfed our caique as it bore down with the power of two dozen oarsmen. At first, I thought it aimed to ram us, but as it approached, the oars lifted from the water, and the helmsman slew the course so its hull would kiss our gunwale on contact. Marianne dropped the tiller and leaped to her gear. Shoulders sagging with fatigue, I gave up. Meanwhile, Corax had recovered enough to sit up and stare at the advancing galley with an expression of horror. I couldn't figure out what Oizys was thinking behind her impassive expression, but she calmly looked at each of us, nodding.

Marianne pulled her bow from the baggage. She fitted an arrow and waited as the galley closed the final gap. A pirate stood on the bowsprit, yelling directions to his crew. With the galley in range, Marianne fired the arrow, burying it in the pirate's chest. He choked out a gurgle, lost his grip on the forestay, and plunged into the water, disappearing under the hull as it slid over him. She nocked another arrow, but the crew grew cautious and peered from behind the heavy gunwale. As the galley bumped against our boat, they dropped a weighted fishing net over the caique, capturing us all with one maneuver.

Marianne slashed at the net in desperation until they tossed another, more finely meshed net, trapping her. She cursed and thrashed but subsided under the aim of pirate arrows. A sudden word salad of invective roared out of Corax, and I worried that the stress had launched him into psychotic mania, but his voice soon trailed away into subdued muttering. Despite the turmoil,

Oizys sat in the same position as if barely weighed down by the net, which draped over her like a shroud. Tired and seeing no point in further resistance, I sat still and tried to accept that we were captives.

Half a dozen pirates clambered down ropes and boarded. They were a hardy lot, tough as nails, no doubt, but surprisingly well-dressed and groomed. It crossed my mind that piracy probably paid well. The slave trade offered the rewards of low overhead and high profits, generating bonus coin for pleasure. The boarding party concentrated on Marianne, holding her down until they could peel off the nets and tie her arms and legs. The pirates laughed at her struggles, taking the opportunity to paw over her privates and boast about their rapacious deeds. The rest of us were similarly trussed like spider prey and dumped on the bottom of the boat. A boom swung over the galley's gunwale. One by one, we were secured to the boom line and pulled up to the deck, where we were stacked side by side. I lay on the outside, with Marianne next to me, then Corax, and finally, the goddess Oizys. If her job was to protect us, I didn't understand her method, but maybe it wasn't her assignment, just my expectation. Marianne had a wild look in her eye as she strained against the bonds. I noticed that she had twice the restraints that I did. The pirates weren't stupid, that was clear.

"I expected six," stated an iron voice from behind my head.

"That's all there was," came the raspy answer. "Some blood in the boat, but that could be from fish."

"They don't strike me as fishermen," replied the first voice.

"No, me neither. That one there is a she-devil. A fine piece of meat, if I say so myself. She'll fetch a royal price. The others—who knows? This one could do the work of an ox, by the looks of him. The other two, the bald guy and the twig, depends.... Baldy has a mouth, we know that much."

The first voice moved into view and my guts twirled just to look at him. The top of his head was shaven clean in a tonsure while the remaining hair dangled as a queue. A long-handled mustache, waxed into sharp tips at each end, rode above sensuous lips. He was lean and hard, with muscles like plate armor adorning his bare torso. A sash held up his baggy pants along with an assortment of alarming knives. But it was the eyes that cut through me: sharp blue spears that pinned me to the deck and left me weak. Accompanying this commanding devil was an ugly giant of a man, completely naked but for a loincloth and a profuse red beard. He lacked an ear on the left; all that remained was a ragged stump. A leather whip curled around his waist like a dormant viper. I guessed this was the raspy one.

"Welcome to the good ship *Hermetic Endurance*. I am Captain Nobody. They call me that because," and here his voice lost its jocular tone to ring like steel, "nobody fucks with me."

The giant chortled, a childish sound that seemed out of character.

"Where are the other two?" demanded Captain Nobody.

We remained silent while Nobody paced back and forth, humming a plaintive tune. After two passes without an answer, he suddenly dropped to a crouch and pressed a knife against my septum. "Off with his nose, then," he said. I tasted a trickle of blood over my lips.

Marianne twisted her head and spat on the captain's foot. "They decided to go swimming," she snarled. I wanted to scream at her for gambling with my body parts, but I didn't dare move for fear of the blade.

"Oh dear," he replied, returning the knife to his belt and wiping his foot on my hair and beard. I didn't mind, relieved to have a nose. "That's not recommended, especially this far from shore. You'd think with their experience on the water, they'd know better. But fishermen are a reckless lot, I'm sure you'd agree." With a twinkle and another devastating sneer, he patted my chest and stood. "Oh well, they've done us a few turns—we'll raise a flagon for them at some point." The bearded giant chortled.

"Pay him no mind," advised the captain, "he is Oruk, first mate, as gentle a monster as you can imagine. Until he's not, of course. And I guarantee you don't want to see that. He can flay the skin off your back in seconds with that nasty whip. Nothing for you to worry about—as long you're good boys and girls and follow orders. You will speak only to me or Oruk—no one else—if you value the retention of your extremities." As punctuation, Nobody whipped out a knife and threw it with a snap of the wrist. It thudded into the deck an inch from Marianne's ear. She grew still.

"Yes, dearie, best lay quiet and you'll come to no harm." He bent to retrieve his knife and stroked Marianne's head. I heard her gasp as he squeezed her breasts, then watched as he trailed the fingers of one hand down her abdomen, digging quickly between her legs. "Aren't you a fine thing? In other circumstances, you murderous little twat, I'm sure we would make a robust duo. But it is what it is, eh?" He kissed her forehead and stood. I studied her face, noting the surge of anger, but Nobody ignored her. When Marianne turned her head to mouth the word "sorry" to me, the ferocity was gone; her proud face now dimmed, chalked pale with vulnerability. It made me realize how easy it was to violate a woman and I offered her the reassurance of a tender smile, though I doubt it was convincing.

Oruk circled our helpless group, grinning at us while fondling the handle of his whip, which dangled suggestively in front of his loincloth. Nobody continued, "I do apologize for the accommodations. Sadly, you will be confined to your current quarters for the duration of our journey. Should you need to use the facilities, well, we have none for your kind, so just urinate as you are. If the stench gets too bad, Oruk will douse you with a pail of seawater. The good news is that the journey is short. By the end of the day, we'll make port on Temple Island where you will be transferred to new ownership. Meanwhile, enjoy your experience on board the *Hermetic Endurance.*"

The captain smiled, pleased with his sarcasm. I contemplated various rejoinders myself until I heard Oruk speak. "I'm not sure about this one, Captain. There's something fey about her."

Nobody joined Oruk in contemplation of Oizys. "What do you mean?"

"Look at her, sir. Take a whiff. She reeks of divinity."

Out of the corner of my eye, I saw Nobody crouch over the limp form of Oizys. He sniffed at her like a dog on the hunt, then poked and pinched her in a variety of sensitive places. "Hmm," he said. "Maybe. A bit on the scrawny side. Still, there's some that get excited about that. Her features are fair and I expect she'll fetch a good price in the market; we'll soon be rid of her."

"I'm not sure that's such a good idea, Captain. Selling her off, I mean."

Nobody looked Oruk up and down with icy silence. "Leave the ideas to me, first mate."

"Aye aye, sir."

The news that we were headed to Temple Island evoked mixed feelings. On one hand, we had transferred to a faster and more seaworthy vessel. On the other, the time gained in transit would certainly be lost by fulfilling new destinies as chattel. Was this, in fact, the end of our mission? I looked at Marianne, whose eyes had narrowed into slits; I recognized the expression and could sense the shuffling of schemes in her imagination. I hoped she had some good ideas. Slaves were known to escape from captivity, as I knew from our caper on the mainland. However, a drunk missing from the slave market might avoid attention, but four expensive thralls on the run from private ownership would hardly go unnoticed. The ensuing bounties and a fugitive life were less than appealing. I didn't understand how we could infiltrate Apollo's temple and gain the lyre while dodging authorities in pursuit. I thought to ask her a question, but no sooner had I cleared my throat than Oruk loomed over me. "No talking," he barked. I nodded vigorously, eager to avoid the whip.

Corax was the first to piss himself, letting out a sickly moan. I raised my head to look and saw that he was on the verge of tears. Oruk strolled over and stood over Corax's face. "Tsk, tsk," said the mate. "Since you've soiled the deck...." Oruk untucked his penis from the loincloth, waving it back and forth as he sprayed urine over all of us. This was followed by several buckets of cold seawater and we lay sputtering in humiliation.

Oruk kept a close eye on us without neglecting his supervision of the crew, which he accomplished through a stream of lewd threats, delivered with volume in his rock gnashing voice. Despite the color and specificity of his insults, the crew seemed content; there was no grumbling that I heard. They applied themselves to their work with a well-practiced order. I imagined myself following the pirate life and for a moment, I wasn't repulsed. Better than slavery, I was certain.

Our skin baked through the hours until the sun swung well past zenith. Laying trussed and supine on the deck, I mostly watched the monotonous sky, schemed, then gave up scheming, and surrendered to idle thoughts punctuated by stolen expressions with Marianne. Our arrival at the island was only apparent by the changed behaviors of the crew: shipping oars, tossing lanyards, and the general bustle of making port. Oruk cut the ropes binding our legs, all except for Oizys. He ordered another crewman to handle her. They helped us to stand and as soon as we were upright, snapped metal collars around our necks. A chain linked our collars and thus bound into a line, we shuffled to the gangplank. I seethed at the collar and the chain—these stigmas of subjection—but kept my face calm out of fear of reprisal.

Captain Nobody greeted us as we queued for deboarding. He motioned to a small net filled with our belongings. "I see no reason to keep these things; the clothes and personal items, even the weapons, will increase your value in the market. This, however," and he hefted two pouches of coins, the money that Marianne had brought to cover our expenses, "can only get you into trouble. I will retain it as compensation for the loss of the crewman you wantonly murdered."

He saluted as Oruk marched us down the plank, followed by two crewmen—one toting the net with our stuff and the other poking us along with a spear. By the tension in Marianne's body, I could tell that she itched to make a break, but as it would only bring the four of us tumbling to the ground, I was glad she merely flexed her muscles and scanned the surroundings while we hustled along in obedience.

The wharf of Temple Island was busy with people and cargo in transit, coming and going amidst the odors of grilled meat, ripe fruit, and the sweat of human labor. I saw many who were chained together and wore iron collars like our own, pushed along with spears or barbed quirts. This was the island of Apollo, the holiest sanctuary of the god, and, from the looks of it, another slave-trading center. A barren, rocky peak dominated this part of the island and I saw that the outskirts of the city ran well up its flank. Pricked from behind by the spear of our guard, I bumped into Marianne, who tried to stay close to Oruk as he shoved his way through the crowd. Glimpses of elegant marble structures provided hints of the inner city, but I was in no mood for architecture. Oruk led us directly to a large, unadorned brick building at the end of the wharf and we were herded into the dank vastness of a slave barrack. With impressive efficiency, an attendant looked us over, made notes in a log, inscribed a receipt on parchment, stamped it with a seal, and handed it to Oruk. The first mate spun around, shuddering, and averted his eyes as he passed Oizys, leaving us to our new careers.

A guard picked up our belongings and I quickly lost sight of him in the dim warehouse. The interior had been fitted with metal cages; separated by narrow corridors, row upon row of these cages lined the main space. Many cages were empty, but some held groups of prisoners sitting on the floor in postures of apathy and defeat. Open chamber pots filled the air with the stench of human waste, and the guards wore long scarves wrapped around their faces. I was glad for the high ceiling and the sea breeze flowing through the wide entry. A few well-dressed customers, cloths over noses, wandered along the corridors, pausing to inspect the cages for the quality of the retail goods.

The guard who took our net returned. "Who's the leader here?" We looked at each other in puzzlement. "Doesn't matter. Here, take it, it's the receipt for your possessions." He thrust a small parchment tag at me, and I took it. "Follow me," he ordered.

We followed him down an aisle to an empty cell where he held the door for us, and once we were inside, slammed and locked it. Still chained together, we sat in a line, facing the entrance, straining for a draft of sea air.

"Shit," said Marianne. "This is fucked. And I have to pee again! What's with this fucking mission—go to jail, need to pee. And we've been going to jail a lot, it seems."

Wordlessly, Oizys reached to the edge of the cell and passed the chamber pot down the line to Marianne. We closed our eyes as she took care of necessity. The pot was passed back and placed as far away as Oizys could extend her arm.

I craned my neck to inspect the grim surroundings. Most of the nearby cells were empty, but there was a solitary old man studying us from the adjacent cage. "First time?" he asked.

Corax twisted his head around. "First time for what?"

"First time to gain the blessed status of property," the old man cackled, started coughing, and hawked a glob of sputum on the floor.

Corax glanced at me and frowned. "No, actually."

"My condolences," said the old man. "I would have took you for first-timers."

"It is for *them*," Corax waved a hand to include us. Marianne snorted and Oizys stared into space.

"What happens next?" I asked.

"You sit here and stew in your juices until someone pays the price. Twice a week there's a big market day. We get paraded outside so's the customers can shop in the fresh air. Even though there's pokin' and proddin', I enjoy the chance to reacquaint myself with the sun. Between market days, eager buyers venture into this stink hole to catch a bargain. Myself, this is my tenth go-round. Bad luck, I guess. 'Course, I'm an old man; nobody wants me, not really. Seems like every time I get settled into a new place, another pirate raid comes along and scoops me up along with my owners. I'm always the last to filter through. But you four, you won't last long. You may not even make it to the next market day. Buyers like 'em young and pretty and all that."

"Yes," said Corax, "we're joyfully awaiting our new owner, having nothing better to do."

The old man stared for a minute, then guffawed, ending in another coughing fit. "A real wit! Some owners like that. But in my experience, it's a quick path to the whip."

Corax grumbled and turned away from the old man. I nodded to the fellow, feeling sorry for him, and resumed my contemplation of the entrance. Or exit, depending on your perspective. "Well," I said to my companions, "at least we're on Temple Island."

"Fuck you," said Marianne.

[18]

Tired, but limited by our chains, we lay in a line, heads on each other's hips to avoid putting our faces on the floor, which reeked of old urine, rotten flesh, and who knew what else. Oizys had been at the front and I was at the end, but I insisted on being the one to anchor our chain and forego a hip, so on a count of three, we tilted my way and managed to recline without choking anyone. I tucked my hands under my head and tried not to look at the grime. Not that anyone slept. I spent hours alternating between praying to various gods and trying to suffocate my panic. Corax murmured to himself a good part of the night and I feared he was drifting into mania again. At least he still had enough control to whisper.

In the morning, a guard walked along the cages tossing chunks of stale bread through the bars. We seized this excuse for breakfast and diligently gnawed on it until we were able to swallow it lump by lump. With relief, I noted that Corax chewed patiently like the rest of us, without any tendency to rant. Shortly after we completed the bread project, a guard came to the door, peered at us for a moment, then motioned for us to get up. "Let's go," he said. "You've been sold."

"What?" I asked. I didn't know whether to be pleased or afraid. Pleased, at least, to leave this shithole.

"Shut up," he replied, gesturing with the point of a spear before unlocking the door.

The old man raised a hand in a resigned farewell as we marched past. I ventured to return the gesture and earned a poke in the ass from the guard. We filed out of the ware-house gloom and into the brilliant sunshine. In front of the building, we were delivered to two men with glowing bronze skin; they were clearly twins, tall, naked, majestically pro-portioned, and flexing muscles of defined precision. Corax gaped at them openly, and with good reason—their beauty shone with unnatural splendor. Even Marianne seemed in awe. Oizys, as usual, ignored them. The duo stood before a large golden chariot pulled by three horses adorned in gaudy harnesses.

"You may address me as Castor," said one of the men.

"And I am Pollux," said the other.

Corax started to laugh, then covered it with a cough. "Not the Dioskouroi?" he asked.

"The same," they said in unison.

"Isn't your name supposed to be Polydeukes?" argued Corax. In an aside behind Marianne's back, Corax whispered to me, "More divinities. Real old school, these two. Dangerous."

Castor snickered. "He changed it to Pollux a while back. Sexier, he says."

"Who in the hundred rings of Hades can remember Poly-deukes?" chirped Pollux. "Plus, this sounds so much better, don't you think? Castor and Pollux, Pollux and Castor. It just rolls off the tongue. Castor and Polydeukes…yuck." Pollux stuck out his tongue.

Oizys stared at the Dioskouroi with a blank expression, but the rest of us looked at each other with astonishment. Were these gods or clowns?

Pollux giggled and gestured at the chariot. "Whatever, get in, get in. We'll take you home."

Marianne, with an air of innocence, asked, "Is this required? We can certainly find other accommodations."

The Dioskouroi burst out laughing, slapping each other on the back. Finally, Castor replied. "Oh yes, it certainly is required! But worry not, you'll be treasured. I mean, just look at you, so adorable…. She's going to love you to pieces."

"She?" ventured Corax.

"Mistress Leto, silly!" said Pollux. "You're now in the service of the household of Lord Apollo. Really, it's a wonderful opportunity. People would kill to be in your sandals."

"But enough chit-chat," ordered Castor. "I'm so done with this place. The odor is atrocious! Let's get you to the Temple and you can learn your duties. Climb in, now—very good."

A guard ran from the warehouse and handed our bag of belongings to Castor, who hung it from a peg on the front of the carriage while Pollux set out a footstool to ease the ascent into the chariot. Awkwardly, tired and still chained, we climbed together over the stool and sat on the wooden floor. Pollux tossed the stool in the chariot and walked around to stand next to the wheel, which came up to his shoulders. Castor took a similar position on the other side. With a tandem yell, the twins leaped in, one over each side wall, easily clearing the Olympic dimensions of the feat. Their synchronization was perfect, and I guessed this maneuver had proved to be a well-practiced crowd-pleaser because spontaneous applause broke out from the bystanders. The Dioskouri waved and blew kisses to the crowd.

I decided to take advantage of the high spirits and chatterbox inclinations of the twins. "Please, can you explain how we ended up in the service of Lord Apollo?"

Pollux took the reins and whistled to the horses, starting us rolling and bumping along the cobblestones. Castor turned and leaned back against the rail of the chariot, looking down at me. I kept my eyes glued to his, trying to ignore his god-like penis swinging a short distance from my face. I derived some satisfaction from noting that, despite its substantial dimensions, it was still smaller than Corax's.

"Divine luck, you might say," Castor grinned. "Mistress Leto is known to have a prophetic dream now and then. She is, after all, the mother of Apollo. First thing this morning, she calls for us and says, she does, 'Now boys, I've had another dream. It told me to find four freshly delivered slaves in the market. Two women, two men, one group. I want them. See to it.' And so we did. She's mad for the dreams, she is. There's no talking her out of it, not once she's got the light in her eyes. After all, mother of Apollo and so forth."

The chariot jolted over a rough spot and Castor turned away. At that moment I felt a nudge from Oizys. When I looked at her, she mouthed the words "my mother." I didn't know what she meant by that, but Corax did. He nodded and said, in a low voice "*Oneiroi.*" I puzzled over that before remembering that Nyx was mother to the thousand boys who made up the *Oneiroi*, the beings that deliver dreams to both gods and mortals. I felt a surge of hope. Something happened by plan and it cheered me to think that it went in our favor. Of course, none of this contradicted the scheme to get the lyre for Dionysos, so if this was the rehearsal, we were definitely on stage. Regardless, the goal remained to steal Apollo's lyre, whether by chance or scheme, and we were now within his household. Could we have engineered a better opportunity on our own? I didn't see how. Oizys, after that surprising effort, dropped back into her fugue state while Marianne, Corax, and I exchanged glances.

"Anyway, as I was saying…" resumed Castor, "you'll soon be meeting the Mistress herself, you lucky dogs. I'm sure she'll have wonderful things for you to do around the Temple. The work is never done, can you imagine? Oh, you'll fall in love with her instantly, I'm sure. She's really something."

"And Apollo?" I asked.

"Not here. He's off on the oracle circuit, you know. Busy busy busy. Should be back soon. Then you'll be allowed to gaze upon his magnificence, wallow at his feet, sing his praises, and all the other little endearments he expects. A word to the wise: flattery is on the menu every day with him. Take another approach and you'll be on the menu."

"Why are you two here?" asked Corax. "I thought you had ascended to the heavens or some such terrific honor."

"Been there, done that. That was supposed to be our retirement reward, but don't you know, it was *bor-ing*. Mistress Leto needed help anyway, so we unretired."

"Help?"

Castor lowered his voice and leaned over in confidence. "It's that bitch that our dear father ended up marrying—Hera. She's got it in for Leto, big time. Along with every other woman Old Daddy's set his eyes on. But Leto, especially. Usually, Leto's darling children fend off the endless assassination attempts, but they're on the road a lot, so we're Plan B. Though since I don't mind tooting our own horn, we're the real A-Team."

The bumping and jerking over cobblestones came to an end as we rolled onto a smooth marble plaza. Across the square loomed an edifice with massive columns and wide steps. Facing away from this classic tabernacle stood a statue of Apollo, the eternal *kouros*, at least thirty cubits tall, dwarfing the worshippers wandering in and out of the sacred space. We turned along the edge of the plaza, passing a miscellany of modest sculptures and monuments before entering an archway that led into a compound of stone buildings, less majestic than the temple but still impressive. Stopping at a broad portal, the kitchen odors and general bustle suggested that we had arrived at the working entrance. An old man pushed a long-handled scoop along the paving stones, scraping horse dung and litter. As soon as we came to a halt, several attendants rushed out of the entry, ushering us off the chariot with gentle hands. The Dioskouroi dismounted by reversing their gymnastic stunt and ducked through the entrance, waving at a servant to take the chariot and horses away.

We stood in a line at the door, not sure what to do. Pollux popped back out. "Sorry," he said, "almost forgot." With a tap of his finger, he sprung open the collars around our necks. Taking the chain and dangling collars, he carelessly tossed the apparatus aside. A lurking attendant dashed over and scooped it up from the pavement, disappearing through another door. "Follow me," Pollux said, and stalked into the building.

Marianne rubbed her neck where the collar had left marks. "Damn," she said. "Fucking barbaric."

We passed through a large room filled with amphorae and containers of all sizes, followed by an even larger room that housed the kitchen. Several servants worked on food preparation and the smells were enticing, but we hurried to keep up with Pollux. He led us into an open-air courtyard at the heart of the structure, ringed with overhanging balconies and polished stonework. Statues grew out of the marble pavement accompanied by miniature gardens of roses, orchids, iris, and flowers I'd never seen before. At the center of this idyllic space bloomed an apple tree.

We caught up with the agile Pollux as he joined his brother and knelt in front of a woman sitting on a bench under the tree. We stopped behind the twins. I twitched in embarrassment, not knowing what to do, but when Marianne fell to her knees, the rest of us followed automatically. The twins rose and stepped aside. Waving a hand in our direction, Castor said, "Your latest acquisitions, Mistress. Should you require further service, we'll be in our quarters." In tandem, the Dioskouroi bowed and marched across the courtyard, disappearing through a doorway.

"Stand up, stand up, so I can get a good look at you. Fawning doesn't do much for me; save it for my son. He eats it up."

We obeyed and looked at our new owner, the goddess Leto, mother of Apollo and Artemis. She looked every bit the part: a voluptuous woman with a head of curly golden tresses hanging in cascades around her shoulders like a personal wilderness. As I stared, I saw a mouse poke its head from a tangle; it wriggled its nose and retreated. I spied another one peering at me from above an ear. When a third mouse squeezed up through the cleavage behind her low-cut bodice and, with a quick sniff of the air, scurried up her neck and into the flaxen jungle, I knew that this was a woman of unusual proclivities.

"Ah," said Corax, "oracular mice?"

Her blue eyes snapped to his face and peered at him, plumbing his depths. "Someone has been educated," she pronounced.

"Yes, ma'am," replied Corax.

"I will name you Sage," she declared. "Do you play chess?"

"Yes, ma'am."

"Then you will serve as a playmate for my son when he is in the house. He's mad about games. Meanwhile, you can, oh, help with the cleaning or something."

She turned her inspection to me, looking me up and down in a way that left me feeling quite exposed; essentially naked. "You, are you afraid of mice?"

A curious question, I thought. "No, ma'am, I love them."

"You do? Not merely unafraid, you *love* them?"

"Yes, ma'am. When I served as a monk in the Western Isles, long meditation confinements in stone cells were only broken by the friendship of mice. I found them to be reliable companions."

"Indeed. Then you shall serve as *my* playmate." A lascivious grin spread over her face. "There are many games we can play with the little ones."

I gulped and nodded, unable to conjure a response of wit.

"Oh, and I shall call you Parsley." Leto turned her attention to Marianne and frowned. "You're a bit mannish. Some kind of Amazon?"

"Yes, ma'am."

"The twins like their playmates to look like women. You know, soft and curvy, *comme ça*," and Leto swept her hand down her body to indicate the desired type. I saw Marianne start at the use of her native language; it did seem unexpected. It occurred to me that if you were a divinity, any language might do as well as another. "You might be useful in helping the weavers move supplies and shift their looms. They're always complaining about the labor involved. I don't dare send any men in there or it'd be rape and more rape every day. Before long, instead of working they'd be nursing their screaming brats."

Leto pursed her lips. "In time, you'll soften around the edges. You'll be Rosemary, a gentle name for the new you."

Oizys stood in a slouch, long hair dangling in her face. Leto investigated her with a slightly puzzled expression. "You look familiar. Have we met?"

"No, ma'am," came the faint response.

"There's something not quite right about you. Have you been to Olympos?"

"No, ma'am."

"I'll figure it out in time. Meanwhile, I will name you Thyme." Leto chuckled at her joke while the rest of us maintained faces of stone. "What about you? Can you do anything? You don't look like you'd be a fun playmate for anyone."

"I can weave, ma'am," answered Oizys.

"And so, you shall." Leto abruptly stood, causing mice to scurry around her body as they secured their perches. "Xanthias!" She yelled.

Promptly, a bug-eyed, rotund man waddled from the kitchen entrance. He resembled a hefty bullfrog as he squatted before Leto, licking his lips and waiting for her command. "Show them their quarters. The ladies to the weavers and Baldy to Apollo's playroom. You," she pointed at my chest, "come with me."

[19]

Reluctantly, I watched my companions follow Xanthias across the courtyard. Corax glanced back with a forlorn expression and my heart lurched at the parting. I should never have mentioned the mice. I don't know why I did; trying to look good for my new master, perhaps. I feared separation from the others. Not that my desires or feelings carried much weight anymore; slaves had no say. That was the point of human chattel, I supposed; you can make them do things they don't want to do. At least I would see the inner recesses of the palace. Maybe I could learn something useful, like the location of the lyre. Then I remembered that I still had Corax's lithium and felt a surge of panic. How long could he remain stable without it?

"Will I see the others again, ma'am?" I trotted to keep up with the goddess as she glided without effort through the halls and up staircases. Her feet never moved as she floated a finger's width above the surface of things, ascending stairs as if they were ramps.

Rotating her head, owl-like, she peered at me while sailing down a long hall on the second floor. "Breakfast and dinner, Parsley. Staff dining just off the kitchen. Do keep up." She accelerated in a gust, forcing me to sprint or lose her. With a giggle, she zoomed around a corner. Breathless, I pursued, turning into an empty cul-de-sac. I advanced cautiously, stopping at an open doorway where I peeked past the jamb into a high-ceilinged chamber as large as a warehouse. Tall mirrors covered the walls, offering the illusion of infinite space.

Situated at the geometric center of the room was a bed big enough to sail the seven seas. Sprawled on the white coverlet, partly propped against the headboard lay the nude figure of Leto, reclining as if she had been there for hours. Across her abundant skin, a horde of mice scampered and played, crawling between her legs and into her armpits, hiding for a moment before popping out with a squeak. She laughed at their antics and motioned me to join her.

Holy shit, I said to myself. Nerves aflame, I approached the bed as slowly as I could without appearing to dawdle. Although I preferred intimacies with men, I was not averse to women, and I prided myself on an appreciation of their unique qualities. Corax, due to his intersexed blend, had a bit of both, which added an interesting spice to our connection. Whether my appetite extended to divinities of any sex was another matter. Based on my brief exposure to this class of being, I had learned that everything was always about them, regardless of what they said. They toyed with mortals for their own satisfaction and the closer you got to the gods the more dangerous life became. These prospects hardly provided an aphrodisiac. Nor did I find the idea of a frolic with rodents to be a compelling twist. However, retreat seemed impossible.

"Here, Parsley, lay here," she patted the bed. I crawled over the expanse of the empty mattress and stretched out on my side, propping on an elbow. "Pick one," she said, pointing to the mice wandering around her creamy flesh. She plucked a white one from her chest while I assayed the mice, not an easy task since they were in constant movement.

"Uh, that one, I guess," I said, pointing to a brown one sniffing at Leto's navel.

"Pick it up, silly. Murmur sweet things in her ear."

I tried to pick up the mouse without touching Leto's belly, but it darted away, leaping down between her legs. I felt the rush of blood to my face, anticipating what was next.

"Go on, go after it," she ordered and spread her legs to accommodate the search. The mouse turned around and crouched over her pubes, looking at me with a curl of the mouth that resembled a smirk. I remembered a trick an old monk had taught me for catching lizards. Sitting up, I extended my right hand over Leto's belly and moved it slowly toward the mouse's face. Interested in the hypnotic approach of my fingers, it watched in fascination. With a lightning grab, my other hand darted from behind the mouse and snatched her up. Not, however, without brushing against the hairy tangle of Leto's mound.

"Ooo! So fresh!" she said and laughed as I blushed. But I had the mouse.

"You want me to whisper to it?" I asked, just to make sure I understood the rules.

"Yes. Tell it something nice. Maybe a secret! Like this," and she held her mouse next to her lips and whispered, like a breeze in the tall grass.

I cradled the delicate brown creature in my hand. It sat calmly, wriggling its whiskers, and staring at me with tiny obsidian eyes. A lovely being, it was a wonder of life in miniature. I recalled the long days in the monastic cell, where out of loneliness I had befriended a mouse like this one, feeding it particles of bread until it trusted me enough to tolerate a touch. Our understanding evolved slowly and naturally, a connection between two tenuous wild things, and I learned the value of shared space. The bond had been real, but it never ignored the boundaries that distinguished our species. Here in Leto's bedroom, that didn't seem to be the case. Typical of the gods, boundaries were an invitation for transgression. Just whisper something nice and get it over with, I thought.

I held the mouse's ear next to my lips and spoke so quietly I couldn't even hear myself. "The lady is quite beautiful," I breathed.

"Okay, now, let's trade mice!" said Leto, handing me the white one, which I took with a free hand while giving her the brown. She held my mouse to her ear, then laughed. "That's no secret!" she said. "Go ahead, listen to *my* mouse!"

Wary, I put the white mouse to my ear and heard, clearly though quietly, "I think this one's a keeper." I blushed and Leto laughed again. Her laugh was full of joy and I smiled even as I squirmed in discomfort.

"Again! This time you whisper to the white one and I'll use the brown. Only it needs to be *more* of a secret!"

It occurred to me that divinities must get bored over the eternity of their lives and they developed games like this for diversion. Plus, if you're immortal, maturity is irrelevant. Childish, cruel, excessive—who was to say you couldn't do whatever you felt like? Pleasure was relevant—nothing else. If the goddess wanted to act the giddy girl, I certainly wasn't going to tell her to grow up. Nor was I willing to confide any true secrets, such as who we were and why we had come to Temple Island. I settled on flattery as the safest choice. She might complain that such things were not real secrets, but I divined that she wouldn't be unhappy hearing them. Anticipating that the game's destination was erotic anyway, I offered increasingly risqué compliments about her body. She eagerly accepted this slight variation on the rules and disclosed her lascivious observations, demonstrating an imagination unprecedented in my experience. Before long, our tongues were put to more tactile methods of exchange, and we explored each other's physical secrets with taste and touch. It was challenging to stay focused while being tickled under the feet of cavorting mice—there must have been a dozen or more—but I applied myself to the desires of the goddess. The mice seemed to understand the details of human sensuality, using their tiny feet to tickle points of sensitivity, or wallowing on their furry backs in hollows of skin. At one point, a mouse dragged a tail along my anus, and I startled, which caused Leto to laugh hysterically. I wondered if this kind of orgy was going to be a daily expectation.

I lost track of time and just let hormones carry me along. Finally, we paused when a throaty blast resounded through the palace, like the bellow of an impassioned beast. "Just the dinner call, sweet Parsley. I'm sure you're famished, and we must keep your strength up." I slid to the edge of the bed and stood up, shedding mice, who leaped to stay on the mattress.

I removed one clinging to my beard and stared into its face. "What makes them oracular?"

"If you're very nice to them, they will tell you things about the future. Important things." I put the mouse down on the bed, hoping that if I *were* very nice, it would keep a few secrets. "Run along and see your friends," the goddess said. "Eat well, gossip a bit, then return to your quarters, the next room down the hall. It has its own bath and I expect you to use it at least once a day. More as needed. When you hear this bell," she suddenly held a small bell which I hadn't noticed before, "you will come to me instantly." She demonstrated the musical tinkle of the bell.

"Yes, ma'am, but it's so quiet, what if I don't hear it?"

"You'll hear it. Now run along and we'll play again soon."

If I could, I would have run out of the room, but I felt like an empty husk, drained of energy. I wondered about the life span of Leto's playmates and how often she needed replacements. With a wave to the reclining goddess and her pets, I left the bedroom.

[20]

I found my way back to the courtyard and the mess hall, following the pungent culinary trail. The clamor of mealtime crashed against my ears after the hours straining at the whispers of mice. Servants, dozens of them, sat in groups around long wooden tables, talking, laughing, and arguing while they sated their hunger from plates heaped with food. In the corner, an old man sat on a raised stool and idly plucked notes on a kithara, but no one paid attention. I saw Corax, Marianne, and Oizys seated together and joined them.

"You look like hell," greeted Corax.

Marianne clucked in sympathy. "Go grab some food before it's gone. Then you can tell us all about it… Parsley."

"Don't start," I muttered as I walked across the hall to get in line.

I sat next to Corax, feeling ashamed of how readily I had betrayed our affections. Not that I had much of a choice. I could have resisted Leto, I supposed, but it was hard to see how that would have helped our mission. Besides, although weird, it wasn't exactly unpleasant. I decided to accept my measure of guilt and move on. Corax seemed to sense my turmoil and put his arm around my shoulder, giving a warm squeeze. "Any sign of the lyre?" he asked.

"I didn't see it, if that's what you mean," I said. The food smelled good and I took a bite.

"What did you see?" inquired Marianne, struggling to keep a straight face.

"Too many mice," I said. I was in no mood to humor Marianne's interest in details.

"I learned a variety of things, at least one of which may be useful," said Corax. "I had a tour of Apollo's quarters, a palace in itself—as you might imagine. When his holiness is in residence, I am expected to entertain him because, don't you know, he gets frightfully bored. These immortals have so much time on their hands, they don't know what to do with themselves. I was made to understand that a bored Apollo is a dangerous Apollo. For example, he's been known to use the courtyard as target practice for his famous archery skills. With the servants, of course, as the targets."

Oizys wrinkled her nose in a rare facial expression. "Such behavior is undignified for a god." After this outburst, she went back to eating in slow motion.

"Anyway," Corax continued, "Apollo is obsessed with board games."

"Board games?" I said through a full mouth.

"That's right. He has quite an extensive collection. I didn't realize so many games even existed. Chess and draughts, of course, mancala, senet, those I've played, as well as a few card games. But who knew about something called mahjong, a game of decorated tiles from the other side of the world? Supposed to be one of his favorites. My job is to curate and master the game collection. There are a thousand of them at least! Apparently, the last curator—who was given the absurd title *Game Boy*—threw himself off the roof of the palace rather than face another defeat at mahjong.

"But... it occurred to me that if Apollo is this mad about games and I can lure him into playing something at which I have a little skill, like chess, it might be possible to distract him for a while so that the rest of you can get the lyre. We just need to know where he keeps it."

"That's something," I agreed. "Though I'm not sure how useful I'll be. I get the impression that I'm not going to get far out of Leto's sight." Suddenly anxious about being overheard, I surveyed the nearby diners in the hall, but no one seemed interested in our huddle.

Marianne grinned. "You poor thing. Desired by the gods— a terrible fate. I do think Rosemary and Thyme may learn a few things, though. The weavers are mostly old women. They gossip nonstop and my guess is that if they know anything, it'll come out. There's a dormitory connected to the weaving works, so we'll be around them day and night. And no one watches us. There's a head weaver who hands out assignments, but it looks as if one can come and go at will. Sometimes, one of the advantages of being a woman is that we tend not to be noticed—we're just part of the backdrop. It also looks like the four of us may be the only current servants to come through the slave market. From what I heard, employment in the temple is a coveted position. The work is easy, the accommodations are clean, and the food is excellent. The hard jobs are the ones you two have—being playmates for the divine. Supposedly the twins—those Dioskouroi—don't hang on to their playmates very long; they use them up in sadistic rituals. Or at least that's what the weavers say."

"The sooner we get out of here, the better," I said. "Of course, now we have no money so I'm not sure how we buy our passage off the island. Maybe we can steal a boat. I don't see how that makes us any worse thieves than taking the lyre."

Marianne looked smug. "You don't think I'm that simple as to put all the funds in one place? What kind of a woman do you take me for?"

"O thank you! I needed some good news."

Servants finished their meals and wandered out of the hall. I sighed at the prospect of returning to Leto's chambers. "Oh, Corax, before we separate, let me give you some lithium. With all our stress, I might need some myself."

"No thanks," he said.

"Don't do this to me," I pleaded.

"Look, I've got a thousand games to study. I need the energy; I need the drive. I need to be at the full height of my powers! This is no time for Mister Mellow. I've got a god to wrangle!"

His eyes showed a spark of that hungry gusto that forecast mania. "Please." I knew that I was pathetically begging him; that once again I ignored the wisdom of Tiresias to let things alone, but wisdom travels an irregular journey and it still had a ways to go. "We need you to keep it together," I begged.

Oizys stared at me with solemn gray eyes. "He'll be okay," she said. I don't know where she got her authority on this matter, but it brought our conversation to an end. The hall was empty but for the cleaning crew, so it was past time to return to our stations. I hugged Corax and we all agreed to meet again over breakfast.

I dragged leaden feet up the stairs. When I came to Leto's chamber, I walked softly past the entrance, stealing myself for the call of her saccharine voice: *Oh, Parsley!* No sound emerged and I made it safely to my room. I closed the door and inspected the bath. A shallow tile basin offered two spigots. One provided a thin flow of cold water, no doubt fed by gravity from the mountain above the city. The other was scalding hot and reeked of minerals from a geothermal source. I mixed the water in a bucket and sat naked in the basin, sponging off the stale sweat and whatever else was left over from the session with Leto.

The room was sparse but clean. Two sets of clothing lay neatly on the bed. I preferred desert robes, but the local style was practical and flattering for those who wanted to flaunt. Given my new status as a subjugated sex toy, the latter attribute was hardly a plus. However, I was too tired to give much thought to the concerns of apparel and I shoved the clothes to one side and fell asleep on the bed.

I awoke in the dark to a clanging noise. Jumping off the mattress, I realized that it was the sound of Leto's bell, somehow magnified within my ear to decibel-crushing volume. Another perquisite of limitless divine power, I guessed. To what greater purpose all this magic tended, I failed to comprehend. But power always provided its own justifications, as I well knew, so I promptly trotted to Leto's chamber.

"Good," she observed, "you're ready to go. I think we're getting on wonderfully, Parsley, don't you? Now pick a mouse."

We followed a similar script during this encounter. I whispered more fawning hyperbole into the mice conduit, and it was received on the other end with glee. I vowed to write a text on getting along with the gods—first axiom: flattery was always welcome and did not require originality. Our verbal overtures segued into repetition of the postures we had practiced in the afternoon, with only minor innovations. I was drained beyond all reserve, but I hung on until she was satisfied, at least for the moment. Then we lay next to each other and watched the mice use our bodies for gymnastics. One was adept at climbing my raised knee and somersaulting down the thigh to land upright on my belly. Leto laughed at this.

"Aren't they adorable? Oh, Parsley, I needed that!" she said. "My son arrives in the morning and I'll have to dote on him constantly. At least until he gets tired of it, which is never very long. It's hard being a mother, I tell you."

"Apollo?"

"I have no other son. He was born here, you know, on this island."

"I didn't know that." I lied. I'd heard the story but hoped that she would talk more and reveal something useful.

"It's pleasant enough on this tiny island, but it's well off the beaten path. I would have preferred living in a more urbane environment. You know, theater, festivals, shops—all that. I would have had it but for that bitch."

"Uh, which one?" It seemed to me that the world was full of bastards and bitches, especially in the divine realm. I knew who she meant, of course, but wanted to encourage her to tell me everything.

"Hera. She can't keep her man in line, not ever, but she blames the women. Go figure. Anyway, her faithless husband got me pregnant. Predictably, she proclaimed a vendetta—against me. She sent that monstrous flesh-eating snake to do her dirty work—Python. I had to drop the babies on the run. Artemis on a rock in the strait and Apollo here on Temple Island. They're both archers, you know. Once I got them out of the breach, they turned on Python and shot it so full of holes it sank to the bottom of the sea. Merely one of the reasons why I love them so much. Especially Apollo—he's just the most beautiful boy!"

I took advantage of her train of thought. "I've heard he sings and plays the lyre and does so better than anyone."

A dreamy look came over Leto's face. "You should hear him—truly divine."

"I'd love to. Is that possible, do you think?"

"Try to stop him. He insists on performing. If he's in the mood, he'll sing the complete *Iliad* in one sitting."

"Okay, good to know. And the lyre itself is remarkable, I understand."

"It is. Hermes made it himself straight out of the breech! As it happened, he crawled from the womb and spotted a wandering tortoise—you know how they get underfoot. He's such a wily one, he killed the sluggish creature, hollowed out the shell, and mounted it with strings and a frame. Before his mother could even get him latched to her teat, he strummed and sang a lovely hymn to her glory. What a clever son! However, he's also a bit of a thief and was soon forced to surrender the lyre as compensation to my own dear boy who, I dare say, has long since eclipsed the inventor in the mastery of the instrument."

"Truly remarkable. Apollo must take good care of such a precious object."

"I imagine. No one is allowed near it. But I'm sure you'll be fortunate enough to hear him play. Now go."

I slogged back to my room. Remembering Leto's admonition to stay clean, I washed again before collapsing on the bed.

[21]

At the sound of the breakfast conch, I shuffled downstairs and into the mess hall like a starving ghoul. Marianne and Oizys were sitting at the end of a table, but Corax was nowhere to be seen.

"Any word of our Games Master?" I asked as I plopped next to Marianne.

She shook her head. "No, but you'll never believe what we heard." Before she could explain, Corax entered the room, skipping and humming to himself. There was too much energy in his eyes, and I guessed that he had been awake all night.

"Ho ho!" He said as he whipped out the chair next to Oizys and seated himself with a maximum of drama and flourish. "What have we here? The merry band of plotters, no doubt!"

"Keep your fucking voice down," hissed Marianne.

Corax looked offended for a moment, then grinned. "Well, excuse me, Madam Who-Put-You-In-Charge. But I'll have you know that I've mastered fifty games since we last shared a table. I'm ready to take on all comers, even the gods!"

"Fifty games?" I said dubiously.

"At least," he replied. "Maybe more. Some of them are quite complicated or I probably could have learned a hundred! My favorites are the ones that stage mock historical battles in a distant future or some alternate reality. The conceits are outlandish, as you can tell by the names: *Gettysburg*, *Blitzkrieg*, *Axis and Allies,* and my favorite, *Stalingrad*. They come with cast metal playing pieces that suggest weaponry of imaginary technology. I have no idea where he got ahold of these bizarre creations."

"Well, he is a god," I speculated. "Matters of time and space present few limitations, as Tiresias explained. Did you learn anything about the lyre?"

An expression of disappointment crossed his face. "God, no. I've been busy with these damned games!"

"I learned a few things from Leto, who was chatty in the middle of the night. His Lordship insists on performing with the lyre when he's at home. Since he prefers large, favorable audiences, chances are good that we'll be drafted for places in the adoring crowd. I don't think we'll wait long for this treat, because he's supposed to arrive today."

Corax showed panic. "But I haven't learned all the games yet!"

Marianne picked her teeth with one of her knives. "Good," she said.

"Where did you get that?" I asked, pointing at the knife.

"I got my stuff back. No one seems to care about weapons, flight risk, or any of that. Astonishing how casual it is here. Perhaps because it's owned and operated by immortals, they have nothing to lose. It's like they can't be bothered with petty concerns and anything to do with mortals is petty by definition. Why worry about runaways when there's no shortage of people anxious to get an assignment here? But enough of that. Oizys and I learned where he keeps the lyre."

"What?" I said.

Corax stopped gnawing at his fingernails long enough to ask the relevant question. "Where?"

Marianne chuckled and even Oizys paused her turtle's-pace breakfast to smile. "It turns out that both of your questions are relevant," Marianne said. "As for *where*, it moves around the slopes of the mountain above the city. As for *what*, Apollo has transformed it into a singing goat."

"Ridiculous," said Corax.

"I'm going to agree with you on that. So, how hard is it to poach a goat?" I mused.

"No one would dare," said Marianne. "Everyone knows about it, but nobody wants to offend Apollo; he's their bread and butter here. Besides, it wears a magical bell that sets off an alarm if anyone so much as touches the goat."

"An itty-bitty bell?" sneered Corax.

"Don't scoff," I said. "Leto uses something like that. When it goes off, it's like your brain explodes—distance is no object."

Oizys stopped chewing. "No bell rings in the shade of Lethe."

"What in the name of maddening metaphors is that supposed to mean?" demanded Corax.

"Lethe is my niece," answered Oizys. "We have shared secrets."

I picked at my beard, anxious about the conversation. The twitching in his face informed me that Corax was gearing up for a sarcastic assault on our depressed goddess. Before the impending explosion, Marianne intervened. "Back off, madman. I've been getting to know our companion while you've been playing games. She's subtle but sharp. Is patience even in your skill set at all? My guess is that she can handle the bell—that's what she's saying. If you want to concern yourself with something, consider this: once again it will be women doing the actual work while you two look pretty and kiss ass. So, don't worry about the bell, okay? If you want to obsess about something, think about getting us out of here and back to the Island of Marble. Because when the time comes, I'm pretty sure we're going to need a brisk getaway."

"There is that," I agreed. "Anyway, sounds like we have a plan. Corax and I will do our best to keep the gods distracted and you two will fetch the lyre. Simplicity itself."

"Funny man," said Marianne.

"If Apollo is as obsessed with playing this instrument as his mother says, I think we'll probably see it soon enough."

The words left my mouth and hung in the air for a moment before being swept away by the music of plucked strings reverberating throughout the palace. The sound carried a purity of tone that slipped into the ears like loving whispers, music that filled the body and emerged in the gleam of the eyes. Without a word, everyone in the dining hall, staff included, stopped what they were doing and filed through the doorway into the courtyard. Except for Corax, who put his head in his hands and slumped over the table. I hoisted him upright and we joined the crowd.

We caught our first sight of Apollo posed on the balcony. In his arms, he held the famous lyre with its tortoise-shell body and oak frame. Next to him stood Leto, bursting with unmistaken pride. On the other side and slightly behind were the Dioskouroi, nudging each other and acting like louts. Apollo outshone them all. A true golden boy, his skin glowed with surreal intensity. His hair hung in long, curly locks the color of straw. He flipped a wayward tress over one shoulder with a twitch of his head, and at least two female servants required a

prop to keep from swooning. He smiled, piercing the expect-
ant atmosphere as the sun drives through storm clouds, chasing
away the rain. I knew that many men and women would grovel
for a touch or a taste of his beauty. Impressive, yet repulsive,
I thought. I'd never been drawn to gaudy objects, unlike the
magpies of the world. Beneath the shiny façade, it wasn't hard
to sense the emptiness of being. He represented a vacuum that
sucked up life, feeding on the vitality of other souls.

When the entire household, a hundred strong, stood in the
courtyard at his feet, he launched into a lively tune on the lyre.
As soon as the melody lodged in our bones, he began to sing,
and the words fell over us with sweetness. He was good, I gave
him that. Many of the bards of my homeland would die for his
skill. A few, though, honed by their incessant contests, would
quickly put him in the shade.

"Apollo sprang forth to the light, and all the goddesses screamed."
He sang about himself in the third person, a privilege reserved
for divinities, royalty, and narcissists. As he ended the first line,
on cue, several younger women shrieked and squealed with joy.

> *"Then, noble one, the goddesses bathed you pure and clean*
>
> *With water fresh and swaddled you in a white sheet,*
>
> *Fine and new-woven and round you they wrapped a*
> *golden band.*
>
> *Nor did his dear mother nurse the lord Apollo,*
>
> *But Themis poured him nectar and lovely ambrosia*
>
> *With her immortal hands, and Leto rejoiced*
>
> *For giving birth to a mighty son who carries the bow."*

Leto beamed at her son, ignoring the put-down in the lyrics where he revealed that his mother didn't nurse him but handed him over to someone else who poured honey down his gullet instead. The sharpness of my observation surprised me, but I decided it was a reaction to the unbearable narcissism of the god and his performance. He tipped and swayed to emphasize certain words like *mighty* and *noble*, and at every gesture, someone else swooned. I studied the audience and tried to understand how the treacly performance served to transport them to ecstasy. Perhaps they were feigning enthusiasm to curry favor. Certainly, Apollo could sing and play the lyre with skill, but he was still a dandy. No wonder Corax's hard-edged agnosticism had pissed him off, even at a distance. This was not a deity open to challenge or authentic reflection.

I turned to see Corax's reaction to the spectacle. His squinted eyes aimed straight at Apollo, an expression I recognized as a sizing of the opponent. It wouldn't be long, I imagined, before they would be locked in gameboard duels. Hopefully, Corax would keep quiet about his career as a philosopher. If Apollo remembered that he had already found reason to curse Corax, this time he might just disintegrate him, like one terminates a pesky mosquito. He might not remember, though. Apollo struck me as someone who never thought much about anything, except himself in the present tense.

Apollo finished singing, flashed one exaggerated wave to the applauding audience, and retired in triumph. Leto saw me in the crowd and threw a kiss. As everyone turned to stare, I blushed. Leto curled her finger at me, calling me to her side as she left the balcony in the direction of her quarters.

"I guess it's time to go to work. Good luck, dear," I said to Corax and gave him a hug.

"Tonight," Marianne whispered as she brushed past. "We're going after it. Hang in there."

I sighed and braced myself for Leto and her peculiar notions of teamwork.

[22]

The bell went off in my head before I made it to Leto's room. It was still clanging when I went through the door, giving me a full-bore headache. Never mind how I felt, Leto and the mice required instant attention and quite a bit of it. When we finally came to a rest, she wanted to talk.

"How lucky for you to see my son and hear him sing and play, just as you'd hoped! Isn't he a wonder?"

"Yes, ma'am, he shines, there's no other way to put it."

"Oh, doesn't he? He's a god among gods! So like his father!"

"Yes, ma'am, a wonder. No doubt about it."

She frowned. "Though you'd think he'd find more time for his mother, wouldn't you? He's been gone for ages, just got back, and all he wants to do is run off to his den with that gnome friend of yours and play games! Humph!"

"A mother is never truly appreciated, ma'am," I offered.

"You do understand! Few men do. Aren't you something? I love how you appreciate me, dear Parsley!" This led to more snuggling and dancing of mice over torso landscapes. I spent the rest of the day either playing with Leto or listening to her babble about her son. This monologue contained excessive praise for the god blended with forlorn complaints, on and on, punctuated by bouts of tears and the occasional brief, support-ive comment from me as I tried to salve her moods.

When I heard the bellow of the dinner conch, I extricated myself and fled to the mess hall. Marianne and Oizys were at the table, but no Corax.

326

"Look at it this way," Marianne said, "perhaps he's so successful at distracting Apollo that he can't get away for mundane concerns like food. That bodes well, to my mind. If you want the optimistic view."

I grumbled and felt helpless within my pessimism. Marianne informed me that the women planned to sneak out of the palace after dark. There was still a good slice of the moon at night, so they would search the mountain to find the singing goat. I wondered how we would transform the goat back into a lyre, or if we could deliver it as is and let Dionysos do his own damn transformation. It occurred to me that a lyre would probably be easier to transport than a goat, but I was too tired to figure out the flaws in the plan. The revels with Leto had left a powerful apathy lodged in my bones. Fortunately, Marianne seemed unaffected by the atmosphere of the palace. Quite the opposite. She radiated energy. Even Oizys caught a little of her glow and ventured a smile now and then as she ate.

"By the way," said Marianne, "I confirmed what I suspected: the port is a major hub. Ships put in often and some even go on to the Island of Marble. I probably have enough coin to buy our way onto a boat. Admittedly, many of them are slavers, but they'll take paying travelers as well. Most are relatively honest according to the ladies in the weaving works; at least most of them aren't pirates, so it seems such a voyage wouldn't bring a new set of problems."

"Perhaps you've forgotten that—at this point—we *are* slaves. I'm not sure how we change that status and buy our way onto a boat like free folk."

"True. I guess we'll cross that bridge when we come to it. There's always the run for our lives option."

"I'm not sure how viable an option that is. Wouldn't they just disintegrate us with a lightning bolt or something?"

Oizys managed another smile. "That doesn't happen in real life, you know," she said.

"Which part?" I replied. "The part about the cosmos-shaking powers of the gods or some other part?"

"The lightning part. There are plenty of threats and posturing and sometimes weapons are drawn, but I don't think anyone really gets blasted out of space. Not since the old days, anyway. Skewered by spears—that's the more common fate."

"I'm certainly reassured," I said, laying on the sarcasm because I was too discouraged to care.

"Anyway, Diarmuid," continued Marianne, "has it occurred to you that things keep falling into place a little too neatly?"

"Neatly? You mean now that we're slaves?"

"No, look. You two had been spinning wheels for months, then as soon as I show up—and I'm not saying this is about me—we meet Manto, find Tiresias, get enlightened, and pointed in a new direction where we meet an ancient goddess who loans us her daughter. Things seemed to go south with the pirates, but not only did they expedite our journey to Temple Island, they also set us up to get close to the lyre. Corax has Apollo's ear, you have Leto's, I'm beginning to think Mother Nyx was right. It feels like a script."

"If so, it's full of holes."

Corax never showed up for dinner. Marianne and I argued about nothing for a while, and I finally trooped back to my room. I waited for Leto's bell, but I heard nothing. Another bath and I fell asleep on the bed, too tired to fret any more about our plight.

I woke with a start before dawn, drenched in sweat. It wasn't the bell this time, just the anxious drama of my mind. I had dreamed that Corax and I lay in a secluded grove of oak trees where we made love with the wild joy of our early couplings. At the height of passion, a curtain rose to reveal an eager and excited audience. I ran off stage in embarrassment and tried to hide under a table, only to be found by Leto, the director, who screamed at me about following the script, lashing me with the stinging blows of her tongue, back and forth. I cringed and writhed but couldn't get away. In a panic, I started flailing and exploded out of the dream.

There would be no going back to sleep after that, so I rinsed off in the bath and dressed, thinking to get an early cup of tea in the dining room. I wondered if Marianne had the lyre yet. I shuffled down to the kitchen as quietly as I could, thinking how tired I was, how ready to move beyond this part of the world and its strange cast of characters. Stimulating and complex, sure, but I longed for a sedate environment, one more suitable to contemplation, which was all I knew how to do very well. If we got out of this predicament, I would urge Corax to leave the region and its interfering gods in favor of a home where deities were merely concepts and not actors. If such a place could be found.

The bakers working in the kitchen agreed to let me brew up some mountain tea if I stayed out of the way. I dodged around their bustle, then took the steaming cup out in the alley and slumped onto a bench. Looking along the passage I saw a portion of Apollo's gleaming white temple with its soaring columns and classical style. I considered the significance of this grandiose structure and the god it honored. Not just Apollo, all these gods were difficult to worship. They were less principled than most mortals. Besides, what was there to worship other than raw power? As I watched the eastern sky ease into light, I thought about Oizys. Despite her moody presentation, she expressed the dignity I expected in a god. As did Mother Nyx, regardless of her breezy manner, who conveyed nurturing attention worthy of the divine. But these other characters, Apollo, Dionysos, even Leto, struck me as monsters of the psyche, somehow made real and infused with a terrible might. Maybe that's what bothered me. In these gods, the whole range of human psychic possibility embodied itself as a cast of immortals, swaggering and fretting around the world just as they do within each of our human personalities.

When we were at the Academy, Corax introduced me to the texts of the founder and I read what I could while we had access to the library. The founder wrote about "the patterns in the nature of things," which he sometimes called forms or *eidos*. What if our recent experiences were a result of Corax's damned *eidectic reduction*? By stripping away the phenomenal gloss of the world, had he exposed the truth of pure consciousness? And it was a realm of profane gods? If so, it was hardly an argument for the application of phenomenology. Unless you wanted to rub shoulders with madness.

I finished my tea and thought about going inside for another cup when I saw Marianne and Oizys hurry around the corner of the palace. I didn't know Oizys could move that fast. Marianne raised a finger in greeting, but Oizys waved with the flair of a ten-year-old. It occurred to me that another week of hanging out with Marianne and she'd be positively perky.

They sat on the bench next to me. "Well?" I asked.

"Mission accomplished," said Marianne, who looked tired.
"No bells?"

Oizys pulled down the neck of her chiton. Hanging around
her neck was a small bell. She jiggled it but no sound could be
heard.

"The dampening effect of depression," explained Marianne.

"So, there's even a use for that."

"I'm beginning to think there are more uses than you could
imagine," said Marianne. Oizys smiled.

"Where is it?" I hoped that the wonderful magic of depression had transformed the lyre into a pebble or seashell for con-
venient transport.

"Hidden near the docks. If we can find a boat today, we're
good to go."

"Well done! Dare I ask what form it's in?"

"It's not a goat, if that's what you're asking."

"I'm impressed. Did you need us, really? Your entourage of
male admirers?"

"Of course. Don't get morose; we need to get off the island.
The sooner the better."

"Agreed. I think they're serving breakfast soon. Shall we eat
and hope that Corax pries free of the gameboard?"

After we sat down to eat in the mess hall, I asked Marianne
for details about the midnight raid. She held up a finger and
attended to her hunger with another mouthful before answering. "We waited a couple of hours until the weavers were asleep,
then we left. Oizys convinced me to leave my bow, which was
hard, though I saw the sense in it. We needed to avoid the
potential commotion of combat. Anyway, it didn't take long
to get out of town. There's not much to it: a few temples, the

docks, the slave market, and residences jammed around the periphery. Beyond that, it's all fields of stone. I didn't see many crops. It's a barren island, but there's enough grass and weeds to keep livestock. Goats, especially. So, we combed the fields bit by bit. When we saw animals, we checked them out."

"How did you know what you were looking for? What is a singing goat, anyway?"

"That was my question. The weaver with the story assured me that we'd know it when we saw it. 'It's loud,' she said, 'can't carry a tune, and won't shut up.' But even with that, there are lots of fields and lots of goats up there. We used a systematic approach, walking completely around the mountain, then hiking uphill a bit and making another circuit. Painstaking, but each time the circle got smaller and we covered all the ground. The moon helped with light, but I was impressed with Oizys— she's sure-footed in the dark and never missed a step. Methodical, too. Anyway, of course, the damn goat would be near the summit."

"Goes without saying."

"We heard it before we saw it. It was bellowing some kind of folk song. Phrases like 'take me back to my country home' and that sort of thing. Not only was the tune off-key, but the goat also staggered through the rhythm. Despite the considerable gusto of its performance, I'd never in my life heard such awful singing. Caterwauling, you know? As we got closer, and this was the damndest thing, I saw that it sat on its haunches like a dog. We walked right up to it, but it kept on with the racket, segueing into another round of appalling lyrics as we approached. True to its Capricornian nature, these were obscene. I have to admit, being leered at by a goat while hearing it sing 'shake that booty baby baby,' was a new one for me."

I couldn't help laughing. Marianne frowned in disapproval before melting into a sly smile.

"I didn't know what to do, I have to confess. But Oizys did. She stepped in front of the lecherous old goat, grabbed the bell hanging around its neck, and yanked. The goat collapsed into a bag of skin; the lyre was nestled inside. As for the bell, it won't sound while Oizys keeps it on her skin."

"Impressive. Thank you, Oizys, for everything. Of course, if Apollo feels the muse and wants to play his lyre, he's going to notice its absence, eh? As soon as he's done beating the socks off Corax in board games, I'm guessing that his attention will wander. We do need to get out of here," I said.

"Precisely my opinion," said Marianne, and Oizys nodded.

[23]

An agonized scream reverberated through the palace, sounding like a cross between a banshee and a bull. Everyone in the mess hall stopped eating and looked around in alarm. The cry diminished into a series of echoing sobs that permeated the building. Before the last sounds died away, Corax skipped into the room, looking pleased with himself. His eyes were wide, he swung his arms about in wild gestures, and when he arrived at our table, he did a few dance steps, ending with a theatrical bow. He was in the grip of mania.

"You're looking at the new chess champion of the known universe," he said, adding another flourish, this time thrusting one arm straight up and setting the other cocked on his hip.

"You... won?" I asked.

Marianne didn't wait for his answer. "Sit down, you fool! You're drawing far too much attention."

Corax ignored her, so I stood up and pushed him down into a seat. "The lady said sit, dammit."

I thought he was on the verge of throwing a punch, but when he saw Marianne rising from her chair with a furious expression, something shifted, and he opted for words. "Bah! You don't know who you're talking to. You lucky mortals are looking at the man who beat Apollo. No mean feat, I guarantee. And he's still whimpering! Poor, pathetic god. Didn't know what he was in for! The big man in the divinity racket, oh yeah, but not quite big enough for the Master of the Boards!"

"Calm down and tell us what happened," I insisted.

"Not much to tell." His feigned modesty was annoying, but I let it go. "If you insist..." he went on with an extravagant flourish of the hand. "Yesterday, after his lame concert, I met Apollo in the game room. I thought he was ridiculous. He lay sprawled across a garish throne draped with lion skins, twitching a foot, and drinking wine. Didn't even look at me. 'Set up a game,' he demanded. 'A new one.'

"'You bet,' I said, humble as pie, 'Do you know speed chess?' 'What? Just chess, is it not?' I could tell he knew nothing about it. 'Just chess, that's right, sir, but played with a strict time limit. Five minutes per player per game. Sand clocks keep the time; run out of sand and you lose.' Apollo yelled for someone to get us two sand clocks with the correct calibration and snarled at me to set up the board. I thought he might be pissed off already, but then I realized that petulance was his normal state."

As Corax told his story, I noticed that he dialed down the intensity a few notches. Usually, in this state, the opportunity for a monologue would only spin him to greater heights, so I puzzled over the change. Then I realized that the proximity to Oizys might be slowing him down, just as being near Apollo seems to have wound him tighter. Clearly, there was a relationship between the gods and madness.

"So, we played speed chess. Nonstop since yesterday, one game after another. Being the first to a hundred wins was the goal. Right away, he lost game after game, which made him furious. He slammed down his sand clock more than once and broke it, requiring servants to fetch another. His game lacks defense and structure, and it didn't take a lot of strategy to ravage his primitive positions. However, he does have an intuition for combinations. And he is a clever bastard. Eventually, he started to learn some tactics from my play and caught up in the tally. We proceeded through the night, back and forth, neck and neck. Servants brought wine and bowls of seeds. He drank the wine while I ate seeds and washed them down with water. I felt great; no reason to dull my wits with the booze! You'd have been proud of me!"

I didn't respond to that; with Corax, it was always one extreme or another. "And you won!" I encouraged him.

"Indeed, I did. Corax the god-killer! I took the hundredth game only minutes ago! That's why you hear the crybaby moaning upstairs. I spanked him!"

"Hmm. How many games did he win in this titanic contest?" Marianne asked.

Corax dropped his eyes and muttered. "Ninety-nine."

"Jesus, Joseph, and Mary," I said, shaking my head.

Corax started bouncing in place like a child with a full bladder. I feared he was ready to do something extreme, like jump onto the table and sing a praise hymn bragging about his triumph. With a swoosh, Leto charged into the dining room, ran up to Corax, and slapped him hard across the face. Her golden tresses crackled with life, whirling about her head like the snakes of Medusa. I caught a mouse as it flew from her hair.

"How dare you!" She yelled at Corax. "How dare you come into my house and disgrace my boy, my child, the light of my life!" She looked wildly at me, then Marianne, and finally Oizys. When her gaze landed on Oizys, the energy drained out of her. She frowned. "I feel like I know you from somewhere. Oh, maybe not." She turned back to Corax and glared at him with a honed edge. "You, ingrate, begone! By rights, I should have you disintegrated, but out of respect for this man Parsley, who somehow claims to be your friend, I will let you continue your miserable, horrid existence. Just go! Immediately!"

Marianne gave me a look that urged action. "Ma'am, mistress Leto," I beseeched, "I could not bear to be parted from him; he is my teacher!" I don't know where that came from and why I thought it might help. As part of my plea, I gave her the mouse cradled in my hand.

Leto took the mouse and tucked it into her bodice. She turned back to Corax and gave him another slap, even harder. "Very well," she said. "Out of my appreciation for your generous kisses and deep understanding of mice, dear Parsley, I will grant a boon. You say your education comes from this odious creature, which I find hard to credit, but I do think you've earned the right to learn a bit more, my sweet. So, go. The whole lot of you. Get out of here. Before I change my mind. Now I must comfort my son. If you're still here when I'm done, consider yourselves blasted." She spun majestically and stalked away.

I saw that Corax was going to yell something after her, so I clapped a hand over his mouth, snatched him in my free arm, and ran for the door. Marianne laughed, linked elbows with Oizys, and followed. In the storeroom, Marianne said that she would fetch her belongings and meet us outside. As I wrestled with the flailing Corax, I asked Oizys to grab a water flask, thinking that now would be the time to force down some lithium. We needed Corax with a level head. Luckily, I still carried the pouch of lithium salts, hanging dutifully around my neck.

I dumped Corax on the bench in the alley and forced him to drink some water with the salts. He started to protest but gave up when I lifted a fist. I was in no mood for his bullshit. Things were going our way and I didn't want him to ruin it.

Leto had dismissed us from service, which meant, as far as I understood, that we were no longer slaves. I wanted off the island before anything changed.

Marianne flew out the door with her archery bag over her shoulder. "Let's go!"

It didn't take long to walk from the temple compound to the docks. By following a few narrow passages, we took a more direct route than the chariot road. As before, the port was crowded with traffic. At least half a dozen ships were loading or unloading commerce. I winced to see a group of chained men herded toward the slave market. Dressed in skins and furs, they appeared to be nomads from the North, the type locals dismissed as barbarians.

"Who are the real barbarians," I muttered, as I watched the weary men shoved along by guards.

"Something needs to be done about that custom," Marianne said.

Oizys stopped and pointed toward the end of the wharf. "There's the *Hermetic Endurance.*"

"The what?" I asked.

"Captain Nobody's ship," she answered. She was right, there it lay, snug against the wharf. Standing at the gangplank was Nobody himself. I watched stevedores use wheeled sleds to push loads of crates from a warehouse and stack them next to the *Endurance.*

Marianne frowned. "I have a score to settle with that bastard. And those crates may be our ticket. Quick, let's get around to the back of that warehouse."

I was loath to be anywhere near the slaver, but it was clear that the ship was loading for departure and I didn't have a better idea. We retreated up the passage and turned into the alley behind the warehouses. This was the backside of the port's business, less crowded and hidden from the dockside traffic. We passed an alcove filled with junk—mostly broken amphorae that had been used for shipping in times past. Marianne ducked in the alcove, reached into an amphora with a broken top, and retrieved a skin bag.

"That's it?" I asked.

"That's it," she said. I wanted to look but thought better of it; we needed to get away from the island first. I kept glancing over my shoulder, anticipating pursuit. Marianne counted the warehouses as we passed and when we got to the right one, she ordered us to mill around by the entrance and pretend to be workers on a break. She shoved the lyre into Corax's arms and slipped into the warehouse.

From a pouch, Oizys produced a short clay tube with a flared tip. She held it between two fingers and stuffed a wad of dried herb into the large end. Both Corax and I watched in amazement as she struck a flame by snapping her fingers. She held the tube to the burning index finger and inhaled through the small end, sucking at it with hearty puffs. Once the herbs glowed steadily, she shook out the flame on her finger and resumed sucking on the tube, drawing the smoke into the depth of her lungs. Holding her breath like she was holding in the spark of life she passed the tube to me. I looked at her with an arched brow and mimed her actions with the pipe. She smiled and exhaled with a great rush of smoke on my face. Taking that as a yes, I inhaled a modest puff and quickly gave it to Corax as I bent double coughing. The pipe load of herbs burned for two more circuits of puffing and coughing for

Corax and myself. Oizys smoked it without effort. When it was empty, she knocked the ashes out of the tube, returned it to her pouch, and leaned up against the wall of the warehouse.

I felt woozy, which I attributed to inhaling smoke instead of oxygen, until I looked at Corax, who slouched with a goofy smile next to Oizys. With rare humor, she smirked, and I understood that the herb provided an altered state of consciousness. However, it seemed mild enough to allow space for my wits, so I decided not to panic. I joined the others against the wall and waited for Marianne.

She popped out before long. "Holy Kraken, are you stoned?" I grinned, which proved to be a confession. "Good grief," she continued. "Well, maybe it's for the best. Here's the deal. A load of goods from the Great City is being trans-shipped to Cornucopia, a major island to the south."

"Oh yes, Cornucopia, the nursery of Zeus and land of the ancient Minoans..." began Corax.

"Not now," snapped Marianne. "Anyway, it'll make a short stop on the Island of Marble. Apparently, the *Hermetic Endurance* often takes on legal cargo to disguise itself as a normal trader. I bribed the Shipping Master to hide us in some crates. Once on board, we can figure out what to do when we're away. But we have to move, now."

I heard her urgency, but my blood seemed to flow in slow motion. "Won't they notice the extra weight if we're in the crates?"

"Probably not. The crates are full of metal ikons and are heavy already."

"Let's hope they don't stack the crates on top of each other, then," I said. Corax giggled at the thought.

"If anyone has a better plan, let's have it," said Marianne.

No one did, so we trooped after her into the dim warehouse. She handed a bag of coins to an attendant, who led us down a corridor between the stacks of items to be shipped. He stopped in front of a coffin-sized crate, untied the knots that cinched the lids, and gestured for one of us to crawl in. He moved on to the next crate and opened it. Before we crawled into our coffins, Marianne handed each of us a knife from her extensive collection. Once we were loaded on board, we could cut the ropes through the gap under the lid to free ourselves if we had to act independently. The contents of the crates were packed in straw, but when I stretched out, the lumpy metal ikons felt like a bed of nails. After the lid was placed, I had a rush of claustrophobia, only slightly relieved by rays of light filtering through a few cracks. I pawed into the packing and clutched the familiar outlines of the Savior. Long ago, that would have provided some comfort; now, it just seemed like cold metal.

I heard more giggles from Corax in the next crate, followed by an insistent "Shh!" from the crate beyond him. I was glad for the herb. Despite the helplessness of being confined, my anxiety dissipated, and I reviewed favorite daydreams. I settled on an image of sitting in a neighborly inn, eating a bowl of steaming potato soup while watching the rain.

I heard voices. "Come on, we gotta take these, too."

"Fucking Mother-Of-Us-All, this thing's heavy."

"No shit. Religious crap again."

"Don't come no heavier."

The stevedores laughed and I felt the crate sliding, followed by a bump as it dropped onto a sled. As the sled rolled along the stone floor of the warehouse, every irregularity of the surface jarred my bones and jabbed me with ikons. I clamped a hand over my mouth lest they hear my gasps.

"You worship this junk?" Asked one of the stevedores pushing the cart.

"No way. Old school here. Give me Zeus all day, every day of the week. It's free."

"Good point. Roast a juicy animal, pretend it's for the god, then eat it."

"That there is a man's religion."

"You got that right."

There was another bump when they unloaded the crate on the dock. The voices receded as the stevedores returned to the warehouse, presumably to fetch my encased companions. Before they returned, however, I heard new voices. I recognized the gruff tone of Oruk, the first mate. He ordered crewmen to lash a sling on my box and after unfamiliar sounds of scraping and brushing on the wood, the crate tipped at one end, then the other, and with a jerk, I realized it was being hoisted on board via the boom. It crossed my mind that with one slip I'd go crashing onto the dock, the box in fragments, and me laying amidst the wreckage, impaled by ikons. I had to practically choke myself to keep the laughter down.

After a swing through the air and a rapid descent into the ship, the crate was unhitched from the boom and shoved along a deck. When it came to rest, I heard muttered curses from the crew as they walked away. I presumed this was the hold. Given the difficulty in managing the weight of the crates, I was hopeful that they wouldn't try to stack them. I lay still, not daring to move as the crew handled more cargo. From the thumps, banging, and severity of cursing, I guessed that the other crates were making their way into the hold. A foolish fever came over me and I wanted to hum a song of the old country. A jaunty ditty, suitable for skipping along a country lane. Maybe we were getting away with the lyre, after all.

[24]

It was silent and dark in the hold after they secured the hatches. Soon I felt the rolling of the sea and understood that we had left the port. I wondered how long we were supposed to lay in the crates, but I wasn't going to be the one to break the silence. I didn't have to, because I heard a tap on the lid and Marianne's softest voice as she cut through the ropes, "Coast is clear." I marveled at her stealth. I crawled out and replaced the lid while she freed Corax and Oizys. As soon as she opened Corax's crate, he started talking and she clapped a hand over his mouth and hissed. Poor man—he'd gone from mania to lithium to herb within the space of a few hours, a *pharmakon* jumble. I helped him out of the crate and gave him a hug.

We crouched behind the stern-most crate and talked in whispers.

"What now, wonder woman?" asked Corax.

"There'd better be a smile with that," she replied, "or you'll soon be wondering about a lot of things."

Corax offered a loopy smile. I was surprised he hadn't passed out from fatigue during shipment, which suggested the mania still coursed in his blood. It would probably take another dose or two of lithium to bring him down.

"This ship won't stop in the village where Nyx lives, but it makes port at the main town on the Island of Marble. I'm afraid you'll have to accompany us there, Oizys, but I promise to see you home before we're done."

344

Oizys smiled serenely. "Thank you, but I may not return home. At least, not yet. I do think I'm developing a taste for adventure!"

This speech—long for Oizys—with its hints of enthusiasm, left us amazed. Was the goddess quitting her job as the merchant of depression? "Well," I took the liberty of proclaiming, "I think I speak for all of us in saying that you're welcome to accompany us as long as you like. I mean, if you want to." It felt ridiculous, speaking that way to a goddess, but I wanted to express my appreciation for her help. And she had been no problem at all. I also had a suspicion that she provided a subtle grounding for Corax. She had an uncanny way of anticipating the utility of his labile mood states and nudging him one way or another.

"Agreed," said Marianne. "I figure it will take at least half the day to make our port, which is the first stop. If we can sit quietly here and wait until the ship docks, I believe we can rush out and get off the boat before they react. I thought about jumping into the harbor and swimming for shore, but I don't want to risk damage to the lyre. We'll have to use the gangway. But if we get on the main deck with weapons drawn, there's a chance they won't fight. We'll have them by surprise. Anyway, they already made their money off us; why risk getting killed?"

"Or," I said, "since you're the most athletic, you could take the lyre and run for it. The rest of us can jump in the harbor. That might work."

Marianne turned to Oizys. "Can you swim?"

"I think so," she said.

"I can't," added Corax.

"What? I thought you could! All that talk of beaches and seafaring and so forth…."

"Nope."

"That settles it," said Marianne. "We're taking the gangway. For now, let's hang tight. Maybe a nap, for those inclined. Still, we should keep a watch. I doubt the crew will investigate the hold, but just in case…."

"I'll watch," I volunteered. "You should rest, all of you. You've been awake since yesterday."

My companions nestled together behind a crate while I positioned myself on top so I could see the ladder to the main deck. The hatch was closed but I could hear the crew as they moved about and relayed orders. At first, the sound of oars swinging in the locks provided a regular background, but once in the open sea, oars were shipped and they hoisted a sail, or so I presumed, and ran with the wind. The swells were regular and hypnotic. The others quickly fell asleep, leaving me with the responsibility for their keeping. They resembled a pile of puppies, and as I watched over them, I felt a pang of love, followed soon enough by worry. What had Marianne said? It all seemed a bit too easy. There was enough truth in that to set me fretting. If things were too easy, pessimism demanded that there would be compensation. I clutched my knife and tried to imagine fending off a dire foe. I couldn't see it, really.

My fantasy evaporated when I heard heavy clomping on the deck. It sounded like horses, which was impossible. Shouting erupted from all parts of the ship and between the voices, distinct, I identified the unmistakable neigh of a horse. Rolling off my perch, I woke the others, who roused with groggy reluctance. Suddenly, the hatch flew open and I heard a familiar voice. "Come out, come out, wherever you are! Don't make us come down there and drag you out like trash!"

It was Castor. The Dioskouroi had chased us down.

We climbed the ladder onto the deck, blinking in the sunlight. The twins stood side by side in shimmering glory while two crewmen held their horses. I didn't understand how they had gotten here on horseback, but figured it was another god thing. A vast flock of sparrows wheeled and zoomed around the ship before settling on the rigging. Captain Nobody and Oruk glared at us, yet they couldn't conceal their expressions of amazement.

"You!" accused the Captain.

Oruk tugged at Nobody's arm. "I said so, Captain. These aren't normal folk. We're well above our paygrade here."

"Shut up," snarled the Captain.

"Fuck you," said Marianne, joining the discourse.

"Such marvelous chatter," interrupted Castor, "I'm sure we could go on for days. But I believe you have something that doesn't belong to you. Hand it over now and your death will be swift and painless. Otherwise, you'll hand it over later—after incredible agony and suffering. Most people select option A." His smirk glowed with divine energy.

Corax spoke with resurgent mania. "Bah. Why sully your divine dignity with barbaric threats? Why not, instead, a contest worthy of your stature? Why not a competition for the lyre?"

"Ooh," said Pollux, clearly pleased, "our own little Olympiad! I wouldn't mind a little fun before we kill them."

Castor frowned. "You do know that we could just take the lyre? I'm not sure how you imagine there is a contest here."

Corax puffed himself up. "You're talking to the mere mortal that stuffed Apollo less than twenty-four hours ago! Oh, I'm sure there's a contest to be had. And I've heard you two love a contest." Corax had a sly look, but I couldn't tell what he had in mind. The twins surely would want to compete in the realm of physical prowess, where it was impossible to imagine getting the best of them. Based on the volume and pressure of Corax's speech, it seemed that the lithium had lost the contest with his mania. "Come on, name your specialties," he ranted. "What are you good at—if anything? Name it and we'll take you on. Or maybe you're afraid of losing?"

"Alternately, we could just give them the lyre and beg for mercy," I suggested.

Corax looked at me with disdain. "Come now, boy, hitch up your britches. We can take them!"

Pollux stepped forward. "I love a contest. Even an unfair one. There's something satisfying about pummeling the shit out of big-mouthed louts. I've taken five golds at the Olympics in boxing. Put 'em up."

Corax shuffled his feet and took a few jabs at the air. Perhaps his victory in speed chess had scrambled his wits. No, it was the mania, glowing with grandiosity beyond all reason. I felt my heart leap into my throat, thinking that his death was certain. We had our conflicts, sure, but I loved him anyway. As a cavalcade of panic rushed through my thoughts, Marianne stepped forward, grabbed Corax by the shoulders, and shoved him behind her. Hands on hips, she stared at Pollux. "If you're fighting anyone, it's me."

Pollux didn't like that. "As a rule, I don't fight women. What's the point?"

Marianne went for the jugular. "Because if you lose, it's a humiliation you can never overcome. Same as all men."

Pollux tightened his lips and squinted. "Impertinent bitch! You wouldn't be able to take a single punch!"

"You'll have to land it, little man. Or do you intend to knock me out with *that*?" She pointed straight at his penis and sneered.

The captain and his crew backed to the gunnels as Pollux stomped and bellowed. Castor, laughing, used his spear to gouge out a large circle on the deck planks. As he did so, I saw Nobody wince and raise his hand, then drop it without a word. Who would be dumb enough to interfere with the business of the gods?

Pollux hurled his spear at the mast and screamed, apparently a signal he was ready for battle. The spear shaft vibrated with a loud thrum as the tip went deep in the mast. Marianne rolled her eyes and unstrapped the infinity of knives from her waist, thigh, and ankles. She handed them to me and shrugged. I wanted to hug her, but it didn't seem like the proper encouragement. Instead, I tried to look nonchalant, though inside I assumed that we would witness a battering to the death.

She stepped into the ring and waited, tall and composed. Pollux entered from the opposite side, skipping in place, and rolling his shoulders. Marianne smoothly separated her feet and brought her hands together in that odd prayer-like gesture, bowing slightly to her opponent. Pollux looked at her in surprise, then shrugged and charged across the ring, one arm cocked back, ready for the killing blow. Marianne dropped into a crouch, ducking well under the swing. She popped up as he went past and shoved him high in the back, adding to his momentum. Pollux stumbled out of the ring and fell on the deck.

"Hmm," said Castor. "One point for the woman."

Pollux yelled and pounded the deck with his fists. He charged back into the ring, running straight at Marianne, who stood quietly in the center. I allowed a spark of hope. She had uncommon fighting skills. They were subtle, devious, and contrary to all the known methods.

Pollux came at her with a high feint, but delivered a low roundhouse aimed at where her head would be if she crouched again. Instead, she leaped into the air while kicking up with one leg, landing a jaw-cracking slam to Pollux's chin. He staggered, giving her time to spin behind him off her landing and drive another kick to his lower back, pushing him out of the ring.

"Two points," noted Castor. "Match point."

"That's not boxing!" complained Pollux.

"True," said Marianne, panting. Yet her eyes gleamed. This was who she was, I thought.

Corax was gleeful. "Hand to hand fighting. No weapons. A mortal woman versus a god. Are you saying it's not a fair fight?"

Pollux pounded his feet on the deck. As he did so, the timbers groaned, and I thought Captain Nobody was going to faint.

This time Pollux entered the circle cautiously, weaving and jabbing. Marianne ducked his blows, occasionally deflecting them with the back of her arm or a palm. She made it look easy, but the darkening bruises on her skin acknowledged the price. They circled each other and I saw that Pollux was trying to get the measure of this strange combat. I imagined that he looked for the one-shot attack that would nail this slippery, pesky creature who danced out of reach. Despite her skill, I feared for Marianne. The powerful fists of Pollux sucked the air out of space; even a glancing contact could kill her. I had to remind myself to breathe as I watched the two circle and test. At some point, I realized that I was biting the back of my hand. Abandoning what little patience is given to the gods, finally, the furious Pollux leaped at Marianne, outstretched hands aimed at her throat. She threw herself onto her back and as Pollux flew over, she delivered a powerful kick to his groin. He crumpled into a screaming ball while Marianne rolled out of reach.

"Enough of this," said Castor. "Match over. My turn. Let's try a different specialty, like taming horses." He stared at Marianne as she gulped air. "I'm going to ride you, you bitch, till you're broken."

To my surprise, Oizys stepped in front of Marianne. "Let her rest; she's earned it. If you are to ride at all, you must ride me. But I doubt you can."

Castor's eyes narrowed to slits as he contemplated this new phenomenon: a thin, moody-looking girl daring his prowess. Castor was a formidable opponent in the martial realm, no doubt, but Oizys contained dark energy beyond the influence of muscle and sinew. If it suited her, she could swallow us all in a moment.

"Very well," replied Castor. "First you, then the other one."

Oizys turned her back to Castor, bent at the waist, and flipped up her chiton to reveal long legs and narrow hips. Placing her palms on the deck in front of her, she swayed slightly back and forth, displaying her bare bottom. Everyone on the boat stared, transfixed. Surely this was not what was meant by a *tamer of horses*, I thought. Castor appeared to be satisfied with the challenge for he had grown tumescent. I winced, sure that he would tear her apart.

Grinning, Castor stepped forward and seized Oizys by the hips, preparing to mount. He got no further. As soon as he touched her, a bone-chilling moan rushed from his throat. He stood behind her, frozen in place. At the same time, the mast sprouted branches growing swiftly along the rigging and scattering sparrows in a panic. The gunwales pulled free of the hull, sending shoots like whips across the deck, winding around Castor, Pollux, and the crew. Every scrap of wood in the boat sprang to life, animated with new growth, runners, twigs, and leaves slithering and waving like the tentacles of the holy kraken. Only Oizys, Marianne, Corax, and I were untouched, other than the occasional caress of a leaf as a branch snaked by.

Castor and Pollux, trussed in vine-cages, were chucked overboard by the arms of the living ship. Their horses were herded into the sea. Rather than sinking, they galloped off at great speed across the waves. Oizys watched the proceedings as she smoothed her chiton and patted herself back into place. She glided over the writhing deck to where Captain Nobody and Oruk were bound to the tree that used to be the mast.

"See Captain, I told you so," Oruk babbled. "We should have freed them right away. Stuff of the gods, I'm telling you."

"Whatever, Oruk," replied Nobody. "I'm a pirate; it's what I do."

In a spurt of growth, the branches holding Captain Nobody enclosed him completely in twigs and leaves, contracting forcefully into a ball of vegetation. The branches opened and slithered back into their matrix. Nothing remained of the captain.

"One less pirate," Oizys noted. She pointed at Oruk. "You're in charge. I'll free the crew if you'll get us to port on the Island of Marble."

"Yes, ma'am. Absolutely, your highness, anything you say."

The vines loosened around the crew and they jumped to Oruk's commands while the vegetation withdrew into the woodwork, and the ship resumed its normal appearance. The three of us stood in the center of the boat and watched in awe. Once the ship was underway, Oizys strolled back to our circle. Simultaneously, we fell to our knees in front of her.

"Goddess," I murmured, "thank you." I kissed the hem of her dress, not knowing what else to do.

"Enough of that. Let's not let a little power spoil our friendship. Say, I've worked up a bit of an appetite. Shall we eat?" She removed her small pack. I suppose she'd worn it the whole time, though it clung so closely to her back that it looked like an extension of her clothing. Laying it on the deck, she pulled the laces on the sides and unfolded it. As each fold opened, the pack expanded in size until it was a pannier filled with cheese, bread, olives, wine, and fruit. My mouth watered as I gazed on the feast. Even if it was magical food, it smelled of delicious reality.

After a bit, Corax winked at Oizys. "Neat trick with the vines and all. Seems very Dionysian."

Oizys smiled. "You're thinking of the story of Dionysos and the pirates, I'm sure. Actually, I taught him how to do that."

"No shit," Corax said. He stared at her as if he might say more. I recognized the look as belonging to his mood of skeptical inquiry, a mood expressed in a barrage of questions that either led to an argument, bad feelings, or both. He let it drop, whatever was on his mind, and I breathed a sigh of relief.

Oizys spit an olive pit into her palm and held it out for us to see. The pit sprouted roots that penetrated the skin of her hand while a stem broke out of the seed and grew into a miniature tree. We watched transfixed as the tree developed through an entire life cycle within minutes, finally withering away in decay and dissipating into the flesh of her hand, if her hand could be called flesh. She smiled. "People get the wrong idea about depression. It's not all bad. There is power there—the power of the earth."

Corax looked at Oizys with open admiration, skepticism banished, at least for the moment. I wished that we could take her with us, she had such a beneficent effect on him. We all admired her. Marianne was smitten once again, that was obvious, and for myself, well, the more I knew her the more I saw that she was a soulful companion, although undeniably strange.

The pirates sailed the ship, kept their distance, and gave us no trouble. We spent most of the voyage watching an escort of dolphins leaping and frisking in the wake of the bow. Marianne leaned over the gunwale, clicking and moaning to them in their language. When asked what had been said, she only smiled. Within a few hours, we pulled into port at the Island of Marble. As we disembarked, Oizys informed Oruk that he and his crew were free to pursue their desires, although she recommended an early retirement from piracy lest they share the fate of their former captain. We stood on the dock and watched the *Hermetic Endurance* sail away.

"Probably not enough time to hike up to Tiresias and Manto," I pointed out. "But Aristotle will put us up. I could use some rest."

Marianne smirked. "Has Leto drained your fiber, you poor thing?"

"Hey, we all had parts to play. I played mine."

Corax laughed, then narrowed his eyes. "Speaking of parts, we never have resolved whether this is all a play or what in Hades is going on." He turned to Oizys. "Being our field expert on divine influence, what do *you* think? Any insights for foolish mortals?"

Pointing over her shoulder at her pack, Oizys said, "If you want hot food, I can do that. Penetrating the secrets of other gods, though, that's another matter. Because of who he is, Dionysos permeates all things; his influence is everywhere. So, yes, it's not impossible; it could be a play."

Corax sighed and shrugged. "A definite maybe, then. Whatever. For now, I'm with Diarmuid. Let's go to the inn. Maybe you'd like your back massaged?" He gave me a wink that melted right through all my stored resentment.

Marianne linked arms with Oizys while Corax led the way, bearing the lyre in its goat-skin, and we strutted along the wharf and up the hill to the Inn of Pure Reason.

[25]

Aristotle beamed as we filed into the dining room. Waving us to a table, he brought out bowls of pork in wine sauce stewed with potatoes and peppers, which earned universal praise. Oizys ate little but agreed that the *stifatho* revealed a skillful use of ingredients. She continued to socialize with enthusiasm, extending small flirtations to Marianne and enigmatic smiles to me. As we ate, Corax bantered with the three of us, but it wasn't long before he stopped conversing and launched into a loud recitation of his chess triumph over Apollo. The boasting was sometimes clever, but the increasing pressure and volume of his delivery incited my worry about his mood. There was too much animation in his manner, and I could sense the mania around the corner. I insisted that he drink lithium water rather than wine. He grudgingly agreed but vowed he would bring out the lyre to demonstrate its divine tones for Aristotle, "the world's greatest innkeeper." A simultaneous and emphatic "No!" from the three of us took him by surprise. I agreed that Aristotle deserved all honors, but it seemed presumptuous and possibly dangerous for a brazen display of our prize. Corax sulked but dropped the idea.

I watched Oizys stroke Marianne's forearm as it rested on the table. When Oizys noticed my attention, she put her free hand on my shoulder and caressed down my back, coming to rest lightly on my hip. Nervous, I glanced at Corax, who ignored us and resumed his move-by-move broadcast of the best games against the god, this time aiming it over his shoulder at Aristotle tending the bar. Marianne appeared mesmerized by Oizys' touch and looked at me as if through dreamy gauze. Where had this bold new Oizys come from? If she had started as a hesitant vegetable, she had grown into willowy, blooming eros. Her hand on my hip radiated a cool sensation much like a dip in the water of a deep spring. I expected to feel moisture, but our contact remained dry even as a flow of desire made its way toward my heart. Yet the desire had no fire; it contained only the impressions of dark rainy nights and prolonged slumber, like the eros of the underworld. It was unnerving in every way. I worried that Corax might be jealous, although he rarely acknowledged such irrationalities. How he could ignore what was happening at the table was beyond me. He twisted in his chair, talking at Aristotle, who listened with dutiful patience; I can't imagine what he was thinking. Well, he said that he always gave us the benefit of the doubt because he had a soft spot for philosophers and their Sisyphean travails, bless his soul.

Oizys withdrew her hand from my hip and focused on Marianne. With a touch of precise delicacy, she traced the kraken tattoo on Marianne's arm, following it from the back of her hand along the hard muscles of her forearm, curling around the elbow and up to the shoulder. Marianne shuddered and I imagined what she was feeling. Maybe we were all a bit loose after our escape from Temple Island. I had the sudden urge to whisk Corax up to bed. And since there was no reason not to, I did, stumbling out of my chair, grabbing one of his gesturing hands, and dragging him after me. He jabbered on for a while about chess, but I soon made him stop.

When I awoke the next morning, I slipped out of our room, closing the door behind me, leaving Corax to his slumber. The stress of the last few days had entangled him in knots, and it was only after heroic love-making that he collapsed into the usual snores. I blinked at the sun, already well above the horizon and promising to bake the earth without mercy. Marianne sat at the table on the terrace and stared across the rooftops of the town, drinking in the expanse of sea beyond the harbor. Her expression was composed, and I sensed that it required some effort on her part. I sat next to her, putting a hand on her shoulder. She covered my hand with hers.

"She's gone," Marianne said softly.

"Gone?"

"Disappeared. When I awoke, she had left, and taken her things. I asked Aristotle if he'd seen her leave, but he had not. Just… thin air." She shook her head. Her face showed a careful neutrality, belied only by tears trickling down her cheeks. Marianne was an intense woman, ruthlessly self-disciplined and averse to displays of vulnerability. I understood, though, that she paid a price for that level of control. I didn't want to see her pain. If she couldn't wrestle it into submission, how would I? But, of course, being who I was, I wanted to make things better.

"I'm sorry," I said. "She seemed like a nice one. You know, for a goddess." Once again, I had found the lamest thing to say. Perhaps Marianne would take it in the spirit of good intention. Apparently, it was good enough because she turned to me with a sudden hug, burrowing her face into my chest.

"You have no idea," she sobbed.

I had never seen Marianne so distraught. Contending thoughts tumbled around in my head while I held her and stroked her hair. As a friend, I wanted to comfort her, but as a dependent on her competence, sudden insecurities clamored for my attention. Who would protect us if our champion needed protection? Who were these gods and how had they penetrated so far into the essence of who we were, spreading their chaos? Or perhaps, as with Corax's archetypes, they had been there all along and we had finally learned how to see them. Marianne sat up and with a laugh, wiped the coursing trails of weeping from her face.

"Thanks," she said. "You're a good friend."

With a warm glow, I went downstairs and placed an order for breakfast. Aristotle soon brought it to the terrace: a platter of fruit, ring bread, honey pastries, and cheese. Marianne applied herself to the food with deadly intent. I recognized the compulsion. Eating was an inviting displacement for emotions; it often gave me the perfect distraction from troubles, at least for a while. Remembering that this was the day we would deliver the lyre, I barged into the bedroom and woke Corax, dragging him off the mattress. Grumbling and batting at my hands, he managed to get dressed and tacitly agreed to join the day.

We finished breakfast in silence. Corax grunted when I told him about the disappearance of Oizys, as if he had expected it. He picked idly at the food, but I couldn't wait for him to feed himself by accident. Drumming my fingers on the table, all I could think about was the endgame of our quest and being done with the curse. Unable to contain myself any longer, I blurted. "You know, getting rid of the lyre before Apollo's minions make another play for it strikes me as prudent. As soon as we get the lyre to Manto and Tiresias, like they said, they'll see that it gets to Dionysos. At any rate, it'll be out of our hands. Let's get on with it. Then we can leave this place and go home."

As soon as I said the word, I remembered that we had no home, so we'd have to figure something out about that. At least we'd have the freedom to choose, a welcome change from being bound to the limited horizon of addiction and madness or stage directions or whatever other godly whims controlled us.

"Makes sense to me," Marianne said. "Come on, grumpy, time to march."

I stuffed the lyre into a pack and gave it to Corax while I loaded myself with food, and Marianne brought the usual array of weapons. As we left town, Corax dawdled like a recalcitrant child. When I urged him to step up the pace, he suggested that we should just pawn the lyre, catch the next boat to the City of Philosophers, and from there, work our way west again. He was certain that he could live with the curse, after all.

I glanced at him to see if he was making a joke, but I couldn't tell, which told me enough. "Let's assume you're trying to be funny. Otherwise, we'd have a problem."

Marianne, clearly in a foul mood, sneered at Corax. "Maybe we should just pawn you."

"Joking!" he said, but I wasn't convinced.

A few hours later, we climbed the last incline of road and arrived at the hut of Tiresias and Manto. The old seer sat in his chair under the sheltering plane tree, staff in hand, staring into the unknown layers of the universe.

"Ho ho," he called as we approached the patio, "familiar faces, it seems!"

His choice of terms struck me as curious, implying that he recognized our faces, but I was exhausted from unpeeling layers of significance; let Corax deal with it. "Yes, Master Tiresias," I said, "we've returned with the lyre of Apollo!"

"No mean feat, I'm sure," he chortled, picking at his beard with a free hand.

"No mean feat at all," boasted Corax. "Where is Manto? Let's hand the thing over, nix the curse, and get on with life. I could use a drink."

"I don't know—that girl comes and goes as she likes. Should be back soon, though. Meanwhile, I wouldn't mind a strum or two on that lyre."

Corax looked and me and shrugged. "Sure, why not?" He slipped off the pack, removed the lyre from the goatskin cover, and handed it to the old man.

Tiresias dropped his staff and drew a sharp breath as he touched the instrument. He turned it over, methodically inspecting every inch by feel, stroking the patterns on the tortoise shell with his gnarly fingers, caressing the lyre like a lover. "I've longed for this; you don't know how I've longed." He plucked a few notes, strummed, and began to chant as he played:

"*Thus while he spoke, the sovereign plant he drew*

Where on the all-bearing earth unmark'd it grew,

And show'd its nature and its wondrous power:

Black was the root, but milky white the flower;

Moly the name, to mortals hard to find,

But all is easy to the ethereal kind."

He struck a few more chords, picked and bent a note, then fell silent.

Corax scratched his nose and studied the prophet. "Tiresias, old man, I've never heard you lauded as a singer, but with that instrument and your command of the lyric, you could pass for the author of those lines."

Tiresias said nothing. We heard a whoop from above and looked up the hill to see Manto striding through the rocks, jumping from boulder to boulder. Marianne smiled and waved, perhaps ready to forget about Oizys. Manto headed straight for the edge of a small cliff, leaped forward into a handstand, and without a pause somersaulted from the brink like one of King Minos' bull leapers, landing on the main path in an explosion of flowers— petals of every hue swirling through the air like confetti. As the floral burst settled around her, Manto's appearance changed in front of my eyes. The same clothes, but with a slight broadening of the shoulders, narrowing of the hips, and a little more weight through the frame. And the metamorphosis continued until she had a sharp beard, long black hair tied with a wreath of ivy, and ornaments of silver. Hardly a woman, yet barely a man. It took a few seconds, but I recognized him: it was Dionysos.

We stood there like rocks. "Jesus Christ!" I said.

"No, I'm from an older vintage," he laughed and performed a flamboyant bow.

"What the fuck is going on?" demanded Marianne. "Pardon the disrespect, your holiness, but I do have a few questions."

"No need for abasement," Dionysos said with a haughty tone, "your questions shall be answered. Here and now, postproduction."

"Postproduction?" I sputtered.

"Yes, silly, the briefing. At the end of the play."

"Oh shit." So, it was true after all, what Nyx had said.

"Look, big boy, despite your tendency to monosyllabic dialogue, one assumes that you're at least minimally versed in the theatrical arts. Especially now that you've performed a major role!" He waggled a finger at me. "And you were magnificent! Mopey, resolute, fretful yet determined, forever loyal, but to what end? The perfect antihero sidekick!"

I stared at Dionysos, aghast, as I ticked through the numerous incidents of our travails, looking for all the scripted possibilities. I was too distraught to get far in what could prove to be a lengthy list.

"And you, my lovely lady," he turned to Marianne, "no need for a macho man to save the day! Every drama needs some muscle, don't you think? And that was you, always you, slaying all comers, not a hair out of place; really, how do you do it?" He minced around a bit, peering at Marianne from different angles, then bent over and hacked out a rush of shrill laughter worthy of a lunatic. Straightening, he slapped his thigh. "Worth the price of admission to see those tedious Dioskouroi sinking into the oblivion of Poseidon! They'll wish they'd stayed in the heavens, no doubt!"

"Oizys deserves most of the credit for that, and much else," objected Marianne.

He stroked his beard. "Oizys, oh yes, a credit to the troupe, for sure!" Dionysos' features blurred and reformed with the face of Oizys, then dissolved back into the bearded god.

"Son of a bitch," I said. "How many roles have you been playing?"

"Certainly not all of them," he said, stroking his beard. His face continued to blur and reshape itself, assuming the visage of everyone we'd seen. When he displayed our faces, I gasped.

"Now you're just fucking with us," said Marianne.

He enjoyed our torment as he grinned and capered. "Wouldn't I like to be fucking with *you*, sweetheart! No, you'll just have to figure it out for yourselves. Can't dispel all the mystery now, can we? For one thing, it would hardly be kosher with the Standards of Practicing Divinities."

Corax looked faint. "And my role?" he squeaked.

Dionysos cackled. "Quite simply: the protagonist! The hapless bloke who's pulled along through a narrative tempest of conflict and mystery! I can see the blurb: a prodigy, a child genius—but his devious bent brought him to wrack and ruin. No matter that he's a god, his luster has dimmed, and Fate has stuffed him in the gutter! Before he rots away, at the brink of desperation, he steals back his first creation from the meanie that took it away. Now, he's back in the game! No more overlooking the wily transgressor! Yes, you played Hermes himself! That mischievous miscreant! And you were insufferably perfect! By the way, my working title is *Hermes Rides Again*. Either that or *Pluck of the Lyre*, I haven't decided which. Whatever, there's tragedy and comedy rolled into one! A true monument to the trickster god, wouldn't you say? Overall, maybe it's more of a comedy. What do you think? I'm soliciting opinions!"

Corax was reduced to a whisper. "Hermes? Why me?"

"Why you?" roared Dionysos, throwing up his arms in astonishment. "Who else? Who else but the great hermeneuticist and Academy misfit? Who else but the author of *Insight Intersex*? Why do you think they call them *herm*aphrodites? Hermes and Aphrodite, ding-dong, nine months later here comes the girly man. Well, some say Hermes never actually did it with her. I think they conceived it in a cauldron, myself. Not sure he goes for the ladies like that. He's more into cock. Anyway, you're perfect for Hermes—spitting image! Tricky, pompous, ignoring boundaries—perfect!"

I struggled to control my anger. I wanted to scream, but it was still a god we were dealing with, not a back-alley fop, even if he acted like one. "So…. What? This was a long, drawn-out theatrical joke? On us?"

"There were times when it felt all too scripted," said Marianne.

Dionysos looked offended. "Of course, there's a script! Impossible to improvise something this subtle, this refined. Did you like it?"

"Not really. No. Can't say that I did," Marianne replied.

I thought my head was going to explode. "And the curse, what about that? An affliction? An addiction? Or was it even real? Feels like a sick fucking joke is what."

Dionysos waved off my concern. "Of course, it was real. We're talking gods and mortals—there's always a curse! But hey, we needed something dramatic to kick off the narrative, and as I like to say: you can't do worse than a curse. It's not like he didn't deserve it, with all his blasphemy and bratty ingratitude. I mean what was that nonsense about *eidetic reduction*? You want to see the world as it is—I'll show you the world! You know, he'd be better off with dietetic reduction! Hell yes, there was a curse. I think it put some real oomph in the acting, don't you? Authentic pathos! I could hardly keep the tears at bay watching googly eyes here drink himself to death! And you whining and wringing your hands in despair! Too rich! But don't call it a joke: no, no. Not a joke at all. Think of it as the making of a myth! Through our little enactment, we have planted a new legend—an epic! Singers like the old man here will spread the tale—before long it'll be the talk of every symposium! The theft of Apollo's lyre! The revenge of Hermes! It will be on everyone's lips, like gossip. My creation! That's when we roll out the play and take the theater world by storm! You see, your little adventure is more than a myth; it's also a rehearsal. Completely original, from start to finish, myth to the stage—no one has directed such a thing. A triumph of the *auteur*!"

Dionysos clutched his genitals and gyrated. His antics were obscene, and I was glad when he stopped. He peered at us eagerly. "So, can I count on you three for the full run?"

We exchanged glances. "You're asking us to repeat this pointless farce?" My anger boiled over. "Because it was so much fun? Or what?"

He pouted. "No, no, not the same events as you've lived them, silly. Don't be dense. A theatrical reification, a reprise for the stage! A few lines, a few days of your time, and in the end, you'll drown in fame and fortune. Your names will be associated with mine forever! Truly, what more could you want?"

"I could think of a few things," said Marianne.

"Immortality may be in the offing!" Dionysos played the trump card of the gods. "Still grumpy? What then? Perhaps the script wants tweaking. What do you think: more action, more sex, more despair, more argument, perhaps a severed limb or two?"

"*Incroyable,*" whispered Marianne. I glared at Dionysos while Corax chewed his fingernails and looked at the ground. I was sure it took all his willpower to stifle an onslaught of sarcastic blasphemy.

"Really, where *is* the gratitude? This opportunity won't come around again!" He flung out his arms and stomped his feet. "Mortals! You don't deserve the gods! Well, you weren't that good, anyway. I rescind my offer. No real loss and there's always more where you came from. The show must go on!"

"So, what was the deal with the lyre? Obviously, you didn't really want it." I said.

"Nah, just a plot device. Let the old man have it. He's wanted one for ages, ever since he stepped on the last one."

"The old man? You mean—now I doubt everything—is this really Tiresias?"

"Heavens, no. You're simply too gullible. Tiresias has been in the underworld for a millennium, at least. This is just some old poet that hangs around. The Singer of Tales, they call him. Anyway, he'll play the dickens out of that lyre, won't you, pal?"

The old man chuckled and strummed a chord.

Dionysos perked up, apparently reconciled to the rebellion of his cast. "Oh well, that's showbiz, as they say. It's been real. Gotta run, start shopping for some real actors. I do think I'll fiddle with the text. The theater is positively moribund these days. We need some of that old pizzazz! But modern, too, you know? Lots of anxiety. And more than a touch of the absurd. Oh yes, much more than a touch. Well, you had your chance." He fluffed his hair, looked into the sky, and disappeared. A single long-stemmed red rose fell to the ground where he had stood.

The old man plucked a few more notes on the lyre—it did have a lovely sound—then started a new song.

"I'll sing you about a man and a lyre,

A curse and a kiss and failing desire.

A line can be drawn across the sand

But the tide comes in and is gone again.

Limits and reason are known to fail

When chaos lurks at the root of the tale."

He had a weathered, soulful voice and I could have listened for hours, especially since he seemed to be singing our story, but I was anxious to leave this place. If we hurried, we might make it back to town before dark. As the old man sang on, my attention wandered. I started to ruminate, to obsess about who was real and who was not. What if the innkeeper had been played by Dionysos, and if he had, did that mean there was no Aristotle, perhaps even no Inn of Pure Reason? It seemed certain that Manto was one of his constructs, but who else? Oizys? That must have been a bluff, because I couldn't imagine that Mother Nyx was anything other than what she said she was and surely, she knew her daughter. But Oizys' disappearance this morning triggered plenty of doubt. What about the others? There was no end to this line of thought. Was this even the real Marianne sitting next to me? I shook my head and tried to purge the circular madness from my head.

"Old man," I interrupted, drawing the stares of my companions, "will you be alright here? I suppose there never was a daughter?"

"No, sorry to say, there wasn't," he acknowledged. "I stuck to the script and played my part. But don't worry about me, the neighbors look in every day—they bring food and clean the place. I'll be fine, as I've always been."

Marianne walked over and patted him on the shoulder. "Do you understand the point of this, sir? I'm reluctant to accept his explanations, all that garble about Hermes and hermeneutics and mythic plot devices. Just to motivate a play? That was the purpose? Wouldn't it be simpler to work it out in your head?"

He chuckled. "It's all about the stories, my dear. We have to keep them alive; otherwise, we will perish. That's as true of the gods as it is of mortals. Pay attention: we're telling stories to each other all the time. It's at the heart of everything we do. And I've had a nice career of it, a career that will be even more rewarding with this lovely instrument." He paused and brought the lyre to his lips and kissed it.

"As for the god, he's dedicated to the theater. The ages have rolled by and the influence of the elder gods has waned, and he's thrown more and more of himself into performances without boundaries, where art and life are the same things. Method acting, he calls it. Plumbing the depths, embracing the essence underneath, renewal through the archetypes—that sort of thing. Perhaps he's trying to impregnate the culture with something of himself. Desperate not to be forgotten, I suppose. Not so strange, really. Anyway, consider yourselves initiated into his reality. Might come in handy for you later."

Corax finally stopped chewing his fingernails and spoke. "Okay, great. I guess we're not the first to be manipulated by a god. I'll add it to my curriculum vitae." Corax waved his hand in the air. "Let's get out of here; I'm feeling the need for a drink of wine. Don't even try to say no," he pointed at me.

"Before you go," the old man said, "the god wanted you to have this. He said you don't need a steady diet, just use it when things get out of hand." He pulled a large pouch out of his robe and handed it to Corax. "Don't be afraid, he said, it's a common element of the earth itself—one of the true essences—and can be found where clear water bubbles from the ground."

I peered over Corax's shoulder as he opened the pouch. Lithium salts. A *pharmakon* for the next stage of life—one that might offer a reduction to the excessive drama.

The three of us said goodbye to the old man as he strummed happily on his new lyre. We took giant strides down the road, three abreast, loudly debating along the way who or who wasn't a real person. It didn't take long to decide that we were taking the first boat off the island, following Marianne westward to her homeland, far away from the madness of Dionysos.

The westbound boat made its scheduled stop at the Island of Marble the next morning. We paid Aristotle handsomely, shared hugs of farewell, and made it to the dock as the boat, another decommissioned warship, tied up to the moorings. Marianne nudged me and pointed out the brat who had lied about us to the soldiers at the festival. He twitched around the gangplank as it was lowered into place, ready to ply his craft. Perhaps feeling our eyes, he spun around and stared in shocked recognition. Corax and I ignored him as we walked up the plank. Curious, I looked back. As Marianne passed him, she made a sudden feint towards the boy. He leaped backward and fell off the dock.

"Now *that* will make a good story," she said.

III: STEALTHY LIKE A WOLF

[Marianne's Story/Osana's Story]

To move à pas de loup is to walk without making a noise, to arrive without warning, to proceed discreetly, silently, invisibly, almost inaudibly and imperceptibly, as though to surprise a prey...

Jacques Derrida,
The Beast & the Sovereign, Volume I

Franny is listening to a program on wolves. I say to her, Would you like to be a wolf? She answers haughtily, How stupid, you can't be one wolf, you're always eight or nine, six or seven. Not six or seven wolves all by yourself all at once, but one wolf among others, with five or six others.

Gilles Deleuze & Felix Guattari,
A Thousand Plateaus

To knot companion and species together in encounter, in regard and respect, is to enter the world of becoming with, where who and what are is precisely what is at stake.

Donna Haraway,
When Species Meet

[1]

I hobbled off through the woods, bloody and bruised, leaning on the broken shaft of my spear like a three-legged beast. I had thought to test myself against the wild boar. What folly! Now blood pumped from a gash on my thigh, gagging me with the odor of sweet, rusty iron. At this rate, I'd never make it back to shelter. If I wanted to live, something had to be done about the bleeding. And I did; I wanted to live. I stopped and removed my tunic, cutting it into strips to bind the worst of the wounds. I shivered in the remaining thin undershirt, knowing that it provided scant coverage for my breasts, an advertisement for cruel sport should I encounter a man. Normally, I didn't fear them; I killed them with ease. Weak and injured, though, I was mere prey.

I willed my reluctant body to push on past dusk and into the night, suffering the dizzy stumbles and sharp rivets of pain as I made my way through the shadows. Most women would have given up and crawled off under the nearest bush to wait for the end. Not me. I couldn't tolerate the thought of laying helpless in the woods, food for the wolves and ravens. Out of fear or pride—take your pick—I ground my teeth and staggered along, navigating by memory and starlight. .

Gray colored the eastern horizon by the time I made it to the ladder below the cave. I clutched the rungs and pulled myself up with grim resolve, rolling over the top and onto the ledge. Flat on my back, I stared into the indigo sky and counted the dwindling stars until my heart stopped pounding.

The sun would rise soon whether I lived or not. I knew the day would come when I didn't care anymore, but this wasn't the day. Standing, I grabbed the ladder and hauled it onto the ledge. Now I could stop worrying about predators, whether four-legged or two.

More an alcove than a cave, the limestone recess was deep enough to overhang the canvas dome I used for sleeping. A stack of firewood lay against the back wall under a crude counter of sapling poles. Not much of a home, but it provided a basic level of safety and shelter. Enough, anyway. I limped to the tent, yanked open the hide that covered the entrance, and collapsed inside.

I had been stupid. No one hunted boars with a spear, alone, on foot, and without dogs. I cursed my hubris. Not that long ago I had beaten a god in single combat, but there had been rules and a bit of trickery on my part. Apparently, now I thought I could kick anyone's ass. But boars didn't play by rules and were tricky enough themselves. Despite my ambitions, in the end, I was like all the others, another vain woman trying to outdo the fucking men.

I experimented with every posture I could manage—none of it allowed even a hint of sleep. The desperate struggle with the boar ran through my head like a never-ending theatrical production, rehearsing the same scene over and over. Alcohol could dull the pain and close the curtain, if I had enough on hand, which I didn't—a deliberate choice. Dedicated drinking had never been an option in my former profession as a merce-nary. Not if you wanted to stay alive. Out of habit or wisdom, I rarely drank and always avoided intoxication. After the last mission, which involved rescuing my friend Corax from the clutches of a mad god and his holy wine, I'd lost my taste for it altogether.

Pain relief was tempting, but I needed my wits for healing. Dawn offered enough light to properly survey the damage, and I wasn't finding sleep, so I grabbed the medical kit and crawled out of the tent for an inventory. Shedding the remnants of my clothes involved whimpering or cursing with each movement, depending on whether it really hurt or just pissed me off. Naked, I tensed against the morning chill while scanning my body. I found lacerations, abrasions, and a few nasty bruises. Below my left breast, purple and yellow skin bloomed around the ribs and it made me queasy to look at it. I shuddered and dragged a wool shawl over my shoulders, wincing as I clutched the edges. My ring finger looked out of line and it throbbed, but I could still bend it a little, so I left it alone for now. Mostly I worried about the left thigh where the boar's tusk had gouged a trough. After delivering the damage, the boar had run off with my spearhead lodged in its neck, and that was the last I saw of it.

The makeshift bandage had grown into a caked and clotted mass, fused to my flesh. Peeling away the crusty fabric required determination. The gash ran diagonally across the outside of the thigh muscle, at least a handspan in length. Just a flesh wound, as they say in war, but an ugly one, soon to be a blazing scar. Removing the bandage opened the scab and blood seeped out between the torn edges. I needed to soak in the hot spring and clean out whatever infections might have been dragged into the wound from the boar's mouth, as foul a cavity as I could imagine. The stink of its breath was unforgettable after it upended me in the charge, goring, and trampling in its spear-riven panic until it broke the shaft and fled. I trembled with the memory. I should have anticipated the speed and power of the beast, but it had caught me ill-prepared. Or maybe I had been too weak from hunger. I'd been fasting for weeks in an ill-conceived attempt to open a portal to the spirit realm; instead, it had left me feeble and slow.

I opened a vial of the potent alcohol given to me by Diarmuid the monk. Besides Corax, he was the only other man I still tolerated. He had named the liquid *uisce beatha* and declared it a fast road to hell, which, he noted, made it a favorite beverage of his people. One whiff of it and you knew it wasn't potable, but it did make a reasonable antiseptic. Dribbling a bit in the wound, the pain seared to the bone. Later, I would walk or crawl, if necessary, to the thermal spring so I could soak and minister properly to my injuries. For now, I cinched a clean bandage around my thigh and watched the sun clear the horizon.

If I wanted to heal, some things would have to change. At the least, that meant an end to the stupid diet of fruit and water. I had been ready to give it up when I decided on the boar hunt; the taste of pork haunted me. Unfortunately, there would be no savory chops to break the fast; I'd have to dig into my stores. I limped to the back of the cave where I had built a rock cist as a storage pantry. It hurt like hell, but I pushed and leaned against the slab that capped the cist, sliding it back enough to reach in. Once I had enjoyed grappling with this rock, satisfied that no varmint short of a bear could get past it. Now, even budging it a few inches seemed like a labor of Herakles. I should have heeded the encroaching lassitude weeks ago, but I can be a bit willful. From the cist, I retrieved a few strips of dried hare meat, some cheese, and a wrinkled old roasted potato. It was tempting to take more but overloading my shrunken stomach wouldn't help anything. The potatoes and cheese came from an elderly couple who farmed some terraces on the other side of the ridge, about a league away. They were happy to trade for furs or wild game and they never posed bothersome questions, which made them ideal neighbors. Lucky for me to have them, because even though I enjoyed living off the land, I hated farming. Don't tie me down and all that.

I gnawed methodically, savoring each bite with a sip of water. It was a feast as far as I was concerned. Before long, the food settled in my gut like ingots of lead, and I returned the rest to storage. Better to eat little bits at a time, I reminded myself. I sat on the edge of the cist and watched the sun clear the horizon and beam its hard, welcome light into the alcove. Time for a bath. Stuffing some clean clothes and the bandage kit into a bag, I lowered the ladder over the cliff. The shawl was enough to keep me warm until I walked the quarter league to the hot spring. Just as well I hadn't gotten around to taking off my boots, still dappled with blood. The morning chill I could handle, but bare feet were a liability on thorns, rocks, or the occasional viper. I also grabbed my quarterstaff because I needed a crutch, and I didn't like to go anywhere unarmed. Just a habit of mine; recent events suggested that I'm not that dangerous.

[2]

I left the cave and set off across the slope, traversing through woods and outcrops to the geothermal spring. The gash on my thigh started bleeding again, so I tightened the bandage. I tried to increase the pace, eager for the bath, but every part of my body hurt in some way and I couldn't muster more than a hobble. It took a good hour to cover the distance.

Scrambling over a rise, I gained the tiny basin of the spring. When I had first found it, I recognized its value right away and dammed the outflow, stacking rocks and clay to make a tub-sized pool. Situated at the edge of an outcrop, I could sit in the near-scalding water and look over the valley below. I had spent many sublime hours in the bath, combing the knots out of my long, troublesome hair, stretching out and staring into the sky with the hope of seeing a lammergeier, yet content to observe the passage of ravens, songbirds, or clouds. I had never owned religious convictions, but since my encounter with the maenads of Dionysos and their earthy, feminine spirituality, I toyed with the idea of finding something to believe in, something beyond my independence and martial prowess. So far, I had no revelations. If I worshipped anything, it was this spring. I doubted that a more rewarding divinity could be found.

The water, hotter today than usual, seared every laceration with needle intensity. I reveled in its cleansing fire. I didn't mind a little pain. To a certain extent, you could say that I liked it. Pain made it clear that I was alive: intensely, sharply alive. Most people would call me perverse, but I never tried to justify myself. Nobody else could feel my pain or understand how it thrilled me. Trying to explain was a waste of time.

I settled back, opening my legs, and stretching the length of my body to accept the water's balm. This body was a gift; I recognized that. It was the envy of some and a desired object for others, or so I'd been told. So why treat the body like it didn't matter? I saw the irony right away: *the* body, like it wasn't me, but something that belonged to someone else. I knew what I was up to: self-abuse. I'd been down this beaten path before. When I started to think about my flesh as something apart, abuse was soon to follow. Either I'd throw myself into violent situations like a berserker or I'd sit in a corner with a knife and carve lines in the skin. Either way, it felt good. Maybe pain broke through the wall and let me back in the body, yanking my head out of the clouds. When the numbness set in, it didn't matter anymore why I did what I did. Of course, an affinity for pain was an asset in a warrior. I recognized that and had been known to boast about my tolerance. Forced to prove it, I never failed to make my point.

The hot bath calmed my ragged nerves. How had I arrived at such a state, a crisis, really, overloaded with self-doubt, weak, and so vulnerable? My eyelids drooped and I let my mind drift back as I plodded through my recent history, searching for narrative keys to unlock the sense of it all. After the last mission, where I had to rescue both Diarmuid and Corax, I felt changed in more ways than I could understand. Our adventures had entangled us with gods and goddesses and all their fickle concerns, including deception, violence, domination, and a dozen other devilments. Despite the ordeals, at times I experienced wonder and ecstasy, too. Yet my soul felt drained and hollow;

all that remained was an ache to touch the world, truly touch it, with reciprocity. I wanted to be seen as myself and not the projection of someone's need. I hesitated to call it a spiritual longing, but of course it was. The maenads had taught me how to drink milk from the earth, and I could always turn to nature for primal nourishment. But I still craved a mother of flesh and blood to fill the void of my heart. I was barely four years old when my own was taken in war, another casualty in the relentless striving of men and their thirst for power. I had long hoped to find meaning in such senseless loss, but perhaps it was true, what the gods declared, that there was nothing behind the drama and farce of life except a theater for their amusement.

Ordinarily, I left such troubling matters to philosophers like Corax and took care of my department: who needed killing, who needed saving, that sort of thing. Corax and his lover Diarmuid were decent men, and I usually enjoyed their company. I say "his," but I know that Corax wasn't precisely a man due to his muddled biology. Still, short of more diverse pronouns, I didn't know what else to call him. That's what he called himself, so I followed his lead. Perhaps he didn't like it, but he never objected, and given his outspoken nature, I think he would have. He was never shy with opinions. Nor was Diarmuid. If anyone embodied dialectical tension, it was those two. Often amusing, frequently brilliant, their analyses were fierce and tended toward the interminable. I had learned how to tune them out when necessary, shielding myself with scorn, but the long sea journey back from the land of the gods broke down my resistance. I started following their dialogues. Before long, the constant wrangles over philosophy provoked within me a turbulence of fascination. They argued about our experiences within the theatrics of Dionysos: did we see true to the archetypes or were we distracted by perceptual fireworks and saw mere reflections? Or was there even a difference? Much of what they said made sense at first, then, confronted with an opposing perspective, it did not. The only certainty was that their opinions changed daily. The discourse worked on me like a gossamer skirt blowing in the breeze, alluring, and always swirling out of reach. In all that twisting language was something I wanted—but what? Was that where I lost my bearings, in the labyrinth of their convoluted discourse?

They argued throughout the two-and-a-half-week journey over sea and land. It was a blessed relief to see the gentle, lush valley that returned us to the headquarters of The Kraken Imaginary and brought an end to the forced proximity of our travels. After we checked in and delivered our reports, including my embarrassing explanation of how I'd lost a large portion of funds to a slave trader, we hung around for a while in that aimless pause that follows the completion of a mission. Corax and Diarmuid amused themselves with eating and fucking between arguments; I paced the grounds or ran up and down through the surrounding hills until my legs felt like deadwood. They might be content to grow fat and lazy, but the idea of any extra flesh gave me a panic. I ate sparingly. If I didn't soon find a purpose for my edge, I knew that I would become obnoxious—even aggressive. But it was too late to mend my ways. People avoided me in the mess hall, the bathhouse, and every public area throughout the compound. Before doing something I would regret, I collected my earnings and fled into the hills. Between my bow and wits, I knew I could live off the land. As for my comrades—fuck them. Maybe that was the crux.

Or it could have been the nasty little thing I did on the way out the door. I stole a text from the Archive of Things, part of the permanent collection assembled over hundreds of years of investigations. Mostly documents and artifacts, the shelves were meant for reference only, but at that point, I didn't feel like following rules. Childish of me, true. Maybe after stealing the lyre of Apollo, I'd developed a taste for thievery. Or maybe I just didn't give a shit. The text I took was written by a woman, anyway; I'm sure they'd never miss it. If they wanted it back, let them find me. I knew they wouldn't; hiding was a skill I'd perfected as a child. Yes, that must have been where I crossed the line.

I slipped out at night and headed south toward the high mountains, purchasing food and basic items in a village along the way. To help carry the load I bought two goats: black, hairy beasts with long, arcing horns; they were good on steep terrain and known for their milk. The farmer said they were named Bertrand and Beatrice, but I wasn't interested. Names meant nothing to me and too much to everyone else. I vowed to abandon my own—the goats didn't need it; why would I?

As I walked through the memories of these events I marveled at the drastic severance of my actions. I had pruned it all away. No wonder I felt unmoored; it wasn't just one thing, it was everything.

The three of us made our way out of the farmlands and into the foothills of the great mountain range that stretched east to west from one sea to another. History told about a general who marched an army with elephant cavalry over these mountains; I never believed it. I'd seen the range with my own eyes: the jagged spine of peaks sliced open the sky, littering canyons and glaciers in alpine chaos, hardly a terrain friendly for armies or elephants. On the lower slopes of the range, though, between the sub-alpine and the valleys, one found meadows and forests, rarely traveled, and abundant with wildlife. A zone of concealment for all sorts of beasts.

A week of steady travel brought us out of the valleys and into the broad expanse of upland beech forest. As soon as we were surrounded by beech trees, I stopped, opened my arms, and took deep, exaggerated breaths. The goats watched me through their inscrutable rectangular pupils. I had an impulse to give them a show, take off my clothes, and climb a tree. I settled for spinning slowly in place, around and around, absorbing the beauty of the woods. These arbors took me back in memories and not all of them were bad. The billy walked over and licked my hand in approval. I laughed and kissed him on the mouth, which earned me a taste of his tongue. Maybe I'd made some mistakes, but under the trees, things felt right. I had come to a good place for a woman to reflect on her errors and deficiencies. As I judged my narrative, I had no regrets about that part.

Far beyond the last town, on a steep hillside where birch and holm oak mingled with pine, I found a spring, just a trickle in the rocks, but sweet and pure. Above that, near the ridge crest, I spotted a cave in a limestone scarp and wanted it for shelter, assuming that it wasn't occupied. Providing both seclusion and security, it would answer my needs, and nearby meadows would please the goats. The face below the cave was too steep for hands and feet so I cut birch poles and made a ladder. As I reached the top rung, I peered over the edge, bracing myself for a charging lynx or a swarm of bats. The recess was empty and dry. Toward the back, I found a midden of old bones and flint chippings from the stone age. Perhaps no one had been there since.

Satisfied that I was free to claim the space, I hauled a dozen saplings up to the alcove and bent and lashed them into a dome frame; with my canvas, it made a serviceable tent. I let the goats graze free, figuring they wouldn't venture up the ladder. Indeed, they preferred the rich grass on the ridge, but one morning I woke up to find them chewing on the corners of my tent. How they scrambled into the cave was a mystery, but the goats were like that—part of the reason I loved them. They wore their weather shelter on their backs, but I did worry that the rare wolf or brown bear might find them. I needn't have bothered—they proved to be crafty survivors, never venturing far from cliffs and outcrops where they could retreat onto impossible ledges. Later, when it snowed, they chewed lichen off the tree trunks. During blizzards, though, they forced their way into the tent so we could curl into one huddle. I couldn't have been happier with my home or my family. I never was very civilized, anyway.

When we first moved in, it was early autumn, days were sunny and warm, and I often followed the goats to their pastures where I could lay among the grass and purple iris while studying the pilfered text. "*Knowing Touch*," it was titled. I found it a chore to read. Every new paragraph offered pronouncements like "*...the flesh is not something one has, but, rather the web in which one lives...*" and "*It is not consciousness who touches or who palpates, it is the hand, and the hand is man's outer brain.*" If I ignored the temptation to batter away at the words one after another but flowed through the sentences like paddling a boat, cresting the swells, and sliding down their backs, then the text reached a place in my brain that approximated sense. Mostly, though, it formed a prelude to a nap in the sun. My flesh was in the world anyway, and I didn't need the contortions of language and reason to know that. Sometimes the naps provoked disturbing dreams where I would be held down and touched against my will. I couldn't identify a perpetrator; that part remained in shadow. Perhaps the text sparked such thoughts, though I resisted that conclusion. Why should I fear my intellect? Being stubborn, I persevered. There were moments when things clicked into place and I felt a rush of understanding. Those were worth the trouble.

Remembering the warmth of naps in the sun brought me back to the bath and my simmering flesh. The searching inventory of my past had exhumed an accumulation of failures and outright mistakes. No surprise there. Could I learn from that? Not fucking likely, said the little demon in my head.

Tired of my thoughts, I opened my eyes to survey the state of the wounds. Soon forgotten, most of them. The gash, however, would leave a dramatic scar. That is, if it didn't become infected, turn black, and ooze a foul pus that ended in amputation or death. As I stared at the ragged meat, pink and bleeding from the hot water, I felt a rush of nausea. Leaning my head over the edge of the pool, I vomited the cheese and dried meat onto the stones. I crawled out of the water and stayed on my hands and knees until my stomach purged it all. The stench of the puddle triggered spasms of retching, but finally, there was nothing left to bring up. Moaning, I flopped back in the water, sliding to the other side of the pool to get away from the smell. I wrapped my arms around my chest, for comfort or to stop the shaking, I wasn't sure. God, I was a wreck. I needed to pull it together. War had taught me the perils of infection. I couldn't ignore this. It could kill me, and here I was, barely thirty years old. There were things left to do. I'd never had a child, unlike most women. Not that I wanted one, not really. But death would certainly remove the option.

Reluctantly, like a corroded machine, I stood, shedding the water's warmth. I forced myself to look at the thigh wound. Yes, raw meat ready for the stew. I told myself to shut the hell up and do the next thing. But then I noticed my ribs—when did I get so thin? I looked like a skeleton. I flexed my forearms; at least I still had muscles. Hand to shoulder, my right arm was embellished with tattoo ink: the detailed form of a kraken, symbol of the tentacular world. People admired the tattoo, then looked me over with narrowed eyes, saying that I was beautiful, but I knew they were liars. I was strong, yes, and desirable, maybe, but nobody named the stain that seeped out of my heart. Why did they pretend not to see it? You can't kill people without wearing it in your face. I'd certainly recognized it in others; even one murder is enough to etch the truth. And I had no idea how many people I had killed. How do you live with that and be beautiful? An impossibility, of course. But they couldn't know me, all those folks mouthing praise because I protected them. They had no idea of the dreams that came at night, the memories of blood, nor could they hear the shrieking souls of the vanquished, thirsty for revenge.

I shivered and stepped out of the spring, casting my eyes across the peaceful valley below, hoping to flee the emotional vortex of shame unleashed in my weakness. A hawk gliding over the treetops caught my attention and I watched it hunt, wishing for the freedom of its wings. Taking a deep breath,

I sat on a flat stone and opened the medicine kit. While the wound was still pink and fresh, I poured *uisce beatha* over it, followed by a bit of vinegar. The sting felt like a hornet jab and I shivered with pleasure. Take that, you bitch. Next, I dribbled a line of honey into the wound to control the inflammation. Now for the fun part. I threaded a curved needle made from steel wire and sharpened it to a point. With the same calculation I used to take down an enemy, I pierced the flap of skin on one side of the wound. Pain exploded, forcing a gasp and a tremble of my hand. Another deep breath and I shoved the wire through the other side of the wound, doubled back, pulled the skin together, and tied off the end of the thread. One stitch done, maybe twenty to go. My body rebelled at the pain yet welcomed it. I forged ahead, running the needle back into the skin to suture the next length of the wound. After the second stitch, I felt the relief of numbness seep into my leg and spread throughout the body. The pain was still there, but it reformed as an echo of ecstasy. I tingled all over. Sewing myself together with increasing detachment, I grew clinical and laid in more stitches than was strictly necessary. Finished, I poured vinegar over the jagged wound, now red with fury. I wrapped it in a clean cloth. Not bad, I thought. Maybe I had a career in medicine after I was done killing people.

[3]

After the soak, I put on clean trousers and a sleeveless tunic, both made from soft, gray buckskin. I didn't own any dresses and wouldn't wear them if I did; I preferred the barbarian look. The silk chiton I brought back from our last mission had been passed on to Diarmuid and Corax for their dress-up games; I had no intention of wearing it again. It advertised much more than I wanted to share.

As I crossed a meadow on the slow walk to the cave, the goats spotted me and clambered down for nuzzling. I had to lean hard on the staff to keep them from knocking me over in their enthusiasm. I hadn't seen them since I went off to hunt the boar, and even though they kept brushing against my thigh, their affections reminded me of our bond. Maybe they sensed that I needed loving. I scratched their foreheads and let them lick my palms. Dropping to my knees, I wrapped an arm around each neck. I kissed the female and earned her slobber. Our companionship was simple but sincere; in lieu of my kind, it would have to do. Since no treats were forthcoming, they grew bored and wandered off to resume grazing. Even for true love, there were limits.

When my parents had been killed during the war, I had hammered my grief into steel, vowing to need or want nothing again. An impossible goal, but I tried. Things got easier when I made myself into a weapon and dared anyone to hurt me. Those that tried, I killed and shed no tears. A few people proved worthy of trust and for them, I dropped a veil or two, but no more. They called me hard and I took it as a compliment. I wanted to be hard, impenetrable. And I'd paid a price for that. Like the philosopher implied, no one stands entirely apart, nor is the heart an impregnable fortress. In the end, the essential state of living contains a measure of vulnerability for every one of us. Including me.

The next day I returned to the thermal bath, cleaned the wound, and applied fresh bandages. When that was done, I worked on my hair as if pouring over the tomes of scripture, worrying the tangles from the strands, brushing it over and over until it hung down my back with the freedom of a wild mare's tail. I thought about slicing it off and shaving my skull into monkish austerity. A practical notion. Still, I balked. I recalled tender moments sitting between my grandmother's legs as she brushed my hair, singing or telling tales. For both of us, I imagine, those were times of grace and intimacy without complication. The memories and the hair were inseparable. No, I would not cut it off. I braided it back into a rope and let it be.

When I wasn't bathing, I was eating or foraging. Some tubers from last year's harvest remained in the cist, mostly potatoes and carrots, as well as a block of cheese, all from the neighbors. I looked forward to the time when the goats might breed and share some of their milk. Meanwhile, I had to work with the limitations of my injury, so I focused on slow scrounging. The forest offered truffles, difficult to find, and lichens, abundant in every direction. Curled fern heads forced their way out of the ground, along with the fresh shoots of clover, thistles, and other greens of dubious culinary value but nutritious, nonetheless. I dug out grubs and insects from under bark, hunted frogs in the vernal pools, and set snares for hares, squirrels, and ground birds. A diet beneath the notice of an aristocrat, but good enough for this former slave.

I spent the mornings creeping around the woods, lame and sore yet trying to be stealthy. I checked the snares, rigged new ones, and sometimes retrieved a hare or grouse unfortunate enough to get caught. Though I welcomed the meat and skins, I mourned each dead creature with a sadness that surprised me. Killing anything, even for food, summoned the darkness of my history. Delivering death to so many had emptied me more than I realized. One of my traps held a hare, still living, a beautiful brown female who lay quiet in defeat. I picked her up and cradled her to my breast, talking softly before I snapped her neck. Immediately I burst into tears. I felt ashamed at my weakness, but I did nothing to check the rush of grief; I hugged the limp corpse and sobbed. After that, I talked to every animal, alive or dead, thanked them for the gift of their lives, and shed as many tears as wanted to flow. Eventually, I understood that I cried less for my victims than for myself.

One day, I found a hollow tree with a beehive. I returned to the cave and made a smudging torch to smoke out the bees. During the last mission with Corax, Diarmuid, and Manto the intriguing maenad, I'd played the hero and removed the wild honey bare-handed, daring the bees to sting me (and they had). Now there was no one to impress, so I took the easy way, sedating the hard-working creatures before stealing their honey. I carried off a full bowl to a safe distance and dug in, biting off big clumps of the sticky comb, licking my fingers in delight. I strained enough of the viscous liquid to replenish my medicinal stock and gobbled the remainder.

The forest provided enough to live on, but not much more. The act of foraging burned nutrients almost as fast as they could be consumed. I devoted myself to the pursuit of food—with success, I admit. Gradually, my ribs lost a little definition and strength returned. When I began to menstruate after a respite of many months, I welcomed the flow as a sign of normality.

I still walked with a staff, whether out of habit or necessity, I wasn't sure. My leg was sore, but uninfected—this reinforced my vague ambitions about becoming a healer. I fantasized about the rewards of saving people instead of killing them. Imagine me in the middle of an adoring cluster of folks kissing and hugging in gratitude. Just thinking about it made me warm and wriggly and a little aroused. Then I remembered how much I hated crowds, not to mention adoration.

On the first warm morning of spring, I hobbled through the woods below the cave, checking my traps and picking the edible new growth. The deciduous trees were nearing full leaf, and a soft wind stroked the canopy with gentle fingers. The traps were empty, usually annoying, but the life force was in the air and the world seemed too wonderful for resentment. I heard a harmony whisper in the breeze and stopped to listen, think-ing it was a curious vibration of leaves and swaying branches. With a shock, I realized that someone was singing. The sound drifted through the trees from below, somewhere out of sight. In the time I'd been here, I'd seen no one, and my mind leaped to wild explanations. As I strained to hear, it grew louder. With-out a doubt, the source was moving closer—someone coming up the slope. I ducked behind a large oak and strung my bow. Humans often represented danger and I was prepared to shoot first and figure it out later. After the boar had left me maimed, I intended to take no chances.

Arrow nocked, I pressed my back against the tree and listened to the voice. It was female and sang with a mellifluous clarity that Apollo would envy. I didn't recognize the song or the style of music; not a local, I guessed. The sounds slipped up through the woods easy as the breeze. As I let the music flow through me, archetypes conjured into form within my mind, evoking the surrounding land with its contours, its forest, even its web of life. How those complex notions derived from the music, I didn't know. Magic? A permutation of eidetic reduction? Seduced, I relaxed the string of my bow. I was no critic of music or magic, but I sensed a eurhythmic soul behind the voice. I kept the arrow in place, though, in case I was wrong.

I leaned far enough around the trunk to look for the source of the song; I wanted to know who and how many traveled with her. I was astonished to see that she was alone. Not entirely alone, a dog plodded at her heels. Or maybe it was a fox; it was slender, with tall ears and a sharp snout. Best of all, the dog wore saddlebags, which met with my approval. I stepped out from behind the tree and stared down the slope at the singer. Her gaze aimed at the ground in front of her, a sensible habit, so I couldn't see her face very well. She wore beautiful clothing, a white top embroidered with many colors and a white skirt, both of which contrasted with her brown, burnished skin. Seemingly without effort, she carried a large pack, gracefully ascending the slope, the patient dog in tandem step. As I watched, the dog sensed me and stopped. They exchanged no sound that I heard, but the woman paused and lifted her head to follow its attention.

We inspected each other for a slow moment, then the woman smiled and waved her hand over her head. "Hello!"

Even at a distance, her beauty filled me with immediate longing. Large eyes and a wide grin beamed in goodwill. Two braids of black hair dangled down her chest, drawing my eyes along her slender curves. I admired her fitness: wiry, yet strong. She looked like she could run all day and leave the wind gasping for breath. A multi-colored headband covered her forehead and reflected the pastel hues of the embroidery on her shirt. This garment, far too lovely to waste on the labors of travel, ended daringly above the skirt, exposing her taut abdomen. And the sleek, reddish-brown dog, now sitting on its haunches, was a fair complement to the woman, posing them as an otherworldly duo. It occurred to me that she might be a goddess. On the last mission, I'd seen enough of them to last a lifetime. But as I studied her, I changed my mind. She glowed with an energy that could only be born of the mortal earth.

"May we approach?" the woman called.

"We? Are there more?" I scanned the woods and saw no others.

"Just the two of us here," she said, laying a hand on the head of the dog. I nodded and relaxed, returned the arrow to its quiver, and lowered the bow. I sensed no threat in the woman or her companion. Besides, curiosity already had me.

The woman hiked up the slope to my position while I admired the economy of her movements. Her steady flow between foot placements and the roll of her hips reminded me of wave sets on the beach. As someone whose life depended on precise body mechanics, such things impressed me. When she reached my level, she graced me with another beaming smile. I couldn't help but smile back as I stared into her dark, rich eyes. Her skin was free of wrinkles and full of youth, though if you asked me to guess her age, I wouldn't know. Younger than I was, probably. I thought of the crow's feet starting to trek from the corner of my eyes, a new acquisition that I tried to ignore. By the ease of her posture and expression, I guessed the woman never practiced guile. She radiated sincerity. I wondered if I ever looked like that. As a toddler, maybe, before the brutalities and losses.

Bending her knees, she propped the pack against the slope and shrugged out of it, then removed the dog's saddle bags, giving it a quick scratch between the ears. It closed its eyes and groaned, exactly what I would have done. Turning to me, she inclined her head in a modest bow. "I am Niokolo-Koba of the Four Rivers, daughter of Fatoumata of the Cascades, herself daughter of Binta the All-Seeing, the daughter of Kadiatou the Leopard, the daughter of Dalanda the Magnanimous, and so forth from daughter to mother back to the Creation. Please call me Koba; it's easier in the mouth. My jackal companion," she waved at the dog, who was apparently not exactly a dog, "is Yidi, the Loving One."

I appreciated her restraint in citing a mere five generations of ancestry. I had the impression she could have recounted the whole legacy. The flood of information would have been wasted on me, a woman with little legacy.

"Welcome to the highland forest, traveler. I guess you've come far. I have little to offer except clean water, fresh onion and asparagus shoots, and a little hard cheese, but I'm willing to share what I have. And I'd like to hear your story."

"How kind of you! I'm very fond of asparagus! As for telling stories, that's what I do," she said with yet another smile that
weakened my knees. "Would it be rude to ask for your name?"

Flustered, I realized that I had failed to introduce myself.
My social skills seemed to have congealed from lack of use.
"This may sound strange to someone with a line of names, but
I'm not sure I have one anymore. Honestly, I like it better that
way. People used to call me Marianne, but I'm not that person
now. I'm done with it. Take the name and add it to your list, if
you want, but don't use it on me." I paused, noticing her slight
frown and I worried that I was the one being rude. Then I
remembered the pirate who had kidnapped us in the southern
sea. "If you need a name, call me Nobody."

"Nobody it is," said Koba, with a straight face, and curtsied.

I blushed at my brusque ways, so different from the graceful manner of this stranger. No doubt I came off as crazy. And
maybe I was. If by hiding in the hills I had intended to go
feral, I had been successful. To disguise the awkwardness, I busied myself unstringing the bow, taking off my pack, and sitting
down in the grass to get the food. Koba sat next to me, crossing her legs under her skirt, and watched in silence. The jackal,
Yidi, lay its head in her lap. Koba stroked the back of its neck. I
watched out of the corner of my eye as I rummaged for food,
noticing her elegant bracelet of beads and cowrie shells.

I set out the water flask, green shoots, chanterelles, and a
block of cheese. On impulse, I broke off a corner of the cheese
and pointed to the jackal. "May I?" Koba nodded and I reached
across her lap to proffer the morsel. Yidi opened its mouth and
swept in the cheese with a large, pink tongue. A gulp and the
ears perked up, ready for seconds. Another chunk, of course.

It was a gorgeous animal, with silky fur, ears like lance tips, and knowing eyes. As I looked at its face, I slipped out of the moment and into a realm of eternal stillness. We had a bond, this animal and I, as if we were related. I don't know how long Yidi and I remained locked in mutual contemplation, but I came back to the present when I noticed that Koba had gently placed a hand on my shoulder. I pulled back with a start, embarrassed at my presumed intimacy.

"Sorry, I don't know what came over me. Your companion is a precious one," I said.

"Oh yes, she is. No need to apologize. She's called the Loving One for a reason." Koba unfastened her bracelet. She took my hand, turned it over, and placed the bracelet in my empty palm.

"Please," she said. "Take it. I brought it for you."

"What?" I wasn't sure I heard her correctly. She had a slight accent, and though her use of the language appeared solid, I didn't want to assume her fluency.

She retrieved the bracelet from where it sat on my unmoving palm and slipped it over my left hand. I felt a rush of pleasure at her touch. "There," she said. "It's perfect for you. And makes a nice oceanic complement to your beast." She pointed at the kraken tattoo on my right arm. Automatically, as if the tattoo had its own life, I lifted my arm and turned it back and forth so she could see the full design. She ran her finger lightly along one of the tentacles, following the outline as it spiraled around my forearm. I shivered and wrestled with the urge to push her down on the grass and bury her mouth with mine.

She pulled back and studied me with pursed lips. "You haven't been touched in a while, have you?"

Was I that transparent? I clamped down on my swoon and busied myself with handing her the water and a few asparagus shoots. "No, guess not. Sorry," I muttered.

She nibbled off the tip of an asparagus shaft and smiled. "Tusks and toads, dear, don't apologize! We're used to it, me and sister Yidi. Our work is all about love. Maybe not the kind you want, exactly. We'll give you what we have to give, *sister* style."

Her emphasis on the word *sister* was unmistakable. I sighed, but felt a bit of relief, too. My choices with intimacy had never been reliable. At best, temporary, at worst, downright damaging. There was nothing in my desires that I trusted, though I seemed powerless to check them. But sisters… maybe I could live with that.

I smiled at her in a way that I hoped showed appreciation for her kindness. "Tusks and toads? What a curious expression!"

She giggled. "Don't mind me!"

She raised one eyebrow and scrunched her nose, a silly and undignified contortion that caught me off guard. A tidal wave of laughter burst from my throat, and all the tension rushed out of me. "Oh my god," I gasped. "Don't do that again, please! I'm afraid I'll die laughing." I took a measured breath. "Please tell me, who are you, Koba, daughter of many?"

"Straight to the point, then. That works. Mostly I am a wordsmith." She fed an asparagus shoot to the jackal, who chomped it without hesitation.

"Wordsmith can mean a lot of things."

"Yes, it can. For me, it means that I write songs and sing them. For celebration, for spirit, for ritual, for peace. Really, for any time you need a song."

"Was that your composition, coming up the hill?"

"Yes. Singing up the land."

I chewed on a chantarelle and thought about her interesting phrase, *singing up the land*. "I sense more layers behind your words than in front of them."

Koba paused her petting of Yidi to touch my knee for a moment. "True! I can't seem to stop talking like a poet. I play with words. Always oblique, a little crafty: what's she *really* saying! In my culture, a wordsmith is a social person, a mediator, a lubricant, and a repository of history. My heart beats at the center of the community. It's both an honor and an obligation. Part of it, as I see it, is to stretch the words and reveal the world."

"Like a bard," I suggested.

"Yes! Kind of."

"I have a friend who's a bard. She's also more than a little full of magic." I stared at Koba, who opened her lips slightly and made a sound of amusement: *tsaaa*.

"Where there are words and music, there is always magic," she noted. "Say, that friend of yours who's a bard, that wouldn't be... Fedelma, is it? I think that's the name."

"What? You know Fedelma?"

"I know *of* her. Here's where you say: small world."

"Consider it said."

"Anyway, two of our people traveled to that rainy island in the North where she was held prisoner, not that long ago—maybe a year or two? They just wanted a chance to talk to her, like a cultural exchange. But there was too much going on. Then she disappeared. They did bring back more of her writing, though, for our library."

I'm sure my mouth hung to my chest. "Amazing! I was there, you know. I helped her escape. And I think I saw your emissaries. Brown folk, like you? Colorful garb?"

Koba's eyes searched my face. "That would be them. But you helped her escape? You saved a bard? My hands are at your feet!" She bowed and placed her hands on my feet, giving a gentle squeeze before sitting up.

"Now I do have to say it: it is a small world! Speaking of which, what brings you here, to this seldom-traveled forest?"

"It's been a long journey! I come from the continent to the south, the other side of the inland sea. My people are dark, and we speak a different tongue, but our hearts beat the same rhythm. I've been sent here on a mission by the elders of my clan." She held up her hand. "Before you ask about the mission, and I know you will, I have to explain the context, or I can't explain why I'm here."

"Fair enough," I said. "I'll summon some patience."

"Thank you. First thing: our society is based on a congress of species. More than human. We've learned how to communicate with different life-forms, both animals and plants. It's our commitment to expand interspecies dialogues, ultimately to facilitate free and easy conversation between life-forms—all of them. I know, I know. I see the skepticism hardening your eyes. No?"

I shook my head. "Envy, in fact. I tried to learn the Language of the Deep to speak with sea creatures, but I never mastered much. And plants? I'm impressed, that's all."

"The Language of the Deep! I love the sound of that! I must learn it one day. Our tongues are land-based only, I'm afraid. Would you teach me what you know? I do want to learn!"

"It's pretty abstract unless we go to the sea. Certainly, I can share what I know. And gladly."

"Okay! Where was I? Oh yes, social context. So, our primary alliance is with the beings known as elephants. I don't know if you've ever seen one?"

"Only in pictures," I said. "And I've heard descriptions from people who have. One of the few land creatures that seem tentacular."

Koba looked surprised, then smiled broadly. "Exactly! You're ahead of me," she said, though I wasn't sure what she meant by that.

"Elephants are remarkable creatures. Intelligent and social—very social. Once you've made an elephant friend, you have a friend for life. Our communities mingle humans and elephants in open association. Families include both. The thing about elephants, besides being loving, is that they're incredibly smart! Applying those giant brains of theirs, they've developed knowledge beyond anything imagined by humans. All theoretical for the most part, occupying their heads and discourse, but of great sophistication. You might think I'm talking about literature or philosophy, and they do work in those realms, but their true love is science. Biology, mostly. Filled with notions—radical ones! The implications of their research are intriguing, to say the least. However, before theory can become practice, it needs a technology of experimentation. The problem is, even though their bodies are beautiful and majestic, elephants are limited in handling tools and materials. They've relied on a partnership with humans to practice the experimental side of science. With their brains and our hands, we've done some very good work. The most incredible discovery made so far is that there

401 James M. Wright

is a chemical code within all living things. They call it genetics, after the old word *genesis*. You haven't heard about this, by any chance?"

I shook my head. Her story was fantastic and would have aroused the ire of someone like Corax. As for me, whatever. I'd heard more outlandish things and discovered them to be true.

"It's a complex subject," she continued. "If you're interested, I can tell you about it at another time—at least as much as I understand. For now, I'm just trying to sketch the background situation. Anyway, our elephants are much loved and we humans would do anything for them. The primary challenge is that they want to manipulate the technical tools themselves, without primate go-betweens. Understandable. However, they're restricted by the instrumentality of their trunks. Their tentacles, as you say. Sadly, elephant trunks, though dexterous, are not as versatile as tentacles."

"Indeed," I inserted, "the cephalopods are quite handy."

Koba peered at me for a moment, then chuckled. "Oh, you," she said. "You act tough but underneath you've a sly wit, eh?"

I blushed again and rearranged the food. I offered water to Koba and she took a measured draught. "Good water," she said, handing back the flask. "So, the elephants have analyzed their biological legacy, extrapolating back in time many thousands of years. One of their ancestors, a type now extinct, possessed a trunk with extended lobes at the tip. These lobes were as deft as fingers, almost. For reasons unknown, this feature disappeared with the animal. The elephants want it back."

"This elephant ancestor, it wouldn't have been hairy, would it?"

Koba clapped her hands with glee, startling Yidi, who lifted her head, studied her mistress for a moment, then sagged back onto her lap. "Aren't you quick? That's it. The mammoth. Extinct everywhere in our world, apparently, but seen in these parts not all that long ago."

"Forty leagues north of here, in an old river valley," I said, "is a cave with hundreds of drawings of mammoths. Our human ancestors must have thought highly of them, for the drawings are precise and well-formed."

"Really? I should like to see that!" Koba said and sighed. "Later, perhaps. My focus must remain on the mission. Let me explain. Several months ago, I had a dream that a mammoth mother lies frozen in the ice of these mountains. I'd like to think there's a possibility of reviving her—however, that's just a fantasy. All I need is a remnant, a sample. Preferably flesh, even frozen or rotted, because traces of genetic code could be extracted. Bones might be enough. Of course, finding her could be a challenge."

"A dream? You came all this way for a dream?"

Koba patted the dog, who rumbled like a cat. "My dreams have agency in the weaving of the world. I trust them. So do the elders."

"Okay, we'll let that pass for the moment. And because of the dream, you just happen to be wandering this way, headed into the mountains to find a frozen mammoth, because you have to start somewhere?"

She looked straight at me, brown eyes wide open like an invitation to her soul. "No, I'm not here by accident. I dreamed about you, too. I need a guide."

[4]

I leaned back on my elbows. "Guide, eh?" Suspicion rushed through my nerves, spreading like a toxic bloom and polluting all those good feelings I'd let in. The friendliness, her gift--was I was being recruited for another mercenary job? I could be so naïve, especially when a pretty face was involved. Still, it couldn't be that simple. Curiosity softened my temper and I vowed to keep an open mind. Still, there were limits. I slid my pants down to the knees to expose the impressive line of stitches on my thigh. "Did your dream show you this?"

Her eyes flared wide. "Oh my," she said. "That's serious." She leaned forward to inspect the wound and softly probed a few places next to the incision. "Did you sew this yourself?" I nodded. "Not bad. Doesn't look infected, but healing will take time. I imagine it hampers your activities?"

"That's my point. Flattering as it is to be dreamed into a job, I'm not up to scampering around the mountains just yet. Never mind that it might not be a job I want. There are others who know the terrain, though."

"Well," Koba said, tapping a finger against her lower lip, "I dreamed about you. These things don't come to me by accident. I'll wait. In the meantime, I have medicine and know a few things; I can help you heal. And I won't impose. I'll set up a camp and stay out of your way."

If I was being recruited for work, she was doing a perfect job of it. My paranoia dissipated in the soothing resonance of

403

her voice. Even though I knew little about her, I found her captivating. She wasn't the least threatening; I needed to trust my senses. Our tangles with Dionysos, though, delivered a full measure of the deceptions possible in appearance. I shouldn't be surprised if I was a little touchy. However, it would be reasonable to assume things were what they seemed until I learned otherwise. Plus, I had nothing better going on. And though I had imagined I could lead a contemplative life, throw me a promise of action and you had me. "No need for that. There's plenty of room at my shelter. I'd welcome the company, to be honest."

"We would be honored!"

"One thing, it's a cave in a cliff and the entrance is a ladder. Nothing fancy. Not sure if your Yidi can negotiate that."

"Oh, she's adept. You'll see."

As simply as that, I picked up a new partner. Two of them because Yidi was every bit as clever and capable as Koba suggested. She clambered up the ladder faster than I could, even with her saddlebags.

After we shed our loads and Koba admired the shelter, I proposed that we hike to the hot spring for a soak. Without warning, she sprang into the air like a kid goat and shouted "Yes!" while Yidi barked with excitement. I stared at her innocent enthusiasm, astonished, but couldn't hold back the laughter when Yidi started bouncing up and down, punctuating leaps with shrill yips. Koba egged her on, burbling silly nonsense and crouching so that Yidi could lick her face at the apex of each bound. Watching them play, I felt a rush of shared delight and wondered if this was part of having a sister. Meanwhile, the less sisterly part of me noticed the sweat stains under the arms of Koba's shirt and the lithe power of her body.

To disguise my desire, I kneeled and stroked Yidi, who had flopped at Koba's feet, and was rewarded with a slurpy kiss. I looked up at Koba. "You have so much joy in things! I feel like a weathered old cynic in comparison."

Koba kneeled next to us. With a forefinger, she gently touched the wrinkles at the corner of my eye. "Is this the weather of your worries?"

I let go of Yidi and sat up. "Crow's feet, we call them. Often the first sign that youth is over. Not sure I'm ready for that."

"Crow's feet.... I like that. Does that mean that crows are walking out of your eyes?"

I laughed at her image. "Never thought of that," I said.

Koba's stared into the distance. "Where crows are walking, can jackals—or what do you have here? Wolves? Can wolves be far behind?"

What a strange thing to say, I thought. Yet it halted my emotional swirl. I preferred to keep self-pity at bay, but sometimes it stepped out of the shadows, and there it was, ready to eat me alive. All over some stupid wrinkles. Surely, there were better things to do. I stood slowly, feeling the strain in my thigh. "This wolf needs a bath."

Koba smiled. "Lead on," she said.

As we walked to the spring, we saw the goats scrambling down from the ridge; they stopped when they saw Yidi. I coaxed them further while Koba clung to the jackal. The goats, always curious, sidled in but would come no closer than twenty feet, so I limped to them and anchored them with my arms around their necks. Koba walked Yidi, firm in hand, and brought her nose to nose for a sniff. We patted everyone and said "friend" over and over, no doubt looking ridiculous. Koba grinned and patted me on the head as well and we started to giggle and fell into a huddle of squirming animals. As soon as we let go, the goats casually wandered away and Yidi squatted in the grass and peed.

"Even if they don't care, it's good to have friends," I said.

"Truth," she agreed.

At the spring, I shed my clothes and lay in the pool. Koba walked to the edge of the cliff and looked over the valley. "Remarkable," she said. "I would live here, too, if I could have access to this." Yidi tasted the spring water and curled up in a patch of moor-grass. Facing away from me, Koba took off her clothes, folding the garments and stacking them on a rock. I watched her, of course, my head buried to my lips in the water, admiring every new revelation. When she turned around, I felt a rush of weakness. Surely this was the same woman that came to me in dreams, calling forth my desires. We stared at each other for a moment, then she stepped into the pool. "What should we do with you? You're like a starving woman." She stretched out so that we lay facing each other with her feet next to my shoulders, her brown skin a rich complement to my pallor. "I'm sorry that I can't give you what you want," she said, her voice so gentle that it did offer some of what I wanted, maybe enough to suffice.

Her frank manner eased my tension. "I don't mean to make you uncomfortable," I said. "It's just that... you're friendly and beautiful and... I've been alone."

"You don't make me uncomfortable. I'm flattered, of course. I feel bad for you because I know about longing. However, I am married. Even though I'm hundreds of leagues from my spouse, I honor the vows. But don't apologize for your feelings—not to me, anyway."

"I'll try not to be too obnoxious," I said. I winced to hear that she was married, because everything about her not only enflamed my desire, but spoke to some deeper need for companionship. I'd had plenty of affairs and crushes, but I had never experienced love, not as a durable bond. Koba radiated energy that made me think such a thing was possible. I'd heard other people say the good ones were already taken, and maybe that was true.

Koba smiled and patted my hand. "I like you. Yidi likes you, too, and she's never wrong about people. I hope we can be sisters. That's something, isn't it?"

We soaked in silence for a while, then Koba began to sing, a loose melody without words, or without any words I understood. She closed her eyes and relaxed, humming at times, vocalizing at others, as if she sang to herself. Her song pulsed, unafraid of repetition, embracing the beat of a heart, conveying faith in the rhythmic nature of the world. The longer she sang, the more I melted into the soul of the earth. It was as if she transformed the experience of the hot spring into music. I lost track of time, which I tend to do anyway in the bath, but whether minutes or hours had passed when she finally tapered off, I had no idea.

"You're a treasure," I said to her. "I thought you were piping love straight into my heart. But, you know, spiritual love," I hastened to add.

Koba laughed. "Now, don't start editing everything you say. You'll make me nervous. I sing many songs, but my favorite is to sing up the land."

"Sing up the land? You said that before."

"Yes, it means to seek the music that dwells in the land and bring it to expression, or, at least, my version of its expression.

I'm only a young woman and have much to learn about listening to the songs in the earth. The older ones, they hear with great precision and sing so clearly that you can envision the landscape from their voices, every ridge and valley. My heart is in it but I'm still a bit childish, it seems."

"You could have fooled me. I heard the hot spring, loud and clear."

"Oh, good! That makes me happy! In my backpack, I carry a lute. Perhaps this evening, you'll allow me to play it for you."

"*Allow?* Ha, your modesty is charming. I look forward to it." She smiled and twisted around to check on Yidi, who hadn't moved but lifted an eyelid for Koba. I studied the intriguing style of Koba's hair; two braids hung down the sides of her head, one in front of each ear. They were long and tightly woven and tied off at the ends with teal-colored beads. She had removed her headband for the bath, and I saw how her hair was woven into tight rows that hugged her scalp.

"Your hair is incredible. I've never seen anything like it."

Koba turned to face me and sat up, stroking her braids. "It's a custom of my people. This is the sedate version; some are flamboyant and festooned with jewelry, drawing the eye like a magnet. If you like, I could braid your hair. You have so much of it; it would be great fun!"

"I'd like that," I said, imaging her hands running through my hair and liking the idea very much.

On the way back to the cave, we detoured down the slope so I could check some snares. We gathered dandelions, purslane, and mint for a salad. Luck was with us; a hare had wandered into a trap and waited patiently for its fate. I gathered it up quickly, stretched, and snapped the neck. Koba hummed throughout this procedure. I looked at her curiously, but she offered no explanation. Two more snares yielded grouse and she hummed again as I executed each fowl. I thought she might be squeamish and made music from anxiety, though she didn't seem the squeamish type. Long-distance travelers have to be hunters and foragers, too, or they don't get very far.

"Do you hum with a purpose?" I asked.

"Yes, I praise the life of each creature and thank it for the sacrifice."

"Fair enough. We *should* be thankful; with these three sacrifices, we'll eat well tonight—one for each of us!"

Koba filled the upturned hem of her skirt with the abundant flowers and greens, including a few onion shoots and chantarelles. She bore the cornucopia in front of her while I slung the game over my shoulder. We made a colorful troupe, me hobbling with my staff, Koba swaying like a flower girl, and Yidi dancing back and forth between us, excited about everything.

At the cave, I kindled a small fire in the stone ring and skewered the dressed hare and a grouse, setting them over the flames. While I adjusted the meat, Koba used a bone-handled knife from her kit to chop the greens. Crouched next to me at the fireside, Yidi held the uncooked grouse between her forepaws, tearing off bits with her sharp teeth. She applied herself to the task with delicacy and focus.

When Koba finished chopping the salad, she sat next to me and tapped gently on my thigh. "Let me help this heal. I can apply medicine while the meat cooks." I nodded; I was not a patient invalid, and I was tired of stumbling around like an old woman. I took off my pants and peeled back the dressing. She unrolled an indigo cloth bundle, revealing an array of pouches and folded fabrics, each of a different color. Out of a red and black swatch, she took a pinch of orange powder and sprinkled it on the wound. This she followed with a greenish salve from a tiny box, applying it lightly with her fingertip. Then she tied back the dressing.

"It's healing well, but I think this will speed things along."

"What did you put on? Or is that a trade secret?"

"No, hardly! A little turmeric to reduce the swelling followed by a mixture of copper, oil, and beeswax to combat infection. I learned from my mother."

"Let's see," I said. "That would be Fatoumata of the Cascades?"

"Correct! I can't believe you remembered!"

Her grin made my heart swell. I couldn't recall the rest of her list, but I was glad I remembered that much.

After we ate, as the sun set behind the ridges to the west, Koba unwrapped her lute. A crude-looking instrument with a narrow body assembled from wood, it had three strings tied with leather ribbons to the stick-like neck. She sat at the lip of the cave and plucked the strings, her gaze wandering off into the waning rays of sunlight. I stretched out on my side next to her so I could watch her play as she launched a simple rhythm. Her fingers marched around the strings with a deliberate pace, while I tapped in time. As she played, she gained speed and soon the rhythms were more complex. I had seen and heard the famous Lyre of Apollo, an instrument made by a god for a god, but it fared no better in comparison with Koba's rustic assembly and the layers of sound she extracted from it.

When she started to sing, the hackles on my neck stiffened and I felt a shiver pass down my spine. I wouldn't describe her voice as pretty or refined, but it contained raw power and rivers of feeling. Sometimes she sang in syncopation with the lute, echoing the rhythm with the words of another language; at other times she let her voice soar or dip in long fronting tones. I sensed layers of meaning in the blend of word and sound even if I didn't understand the tongue. What I did hear, very clearly, was a form of music that expressed something deep and true. I stopped twitching to the rhythm and rolled over on my back, looking into the sky and the first stars, letting the music wash over me like waves from heaven.

[5]

After the next day's bath, Koba braided my hair, a complicated procedure that took hours. While she worked, I closed my eyes and luxuriated in the firm touch of her hands as she tugged and twined small strands into tight weaves along my scalp. The pain of it was a bonus, of course. I ended up with four long, thin braids trailing down my back, each one tied off with red or black clay beads that I selected from her pouch. She handed me a mirror and I admired the new look; it was elegant and dramatic, yet also sleek.

"*Incroyable*," I said. "Whoever this person is, she looks kind of dangerous."

Koba laughed and watched me as I pranced around the cave demonstrating my self-defense moves, testing the feel of the hair style in action. I felt tight, like a new woman. "I tell you," she said, "where I come from, if you wanted a mate, you wouldn't want for long. With those blue eyes and that body, they'd be lining up. All types."

"Yeah?" I asked, a lot of questions hanging behind that one word.

"You'll find no shaming in our community. We honor species, races, and gender connections of every sort. Whatever makes folks happy."

"Sounds like paradise."

"Well, something to think about," she said.

"What's something to think about?"

"Coming home with me when we're done. You would be welcomed."

I froze in place. Go home with Koba? My insides churned with a combination of excitement and anxiety. I would have to leave behind everything I knew. As I thought about it, that might be a boon. My life here was hardly the fulfillment of dreams; it seemed to be more of an overstretched interim waiting to snap. Why not go with her?

"You're not very hard to read right now," Koba said. "Just sit with the notion. I'm not asking for an answer. You'll decide later."

I was too confused to talk about it. Later sounded good. Meanwhile, there was always a chore for distraction, so I tidied up the firewood pile, the dishes, and everything else in the shelter that could be rearranged.

Whether it was from Koba's medicine, her company, or the salve of time, my mobility increased each day. I decided I was ready to hunt for a bigger game. Running trap lines further up the valley, I had found a deer trail thick with tracks. My imagination swiftly conjured a venison feast. I didn't even try to stop myself from imagining Koba wearing a soft white buckskin, carefully tanned by my own hands. I didn't expect to sway her to me in the way that I wanted, but that didn't cancel the pleasure I got in doing things for her. We'd only known each other for two weeks, but I had started to feel that sisterly bond she talked about. Her gratitude was joyful and sincere; I invented things to do just to see her face light up. When she helped me, in any way, she did it with a tender manner that seemed the epitome of care. Sisters or friends, whatever you wanted to call it, I felt the love and tried my best to return it in the same spirit.

Ready for a solo trial, I woke early in the morning while Koba and Yidi snored, curled together in a comfortable heap.

I had mentioned before nightfall that I might go hunting, so I assumed she'd understand my absence. We shared the tent like comrades, scooting closer on colder nights, and her odor filled my dreams. It was frustrating, but the rough stone of unfulfilled desire sharpened my daytime energies. I liked the intensity of it; it made me feel alive. Sometimes we'd lay awake at night and Koba talked openly, sharing stories of her history of unreturned passions, laughing over her anxieties, and normalizing the fickle alignments of Eros. She never belittled my desire, which, of course, only made me fonder. As I left the tent, I looked back on the sleeping woman and her jackal and thanked the world for giving me the gift of their companionship.

Feeling optimistic, I didn't take the staff, just my bow, arrows, and a small pack with tools for gutting and skinning if I got lucky. I limped a little, mostly from stiffness in the muscles, but it wasn't bad. Liberated from the three-legged gait of the staff, once I warmed up, I allowed myself a longer stride. It felt wonderful, even if now and then I stretched too far, triggering a jolt of pain. I also enjoyed the swinging rhythm of my new braids as they bounced along my back. The braided rows, on the top of my head, were so tight that my scalp felt every rustle of air like a brush. I found myself humming one of Koba's songs and realized that I was happy.

I descended across the slope at an angle, heading in an upstream direction. After maybe half a league of walking, I found the game trail in the valley bottom. The cascading stream remained in the morning shadow of the ridge and I paused to splash my face and drink. All the fresh tracks ran back up the slope; the deer had already come and gone for the day. To catch them here, I'd need to arrive before the first light. Regardless, the hunt was on, and I followed the tracks uphill, walking as gently as I could. I didn't want to overtake them suddenly and send them scattering like rabbits. I stalked with caution, stopping every dozen paces to look and listen. A squirrel chattered at me, advertising my sinister presence, and a woodpecker drummed in the canopy, otherwise, I heard nothing but my breath.

The path worked its way up the slope in switchbacks, zigging and zagging with deer logic. I had the impression that I had somehow doubled back and was now heading in the general direction of the hot spring, which surprised me. I'd never seen deer or their tracks in that area and I assumed they would steer clear of human activities outside of agriculture. But the cautious ruminants had their ways. To find them, I needed to follow them. I felt certain that the tracks meandered to the meadows of the ridge top where they could graze among the spring flowers and shoots. Knowing that and finding them were two different things. From tracks and trails you could think there were thousands of deer, yet never lay eyes on one. Or round a corner and suddenly, there they were.

Thinking ahead, I strung the bow and carried it and an arrow in my left hand. I slowed my pace as I approached the upper section of the slope. The trees thinned and patches of grass and rock ledge periodically removed the opportunities for cover. I stopped at the verge of each open section and carefully studied it, then moved swiftly through to the next grove. The angle of the slope steepened, then let off as I climbed onto the margins of the broad ridge. Game trails branched off and went in all directions. Deer tracks ran amok, back and forth, so there was no telling where the elusive creatures were. Now I wanted some luck. I decided to keep heading toward the crest where the sun beamed its morning warmth. The animal in *me* was drawn to it, so why not the deer?

A broad meadow sprawled across the top of the ridge. I paused and crouched behind a thick oak, peeking around the trunk. Startled, I saw someone lying in the grass about twenty yards away. It was Koba, and Yidi sat on her haunches nearby, alert and scanning the surroundings. I withdrew behind the tree before she sensed me. Slowly, I looked around the other side of the trunk. I don't know why I was being sneaky, just a habit of the hunt, perhaps. Or an ingrained respect for privacy. Koba had her skirt hiked up to her waist and her hands were busy between her legs. I was shocked—I don't know why— then amused, then embarrassed. It was time to retreat down the hill and pretend I never saw anything. But I didn't. Instead, I slumped down behind the tree and let myself feel the excitement of what I had seen. I'd never spied so crassly on a friend, but there I was, doing it.

I felt a little melted myself, but the mood evaporated when I heard Yidi bark—a sharp, insistent bark, the kind that meant trouble. I peered around the trunk. Koba sat up and swiveled her head quickly, scanning the meadow while Yidi jumped in place and yapped. I thought it might be a phantom presence known only to canids when I saw movement at the far edge of the trees. It was a wolf. No, not one: two, three, four wolves fanned out in formation. They advanced slowly, heads down, slinking towards Koba, but she had seen them and was on her feet. She clutched her paring knife, for all the good that would do.

The time had passed for embarrassment, shame, or whatever related to my earlier thoughts. I stepped out from behind the tree, nocked an arrow, took aim, and let it fly, absorbing the power of the yew bow as it thrummed in my hand. The arrow buried itself in the neck of the closest wolf, but I didn't wait to see the result. I loaded another arrow as I ran to Koba. The wolves paused when their pack member crumpled to the ground, but instead of slowing down, they accelerated toward the target, eager to snatch something for their troubles. On the run, I loosed another arrow that drove hard into the belly of a charging wolf. It howled and dropped, then turned and headed back to the trees, dragging its hind end. The last two attackers immediately stopped and circled the first one I'd hit, now twitching on the ground. They whined and sniffed at their dying comrade. I yelled as I ran, hoping to imitate a blood-curdling banshee or something formidable enough to scare them. Koba whirled around, eyes wide, as I made the last strides to her position, another arrow ready to fly. Yidi, emboldened by the changing odds, darted at the wolves, barking in shrill anger. This had the desired result, and the wolves ran off into the woods, leaving their companions. Proud of her accomplishment, Yidi trotted back with head and tail held high.

As the fear drained out of her face, Koba dropped the knife and threw her arms around my neck. Still weaponized, I couldn't hug her back. Sniffing at my legs, Yidi licked my hand as I limply held the unused arrow. Koba sobbed onto my collarbone for a moment, then stepped back. "Am I glad to see you! Out of nowhere like a guardian angel. Where were you?" I saw the thought come into her eyes. "Wait a minute. You weren't watching me, before… Were you?"

The moment of truth. "Not watching, no. Not exactly. I mean, I saw you, yes. But I looked away." I could hardly believe how lame I sounded.

Koba studied me, expressionless. Then she burst out laughing so hard she doubled over and pounded her thigh. I giggled nervously with no idea of how to respond.

"Oh my lord," she said when she caught her breath. "*I looked away.* You're too much! Did you really?"

I nodded, blushing. She leaned forward and kissed me on the cheek. "You're very sweet," she laughed.

Eager to change the subject, I pointed toward the dying wolf. "Time to clean up, I think."

The first wolf I hit lay on its side in a puddle of blood. As I listened to his rattling breath, he stared at me with open eyes. I thought I saw resigned acceptance. Covering his sight with one hand, I slit the throat with the other to end his suffering. I loaded the bow and followed the trail of the wounded one. Dragging itself through the meadow had left a trail of crushed vegetation and streaks of blood. I wanted to finish it off, but I didn't want to be taken by surprise in case its remaining companions lingered. As I approached the edge of the woods, I moved cautiously, straining to see into the shadows. I looked back once and saw Koba, crouched over the dead wolf. I heard her singing.

As I stepped into the forest, I tensed. Wolves were smart; would they know I would pursue into the woods, which offered a chance for ambush? I had no desire to underestimate any more four-legged beasts, so I pulled back the arrow, ready to fire. Only a little way into the trees I spotted the unmoving wolf, sprawled out for the final rest. I inspected each sector around the corpse, which I could see was female. Nothing stirred, no bird or squirrel tore the shroud of silence. I invented feral eyes in every bush, and it took hard stares to dispel my predatory imagination. Never had the woods seemed so full of menace. I could retreat into the meadow, back into the sun, and let it go. But a wolfskin was a prize and the meat was good. I held my ground and continued to study the suggestions of leaf and tangle.

On an impulse, I looked up. A raven sat on a low branch, inspecting me from its stoic blackness. It barely moved, just a slight tilt of the head as it lifted the crests of feathers above its eyes like raised brows. It would be interested in the carcass, too.

I spun around and went back to the meadow, calling for Koba. Yidi could stand watch while we rendered the corpse. Between the two of us, we could pack out the skins and most of the meat. The offal and bulk of skeleton could be left on the ground for the convenience of the endless scavengers of the world. We'd do a favor for the raven and her companions, no doubt soon to arrive.

"You're quite good at this sort of thing, aren't you?" said Koba.

"We'll tan these hides and make you a coat," I said, ignoring the question. "You'll want it for the high mountains."

She smiled and nodded, pleased at the idea, I could tell. After retrieving my arrows, one of which was broken beyond repair, we skinned the carcasses from tip to tail, then sliced off as much of the flesh as we thought we could carry. We filled each skin with cuts of meat and tied them together in two bags. Throwing these over our shoulders, we walked slowly, bent under the burdens. I gave Yidi a rib to carry in her jaws, though she stopped occasionally to crunch on it. As we trudged along, Koba found the energy to sing. I listened to her while monitoring the strain on my bad leg, throbbing after the sudden exertions of combat. Her song used our common language and I listened idly until I realized that it was about me, the killing of the wolves, and her own rescue. The way she told it made me into an epic hero, which seemed outlandish. I could have objected, but I didn't. Instead, I basked in her exaggerated praise, attaching it to the memory of her warm body close to mine.

She sang for a long time, embellishing the event so broadly that it might as well have included the creation of the world. Finally, she tapered off to some wordless humming, then stopped.

"You know, you're not Nobody," she said. "You never were, of course, but now that you're in a song, you're definitely not Nobody no more." She laughed at herself. "Look, we can't have a nameless hero—that won't do at all—and we can't use your old name, either. You've put it aside, which is your right. Hmmm. One of my duties as wordsmith is to name people and things. I want to offer you a name."

"Sure, I guess. I mean, I'd be honored. I think."

Koba grinned at my ambivalence. "Plunging ahead, then, here's what I'm thinking: what word do your people use for a she-wolf?"

"My people? Do I have a people anymore?"

"You grew up somewhere, right? And not speaking this language, I'm guessing. I know a dozen tongues, but your accent is new to me. So, what about the she-wolf: what word did your grandmother use? You must have had a grandmother."

That triggered an unwelcome reverie about the destruction of my family. Sure, I had a grandmother. And before that, a mother and a father and even a sibling. All killed, slaughtered like the rest of the village. Somehow, I was spared and spirited away into fosterage, where they called me "Marianne" and encouraged me to let go of the past. An easy thing to say, impossible to do. I shook my head to clear out the cobwebs of unwanted memories. "Sorry about that. Long story. Maybe I'll tell it. Sometime. Yes, I had a grandmother. I adored her until I lost her. She always had a story and sweets—isn't that the way it should be? She'd let me sit next to the stove while she spun endless tales of animals, trees, and magic. More than a few featured wolves. Maybe she even had a thing about them. She called them *osana.*"

"Osana!" Koba clapped her hands together and laughed. "A beautiful name, suitable for a she-wolf. I place it on your head like a crown, if you'll wear it."

I blushed because I liked it, even though I didn't want to admit it. "If you insist; I still don't feel the desire for a name. But if you need one for your song, you can use that. Osana," I let it roll around my tongue and enjoyed the feel of it. Could be a lot worse.

Koba's smile brightened, sluicing into me like a stream full of gold.

[6]

We spent the rest of the day at the cave working on the wolf remains. While Koba cut the meat into thin strips and hung them on a rack to dry in the sun, I scraped the hides, a painstaking process of raking every bit of flesh from the inside of the skin. Once that was done, I used the brains to make a tanning mash. Koba finished her project, aided by the gulping mouth of Yidi, and joined me. With brain muck up to our elbows we each massaged a hide, working the mash into the skin with our bare hands. By the time we rolled the hides into cloth bundles to soak, the sun lay low in the sky and there was just enough light to get to the hot spring for a much-needed bath.

I brought my archery tackle and a torch and gave Koba the new spear I'd made to replace the old one. Wolves roamed these hills, though usually at the higher elevations; I'd heard them howl but never seen one. Beautiful and interesting as they were, I'd be content not to see any again. If that happened, I wanted to be armed to the teeth. Koba accepted the spear without comment.

As we lay in the bath, soaking the sweat and blood out of our pores, I asked about something that had been flitting in and out of my attention since we'd met. "What can you tell me about your dreams? Are they always prophetic? How does it work?"

"I did promise to explain, didn't I? Not sure how rational it will sound! The dreamworld doesn't follow the logic of the dayworld. In the words of one philosopher, *the nights tell the things of which the days will be made.* But then another said, *one never knows what one may be releasing when one begins to analyze dreams.*"

"I'm well versed in the contradictions of philosophers, believe me," I said. Koba nodded, no doubt recalling some of my less-restrained rants. Probably I wasn't fair in my descriptions of my former companions, but it had felt good to unleash the turbulence of my memories and Koba was a sympathetic listener.

"The trick—if that's the right word—is in the interpretation of the dreams. As we know, they can be a confusing mosaic of images and actions. It's tempting to drill into a dream like it's a foreign language, full of symbols that need translation. That would be logical, and that's the approach taken by many, all the way back to the ancients. By that method, if a man dreams about sucking his penis, it means he won't have children because the penis represents children, and the mouth is a tomb. That's what you get if you consult a professional dream reader. Now and then their interpretations make sense, but usually at the cost of cheapening the imagery, as if sucking a dream penis is a simple code. Sometimes a penis is just a penis!"

"Do you think they do that, men? Suck their own penises? No, don't answer—of course they do—if they're limber enough." I tried not to laugh at my own humor, but Koba's giggle broke me down and we cackled like adolescents. "Anyway, what do *you* do with a dream? I've heard interpretations like you mention; they seemed a bit silly to me, too. But I haven't given it much thought."

"Well, dear protector Osana, tell me a dream and we'll go to work."

Dusk eased into darkness, but I was too intrigued to stir from the bath. "Okay. I've had a dream that keeps returning, ever since childhood. Not every night, just here and there."

"Ooh," said Koba. "Those are the best kind. I'm all ears."

"There isn't much of a story to it. It's a nightmare, I suppose, but nothing really happens. It starts when I wake up from sleep—only I'm still dreaming, of course—and a few steps away is a kind of portal. The portal is only an outline, shadowy and vague, reminiscent of a megalithic trilithon. All my attention is drawn to the portal opening, which is filled with cold light. I'm completely mesmerized by the light. It pulls me like a magnet. I get out of bed, take a leaden step, then another, and stretch my hand toward the light. All this time I'm moving without any volition, driven by an external force. Drenched in fear and wanting to scream, I can't break the spell. Somehow, I know that if I even touch the light in the portal, I will disappear. I'm terrified because I know that disappearing also means never having existed. But I can't stop myself. An inch from the portal, I wake up, covered with sweat. Getting back to sleep is a real challenge; it takes hours to calm down."

Koba's eyes gleamed with the waning light. "What a marvelous dream!"

"Not sure that's how I would characterize it."

"No, of course not. You have to suffer and endure it. Sorry to sound glib. Still, it is rich."

"How would you interpret it? I don't experience it as rich at all. It takes place in a gray world, impoverished of detail and riven with terror."

"I don't dare interpret it. It's your dream and only you can say what it means. That's the problem with all these professional dream interpreters: they're explaining things beyond their realm. To put it bluntly, they're full of *shit*."

I laughed at her emphasis. "But where do I even start?"

Koba sank under the water's surface, soaked her head, and emerged with a shake, flinging droplets from her braids. "What's on the other side of the portal?"

"How should I know?"

"Just let your imagination work. What could be on the other side?"

"Hm. I grew up hearing tales about the Otherworld. Maybe that."

"What do you know about this Otherworld?"

"It's where the fairies live. And magical women and beasts. Alluring it may be, in some ways, but deadly. You can get seduced in against your will and never get out." I fell silent.

"Oh my," prompted Koba.

"Just like my dream! I have no control over my body; it's like being a puppet."

"Now we're getting somewhere. Tell me more about the Otherworld. Who else lives there besides fairies and women?"

"The dead. Though I guess that's not living, is it? You can find them there, anyway. It's a fluid zone and changes from tale to tale. Sometimes it's ruled by powerful women who charm you until you lose all sense of time. If you hear music or eat anything, you'll never get out. Lots of trickster little fellows who'll promise you treasures but con you into slavery instead. It's also supposed to be very beautiful, but a kind of terrible beauty, dangerous and sharp." I paused. "I just thought of something else. The Otherworld is all around us as a vague presence, at least that's the way I heard it as a child, and you can't predict how it might brush up against our world, but there is one reliable way to get there."

"What's that?"

"Through the trilithon stones of a barrow mound. Just like the portal in my fucking dream."

I fell silent, stunned by the insight. Koba watched me closely but said nothing, just let me chew it over for myself. There was much to ponder. I dreamed of the portal to the Otherworld. How could it be anything else? But what did that mean?

"Okay, so the dream depicts an opportunity to go into the Otherworld," I admitted. "Not an opportunity people go looking for, by the way, as the stories tell. Not something I'm keen on doing."

"No?" Koba asked. "You're sure about that?"

"Why would I? It's a bewitched place—some never return."

"And those that do, what do you know of them?"

"Oh… I guess you would say those are the heroes, the ones that go into the Otherworld on quests and get out alive."

"Does something happen to them or do they just return with their skins intact and bragging rights and that's it?"

"No, you're right. They are changed, often in profound ways. More powerful, more focused. Sometimes they bring back a boon for their people."

"So, it's a kind of initiation, you might say?"

And damn her, she put her finger on it. "Yes," I said, "like that. Hey, we should head back to the cave before it gets completely dark." Plus, I needed some time to sift through the conversation. I felt a shuffling of the detritus in my head, components clicking into place like the tumblers of a lock. For years that dream had scared the hell out of me, all through child-hood, and it still hit me like an anvil. Now, Koba's inquiry made it seem like something else altogether. Not just a nightmare. Something of value, perhaps.

We dressed quickly and hurried back to the cave. There was still enough light from stars and the rising moon to find our way. We clutched our weapons, but I thought the chances of another wolf attack were small. They were too smart to mess with humans most of the time. Yet they were opportunists and finding Koba must have suggested an easy meal. A hungry pack, maybe, though they looked well-fed. Despite the mild winter in the foothills, perhaps the mountain snows held their usual hunting grounds in thrall. If that was the case, it could delay our search for Koba's mammoth. Which reminded me that she'd never really explained that, either.

At the cave, we sat next to the fire and roasted strips of wolf meat, licking the fat from our fingers. We leaned back on bedrolls and shared a blanket. I was proud of myself; I accepted the tingle of Koba's proximity without expecting more than the warmth of her companionship.

"I'd like to hear more about your mammoth dream, the one that brought you here."

Koba opened her side of the blanket to let Yidi crawl in and snuggle. The jackal poked her thin snout from under the cover and lay her head on Koba's breast, triggering her companion's hand to scratch and stroke between the tall ears. "We never have gotten around to the full story, have we? Overdue, for sure. Anyway, our elephant elders are convinced that the mammoth genes would be useful."

"I'm not sure I understood the gene thing the first time."

"Each living thing—plant, animal, fungus, whatever—carries within the elements of its flesh a kind of code, a genesis, that determines how it grows. The code is inherited from generation to generation and is like a script that controls the structure of the form. Your height, fair skin, and blue eyes, for example, come to you through your parents and to them from their parents, and so on back into the dim recesses of time past."

"And the same for your brown skin, I presume."

"Exactly. You can't see the code—it's too small—but it's there."

"So, if a dark-skinned person and a white-skinned person mated, they would blend color?"

"Yes. But the child could be anywhere on a spectrum between black and white; there are a lot of factors controlling the blend. It's not a simple 50/50, mix and stir. There's a lot to learn, but we're far enough into it that our elephants can influence genetic blending in plants and mice. Now they believe they can alter their own structure. They are passionate about wanting to manipulate their technical world more efficiently. I get it: even three tons of beautiful body can't do everything. Which brings me to my dreams."

"I'm all ears, as the elephant said."

Koba groaned. "I'm going to pretend I didn't hear that. As for the dream, or dreams—I had a series of three. In the first one, while wandering through a forest, lost, I met an elephant who proposed that we swap heads. Within the logic of the dream, that seemed reasonable, so I agreed. Instantly, the exchange happened. Our heads switched and changed size to fit the body. So, I became a giant Koba head on an elephant body, looking at a human-sized elephant head on my body. The elephant was pleased and leaped and danced, snapping its fingers, and patting its trunk and ears as if nothing could be more amazing than the dexterity of hands. Which is true, I think. Meanwhile, I stood in place on my enormous body and wondered what to do. Then I pissed all over my hind legs. And woke up."

I laughed at her telling of the dream, though it sounded as frightening, in its own way, as any of my own.

"When I told the dream to my elephant mother—mother by adoption, in case you're wondering—she became excited and wanted to know what I thought about it. I remembered the many stories of shapeshifting and metamorphosis in our culture. Like you, those were stories I first heard as a child. But I also recognized a theme of integration with our elephant kin and how blended I've become in my heart and mind. And then, in the background, there was something bigger, about how life-forms change over time, what we call evolution. So that's what I said: it's about evolution."

"Okay, I can see that."

Koba leaned her head against my shoulder while I gazed at the stars beyond the cave's overhang. "The code passes through generations, but it doesn't seem to be static; rather, it trans-forms, influenced by environmental pressure, mutations, and so on. That's why there aren't any mammoths now. They may have had more dexterous trunks, but for some other reason, they couldn't cope over the long haul. Climate change, maybe; we don't know."

I slipped my arm under Koba's neck and added my hand to Yidi's petting. It was nice, the three of us.

"Anyway," Koba continued, "in the second dream, I was a vulture, flying high over mountains. I was so high that I could see a whole mass of land from sea to sea. I didn't know it at the time, but it was this land, these mountains. I found a downdraft and spiraled out of the heights, circling in on a solitary rock tower projecting from alpine meadows. At the base of the tower, I saw a burst of light and I dipped into a dive, zooming straight toward it. The speed rush was a thrill like no other. I felt wild and free and more than a little crazy. Instead of pulling out of the dive, I let it take me into the rocks. Just before splattering on the stone, I was a human again, standing at the entrance to a cave. Within that cave, I knew, was a mammoth queen. And I woke up."

"I always wanted to fly but plummeting like a stone... not that! What an image!" I said.

"I'll say! When I told the dream to the elders and they asked what I thought it meant, I wouldn't answer them. I just said: *I'm going there.* They understood and helped me research the topography of the dream. Eventually, we figured out the physical location. So, I left, traveling mostly by ship from my country, through the great pillars and up the coast to a port of the inland sea. And overland to here. The sea journey took a couple of weeks. One night as I slept, I dreamed about a woman in the woods. I had to chase her through the trees, but when I caught up, she said she recognized me and would take me where I wanted to go. She had a body like yours, strong and beautiful. But two things stood out: she had tentacles instead of a right arm and her head was the head of a wolf."

"I see," I said, as tingles snaked up my back.

[7]

Each day we allowed ourselves a lengthy session in the hot spring, soaking out the grime and letting our tongues loose. Otherwise, we focused on chores and our thoughts. I was glad Koba didn't talk without something to say. She filled the spaces in between with humming, singing, or practicing her lute. I didn't mind that at all.

One day when I stood up to leave the bath, Koba's eyes narrowed. "Look at you now," she said. "When I got here you were thin as a wraith. These days you've worked up a true goddess glow."

"Yes, I feel great. You deserve a lot of the credit for that. I owe you."

"No, you don't! But I was wondering... are you ready for the mountains?"

"I think so. In a few days, let's make a foray into the village to stock up, but once we've done that, we can head out. Between you and me, the goats, and Yidi, we can carry a lot of supplies. It's going to take a while: weeks, at least, with the traveling, searching, and whatever else. Hard to estimate how long we'll need to stay in the high country, but we might as well prepare for a month."

"You're the guide," Koba said. "And I've got funds, so whatever you need...."

Koba wanted to draw a map of the mountains as she remembered it from her aerial dream. I gave her the scroll of *Knowing Touch* and she used the backside of the parchment,

431

some oak gall ink, and a sharpened heron feather I'd found in a marsh. She bent over the parchment on her knees and elbows and worked on it for a couple of hours. The details were finely drafted and duplicated a bird's eye view, at least as I imagined it. Corax would kill me for letting her mark up a sacred text, if he knew. Well, he wouldn't kill me because I wouldn't let him, but he'd want to. The thought of his explosive rant made me smile; he was so predictable. I thought it was an excellent use for the phenomenological text. The author had belabored her thesis that the physical world was an inextricable part of our perceptions and consciousness, so what better application for an embodiment of that consciousness than a map of the actual world? Maybe it was just my twisted humor, but I thought it a suitable irony.

Koba had started her drawing in the center with the rock tower. She spiraled out from there, incorporating the features of the surrounding landscape. I recognized some of the geography from past travels. My memory was not as precise as hers, but I added enough information for her to chart the major valleys and ridges that lay outside her dream, gradually filling in the region between our cave and her tower. *Our* cave, I thought. I'd accepted the domesticity of our relationship. And why not? Her companionship filled a lot of holes. I would be sorry to see her leave when everything was over. But she belonged elsewhere, with the elephants and her people and her… partner, the lucky soul. She remained quiet about that, and in truth, I didn't want to hear about him or her or what. Of course, I could accept the offer to go with her. There was always that.

I applied myself to the wolfskins after they were fully tanned. My fingers, thick from weapons practice and combat, were ill-suited for detail work like sewing, but I fashioned a suitable coat with only a minor amount of cursing. On an impulse, I used the skin from the heads to make us each a cap, padding it so that it fit over the skull with the snout as a brim. I put mine on and howled at Koba, who laughed while Yidi barked madly and ran over for a sniff, perhaps to make sure it was still me. Koba tried on her cap along with the coat and stalked back and forth, growling, and radiating a feral beauty. I wanted to eat her to the bones. Maybe I did have a wolf spirit lurking within.

On the day of our trip to the village, we rose at first light and hiked up to the ridge to find the goats. As soon as we gained the meadows, Koba whispered in Yidi's ear and she dashed off, faster than I thought possible, even for a creature on four legs. Koba smiled absently and slowed down to pick a daffodil and a narcissus, tucking the yellow into one braid and the white into the other. "What?" she said as I watched her, my hands on my hips. I made no attempt to conceal my impatience. It was a long walk into town, and we needed the goats; I didn't understand why she was dawdling.

"Oh, I don't know," I said, trying to decorate my words with sarcasm as pungent as her flowers.

"Just you wait," she said.

She ambled along and I had almost decided to leave her to the wolves when I heard Yidi yapping in the distance. Soon enough, the jackal came bounding into the meadow, chasing the goats. Or they were chasing Yidi, it was hard to tell as they leaped around each other like children playing a game of tag. The goats tumbled into me, pushing against my hips with their foreheads, knocking me backward. I had to grab their horns to keep from falling. These antics excited Yidi, who leaped up and down on her hind feet. Koba laughed and clapped her hands.

As I pulled out leashes, Koba said, "I don't think you'll need those. Yidi's an expert herder—as you see."

I felt an unexpected resistance to her smugness and wanted to be obstinate about it. Sharing control wasn't one of my favorite things and sometimes Koba, sweet as she was, could be a little bossy. These thoughts surprised me and made me wonder why I kept drifting back into irritated moods, even when I was happy. Just scratch my surface and there it was. No wonder I'd never had a long-term companion, not in any meaningful way. Stubborn pride stiffened my joints. The leashes dangled from my hand, but I didn't put them away, either. Instead, I flicked them absently while my mind ran amok. However, it didn't take long to picture the annoying hassle of dragging the goats on their leashes to town, or being dragged by them, more like it. Calm down and learn something, wolf woman, I said to myself. I coiled the leashes and stuck them in my pack, saying nothing and pretending that's what I intended all along. When I looked up at Koba, she stared off across the meadow, leaving me to sort out the crisis on my own, bless her.

And she was right, Yidi kept the goats in line, and made it look like play. They scampered around us in circles as we walked, staying close and moving in the same general direction, exerting more energy than seemed possible.

"Once we load them up in town, they'll fall in well enough," I said to Koba.

"Oh yes," she replied, peering at me out of the corner of her eye while a smile quivered around her lips. Was I that obvious? Yes, of course, I was.

We stopped at the cave because Koba wanted to change clothes. She put on a fresh shirt and skirt, and I admired the contrast between the white and pastel garments and her brown skin. Seemingly without effort, she always looked elegant. I wore the same grubby buckskins I always wore, adding as adornment a quiver of arrows and my bow. Koba watched me, wordless, when I handed her the spear. She nodded. Wolves weren't the only predators in these hills; we were heading into the realm of men, the most ferocious of all. Two women suggested easy pickings and visible weapons sometimes discouraged the random opportunist. We finished our preparations by strapping on empty packs and set off down the hillside to the valley.

An hour or two of tramping brought us to the river, just above the ferry crossing. We had the river path to ourselves, though we saw a dory with two fishermen drifting down the current. We waved at each other. At the ferry dock, nothing more than a couple of planks and some crude pilings, we raised the flag to signal the boatman. He sat on the far shore, eating and drinking. He raised his hand to acknowledge the flag but made no move to conclude his meal. Koba and I sat on the dock, removed our boots, and dangled our feet in the water. The goats grazed the ample weeds and grasses along the shore, watched closely by Yidi. The sun still climbed towards zenith while an occasional cumulus extended a brief shade. We rubbed shoulders and shared pieces of cheese and dried wolf meat. My irritations had dissolved in the trek—action always smoothed my edges—and I was content to sit in the sunshine with my... sister.

"I'm looking forward to our expedition," I said.

"Glad to hear you say that. I wondered if you were having second thoughts," said Koba.

"No, not that. I could use some activity; it's been a while. Well, if you don't count my blunder with the boar, and I prefer not to. Mostly I'm trying to come to grips with what happens after we find your rock tower and you get what you need, mammoth genes or whatever. Then, I guess you'll go home."

"Yes, I'll go home. That's kind of the point."

"I know." I took a breath and let it out. "I'm going to miss you."

"Well… that works both ways. I think you should come with me. I want you to. Have you given it any thought?"

"Yes, I have. Truthfully, I haven't thought of much else. I just can't decide. And that's unusual. I don't know. You've got your spouse and your place in the community. Where would I fit in?"

She put her arm around my shoulders. "Osana, my dear. We should talk more about my family, who's in it, and how it works. Of course, you have anxieties about that. Let me assure you that you will fit. Like a gem in its setting."

"I have a thousand questions."

"I'm sure you do. Later, though—looks like our ride is coming."

The boatman had finished his meal and started across the river. He propelled a small barge by expertly placing the long pole and pushing to keep the craft on a course for our dock. I fetched the goats and coaxed them to the shore. Yidi barked in excitement and the goats bleated back.

The boatman was a strapping man with a long beard. Shirt-less, he had as much hair on his chest and back as he did on his

it

face. In compensation, the top of his head was completely bald. I didn't recognize him, because on the rare occasions I went to town I usually went further downriver and used the bridge. We could have done that this time and saved the crossing fee, but it added another league of travel, and Koba insisted on paying.

She tossed the man a coin once he made fast to the dock and I herded the goats on board. The barge was big enough for a horse, maybe two, so we put the goats in the middle and sat cross-legged on the flat deck. The boatman filled his eyes first with Koba, then me. He grinned, revealing one or two remaining teeth.

"We don't see many of your folk here in the hills," he said in a surprisingly melodious alto.

"You mean women?" I asked.

He giggled, an interesting contrast to his stature. "No, I meant your companion. Dark people."

"You're right, I'm from a land far to the south. Are you a singer?"

"Why, yes, why do you ask?"

Koba didn't answer, at least not in words. She began to sing, using mouth noises like blocks of wood to strike a rhythm. Smiling, the boatman listened for a minute, nodding his head in time while he polled us out toward the current. Once he spun us around to head for the other shore, he joined in with his blocks of sound, overlapping Koba's rhythm with one that landed on the beat and sometimes in between, establishing a new rhythm. Koba responded by varying her own and the two of them improvised so tightly it sounded rehearsed. Yidi added her yips and barks, blending skillfully with the rhythms. I tapped my foot, pretty much the extent of my musical ability.

They sustained the chorus across the river. When we docked on the other side, Yidi promptly jumped to shore. The boatman held each of our hands with a dainty grip to help us step to the pier, then gently lifted the goats to join us. Safely ashore, he bowed. "Ambios, my ladies, at your service. You know where to find me," and he motioned to a hut at the top of the riverbank.

"By the way," he added, "your goat is pregnant. Good fortune!"

My eyes flew to the female. These goats had such long, hairy fur that it was hard to see changes happening on their bodies. I should have been paying closer attention when I strapped on her saddlebags. She had seemed a little plump but if I thought anything about it, I would have attributed it to the lush grass of spring. I didn't like it when I missed details. Too distracted with uncertainties, perhaps. All winter I'd been alone, watching my head grow fat with nonsense. I'd always thought I would flourish in solitude, but Koba's presence had reminded me that I needed others. And not just any others. The right others. Suddenly, I understood that I had to go south with her.

"Thank you!" I said to Ambios and returned his bow with a flourish. Koba arched a brow and we turned to walk along the path toward the village. I felt the eyes of Ambios on our backs.

"He's watching us, you know," I whispered to Koba.

"Let him watch," she said with a grin.

"Just be careful," I admonished. "I'm sure you know how to handle yourself, but you'd be an exotic prize for a lot of men around here. When I come to the village, I wear old clothes hoping they'll see a flea-ridden peasant. But that's me; probably not much you could do to dull your radiance."

She smiled widely. "I think most men would risk the fleas if they had a chance with you! Of course, you're right. But sometimes I just want the frills, you know? Pretty sure I can take care of myself, one way or another. I do know how to use this." She brandished the spear and brought the point forward with a quick, practiced thrust. "Besides, I have a she-wolf protector."

She saluted and fell into a march, inspiring Yidi to bark and match her steps. The two of them looked ridiculous. Their silliness flushed away my sour mood, as intended, no doubt. I ran after them and fell into step, adding my long legs to the parade. As we stomped around a bend, we heard a whistle and turned to look where Ambios stood on the dock, waving.

[8]

"Wait," I put up my hand and we all stopped. "That wasn't there before." I inclined my head to a kiosk on the side of the path about a hundred yards ahead of us. Hanging from a wall of the kiosk was the orange and black flag of the local autocrat, Duke Ganelon. A simple pole gate blocked the entrance to the town. Looking bored, four soldiers leaned against various parts of the roadblock.

"And it wasn't there when I came through," said Koba. "What does it mean?"

"Not sure. Nothing good, I can guarantee that much." I pulled out the leashes and secured the goats. "I guess we'll find out shortly."

As we approached the gate, the soldiers took notice. If I didn't know that such men were dangerous, I would have found them comic. At first, they stared in a kind of amazement, no doubt due to Koba's brown skin and foreign dress along with the diverse menagerie and our lack of male escort. Having sized us up, they leered and grinned openly, nudging each other with obvious excitement. Of course, there would be trouble. I couldn't very well shoot them down with my bow just to relieve some anxiety, but I was tempted, despite my resolve to stop killing. I settled for touching the knife sheathed on my thigh and looking into the woods with longing. If I'd known about the gate, we could have detoured through the forest.

"Halt!" The soldier in the middle stood up straight, thrust his chest forward, and pounded the ground with the butt of his spear. They were all dressed in leather armor, battered and ill-maintained. Gate-keeping duties, I was sure, rarely involved combat. These were men who were used to being obeyed solely because they represented the power of the state. Obedient, we stopped just beyond the reach of the guard's spear. I looked him in the eye with all the weary ferocity I could manage. The other three guards continued to slouch, grinning like fools, and running their eyes up and down.

I could have taken all four apart in less than a minute. I had no taste for playing the meek maiden, but it seemed prudent to find a middle ground, so I softened my posture. "Yes? We've halted. What next?"

The leader scowled and pounded his spear twice more. "Shut up! State your business!"

I looked at Koba and was pleased to note that she had stopped behind me. Her expression was composed and neutral. Yidi sat on hind legs, unmoving except for a twitching nose, no doubt absorbing the pungent aromas rolling off the soldiers. Without a word, Koba gently removed the goat leashes from my hand. I could feel the twitch for combat in my muscles and there was nothing about these louts that gave me pause. The consequences, however, would doubtless mean more trouble than it was worth.

"Who's asking?" I replied.

"The Duke, bitch!"

"I'll wager you're not him," I replied.

"Insolent twat! State your business! Now!" He was on the verge of screaming and I thought it sensible to defuse the situation, as much as I wanted to wind him up.

"Shopping in the town market," I said.

"And where are you from? I haven't seen you before. I'll wager *she's* not from around here," and with contempt, he jabbed his spear toward Koba, as if her appearance was an insult.

I exercised more restraint than the goon deserved. "She's a distant cousin."

"Is that so? And I'm your fucking uncle. So where do you two cunts live?"

I ignored his swearing, which was more ridiculous than threatening, and smiled with all the sweetness and innocence I could muster. "We're from up the valley about three leagues."

He sneered, then motioned to one of the other guards, who ducked into the kiosk and returned with a scroll. The leader snapped his fingers and another soldier hustled over with a wooden contraption which he unfolded into a small table, placing it in front of his commander. Laying the scroll on the table, the leader opened it to reveal a map of the area. My heart sank. A census? It was clear that Duke Ganelon had ambitions of regional control. "Where?" He barked, pointing at the map.

I stepped forward and bent over the parchment. Good to know what they know, I thought. I was relieved to note a lack of detail anywhere near our cave. The valleys and ridges were out of proportion and featured substantial amounts of blank space. I pointed vaguely at a place in the valley a long way upriver from the ferry crossing.

"Exact!" He yelled, spittle flying. He snapped his fingers again and the soldier who had done nothing but smirk, quickly fetched a quill and ink. Thrusting the quill into my hand, he indicated the map. "A simple X, if you're not too daft. Like the captain says, *exactly* where you live."

I stared at him for a moment, noting the food particles in his beard and the waft of bad breath. Taking the quill, I dipped it in the ink and made an X on the map, careful to locate it far from the cave or any place easy to access.

"Sign your name," he commanded, pointing next to the X. I did, writing *OSANA* in neat block letters, more amused than angry by this point. It was almost like getting an official name change. Except, if any officials went looking for me, they'd discover the wolf had slipped her tether.

I gave him back the quill and he gestured at the others to take it all away.

"Five crowns," he said.

"What?"

"Listen bitch, I'm not saying it again. Five crowns. Gate tax. Or you and your little barnyard buddies can turn right around and go home."

"Captain!" One of the men caught his attention and gestured rudely, forming a circle with the forefinger and thumb of one hand and running his other finger in and out.

The Captain guffawed and turned back to me. "Or, if you're willing to take each of us down in the bushes for a spell, you can earn a discount!" He snickered at his cleverness. I suddenly remembered that I had wanted to kill them, but Koba stepped forward and tossed a five-crown coin at him. He snatched it off the ground, frowning, then shrugged and nodded at his men, who swung open the gate.

As we walked by, he called out. "Don't forget the property tax! We'll come by to collect!" He and his men laughed and hooted. We passed through the gauntlet of their leering airs and didn't look back. .

Once we were in the village, Koba drew all the attention; I seemed to be invisible. A few furrowed their brows into hard looks of disapproval. Koba pretended not to notice, but her proud, upright posture told me that she was aware of her status as the only dark-skinned woman in town and she intended to make an impression. It's something most women learn young: we're either in the shadow or on display. Both made me uneasy.

We tethered the goats to a rail in front of the marketplace and left Yidi to guard. The market was an open-walled, roofed barn where farmers could sell their products in all types of weather. We meandered along the crowded central aisle. The aroma and bustle of the market excited Koba and she bounced back and forth from vendor to vendor, taking samples and smiling at everyone. I cruised in her wake, enjoying her delight while also studying the people, looking for the potential problem. But this was the active heart of the community, and as long as goods and coins exchanged hands, there were no hostilities. We emerged with bags of cheese, hard sausage, barley, dried grapes and berries, pine nuts, walnuts, and wheat flour, all good for traveling. We couldn't resist a large apple tart which we ate standing on the front porch while Yidi waited at Koba's feet for falling crumbs.

As I licked sweet filling from my fingers, I heard a voice bellow across the road. "Marianne! Marianne!" Even though it wasn't my name, not anymore, I turned out of habit. Waving and dashing through the traffic of horses, carts, and people, I saw my old companion Corax. I'd anticipated trouble, but not this kind.

He charged up the market steps with alarming vigor, wrapping his arms around me in a bear hug. Because I had the last bite of the tart in one hand and the other was drenched in fruit filling, I let him get away with the enthusiastic greeting. I popped in the remaining tart, wiped my fingers on the back of his shirt, and pushed him away. None of this bothered him. As always, he was oblivious.

"I can't believe it's you! I've been searching.... You're an elusive one, aren't you? Interesting hair, by the way." He pointed at my cornrowed braids and stared at Koba, who by this time was stifling laughter. Corax raised and lowered his eyebrows as he tried to sort identities and relationships.

"Corax, well met," I said thinly. Although I counted him as a friend, I knew that he would eventually get on my nerves. Usually, it didn't take long. But I had saved his life several times and would again, if necessary, so I held a measured fondness for the man. Though he was not exactly a man, having the characteristics of two sexes, and this peculiarity made him someone to cherish, at least in my view. If he would only stop talking....

I placed a hand on his shoulder and waved at Koba. "This is my friend Niokolo-Koba and her canine companion Yidi. The goats, here, have yet to disclose their names. And by the way, I no longer use that name you were yelling. If you really must call me something, call me Osana."

Corax wrinkled his forehead, pulled at his wisp of a beard, and stared at me, trying to fathom if I was teasing him. Finally, he shrugged. "Okay, why not? After all, you did rescue me from the demented theatrics of Dionysos; you've a right to call yourself whatever you want." He curtsied to Koba. "Pleased to meet you, Mistress Niokolo-Koba. And Yidi. I am Corax, an out-of-work logician." Koba giggled and curtsied back. Yidi lifted her paw and extended it toward Corax for him to shake. He took the paw and bent over it with a solemn kiss. Koba beamed and I felt a slight pang of… what, jealousy? Koba and I had been together constantly for a month; I loved our connection and didn't want to share. Corax, with his unstable moods, his ranting, and his penchant for turmoil, inevitably became the center of everyone's attention.

"Just call me Koba," she said, extending to Corax the last corner of the tart. He took it and stuffed in the whole chunk.

"Let's find somewhere to eat," he said, crumbs bouncing out of his lips. "I know there are stories to tell!"

"We're in a bit of a hurry. What are you doing here, anyway?" I asked.

"Looking for you, of course." Hands on hips, he bobbed his head.

"I was afraid of that. I'm on sabbatical, or in retirement, even. No matter how many people you need killed, you'll have to find someone else."

"No, no," he objected. "It's not that. You have an overdue text from the library."

He said it with a straight face, though the twinkle in his eyes gave away how pleased he was with himself. I was sure he'd been practicing that phrase. I stared at him and picked my teeth.

"Since I stole the damn thing in the first place, I'm not sure how that makes it *overdue*."

"Ha ha, good point. Sharp as ever, eh, Mari… ah, I mean… Osana. Is that it, Osana? What kind of name is that, anyway?"

"Native tongue. Needless to say, I don't believe that you came all this way to retrieve a scroll. Though if anyone would do such a thing, I suppose it would be you."

He chuckled. "Well, good to have it back in the library at some point. I wanted to bring you the companion volume, *Invisible Threads*, the one that takes it to the next level."

"Companion volume? Thanks, I guess. Speaking of companions, where is your shadow, Diarmuid?"

Corax blinked and looked down at his feet. I thought he was on the verge of crying. "Oh, him. He went back to his home on that island of fanatics. He said he wanted to tie up some loose ends. I, of course, being *persona non grata*, can't go back."

"No, I don't suppose you could, not after what we had to do to get out. I'm surprised Diarmuid thinks he can return. Weren't we all implicated?"

"Indeed. But he wasn't about to be talked out of the venture. I tried, but he left anyway." Corax wouldn't look me in the eye, choosing to stare over my shoulder at some distant point.

"Now I get it. You're alone, at loose ends, and looking for something to do."

He looked down and kicked the toe of his shoe against the wooden porch. "Guilty as charged. But I did want you to have *Invisible Threads.*"

Koba swiveled her head back and forth to watch our exchange. Her expression remained neutral, but I could see she was trying to puzzle out the emotional subtext of our words. Several times she opened her mouth as if to say something, but each time let it pass.

"Look," I said to Corax, "we don't have a lot of time for chat. We're stocking up for a journey into the mountains. We need to finish here, return to the ferry, then hike a couple of leagues into the hills to get back to our shelter. You're welcome to come with us. There'll be more time to talk."

Corax smiled. "May I? I do love an expedition! Let me run back to the inn and grab my pack. I'll be right back!"

He bolted off down the street before I could clarify my invitation.

"That's not exactly what I meant," I said to Koba. "I wanted him to come for a visit, not join our quest. He seemed so excited. But I can still tell him no."

"Don't be too hasty. I have a hunch that it's meant to be this way. Anyway, I have no objection."

"He is a good man. Infuriating at times, but aren't they all?"

While waiting for Corax, we packed our provisions. I decided to give a lighter portion to the female goat now that I realized she was pregnant. Yidi accepted her load like a soldier, but both of the goats grunted and bleated, unhappy with the burdens. I hugged each one and said nice things, for what that was worth. Not much because they scraped the saddlebags against the hitching post or tried to shake them off. I dashed back into the market, returning with an offering of carrots, which they accepted as a worthy distraction.

Corax soon came trotting down the street with a pack flopping over his shoulder. Pudgy when I first met him, he'd lost weight over the past year and now looked quite fit. That meant I couldn't use his condition as an excuse to deny him a place on our mountain journey. I sighed and resigned myself to his company. There seemed to be no way around it, other than a callous dismissal. I could be aggressive, but I wasn't that mean, at least to my friends. So, together we walked up the street, listening to Corax babble about his recent studies in phenomenology. Koba flashed me a questioning look at one point and I just shrugged. I had tried to warn her.

At the mercantile, we purchased three hand-held lamps and a flask of oil. I gave a lamp to Corax, who beamed with excitement and fondled it like a relic. "This reminds me of the subterranean journey through the Holy Island. We only had one lamp for three of us, which led to more than a few stumbles. What do we need these for? More spelunking? I'm impressed. But you always were well-prepared." I analyzed his comments for sarcasm but detected none. Despite his chirpy talk, there was no sign of the mania or depression that had nearly ruined him a year ago.

"By the way," I said, ignoring his questions, "I hope you have plenty of lithium. Just to cover the bases."

He blushed but nodded. "Yes, yes; I learned my lesson. Trust me."

"I also trust you have some warm clothes; we're going to be at high altitudes."

"Don't worry. I know mountains: snow and all that. And why are we going there? Not that it matters; you can't get rid of me that easy!"

"The usual," I said. "Looking for something that may or may not exist."

"Of course," he said, nodding his head rapidly. "It would have to be something like that. Are you pursuing a specific category of may or may not, or just anything in general along those lines?"

Koba laughed. "Quite specific. It's my search and Osana has agreed to be the guide. We're looking for a mammoth, frozen within a cave high in the mountains. My elephant relatives sent me to find it."

"Elephant relatives?" Corax scrunched his face in a combination of query and disbelief.

"Yes, my family is part human, part pachyderm; it's quite interesting."

I saw a dozen questions arranging themselves on Corax's lips. "We can puzzle over the details later, yes? Time to move," I said.

A trumpet blast interrupted our conversation. We spun to see a military guard, all mounted, parading down the road, three abreast, scattering townspeople and farm animals in front of them. They advanced in a rhythmic procession, a single drum keeping the beat. Every lance flew Duke Ganelon's colors, and every lancer scowled at the citizens as they passed. Half a hundred of them, churning the road's dirt into a muddy mixture of earth and horseshit. I froze, glaring at the callous display of power. Vaguely, I felt my fingers open and close.

"Osana! Are you okay?" I blinked. Koba clutched my arm.

Corax peered at me with genuine worry. "I thought you were going to stab them to death with those blue eyes of yours!"

"I'm okay. I don't like soldiers, but I guess that's no secret!" I managed a thin smile. "Fuck those fuckers. And fuck their gate tax. Let's find a way around it."

"By all means," said Corax. "A hideous crew, aren't they?"

We headed up the hill on a side street until it ended at terraces full of freshly worked soil and new shoots. Turning, we traversed along a garden path. Where it switched back to the terrace above, we continued straight into the forest. Beech, pine, chestnut, and oak formed a dappled sanctuary. I handed the goats' leashes to Corax and took the lead. Instinctively, we walked in silent single file as we traversed the slope, staying high enough to avoid being seen from the road, but low enough to spot the ferry crossing. Through the canopy, I caught glimpses of giant cumulus clouds rolling overhead, blocking the sun, plunging the woods into gloom, and then passing to sprinkle sunshine through the leaves like jewels. Without warning, I stopped.

"What?" whispered Koba.

"Shh." It was difficult to see through the woods. I thought I'd heard a rustle of leaves accompanying a flash of movement. Nothing I could identify. Perhaps a raven in the branches, watching our passage. I felt it, though. Something watched us. In the forest, something always watched; not necessarily harmful, just another monitor, keeping an eye on things. But there were plenty of hungry creatures, too, and those I wanted to see before being seen.

"Nothing there, I guess." I saw by their wide eyes that my caution had spooked my companions. I hadn't meant to alarm them. Or maybe I had—from my point of view the best way to outwit the stealthy hunter was to be stealthier. If everyone walked a little softer, all the better. Certain that we had passed beyond the gate and were near the crossing, I pointed down the slope. I motioned for them to stay while I crept through the woods, stopping behind a bush along the road. A cart rattled toward my position, pulled by a donkey. Two herdsmen walked alongside. As they went past, I heard one say to the other, "What a bunch of assholes." "Yes," said the other one, "it doesn't bode well. I hope they don't bring their damn war with them." The complaints rolled on as they headed down the road. My stomach clenched at the mention of war. Anger flared into a brief rage that made me want to run back to the gate and kill those men. And why stop there? Kill them all. As quickly as it flared, the rage dimmed into numbness. I couldn't control the forces of war, I knew that. Shaking off my despair, I scrambled back up to where I could see Koba and motioned them to join me.

We arrived at the ferry in a somber mood. Ambios, though, was happy to see us. I had cautioned the others not to discuss our expedition in front of him. He was a gentle fellow, but ferrymen had loose tongues and were obvious conduits of information. Was I paranoid? Maybe, and I could live with that.

Ambios and Koba resumed their chant as soon as the boat was away from the dock, and we made the short crossing under the spell of their music. Corax studied the two of them while I studied him. Why was he really here? I had heard his explanations, but I thought there must be more to it. As to what else might be going on, no doubt he would tell us when he was ready. My nerves were bowstring tight, and between trying to read Corax's mind and peering downstream for pursuit from soldiers, I couldn't relax.

Koba paid the crossing fee with a bonus; Ambios bowed and blew her a fingertip kiss. I waved, glad to be free of civilization, and set off along the shore trail. This side of the river was rarely traveled, and it was hard to understand how Ambios made a living with the ferry, but with his hut, a garden, and the fish in the river, maybe he had a fine life. As I well knew from living in the cave, people didn't need much. Give them peace and they will get by. A war would change all that. .

Still tense, I scanned the woods as we walked, looking for signs of spies or ambush. I also searched for the three-stemmed maple that marked the place we'd leave the path. We could take any number of routes through the woods to the cave, but the slope above the maple offered the easiest grade. Loaded with supplies, that would mean something after a few hours of uphill toil. I stopped at the maple as a red squirrel on a low branch scolded us for disturbing his sovereignty. Yidi barked once and the squirrel scrambled up the tree, ran along a slender limb, and leaped across the gap to another tree where it paused to resume its chatter. I insisted that we take three separate routes up the slope from the river path rather than scuff the earth with the sum of our tracks. Corax raised his brows at my instructions, and I saw the retort perched on his lips. I stared at him, and he closed his mouth. Shooing everyone into the woods, I took a last look around before slipping into the trees.

About a hundred yards up the slope, I called us together and we merged to a line, switch-backing up the gradually steepening flank of the ridge. I took the lead, followed by the goats, unleashed now because I knew they would stay close. Experience had taught them that the sooner they got home, the sooner they'd be out of the saddlebags. I asked Koba to take the sweep position, which left Corax in the middle. It was always best to have him as the middle. Otherwise, he tended to get distracted with philosophical fancies and wander off, never a word to his companions, who may not notice his absence except in the blessing of silence.

Corax kept pace, though, I had to give him that, and without complaint. For him, that was unprecedented. An hour into the hike, we stopped for water and food.

"So, what's the big deal with the name thing?" Corax asked as he broke off the end of a loaf of bread.

"It's not a big deal," I said. "I just don't like them. They pull things apart."

"Things are apart, that's what makes them things," he said.

"We *think* they're apart," I said, "but are they? To what extent? And how do we know that?"

"Ooh, you've been reading that text, haven't you?"

"Of course, I've been reading it—do you think I took it to wipe my ass?"

Koba watched this exchange with growing amusement. "Watch yourself, Mister Corax, she's got edges."

"Don't I know. But what's with this *Osana* name? What was wrong with Marianne?"

I hesitated, not sure how much of this I wanted to discuss, and in the pause, Koba intervened. "I gave her that name as an honor. It means *she-wolf*. That was after I watched her kill two wolves with two arrows in about two seconds. Since she'd thrown away her old name, I thought she might need a new one, at least for some occasions. But it won't be a true name for her until she dreams it."

"Dreams it? What are we talking about here? The taxonomy of the unconscious?" Corax stopped eating and tugged the goatish hairs on his chin.

"The naming isn't complete until she claims it with her inner being," Koba said, feeding a scrap of bread to Yidi.

Corax looked at her with a pained expression, then turned to me. "Please don't tell me you've derailed into some unbounded mystery realm where everything is mumbly-jumbly."

I laughed and rubbed my knuckles on the top of his head. He winced. "Well now. It's not too late to reconsider your desire to spend a month with two mumbled and jumbled mystics seeking the mammoth mother in the mountains."

He grinned. "Don't try to change the subject or distract me with alliteration. We are, all of us sitting here, quite separate. Yes, our senses merge within the field of the world, but each of us, as well as all the things we perceive, have identities. A name just provides a reference."

"Good point," said Koba.

"And then the identities start assuming more importance than the connections and perspective is more reflective than perceptive," I said.

Corax looked at me with an open mouth. "Neat. You haven't been wasting your time in the hills, have you?"

"I never waste my time," I grumbled, "except when it came to listening to you and Diarmuid grind logic until my teeth hurt."

"Ouch," said Corax. "Was it that bad, then?"

"Sometimes. What was it that the Tiresias imposter called it? Chopping logic?"

"Do you suppose he's still singing his epic song about us?"

"I don't know what to believe about any of that. Given all the shape-shifting and role-playing, names and identities didn't seem to amount to much, did they?"

"Good god, no, that was insane." Corax took a swig of water from the flask. "You know, the more I think about it, the more I like the name Osana; it's a good fit for you. It's got more flavor than Marianne. So, dream it up real soon and we can move on from the fuzzy-wuzzy, all-is-one stuff."

"I didn't say all is one and never will. Diversity is the rule, not unity. But enough fencing; let's get moving. We've still got a hill to climb."

[9]

It was almost dark by the time we made it to the cave. I relieved the goats of their packs and let them scramble off to their meadows and crags. The rest of us satisfied ourselves with a quick meal followed by a cup of tea, including Yidi, who lapped the cooling liquid from my palm. Corax did a quick circuit of the shelter and laid out his bedroll as far as he could from the dome tent. Given my affairs during our last mission, I'm sure he assumed it was a cozy pleasure palace for women. Remembering his tendency to snore, I saw no reason to dissuade him.

In the morning, we had a light breakfast and strolled to the hot spring for a long soak. On the way, Koba told Corax the details of her family culture and the importance of the mammoth. He listened with few questions, something that surprised me. He seemed a bit in awe of Koba, which I understood. At the pool, there wasn't room for all three at once, so we took turns sitting on the rim, soaking our feet while the others stretched out. Being the host, I took the first shift on the rim. To my delight, Koba put my feet in her lap and started to massage them, using her fingers to squeeze out the pain and stiffness.

"You can do that forever," I said.

She snickered. "It's a simple magic."

"No magic to it," objected Corax. Here we go, I thought, just like old times. "It's simple body mechanics," he said, adopting the tone of the unrepentant scholar.

Koba smiled at him. "Next, I'll do your feet and you can tell me how it's just body mechanics—whatever that means."

"What you're doing to *my* feet, it feels more magical than mechanical, I'll vouch for that," I said.

Corax opened his mouth, no doubt interested in spurring on a dialogue full of thrust and parry, but Koba spoke first. "I wonder, did anyone have a dream last night?"

"Yes, now that you mention it, I did," said Corax. "And it was most unusual!"

Koba looked at me; I shook my head, having slept like a stone. "I also had an interesting dream. But please, Corax, share yours!"

He pulled at his long goatee. "I don't remember it very well, is the thing. And what I do remember is a little embarrassing."

"We're all grown up now, Corax," I said, curious.

"Okay, you asked for it. But like I said, I don't remember much. What I do remember is being in a dark place. In front of me, I saw an enormous, shaggy mound. For some reason, I was drawn to this thing. The attraction was intense, physical, and... arousing. I wanted to touch it, but an unseen force stopped me. I could see the mound, yet I couldn't circumvent or penetrate the barrier, no matter what I tried. I started to cry, then I woke up."

There was a sparkle in Koba's eyes. "Was it alive, this thing?"

Corax's cheeks were red, either from embarrassment or the hot steam. "I guess so."

"The mound was shaggy? What did you make of that?"

"Yeah, it had long hair or fur, kind of matted. Reddish-brown, I remember that. Some kind of animal? I suppose, though I couldn't identify body parts; it was just a big lump."

Koba looked at me and silently mouthed "mammoth."

"Hmm," I said, unconvinced. Sounded to me more like a back-to-the-womb fantasy, but I knew enough about his past to realize it would be cruel to suggest anything of the sort. Instead, I decided to make a joke. "Corax, you must be missing Diarmuid, he's about that big and hairy."

I thought my wisecrack would at least merit a snort, but he put his face in his hands and sobbed. I scooted around the tub and touched his shoulder, leaning over to kiss the top of his head. "I'm sorry," I said. "I meant a jest. Is something wrong?"

He wailed and gasped so hard I thought he would vomit. I patted him until he trailed into sniffles and wiped his face. "I'm not sure I'll ever see him again!"

"I wondered about that. Please, tell us what happened."

He closed his eyes. "Things were going well after we finished that absurd Dionysos business. The library at The Kraken Imaginary base was excellent and I toured back and forth through the collection. Not as good as the Academy, of course, but some real gems. Diarmuid and I had regained our fondness and ease with one another, or at least I thought so. Then you disappeared, and it seemed to shake him up. He wouldn't say why, but I think his feelings for you are probably a bit more than he lets on."

"What? I mean, he's a good man, I like working with him, and he seems to like working with me, but I never picked up on anything else."

"Really? I'm surprised you're that dense. I saw it, and if I saw it, it couldn't have been too obscure. Plus, I think he's a little confused about his desires. When Fedelma showed up and said she was returning to the Holy Isle to continue her research on the kraken, he jumped at the chance to run off with her."

"Fedelma! You didn't mention her before. I thought you said he went back to see old friends," I said.

"Well, I wasn't ready to tell the story, was I? He said he was keen to help with her research, but I have my doubts. Maybe on one level. She was his first lover, you know that, right? I couldn't go, not after all that business with the monks. So that was that. Goodbye and good luck."

I thought about commenting on the fickleness of men, but decided against it, opting for sympathy instead. Besides, men could rarely tolerate the banter they freely dished out to others. "I'm sorry to hear that, Corax, I truly am. You two have been through a lot together."

"See now why I had to get away?"

Koba joined in by patting him on the other shoulder. "I'm glad you're here. That dream of yours seems important, but I don't want to mash it through a symbol sieve and miss the true meaning."

"Symbols? Don't tell me!" Groaned Corax, armoring himself with sarcasm. "Are you one of those dream interpreters like that Artemidorus crackpot?"

"I know his work," replied Koba.

Corax arched his eyebrows. "You do?" I could hear the skepticism. At least, he seemed to have forgotten his grief.

"I've been around. Even to the Great Library," she replied, unruffled. "But I don't work like Artemidorus. I'm more of a dreamer than an interpreter. I'm interested in dreams, but I don't rely on a rule book to understand them. For one thing, I don't believe there are standard, unchanging meanings for dream images. Secondly, I believe that only the dreamer truly understands the dream, and it is for her to figure it out. Others can assist, but the answers have to come from the dreamer, no one else. So I won't translate your dream, but I do sense that it's relevant to our journey. We can talk about that later. Right now,

I think you two should switch positions so Osana can soak, and I can persuade you of my foot magic."

I could sense the tumble of questions Corax wanted to ask. I had a few, myself. I can see where his dream mound might be a mammoth—asleep, dead, or comatose—but what the devil did the rest of it mean? And what was a mammoth to him? I kept my mouth shut and slid into the enveloping waters of the bath while Koba started to work on Corax's feet.

"My dream is relevant, I think, but I'm not sure how," Koba said. "It was a simple dream, but sometimes the simple ones are the hardest to understand. As usual, it started in the middle of things. In this case, in the middle of wading across a wide stream. The bottom was sandy and shallow, but the water was dark, so I had to test each step with my toes. Just after crossing the mid-point of the current, I felt something sharp underfoot. I couldn't tell what it was, and I stopped. All of a sudden, the water turned bright red and started to rise. I knew I needed to get to the other side, yet I couldn't move. The fear overwhelmed me with paralysis. And that's it. I woke up with my heart pounding like a charging bull."

I had slept through all that, apparently. "That sounds awful. You should have woken me. You're not alone, you know...."

"I know. Your sleep was serene, which is not often the case. I didn't want to take you out of that peace; it didn't seem right."

Her sentiment warmed me, offering another hint of what it might be like to have a sister, someone who truly cares about you. "Well, thank you. But I wouldn't have minded. Anyway, what do you make of the dream?"

"I hate to say it, but it feels like something bad is going to happen. I have no idea when or where. Or what. Ultimately, it's just a feeling and could be reflecting my anxieties. Maybe not prophetic at all…" but she didn't sound convinced.

"I think we'd better be on guard, just in case." I remembered the hostility of the Duke's men and their threat to extort further taxes. And there had been the unusual wolf attack. Put that alongside my mishap with the boar and no wonder I was edgy. It seemed I wasn't the only one. I was always on guard, but what the hell, might as well take it up another notch. Koba didn't look particularly frightened, though that meant nothing. She had admirable self-control and would have made a brilliant actress. She angled her head and eyes to suggest that I peek at Corax. He was in a trance, lids heavy, hands on his belly, oblivious to the world while Koba rubbed his feet. For him to remain silent this long was true magic.

Meanwhile, a cloud cover had crept down from the mountains. "Probably going to rain," I said.

Corax blinked and groaned, clearly reluctant to leave his bliss. He nodded toward Koba. "Thank you! We may have to do further experiments before I concede that it is actual magic, though," he said in a sly voice.

"I'll take that as an endorsement," said Koba.

We stepped out of the bath and let most of the water run off our bodies before donning clothes. Yidi stood and stretched her forepaws while wiggling her bottom in the air. Just as we walked away, the first drops fell.

Subdued into silence by the hot soak, we traversed the narrow path I'd worn between the spring and the cave. It stayed on the contour, for the most part, winding in and out of trees and meadows and intersecting with the cave outcrop from above. To allay my hyperactive caution, today I'd removed the ladder and hidden it in the bushes, covering it with boughs. Corax had watched while Koba and I had done all the work. At the time I had wondered at her lack of questions but having heard about her dream, it made sense.

The rain picked up its pace and I relished the way the drops ran along my skull between the braids like furrows in a field. A cool shower after the boiling spring made a pleasant contrast. As we neared the cave, around the corner of the outcrop, I heard a horse whicker. I dropped to a crouch and motioned the others to get down. Pointing to a large beech above the path, I gestured for them to hide. I strung the bow, placed it back over my shoulder, and crept uphill on hands and knees. Fearing the worst, I needed to see what was going on. Along with the rain, a little fear-sweat trickled down my nose, salty on my lips. Every muscle in my body hummed with tension, welcoming the familiar rush of action. I enjoyed this. I was twisted, no doubt about it. Later, I would analyze it… maybe.

Trees grew sparsely on the slope above the cliff, but brush and boulders were plentiful. Enough cover to find a perch where I could survey the area in front of the cave. What I expected to see was at least one horse at the base of the cliff. The problem was the rider or riders. This was hardly the terrain for a casual outing. My nerves clenched lute tight because I knew who was there: soldiers, of course.

At the crest of the outcrop, I spotted a couple of shrub junipers, perfect for a spy. I slithered toward them on elbows and toes, inching my torso through the dirt. So much for the bath. From below, I heard several horse noises. More than one, then. The rain fell steadily but I was so keyed up I didn't notice. Whoever was down there wouldn't like the rain, either—which might help. At the juniper clump, I removed my bow and slid into the middle of the tree, raising my head slightly. Still no sightline. Whoever had come to visit was parked directly below the cave. The juniper was thick, so I took the risk of sitting up, contorting myself to fit around the sturdy branches next to the trunk. I leaned forward, staying within the halo of leaves. Three horses, three riders. One of the riders held a lance; Duke Ganelon's pennant hung limply from the shaft. All three sat hunched over their mounts, clearly unhappy with the weather.

"Who the fuck lives somewhere like this," said one.

"Someone who doesn't want to be found. Someone up to no good."

"Bah, looks like the dwelling of a witch. Not those cunts we saw the other day." I recognized the voice of the captain from the gate.

"That one, the black one—she was decked out. And looking good. I never seen a witch like that."

"Lot of traffic here, though, so it counts as a dwelling for the census. Whoever it is, witch or bitch or troll, they'll owe the tax." The captain spat on the ground. "Well, we know where it is. Next time we'll bring some rope and take a closer look. For now, I'm wanting some grog at the inn. Let's go."

They turned and started down through the trees. The horses stumbled here and there with the steepness, but none of the soldiers moved to dismount. I watched them plod into the dim light of the wet forest. Even though it seemed they hadn't gotten into the cave—and I applauded my caution in stowing the ladder—I felt violated. Soldiers knew the location of my sanctuary? It was ruined. We had to leave. Immediately.

I ran down to the beech tree where I found Koba giving Corax a neck massage as they huddled behind the trunk. If I wasn't racing on adrenalin, I would have laughed. Instead, I was a bit curt. "Come on, we have to go. They've gone."

"Go?" said Corax.

"Who was it?" asked Koba at the same time.

"Soldiers. Same louts we met at the village. They must have followed us, or tracked us, despite our precautions. Pretty sure they'll be back, though probably not today. And yes, dear Corax. No better time to head into the mountains."

"We couldn't wait for better weather?" There was a whiny edge to his voice.

"Sure, we could. But I don't want to give those idiots a chance to catch us at home. The weather provides excellent cover."

"Marianne would have just killed them and taken the horses," grumbled Corax.

"Marianne isn't here, though is she? Osana is different. So, tuck your tail between your legs and let's sneak out of here before somebody does get killed."

Koba watched our exchange without comment. She smiled at me, which I took for support, and volunteered to go up the ridge with Yidi to find the goats. Sensible woman, I thought. Grabbing Corax by the hand, I pulled him along to help retrieve the ladder. We carried it over to the cave and I dashed up to make sure the soldiers hadn't gained entry. Things were as we had left them. Relieved, I went to the storage cist and removed all our food supplies, stacking them in piles for loading.

"It didn't take long for things to get interesting," Corax said.

"You know me," I replied. "No time for dull moments."

He laughed. No longer annoyed, he looked excited as he put things in his pack. He waved a small bundle. "What should I do with this? The scroll I brought for you."

"Keep it for now. And here, put the other one with it, if you don't mind. You'll probably take better care of it, anyway." I slid the scroll of *Knowing Touch* into its oilskin sleeve before he could see that we'd been drawing on it. "And keep this handy, too." I gave him one of my combat knives, certain that he owned nothing of the sort.

He pulled it out of the sheath and waved it around as if to demonstrate his lack of skills. "Just like old times. Seems like you're always trying to weaponize me."

"Humor me."

"I always do," he said.

Koba soon returned with the two goats and tethered them to the ladder. We loaded their saddlebags with food, mostly, but distributed it as evenly as we could for all of us. It was daunting to triage the odds and ends of my possessions, the practical stuff of a home. I couldn't take it all, but I didn't want to leave anything of value. No doubt the soldiers would return and pillage the place. I felt a stab of grief at the anticipated loss, and quickly pushed it down. No time for tears. Instead, I followed the anger and fumed at having to leave under coercion and the implications of oppression. I didn't like to run away. But I saw no future in declaring war against the Duke, either.

I removed the canvas cover from the dome and cut it in half. The whole thing would be too heavy to carry, but a section big enough to shed bad weather would be useful. I gave Koba an oilskin hooded cloak, which she promptly slipped over her blouse and skirt. It was a pedestrian garment, the cloak, but she wore it like high fashion. Corax reached into his pack and hauled out a similar cloak, holding it up with pride. I was surprised that he had such a thing. Apparently, even philosophers could learn.

Our packs were near bursting, but they would lighten as we ate our way into the mountains. Koba went to the spring to fill our water bags while I saddled the goats. The rain fell, steady and drenching. Our warmth would have to come from our labor, but there would be no shortage of that as we lugged the packs uphill over difficult terrain. Koba returned and handed out the full water containers, fat leather bags that we lashed to our packs as if they weren't already heavy enough. We stood for a moment in glum silence, staring at each other from under our hoods, watching the drops bead up on the fabric and slide down to the ground. Finally, Koba laughed and broke the spell.

"I'm sorry to leave this place. It's been more like a nest than a shelter. And the baths… oh, I'll miss them!"

I liked that she called it a nest. "Maybe we'll make it back here someday," I lied.

"Okay, what's next?" said Corax, stamping his feet.

"We'll hike up to the crest of the ridge, then follow it. It runs south for many leagues, slowly ascending into the mountains. By staying on the crest, our way will be straightforward. Once we get into the high peaks, though, we'll need to do some route finding. But that'll be a while, yet. There should be plenty of springs and run-off along the way, but keep your eyes peeled for water and let's refill at every opportunity."

"For today, though, we can just tilt back our heads," and Corax demonstrated his point, widening his mouth to lap the rain.

In a rush of feeling, I pulled Koba and Corax to me and wrapped them in my arms. They laughed and we wiggled together like puppies. Yidi barked and pushed between our legs. When we parted, Koba grinned. "Wolf pack on the prowl," she said. There was something about the way she said it that sent shivers down my spine.

[10]

We trudged along in silence as the rain drummed on our hoods, though Koba entertained us sporadically with her humming. The occasion seemed too somber for more than that as we carried our loads in a slow file, working our way along the crest of the ridge. The clouds stayed low, and the rain fluctuated between heavy and not-quite-so-heavy. The oilskins kept the rain out, but they also retained enough body moisture to keep us damp. Even the animals plodded in an unwavering focus on one step after another.

We took frequent breaks to nibble food and replenish our thirst, cramming in a few bites before the ambient chill brought us back to our feet and the warmth of movement. The weather hammered at us all day and we looked forward to dusk when we'd be forced to stop. I estimated that we'd traveled between two or three leagues when we found a rock outcrop with a slight overhang and decided that enough was enough. Using sticks jammed into horizontal cracks of the overhang, I strung one edge of the tarp, pegging the other side to the ground to extend the shelter. Nearby, I found a small stand of birch and harvested enough bark to start a fire, which I fed with branches snapped off a dead pine. Not enough heat for cooking, but it was something to look at as we huddled under the overhang, sandwiched between the flames and the rock.

The next morning dawned clear. Every leaf and stem moist from the rain sparkled at the touch of the rising sun. The nonchalant goats sampled the grasses and weeds of the adjacent meadow. I saw Yidi sitting on a boulder nearby, watching. When did she assume this responsibility for watching over the goats? I wasn't sure; it just seemed to happen. Appreciating the cooperative spirit of the jackal, I felt a surge of pride in our group. As if the most natural thing in the world, we took care of each other. Almost like a family, it occurred to me. I wondered if this was love, the real thing, not the romantic crap.

When I turned back to our shelter, Koba stood in front, yawning. She waved briefly and started a routine of linked, graceful stretches. It reminded me of my practice forms for hand-to-hand combat. I mimicked her movements, to the best of my ability, but soon we were giggling uncontrollably and had to stop. I took a length of rope from my pack and we rigged a clothesline so we could dry our wet clothes. By the time Corax crawled out from under the tarp, our garments drifted in the breeze while Koba and I, naked, continued the exercises.

Corax stood and watched us for a moment, scratching his belly and grinning. "What is this, some Stoic self-improvement thing?"

Koba stood on one foot with her free leg wrapped around behind her knee while twisting her arms together. I had good balance, but I kept fumbling my attempts to duplicate her stance. She calmly unwrapped herself, then rewrapped while standing on the other foot. Without a quiver, she said to Corax, "I think it pre-dates the Stoics. I learned it when I studied at the Great Library. I met a woman from the East who was kind enough to share her knowledge. I think you're right, though, that it provides an improvement to the self. Join us!"

I anticipated a sarcastic response, but he shrugged and said, "Okay," throwing his clothes over the line and joining our efforts at grace.

We dawdled through the morning, taking the time to cook a large breakfast and to let our gear dry in the sun. I thought it unlikely that the Duke's so-called tax collectors would search for us beyond the cave. And if they did, the heavy rain would have obscured our trail to all but the most seasoned trackers. The view from the ridge was commanding, surveying two valleys and the distant peaks. I could see the tallest one, the Mountain of Flowers, a gleaming beacon of rock. Somewhere around that mountain was the tower of Koba's dream, or so we had determined from our mapping. Maybe a pedestrian week away, over ridges, plateaus, and high valleys.

By mid-afternoon we had covered another couple of leagues, marching along the meadows of the broad ridge. Occasionally, we'd have to scramble up rock steps or detour around steep ledges and groves of dense juniper scrub. We spooked a grouse and I thought how good it would taste but hunting and packing loads are two different endeavors. If we made camp a little early, there would be time for a hunt. I salivated at the thought of fresh game and set my mind on it. When I mentioned it to the others, I heard no complaint.

The fantasy of roasting meat carried me through the drudgery of our progress. Sometimes Koba would sing for a while or Corax might venture a provocative comment, but no one had the energy to sustain such diversion. The work was mostly head down and straight ahead, walking in single file. My job was to lead, keeping us on the route of least resistance. Now and then I'd pick up a deer trail and follow it briefly, but their paths always diverged toward their ends. Other than that and the occasional scat or paw print, there was no sign of traffic. Yidi and the goats plodded along with us. The sun, welcome in the morning, warmed the world until it was too hot for labor. We stopped often for sips of water. The ridge offered a direct route into the mountains, but it wasn't exactly easy: our steps always seemed to go up or down, never level, and the exposure to wind and sky was unforgiving.

I was scanning for a campsite when I spotted horse tracks. I stopped and flagged the others to halt. I turned slowly around, evaluating every direction. The ridge was quiet. A slight breeze blew down from the mountains, but it carried no sound or scent of trouble. I slipped out of my pack and crouched to inspect the hoof prints. There were too many. I backtracked them to the other side of the ridge and saw where they had come up a long, gradual spur from the valley below. And where were they going? Our direction, up the ridge toward the mountains. Judging from the droppings and the impact on the vegetation, there were at least a dozen horses.

I walked back to where Koba and Corax had stopped. "Soldiers, count on it."

"Shit," said Corax. "That's not good."

Koba took off her pack and bent to hug Yidi. Eyes wide, she stared up at me and I felt her distress. "What do you think this means? Are they searching for us?"

"I don't know why they're here. From the depth of imprint, these are heavy horses. Soldiers with full gear, maybe. A search party would want to move fast and light. So I'm guessing no, they're not looking for us. Clearly, this Duke is up to no good. War, looks like. These mountains form a border with another nation—my grandmother was born there. An ambitious duke would certainly consider how to expand his domain in all directions, including this one. As for us, it means we can no longer stroll in safety along the top of the ridge. My guess is that they came through this morning, so they're probably several leagues ahead by now."

"It's come to war... so soon," said Corax, pulling at his beard. "Didn't they just have one?"

"Of course," I said. "They've been having them regularly for a hundred years or more, ever since the Empire pulled out of this region, or was chased out, pick your narrative."

"We'll destroy ourselves, we will. Humans. What a pathetic waste of existence," he said. He continued to yank at his beard until he winced in pain.

"We have wars, too," added Koba. "Not as much as in the past. Allying with the elephants gave us some unexpected protection. Neighboring people are in awe and think we possess great magic. We have commerce, but only because we seek it. Otherwise, they leave us alone."

"I've always wanted to see an elephant," mused Corax.

"Maybe you'll get to see an extinct version—if we can find this mammoth. But we can't afford to get sucked into a war, whether as combatants or victims. And in war, those are usually the only choices. However, I think we could try something different. We could put on our wolf clothes and sneak right past."

Koba looked at me with open-mouthed admiration. "I love it!" she said.

"Anyway," I said, "we can't continue on the ridge. If they decide to turn back, or if there are reinforcements coming this way, we'll be completely exposed. No safer in the valley bottom either, so I suggest we drop down a couple of contour levels and traverse the slopes. Slower going, but we'll be in the woods and under cover. From here on, stealth equals survival."

We donned our packs and angled down from the ridge. As we entered the woods, I stopped to cut a sapling and made us each a walking stick to help with the traverse, a little extra insurance to keep from toppling down the hill. As I handed them out, I said, "Doubles as a weapon, too."

Corax thumped the butt of his stick in the ground. "If you say so," he said.

The anxiety that pursued us all through the previous day's flight from the cave had evaporated in today's sunshine. But now it was back in full force as we marched across the slope, one after the other, in glum silence. The sun dropped to the west and beamed into the forest, a final dazzle before darkness. I picked up the pace, eager to find a reasonable campsite. We all felt it, the fear of being overtaken by violent chaos, as we leaned into the march, planting our staves for support as we shuffled along the hillside.

We came to a gully with a small stream. I walked down the stream and looked over the edge of a small outcrop where the water plunged into a pool. There was enough flat ground to stretch out without fear of rolling downhill in the night. I abandoned the idea of hunting, even though there were certainly grouse and hares in the vicinity. The column of smoke from a fire would declare our presence to anyone with eyes to see it. No, we'd have to live without cooked food.

As we sat together next to the pool and chewed on jerky and cheese, I watched the goats nibble at ferns, lichen, wintergreen, and pretty much everything else that had leaves.

I leaned against a boulder, savoring the ache in my muscles, that reminder of what it's like to be alive and use your body. Koba stretched out, putting her head in my lap and her feet in Corax's. He lifted his arms in surprise, but quickly settled his hands on her ankles. Yidi, always interested in a cuddle, nosed into Koba's belly. Somehow, despite the problems we faced, or maybe because of them, we comforted each other.

"I know we're in the thick of things, danger and all that, but I'm glad I came," said Corax, absently rubbing Koba's feet.

"Ow!" She finally objected when he squeezed too hard. "Okay, that's better. Yes, like that. We all have the magic, really."

When it was too dark to see, we unrolled our blankets and snuggled together, three humans, two goats, and a jackal. A hodge-podge of limbs and odors; but we were warm.

In the morning, after filling our water containers and washing in the cold pool, we continued our long traverse. Eventually, we would arrive at the head of the valley where we'd be forced to ascend into the high country. I hoped by that point that the soldiers would be well away, off to a distant zone of combat. A naïve hope, no doubt. War consumes land with omnivorous gluttony, oblivious to the wishes of peaceful citizens like myself. And combat erupts like disease, often where you least expect it. It would take more than luck for us to stay out of it.

Above the valley and its tributaries rose a high plateau, a plinth for great mountains. Each massif dominated a sector of the plateau with its labyrinth of flanking ridges and gullies. The crest of this range provided a boundary of sorts between the domain of Duke Ganelon and the larger realm of King Blancandrin. I knew little of the kingdom over the mountains even though it included my maternal ancestors. My grandmother tried to teach me things, but the raid that killed her left me, at five years old, orphaned of the last family member. Memories remained, but they were clouded with the taint of grief.

No doubt Blancandrin, like Ganelon, was a petty tyrant, a category which never seemed to exhaust itself. If there was war, their ambitions would encompass every rock and scrub of the high plateau. Yet, it was poor terrain for mass combat. Any war in such a complex and convoluted topography would primarily involve skirmishes between mobile units. I envisioned scores of armed men roaming around, ready to do battle with anything in front of them. Given that so much of the high country was treeless, or nearly so, our chances of walking around unseen were minimal. We'd have to apply every principle of stealth we could muster, including forgoing all fires, no matter how cold the night or how raw the food.

Our progress slowed considerably, and we'd only traveled a league or so when we stopped for a mid-day meal. While the others retrieved food from their packs, I slung the bow and quiver over my shoulders.

"I'm going to sneak up to the ridge and look for signs of soldiers. I won't be long."

"Take your wolf hat," said Koba.

"Good idea!"

"And Yidi," she added.

"Okay. I'll be careful."

I hugged Yidi, who always seemed to understand every-thing expected of her, and we stalked up the hill, ascending via short switchbacks. When I pulled on my wolf hat, she angled her head to the side and stared at me. I knelt to let her sniff. A low growl rumbled in her throat, then she licked my lips. I remembered my disorientation at seeing the hat wrapped snugly over Koba's skull; it looked as if a wolf's head had been spliced onto the human. When she had tilted her head forward and crawled across the cave, the hat became the face, and the woman vanished.

I moved slower as we approached the top of the ridge. Yidi followed directly in my tracks, pausing when I paused. The trees thinned and we lingered behind the larger ones while scouting the open ground. I heard several ravens further up the ridge; otherwise, it was quiet.

At the crest, it didn't take long to spot the beaten path left by the mounted soldiers. We approached with caution. The trail was cold but easy to read as they had scuffed and trampled their way through the grasses and heather. Yidi's nose twitched, and she turned to sniff the air further up the ridge. I followed her example and caught the odor of decay. Stringing the bow and nocking an arrow, I advanced along the soldiers' trail. Ahead of us, ravens came and went, talking to each other in their inscrutable language. I understood enough to know that something was there.

About two hundred yards further along the ridge we found the carnage. Scattered across a meadow were the corpses of half a dozen wolves: speared, trampled, and dismembered. Two days of sun had catalyzed the beginning of rot and clouds of flies formed gray auras around the remains. Yidi growled and stayed close to my side. I gave up counting the ravens; there were fifty at least, hopping around the cadavers, pecking at the flesh where it was ripped open, occasionally flying to nearby branches, or gliding back down to rejoin the feast. They ignored us, only hopping away when we got too close. As I studied the scene, I realized that this was a den. I spotted three more corpses: pups, their skulls crushed. There must have been a burrow here, but the only entries I saw were caved in, as if the soldiers had smashed them with the hooves of their war horses.

Speared with heartache, I crouched next to Yidi, who snuggled close. Wanton destruction—was there no end to it? Always men and their malevolent ways. From the looks of it, the soldiers had quartered the wolves, tying them to horses and pulling them apart. I desperately wanted to kill something, to hurt something. I dug my fingernails into my arm, seeking blood, until Yidi whined. No, self-abuse didn't help.

I stood and walked through the devastation, scattering ravens as we inspected the massacre. The two wolves that I had killed several weeks ago to save Koba were probably from this group, I thought. Seeing the remaining family laid out on the ground, still beautiful despite the mutilation, made me grieve for my deed, even though it seemed necessary at the time. Who had I killed? The leaders? Not improbable. Had I weakened the family and made them vulnerable to this kind of attack? No, that was hubris. The soldiers came here, the wolves made a stand, they lost, and the soldiers went on. These were more victims of war, just like my own family.

Yidi walked around, sniffing, as I surveyed the carnage and wept. On the other side of a rocky hummock, she pointed her nose and whined. I wiped the tears and went to see what had drawn her attention. There was another burrow entrance, either not seen by the soldiers or passed over because it was hidden by the ledge formation. Yidi's nose poked insistently into the entrance. I kneeled next to her and heard a faint whimper from within. Dear God, I thought, there must be another pup. I moved Yidi aside and lay prone in front of the burrow. As I stuck my face against the entrance, I heard the sound more clearly and, as my eyes adjusted to the light, I saw a bit of movement. It was too narrow to squeeze in. Then I remembered the hat. I tilted my face down to the dirt, presenting the wolf head, and I talked. Saying nothing, really, just soft, gentle things—the things I wanted someone to say to me. The whining moved closer. I felt the breath of the pup and I smelled its fear. But the hat offered something familiar, after all. When it licked the snout of the hat, I slid backward, keeping my face down, and the pup stuck its head out of the burrow.

He or she struggled momentarily, but as I pulled the pup into my lap, it went limp. Yidi licked its face repeatedly and was offered a few kisses in return.

I couldn't believe it. I sat there, holding the wolf like a baby. Fuzzy ears and paws as big as my hands, it snuggled against my belly. The eyes, though, were enough to conjure love in the hardest heart, I thought. At least for those of us who had a heart. I figured it was hungry, so I used the trick I had learned from the maenads of Dionysos: I dug my fingers into the dirt and raked a trench. Milk bubbled from the earth and filled the depression. I shifted the pup so it could drink and I raised a hind leg to check the sex: male.

Yidi joined the pup in slurping the contents of the trough, which refilled as fast as they lapped it up. I stroked the pup's head while he ate, relishing the soft, thick fur. The milk ran dry and the pup turned his head to look at me with forlorn eyes. At the same time, I felt a stream of warm piss running down my leg. I laughed, startling the pup, who flopped off my lap. One of the perils of parenthood, I knew that much.

The pup stood and shook himself. I saw that he was quite sturdy on those oversized feet. Taking in an orphan wouldn't help our mission, but we had no choice. I certainly wasn't going to abandon him to loneliness and starvation. He could walk; therefore, we'd take him. He might need a leash for a while, and I had plenty of rope down the hill in my pack. I picked him, all thirty or forty pounds, and set off down the slope. Yidi stayed close, leaping up to nip at whatever parts of the pup dangled within her reach. Despite the tragic circumstances, I couldn't help but smile at my cargo as we hurried down to our waiting companions. I didn't care that the pup peed on me once more.

It was worth it to see the looks on their faces when I approached with a wolf draped over my arms. Koba smiled like a sunbeam while Corax just stared slack-jawed, eyes full of wonder. I anticipated the usual sarcasm from him, but when I put the pup down, he fell to his knees and embraced him.

"What a beautiful creature," he said as he buried his face in the fur. "We're keeping it, aren't we? Please say yes. I'll carry it if we have to."

"It's a *he*, for what that's worth. The only survivor of his family. Their den was on the ridge above us, but the soldiers sacked it and slaughtered them. If it wasn't for Yidi, I would have missed this guy, still hunkered in the den."

"Do you think this is the same wolf group that attacked me?" asked Koba.

"Probably," I said. "I'm sorry now that I killed those two. Maybe there was a way to scare them off without that. At the time, I wasn't willing to take a chance."

"No, they looked serious. I'm not much good at scaring things off. Usually, I have the opposite effect," said Koba, patting Yidi as she rubbed against her legs. "Anyway, you did what you had to do; you'll get no complaints from me. You saved my life!"

"She has a way of doing that," said Corax.

I'd had enough of hearing praise and changed the subject. "Yes, we're keeping him. Don't ask me why. There's no good reason, except that he's an orphan."

"That's the best reason in the world," said Koba, who stepped over and hugged me, kissing my cheek. She was sweaty and smelled like a working body and being the kind of woman I was, I liked that. I kissed both her cheeks, the way we do, and bent over my pack to get the rope. I cut off a short length, tied one end loosely around the wolf's neck, and handed the other end to Corax.

"He may not need this for long, maybe not at all, but there's no reason for you to carry him," I said. "He's a bit big for that, unless you just want the exercise."

Corax patted and hugged the pup, who slobbered on the bald top of his head like it was a salt lick. "I'm going to name him Lykos," announced Corax. "Our name for wolf. Unless there are objections."

I shrugged. Another name—there was no getting away from it, it seemed. Koba grinned at Corax. I think she was pleased to see his affection. I felt the same; when he was depressed, all hell could erupt. For now, the pup would help replace Diarmuid.

We pushed on until dark and made camp on the uphill side of a large chestnut tree. If we huddled close, there was just enough room for all of us. Corax slept with the wolf pup cradled in his arms. I spooned with Koba and Yidi under a blanket while the goats curled against Corax's back, forming an animal sandwich. I couldn't sleep and listened carefully to every sigh, breath, and snort from my companions. There was too much to worry about, especially the things that were out of my control, like troop movements, war, and the goat's pregnancy. Maybe I could do something about the latter by lightening her load. But most of the problems that crossed my mind remained unsolved by the time I faded into sleep.

I awoke at the first hint of light and sat up. I noticed the wolf pup licking at the front of Corax's shirt, which seemed odd, but thought he might be tasting the salt in the dried sweat. I'd have to draw more milk from the earth or hunt down a rabbit. The pup had chewed up some dried meat well enough when we had supper; I felt bad knowing that the meat came from one of the members of his family, but he ate it. Pups needed raw meat, though, I was sure of that. I slipped carefully out of bed, took my bow and quiver, leaving the sleepers to their dreams. Yidi, though, lifted her head and watched me go.

I nocked an arrow suitable for small game and crept down the hill. Hares moved to water at dawn, so I might have a chance. I picked up a stream and followed it downhill on a parallel course, staying far enough away to scan the banks without being seen. Or trying not to be seen, anyway. I walked in slow motion, barefoot, feeling the ground and its array of potential noises, every muscle of my body working in precision. Although stalking required a certain tension, the performance of it relaxed me, flushing away the anxieties of the night. Here was something I could do. And I was good at it; I liked doing things I was good at.

By the time I got to the valley floor, I'd bagged two hares and lost no arrows. I tied the hares together by the feet and wore them around my neck. Two was enough, but the sun had yet to rise, and curiosity led me on. I wanted to see the river. A few peasants farmed the east-facing slopes on the other side of the valley, and I knew there was a rough cart trail along the water. Traffic had been rare in previous years; it might be worth knowing if that was still the case.

This far up the valley, the river wasn't much of a river, and I waded it without trouble. The bank was rocky; just above it, I found the trail. I didn't like what I saw pounded into the dirt: dozens of hoof prints. All of them pointed toward the mountains.

Dismayed, I crossed back over the stream and worked my way up the slope to our camp. I saw some movement and gave a bird whistle as I approached; Koba waved.

"Something amazing has happened!" Her face glowed with delight, and I set aside my worries about troop movements.

"Corax is lactating!" She pointed excitedly to the philosopher, who lay bare-chested on the ground while the wolf pup sucked at a teat. Indeed, his breasts had puffed out a little, taking on a roundness that wasn't there yesterday, and I saw that his exposed nipple had darkened. As the wolf nursed, Corax's eyes gleamed with pride.

"Can you believe it?" he asked me.

"This happened overnight? *Incroyable!*" I removed the dead hares from my neck and set them on a rock. "I wonder, since the kraken altered your biochemistry, have you noticed other transsexual traits? Do you even know what it did to you, exactly?"

"No, I don't, it seems. I thought it merely improved my vision, but… maybe more than that."

"Whoa!" interrupted Koba. "I heard you mention the kraken before, but what's this about transsexual? I want to know about this! If you don't mind," she added.

"Go ahead," said Corax. "I'm just going to zone out here in maternal bliss."

"Okay," I laughed. "Just butt in if I get it wrong. I think I mentioned before that our master logician was born with the genitals of a man and the chemistry of a woman. A hermaphrodite, in essence. When we met in the Western Isles, we came from different directions to rescue Fedelma, the bard, from the clutches of a crazed sect of monks. You know about that part. What few people knew was that she was on the Holy Island searching for a kraken rumored to live in the vicinity. During the escape from the monks, Fedelma and Corax and Diarmuid found the kraken. Fedelma, because she knows the Language of the Deep, asked it for—what? A blessing? Anyway, it massaged them with its tentacle pads and altered their chemistries. But it didn't change the essence of who you are, right Corax? Or did it?"

"Who knows?" said Corax, eyelids drooping as the pup lounged at his breast.

Koba clapped her hands. "I love it! And you're the one who doesn't believe in magic?"

"Oh, it's science," muttered Corax.

"So is magic," she replied.

"Before that pup drains you to a puddle, we need to get going," I said.

"Lykos," he said. "The pup is Lykos."

"Lykos," I replied automatically. "Lykos will need to get going, as will his attendants. Plus, I have some fresh meat for him and Yidi. Not to undermine your maternal bliss, Corax, but solid food is important, too."

Corax grumbled but removed Lykos from his teat and sat up. The pup rolled onto his back and waved his legs in the air, then flipped upright. I lashed one of the hares on my pack and handed the other to Yidi; Lykos grabbed the free end. Within minutes they had torn the carcass to shreds and were chewing the last meat off the bones. Side-by-side, the pup was as tall as Yidi and a bit heavier. He would be enormous, I thought, when fully grown. A hundred pounds, maybe.

As we packed up for the day's trek, I decided to say nothing about the tracks in the valley. Everyone understood the need for caution; why infect them with my anxieties?

The hardest part about traversing the slope of a long valley is that your gait is limited by a shortened upper leg and an extended lower one. This results in an awkward loping shuffle. Holding the staff on the downside of the slope helps a little, but not enough to prevent the ache of a constantly tilted pelvis. The goats didn't seem to mind; with their narrow hooves, they could even walk sideways. The wolf pup followed so closely in Corax's steps that it was like his shadow. I reminded myself to call him by the name Corax gave him, Lykos. So now there were two wolves in the family: Lykos and Osana. Or maybe three, if we counted Corax as the official canid lactator. Then I remembered that his name, *corax*, was another name for the raven. We were all animals. What about Koba? She belonged to an elephant family, so there it was. A pack of wild beasts. Let them try to find us, I thought. We've got wolf stealth, caprine balance, and elephant ears. And if they do find us, we'll stomp them with our hooves and tear them to shreds with our teeth! I laughed out loud at my thoughts.

"You're having an awfully good time up there!" observed Koba from the end of the line.

I paused and everyone clumped around me, shedding our packs for a break. "Would you consider yourself an elephant?" I asked Koba.

She looked at me with an arched brow and wrinkled forehead. Her lips pursed and her eyes sparkled. It was a complicated look, open and full of character. No wonder I loved her. She extended her arms, pressed them together, and swung them back and forth as she swayed from side to side. Right away, I saw the elephant. Yidi stood on hind legs and pranced around Koba until Lykos slunk over and sniffed the jackal's bottom. Suddenly, we had a carnival. I snickered convulsively until it rose into a wave of laughter. Plopping on the ground, I bent over in a fit of hysteria. And then, of course, I was crying.

Corax was confused. "What the fuck is going on?"

Koba sat down next to me and put an arm around my shoulder, pulling me onto her chest, enfolding me with a firm touch. I felt Yidi's tongue on my hand. For reasons I don't like to contemplate, all this only made me cry harder. Koba stroked my head as I bawled shamelessly.

Corax understood enough to keep his mouth shut and I felt him sit down next to me and put a hand on my hip. It wasn't the best place for a comforting touch, but I gave him the benefit of the doubt.

Koba hummed a lullaby for a few moments before saying, "Actually, my dear, I'm more of an antelope." I lifted my head and looked at her. "That's what we call the roan antelope of our savannah: *koba*. My mother gave me that name because of my skin color. Also, maybe she wanted me to be big, strong, and fast like the *koba*. Of course, I turned out like I am."

I caressed her light brown cheek. "You're perfect," I said.

She smiled. "Not even close. But thank you for saying that."

I could feel Corax's impatience, and I pulled away from Koba. Hands on hips, he glared at us. "I hesitate to even bring this up," he said, "but what in the howling halls of Hades are you talking about?"

Koba giggled and I wiped away the tears and snot from my face. I saw anxiety in Corax's face. Understandable, since to his mind, I was rock solid, always. Whoever now blubbered away in front of him, it wasn't the old reliable Marianne. "Well," I said. "You know how the mind can wander on long walks, especially if you're carrying a load?" He nodded. "I was thinking about our little band here, how we're a real ragtag collection of creatures. Somehow in all this, those of us that are human are also animals, or we're becoming animals. And not just by ourselves, but with each other, we're becoming a pack or maybe family of beasts. By my count, we've got two wolves, a jackal, two goats, an antelope, and you, the raven, or maybe raven wolf since you're nursing the pup. And, I don't know, it just seemed funny."

"I'm not actually a raven," said Corax, "though, sure, I have that name."

"Well, you certainly act like one most of the time," I said.

"Do I?"

Koba and I nodded at the same time. "Exactly like one," she said.

Corax sighed and ran his hands through Lykos' fur. "Maybe you're right," was all he said before rolling on his side and lifting his shirt so the pup could nurse. I noticed that his breasts had grown since yesterday. He was a raven sort of man becoming a woman wolf. Or a fluid embodiment of transformational betweenness.

"I know something is bothering you," said Koba.

"We're getting caught up in a war," I said. "I saw signs of heavy troop movements in the valley below. So, they're above us and below us, all heading into the high country. I'm worried about what we'll find. The border is up there, such as it is, and they'll be fighting over it. Unfortunately, tree cover is minimal and passable routes are few. We're going to have to work hard to avoid the conflict."

"Is that possible—to avoid the troops? My mission is useless if we don't survive it. I'd rather give it up than have any of us killed or injured. I trust your judgment. Is it foolish to go on?"

She took my hand in hers and we sat quietly while I thought about how to answer. "Maybe. But you're talking to the wrong person about that. I don't like giving up. It's galling to me, especially, to have to abandon our goal because of the stupidity of men and their idiotic wars. We've still got a couple of days before we enter the high country. Let's keep on for now. At the head of the valley is a peasant hamlet, shepherds mostly. Maybe we can learn more there."

"Sounds good. Lead on, my brave Osana."

[12]

We covered several leagues that day, continuing our traverse of the valley slope, winding in and out of the numerous gullies and run-offs that carved their way down from the ridge to the river. Exhausted by late afternoon, we made camp next to a small cascading watercourse, drank our fill, and rinsed off the sweat. Provisions for the evening came from the female goat's bags to continue lightening her load, though she kept pace without any obvious strain. I fed Yidi and Lykos the hare leftover from the morning. While they tore away at the carcass, I slipped into the woods to look for more. Within a few minutes, I bagged another one. Before giving it to the canids, who waited eagerly, I skinned it and sliced off thin strands of breast meat for Koba, Corax, and myself.

"Why cook out all the nutrients?" I said as I offered the meat.

Corax let the strip of pale flesh dangle from his fingers. "You're kidding," he said.

"It's good for you," I said, chewing a piece with mechanical diligence. "Gives you the legs of the hare."

"This is the best argument I've seen for vegetarianism," he pronounced, and fed his pieces to Lykos.

Before we settled down to sleep, Koba took her lute out of its bag, inspected the strings and tuning straps, and fingered the wooden body with affection. She plucked one low note and hummed in tune, drawing out her voice until it sounded like the sighing of the forest.

"If you play softly, like that, it would be okay," I said, wanting to hear more.

She shook her head. "I appreciate your saying that. I'm not very good at modulating the volume once I get into it, though. I'm afraid I'd launch into a racket that would summon even the armies of the dead." She laughed. "But when it's safe, I'll cut loose. I've been working on an epic for our adventure. It will take days to sing!"

"We're already characters in one epic, but it can't hurt to be in another," said Corax, contentedly nursing the wolf.

"That's right," I said. "Part of that wacky business with Dionysos was getting sung into an epic by the old man who couldn't stop scratching his beard—the Singer of Tales."

"You met the Singer of Tales?" asked Koba.

"Yes. You know of him, too?"

"Certainly. Some say he is the greatest wordsmith of all time. I don't know about that; there's always another candidate somewhere. But I've heard his two famous epics."

"He's not so hot," muttered Corax from his lactating bliss. "I'm sure you'll outdo him."

The next morning dawned gray through a solid overcast. I smelled the promise of rain. In addition to the weather gloom, I felt edgy. Worries about the military presence lingered in my thoughts and a night of exhausted sleep had failed to vanquish the anxiety. As I packed my gear, I kept looking over my shoulder, as though I might find someone watching. There was no reason to worry that I could identify, but the dis-ease remained. Rarely did these gut feelings come from pure imagination. I'd sensed something watching us leave the village and dismissed it because there was nothing to see. Yet the next day soldiers tracked us to the cave. Perhaps they'd spied on us, as my nerves had tried to tell me. I vowed to stop daydreaming on the trail and maintain vigilance. I'd keep my fears to myself, though; it was my responsibility to take care of the group.

It started to rain soon after we broke camp. Not a hard rain, but steady, dripping through the leaves while meandering to the forest floor. We put on our cloaks and pulled up the hoods. As soon as the cowl settled around my face, I flipped it back. I didn't like what it did to my peripheral vision or hearing. It was worth getting wet to know what was going on. I asked Koba to take the lead so I could keep an eye on everyone. By the end of the day, we'd be at the head of the valley, which meant that we'd have to decide where to ascend into the high country. For now, our route was straightforward: stay on the contour and slog. With a smile that contained more sunshine than seemed possible for the day, Koba set off. Yidi and the goats marched behind, dutifully followed by Corax, hunched under his cloak and pack. We had no saddlebags for Lykos, so he trotted behind Corax, stopping here and there to sniff or swivel his ears. I fell in line as they passed, turning my head from side to side as I walked, scanning the woods, and considering the different ways my staff could be used as a weapon.

Lykos, whose senses were keener than my own, responded first. He paused in mid-step and turned his head to look up the slope. Ears rigid, nose twitching, he strained at some detail beyond my ken. Then I saw it, a slight movement between the trees, followed by stillness. Meanwhile, Corax had noticed the pup was no longer at his heels and he'd stopped. I herded Lykos along to rejoin Corax.

"Something moving up above," I whispered. "Could be nothing, could be a deer. Probably nothing. You should keep going, but I'm going to check it out. Let Koba know and I'll catch up. Wait for me at the next water crossing if I'm not back sooner."

He frowned, then nodded and resumed walking, coaxing Lykos to follow him. I dawdled behind Corax, extending the distance between us. When he disappeared beyond a tree, I stopped and put down my pack. I was sure that whatever it was I'd seen, it was not a wild animal, but a beast of my own kind. Certain that someone watched me, I made a show of crashing down through willow shrubs and tall ferns, pretending to look for the perfect spot to empty my bowels. As soon as I got into dense cover, I crouched low and crawled back to observe my pack. Before long, I saw a cloaked and hooded figure descend the slope, pausing repeatedly to scan his surroundings. I couldn't see the face, though I caught a glimpse of a beard. He bent over to look at our tracks and I performed a quick tally: short sword, bow, small pack, rugged clothes. The garments were brown or gray, suggesting someone who wanted to blend into the environment. He followed our trail a few yards and saw my pack. Approaching it with caution, he peered downhill into the bushes where I hid. I was sure he couldn't see me, but I held my breath anyway. As he looked, I got a better view of his face: olive skin with jet black hair. I guessed by his stealthy manner that he wasn't one of Duke Ganelon's men. A spy, rather. I didn't understand why he was interested in us, but I was determined to find out.

After a brief inspection, he left the pack untouched and slipped behind a nearby chestnut tree. I sighed. I assumed he wanted to ambush me, either for interrogation or rape, or both. Whatever his agenda, it didn't coincide with mine. Simply, I wanted him off our tail. It was hard to say what kind of threat he posed, but the fact that he followed us, and had probably been doing so for a while, suggested that his intentions were hardly favorable. I had no desire to fight him here, especially since he had the upper hand, but avoiding combat seemed unlikely. My advantage was that I knew about his ambush. I fussed around in the bushes like I was finishing my business and stood up, loosening the throwing knife from its sheath on my thigh. I would have to be quick, but less than lethal if I wanted his information.

I walked up the slope to my pack, whistling to pretend nonchalance. I turned my back to the chestnut and fiddled with the pack as if getting ready to hoist it over my shoulders.

"¿Qué pasa?" His language answered my question about where he was from. I spun around as if startled. The spy stood by the tree, bow pulled taut, with an arrow aimed at my belly.

"Hey, wo-man," he said, enunciating the label with an emphasis that stiffened the hairs on my neck. I could tell he wanted a helpless female, so I laid it on thick, shielding my breasts and adding a squeal of fear.

"Who are you? What do you want?" I shrieked at him as he stepped forward. I squeezed out a tear. "I have no money!"

I knew my acting skills were thin, even though they had been praised by Dionysos, but I counted on the spy's belief in his superiority. He relaxed as he came closer, sure of himself like all men when they have a woman at the point of a weapon. I flapped my arms in mock agitation and saw a smirk cross his lips. That was my cue; I grabbed the knife and hurled it while diving to the ground. His arrow whooshed past my torso, barely missing, while my knife buried itself in his left bicep. Cursing, he dropped the bow and clutched at the knife, pulling it out with a hard yank. Blood gushed down his arm. He drew the short sword with his good arm and charged. Meanwhile, I'd had enough time to roll up to a crouch and grab my walking stick. The rain fell harder and in one of those curious moments of awareness, I felt it trickling down my scalp. Something else happened at that moment; I changed my mind about tactics. Fuck his information; I intended to kill the son of a bitch. The spy closed the distance between us and slashed at me with a wild sweep, the kind of mistake made by the arrogant or desperate. I dodged and brought the staff down on his wrist with a solid thwack. The sword fell from his limp fingers. I spun the staff around and delivered a hard blow to the side of his head, hard enough to break the stick. He staggered and flailed for balance, giving me enough time to pick up the sword and plunge it into his upper abdomen. I slewed it back and forth to cut the major vessels before letting go of the handle. An expression of incomprehension flickered in his eyes and he slumped to the ground.

I didn't want to kill anyone, yet I had just done so. Why? I knew very well. No matter how sincerely I vowed to walk the path of peace, there were limits. Family was a limit. So what if I didn't know what that meant? It wasn't my fault that my parents and siblings and grandparents were all dead, murdered long ago. Maybe my current companions weren't a real family, but they were all I had. Worth defending, no matter the cost.

After retrieving my throwing knife and cleaning it on his cloak, I dragged the corpse behind a shrub. Searching through his pack and pockets, I found a map with an array of numbers and arrows, perhaps his observations of troops. I kept that along with a pouch of coins. The rest I left for the ravens and wolves.

I cut a new walking stick from one of the hazel stems, then pulled up some rain-soaked moss and used it as a sponge to wipe the spy's blood from my arms and clothes. I wanted a bath to rinse away the aftermath of murder, but it was time to catch up to the others before they came back looking for me. They didn't need to see this. Maybe I would tell them about the spy and what happened or maybe not. I hadn't decided if I wanted them to look at me the way I knew they would when I confessed.

Donning my pack, I headed off through the woods, forcing the pace. Had that been a necessary kill? Maybe not—I could have captured him, but then what? Bring him along as a prisoner? That offered no benefit to our goals and plenty of risk, like carrying around Pandora's box and waiting for the lid to fall off. His intentions toward us would have to remain a mystery. However, there was no mystery about the sneaking or the ambush. I couldn't wrangle any interpretation that put him in a good light. Our mission depended on stealth and being followed by an agent of a state, any state, didn't fit into my plans. My justifications spilled out with irresistible logic, but they didn't bring me any peace of mind. Killing is still killing, no matter how adroitly reasoned. So, add it to my litany of psychic burdens. I wiped the rain out of my eyes and walked faster.

When I caught up, they sat next to a stream, Koba and Corax huddled under their cloaks while the animals stood next to them, fur coats sleek with rain. I whistled to announce my presence and both Yidi and Lykos trotted up to me, sniffing hard at my hands. They smelled the blood, I realized. Koba stood and offered a welcome smile.

"I see you have a new walking stick," she observed.

Here was a moment of truth. I dropped my pack and sat on it, feeling exhaustion occupy my bones. "I broke the other one," I said. Corax raised a brow. "We've been followed. Tracked, actually, by a spy from the south, one of King Blancandrin's men, or so I surmised. We didn't have an extensive conversation."

"You talked to him?" asked Corax.

"It was a brief encounter," I said. "I persuaded him to take up other pursuits."

"I'm sure you did," observed Corax.

Koba stood next to me and put her hand on my head, stroking it gently. I liked the feel of her palm on my braids. It reminded me that they were coming undone, and I'd need her to re-weave them soon.

"It's okay, Osana," she said. "You can say. No need to pretend it was nothing."

Her tone, gentle with affection, went straight to my heart, allowing me to feel the measure of my deed. I started to cry. I didn't have to be a monster, after all. "I killed him. I'm not sure what his intentions were about tracking us, but he meant no good. Perhaps I had a choice, but I did what I did."

Koba crouched down and put her arm around my shoulder, kissing me on the cheek. "My champion," she whispered in my ear. I shuddered at the tickle of her breath.

"Bah, don't be so hard on yourself. I trust you," said Corax. "You've saved my life so many times that I have nothing but respect for your decisions. So, you killed another bad guy. The gods don't care." He patted my forearm.

Was this family?

[13]

At the head of the main valley, the drainage forked into three gorges slicing down from the mountains. The preponderance of fir, pine, and aspen in the woods suggested that the sub-alpine region was not far above us. From here on, our route would become complicated. I shinnied up a pine tree overlooking the first of the gorges and had a clear sightline to the high country. Snow covered the flanks of the tallest peaks and patches lay in the shade but most of the ground was clear.

If we crossed the valley and ascended the far slope to the meadows of the western ridge, we'd come to a shepherds' hamlet. It wasn't a permanent community, just a summer congregation of herding families who spent the winter at lower elevations. Good folks, though, who I remembered from earlier wanderings, always happy for an excuse to feast on their lambs and drink a little wine. They would have knowledge about troop movements since the valley road climbed into the high country through their settlement. We might risk using that same road to make the ascent; it would save us time and toil.

I climbed down the tree and shared my observations with the others. The rain had stopped, and the declining rays of the afternoon sun filtered through the sparkle of the wet forest. We agreed to camp at the gorge, wash in the stream, and dry out in a nearby glade. I settled for a quick rinse and went hunting, thinking that Yidi and Lykos would like some fresh meat.

I brought down three grouse and a hare while ranging across the river to the other side of the valley. The road showed recent horse prints, but none since the rain. I tried to imagine what our tracks would look like to anyone following and decided they'd resemble typical peasant traffic, nothing remarkable. I thought again of the spy I'd killed only hours before. Despite the encouragement from Koba and Corax, the deed hung in my gut like lead. More material for nightmares, not that I needed more.

I felt a bit reckless that evening and ventured a small fire after dark, using it to roast two of the birds while letting the canids devour the raw remainder. While the game cooked, I pulled out the spy's map and showed it to the others.

"Corax, can you retrieve the *Knowing Touch* scroll?"

"Sure. A little reading before dinner?"

I said nothing, just unrolled the scroll and turned it over to compare the spy's map with ours. Corax stared at the back of the scroll with an open mouth.

"You… you defaced a scroll?" He practically choked on the words.

"I don't know if deface is the right word, since this is the obverse. Come on, no harm done."

Koba giggled as Corax sputtered. Finally, he shrugged his shoulders. "Women," he said, as if that meant something. Although the spy map was more of a sketch, its principal features aligned with Koba's artistic rendering. I used a stylus to draw in a few additions to the spy map, figuring it would be useful to keep handy while the scroll could stay tucked away in Corax's baggage.

The cooked meat tasted wonderful, and we nibbled down to the bones and licked our fingers. In a soft voice, Koba sang to us in her native language. Though I couldn't understand the words, it felt like a love song, tender and sensuous, and I wondered if she sang for her distant mate.

When she finished, we lay together under our blankets, but none of us were sleepy.

"Tell me about your family," I asked, hoping to tease some information out of her. I hadn't wanted to know, but of course, that had been a lie all along. Of course, I wanted to know.

"I'll admit to more than a little curiosity, myself," said Corax.

"Okay. I call it a family, but the elephants would probably call it a group. I know you get tired of naming things, Osana, and in this case, I can understand that. There are seven of us and we're all very close. We're kin even if we're not blood kin. Our matriarch is an elephant elder named Poesy; her youngest female offspring, Butter and Froth, also live with us. Poesy had a previous female child who has formed her own family; we socialize with them a lot. Both of her male children have gone off on their own, as is the elephant custom. Two of my sisters live with us, as well as Yidi, a full-fledged partner, and my husband, Nahantsi."

"Ahh," I said, trying to balance disappointment with a vague relief at knowing the situation.

"How does this work, then, living with elephants and calling yourselves kin and all that?" asked Corax.

Koba nestled against my shoulder before answering. "Pretty much like we work, the seven of us right here."

I looked over at Corax and wasn't surprised to see the wolf pup slurping at one of his nipples. "You know, those breasts of yours have grown quite full. If you shaved your beard and wore a wig, you could pass as a woman."

He pulled the blanket down to his stomach and cupped the idle breast in his palm. "You think so? I always wondered what that would be like. If only Diarmuid could see me now...." He trailed off and grew quiet.

"Corax," said Koba, "why don't you come with me to where I live? You'd be welcome in the family and the whole community. I've been trying to lure Osana into joining me. You could come, too. And we do need a librarian."

"I'll come," I said, suddenly decisive. So, she had a husband. We could be sisters, like she said, and I'd come to appreciate the value in that. Plus, what was here in this troublesome land? War, the ambitions of men, death, destruction? Not to mention the loneliness and grief.

"Really?" said Koba, and the tone of her voice conveyed genuine happiness. Instantly, I knew I'd made the right choice.

"Thanks for the offer," said Corax. "I don't know if I'm done with Diarmuid. Maybe. You did say you had a large library, though?"

"We do. Rare volumes. Most of the wisdom of the continent can be found there."

"Hmm," he said. "Tempting."

Snuggled under blankets, we teased each other with threats of sneaking the heaviest items we carried into each other's packs, which prompted extravagant threats and giggling. Then someone mentioned killing and everyone fell silent. Sobered, we withdrew into our tired bodies and slept.

The next morning dawned with a solid blue sky. I checked the she-goat, palpating her belly. Definitely pregnant, though she probably had a couple of months left. Koba knelt next to me. "I'm so glad you're coming home with me!" Without waiting for a response, she put her ear to the goat's belly and smiled. "A female," she announced.

"You can hear that?"

"I can," she said proudly. "You can, too."

I put my head next to the goat's belly as Koba had done and listened. I heard the gurgles of its stomach and the flow of blood, or something like that. I shook my head.

"Sure, it takes practice," said Koba.

I looked at her for a minute, then laughed. "I get it," I said. "You don't know, do you?"

"No," she grinned. "Not really. But it's a good guess, don't you think?"

I'd become accustomed to Koba's optimism, but now she seemed downright giddy. Because I agreed to go south with her? Did I mean that much? Warmth tingled through my body. Maybe I did.

Grunting, we hefted our packs. Theoretically, they were getting lighter, but no one thought so. We wasted a few minutes accusing each other of shifting items, but once the loads were secure in place, we adopted the stoicism of beasts fresh to the burden.

When we approached the river, I asked everyone to delay fording while I scouted ahead to make sure the road was clear. I left my pack on the far shore and scrambled up the bank. A thin band of trees separated the road from the water. I quickly identified new tracks of deer, foxes, and hares, but no humans, no horses. I went back to the shore and waved them over.

The road climbed the slope through numerous switch-backs. I started counting them, then lost track after ten and couldn't persuade myself whether I had missed one or tallied too many. We walked slowly and in silence, straining our ears for the sound of troops. I kept calculating escape routes into the trees. Where the adjacent cover was thin, I picked up the pace. All this made for a stressful yet speedy march to the ridge. As the angle lessened, the trees grew scattered and stunted, and meadows took over, forming chaotic patterns of lush green amidst boulders and outcrops. We ascended the last rise and stood on the crest. The mountains dominated the skyline with startling clarity, looming like gods. I knew from experience that each rocky summit and white-shielded massif lorded over a labyrinth of attendant ridges and drainages. Flat ground was a rarity, mostly found in the basins between crags, and what there was of it could only be considered flat in comparison with the rest of the daunting topography. I inhaled the thin air flowing down from the peaks, excited despite our predicament. I loved this terrain.

About a quarter league away along the ridge I spotted a cluster of buildings—the shepherd's hamlet. Beyond that, the crest broadened and merged into a higher ridge. Somewhere to the west lay Koba's tower, still out of sight. From here on, our survival required awareness at every step. I did not want to be discovered and plucked off a meadow by the superior forces patrolling the range. The best course to avoid that was to climb into the steepest, most foreboding terrain. Places for goats and maybe wolves, but not horses.

We passed around a water flask. Koba poured some into Corax's cupped palms and the canids eagerly lapped it up.

The billy goat pushed at my hand with his nose, wanting his saddlebags removed, while the female, who knew better, munched succulent forbs. A mild breeze glided down from the peaks and I felt a moment of peace. But this was open ground and no place to linger. As we hiked toward the hamlet, I saw and heard a commotion of ravens. Not a good sign. I looked back at my companions and noticed the twitching noses of both Yidi and Lykos. Another hundred yards and I smelled it, too. Carrion. At the first hut, there was no sign of activity. The door hung open and the implements of living were strewn across the floor.

"Fuck," I said. No one answered because there was nothing to say. Punctuated only by the flapping and cawing of ravens, the eerie stillness forecast little hope of survivors. As we approached the second hut the stench of rotting flesh grew stronger. Crucified to the door, naked, slumped an older woman, mutilated, and dead. A long cord of sheep entrails dangled from her neck like a gruesome scarf.

Koba wept while Corax muttered harsh-sounding words in an ancient language. The smell of ripe flesh hung like a pall over the hamlet and my head spun slowly with nausea.

"Come on," I said. "There's nothing for us here."

Beyond the last two huts, we found three more bodies, men, hacked apart and thrown in a pile. The ravens hopped away from us, barely out of reach. Next to the pile half a dozen sheep had been slaughtered and crudely butchered; the easy meat had been taken, while the ravens picked over the rest. The hoof prints of heavy horses could be seen everywhere. I turned around, scanning the landscape for soldiers or survivors or any sign that could fix my attention besides the carnage on the ground. The beauty of the surroundings urged me to look away and escape the horror at my feet, but there was no escaping the smell.

Corax bent over, retched at his feet, and Lykos slurped it up. Struggling to hold back tears, Corax covered his face with his hands. Koba stood tall and let the moisture roll down her cheeks, proud in her grief. They had their masks, but I felt naked. Without control of myself, the anger would ignite a fire inside that couldn't be quenched until it ran its course. Or that was how it usually went. Now, who knew? Not wanting to find out, I waved for us to walk on. As my hand brushed my cheek, I noticed that it was wet.

"We've got to get out of here, and fast. Unless you want to end up like them," I announced. Without waiting for a response, I marched off, shooing the goats in front of me.

The beaten path gradually ascended the remaining half a league of ridge. Where it joined with the higher ridge, the path steepened and switched up a series of broad terraces that ended at a pass. As I recalled, beyond the pass was a vast basin. Well to the right of the terraces was a diagonal slash of rocky ledges and gullies that angled all the way to the crest of the ridge. Unsuited for horse travel, but perfect for us.

I kept glancing up the trail to the pass, as if such diligence would prevent the appearance of troops. We didn't see any, so perhaps it worked. I breathed easier when we started scrambling up the ledge system. It divided the rocky face of the cliff in a long ramp cluttered with gravel, scree, and talus. Patches of heather and other grass grew where they could find a foothold. We left below us the zone of limestone and entered a world of granite. Progress up the ramp required careful steps;

we used our staves and placed our feet with detailed attention. The surface of the ramp sloped out, toward the edge and
the prospect of a sudden fall. Just to imagine seeing one of
my companions plunge over the precipice gave me shudders.
I quickly turned back to my guide's work, finding the safest
ascent. Occasional boulders blocked the way and had to be
surmounted. The goats enjoyed this terrain; even with their
packs they leaped and pranced along, stopping here and there
to stare over the edge. Lykos, like Corax, didn't like the edge
and the two of them whined while following in my steps as
closely as possible.

When the ramp petered out, we were just below the crest of
the ridge. On approach, it had looked like a knife-edge, but up
close, it was broader and more accommodating, although still a
jagged complex of stone. While the others took a short break,
I climbed the remaining face to see what was on the other side
of the ridge. It felt good, dropping my pack and dancing from
hold to hold up the slab; no wonder the goats liked it.

I crept to a chest-high boulder and peeked over the top.
Spread out below me was the basin. A small lake pooled in
the middle, fed by streams from the surrounding peaks. Dense
clumps of shrub-like trees grew where they could find protection from the prevailing winds. The basin was a grassy park
dotted with outcrops of silver granite gleaming in the sun. The
northern side of the enclosing peaks and ridges still had areas
of snow, but I was glad to see little of it. In some years, much of
this would be under the pack.

A scene of pristine beauty, except for the large encamp-
ment of soldiers next to the lake. I saw two dozen tents and at
least fifty horses. Smoke rose from several campfires. I assumed

that these were the same people that slaughtered the peasants and their sheep. Ordinary men sent to war, given license by the state to become demons. I hated them without knowing them because, as a woman, I did know them. Men with power. I would sooner kill myself and my companions than fall into their clutches.

"Lots of soldiers over there," I passed on the information when I climbed down to the others.

"Where's a kraken when we need one?" mused Corax.

"You're accustomed to the *deus ex machina*, but I don't think there's a god to get us through this. We'll have to do it ourselves," I said.

"Coruscating Chaos, woman, don't be so concrete," he retorted. "Who, more than I, knows how much trouble can be caused by a god? No, I'm putting my faith in you."

I blushed; I don't know why. The exchange put a smile on Koba's lips. She caressed my head, saying, "We're going to have to re-braid your hair before long, though as it unwinds it does reinforce your aura as a woman of action."

"Stop it, you two," I complained, weakly.

"I'm with Corax, my dear. Lead on; we'll follow."

"No complaints about our route, then. I'm sure those soldiers prefer to patrol on horseback, so we'll stay high on the steepest terrain. More work, but safer."

"If we're going to be climbing more, can we lighten our loads? What about this food we're carrying that needs fire for cooking?" asked Koba.

"I haven't thought much about what happens after we achieve our objective, assuming we do, but we may be able to use it later. It might be critical to our success. We've carried it this far; I'm loath to ditch it. I don't intend to stay in the war zone any longer than we have to. If we skirt these ridges, maybe we can keep enough rock between ourselves and the conflict to stay unseen. I think that's the key. At some point we'll leave the war; we just need to stay mobile and stay alive. So put on your best sneaky hats and let's go."

Koba reached into her pack and pulled out her wolf hat. It seemed like a good idea, so I donned mine. Lykos perked up and went into a licking frenzy on our hands and faces.

[14]

We scrambled along the ridge, staying below the crest and out of sight of the basin. Progress was slow and involved clambering over rock slabs, faces, and every size of eroded debris. With our loads, it was grueling work and required persistent attention to the placement of each step. Typical walking rhythms were impossible because every movement was different than the last. Yet I saw with satisfaction that we learned to do it efficiently, and in the efficiency, we developed a grace. According to the map, we had to traverse at least seven leagues of similar terrain to find the rock tower, assuming we could travel in a straight line—which, of course, not having wings, we couldn't. At best, it would take several days. I hoped Corax could generate enough milk for the pup. Hunting opportunities would be limited, and I doubted that I could draw any maenad's milk from the thin soil of this rocky domain.

Following the ridgeline, we labored for hours beneath the unfiltered sun while the constant wind leeched away any moisture we hadn't already lost to sweat. Eventually, we encountered an intersecting spur ridge and contoured over it. Below, a new drainage lay revealed. Down a thousand yards of cliffs and heather, we saw the upper reaches of the forest. I suggested we descend and make camp in the trees; no one objected, despite the implications of regaining all the lost altitude tomorrow. Tired of exposure to the elements and the fear of being seen in the open, we welcomed the promise of shelter.

I flushed a grouse on the way down the slope. Yidi dashed after it, saddlebags flapping, and pounced. Head high, she trotted back with the fowl in her jaws, and to everyone's surprise, she dropped it in front of Lykos. We praised her, with abundant pats and ear scratches, while Lykos started tearing into the bird. When we continued the descent, he carried the carcass firmly in his teeth, growling.

"Wolves—what an exquisite food-rendering machine," I said to no one.

"Then why do we call them *ravenous?*" asked Koba.

"Good point," I laughed. "I guess everyone is hungry in the end."

We pushed through a thicket of willow and entered a birch grove, shrugging off the packs with relief. The flat ground of the grove seemed a blessing after the steep rocks and we leaned against our packs, gnawing on dry rations while we allowed our collective exhaustion to replace any thought of conversation. Light faded from the sky, and I fell asleep listening to the distinctive "uuu…uu…u-u-uuuh" call of a tawny owl rising from the deeper woods below.

I woke with a start in the middle of the night. The quarter moon, on the wane, cast its cold light over the mountains. Corax and the pup snored in polyrhythmic oblivion. I turned my head to Koba and looked straight into her watching eyes. She had pulled her wolfskin coat snug around her neck, giving her the appearance of an exotic animal. A tiny reflection of the moon's half-circle shone from each pupil.

"You dreamed," she whispered.

I nodded.

"Tell me," she said, scooting close and placing her ear next to my lips. I wanted to tell her many things—things better left unsaid. So, I stuck with the dream.

"I was adrift in the ocean. Bare naked and no boat. I alternated floating on my back and dog paddling. When I dipped my head underwater, I saw the edge of the continental shelf sloping away, disappearing into the haze of the deep. That vision evoked a kind of fear—a terror of infinity, I guess. A sharp metaphysical anxiety about dissolving into unbounded nature. I can't explain it very well; I just know it scared the shit out of me. The longer I worked to stay afloat, the more anxious I became. Then I remembered the Language of the Deep. I didn't know much, but I sang what I knew. I have no idea what I sang or why, but in between gulping and spitting out the waves that lapped over my head, I did my best. I sang until I exhausted myself. Then it was time to give up and sink into the depths. But something came. Something big, something powerful, something I never thought to see again."

"My God," whispered Koba.

"Yes," I said in her ear. "The kraken. She came to me. That's when I woke."

"I would have died!" she said.

"Maybe. But her power was so immense, I had no resistance. I could do nothing but give myself to her however she wanted me. Whatever that might have meant. Her tentacles reached for me, and I woke up. I can't imagine what would have happened next. Pulled into that toothy maw? I shudder to think of it. I guess it doesn't matter; I gave myself—all I had."

"The sacrifice," Koba said.

Hairs tingled down my back. "Exactly."

"What else do you feel about the dream?"

"Not sure. I'll have to digest this one for a while. Something about going to the sea. I guess that's obvious. After the mountains."

"Yes, after the mountains, we'll go to the sea," she said with a certainty that sent more chills down my spine. She stroked my tattoo. "You called for her and she came."

I don't know what came over me then. I started crying. Me, who never cries, now seemed to be crying all the time. Koba pulled me into her arms and hummed softly in my ear until I fell asleep.

I woke just after dawn and shinnied up a birch tree to scout the route ahead. The far side of the basin featured slabs of granite ledge that steepened into a headwall. The abundant scree and talus below the scarp testified to the frequent rockfall. The face itself offered abundant gullies and crevices for an ascent. Steep and exposed, but no more complicated than climbing a staircase; we'd be atop the ridge in an hour of effort. Otherwise, we were in for a long detour around the cliff band. Or we could go back up the meadows the way we came down, continue traversing the ridge crest, and eventually get to the same spot above the cliffs. We knew the terrain; that seemed the most reasonable option. I slid down the birch and said so to the others over breakfast.

Corax groaned. "Not that I'm eager to climb those rocks either, mind you," he said. "But going backward goes against my grain, if you know what I mean."

"You are quite forward," I said drily.

"Ha ha," said Corax.

"I don't think we have a choice!" observed Koba, pointing to the ridge crest. I spun my head and saw half a dozen men leading horses, angling back and forth as they worked their way down the slope where we had descended. They proceeded slowly, pausing to study the ground, as if following tracks. I leaped to my feet and started grabbing things and stuffing them into packs and saddlebags. I didn't believe a mounted troop could have tracked us along the craggy ridge. This must be a routine scouting patrol. Maybe they saw our goat droppings, which would have made them think of food. But it didn't matter who they were; they represented a threat.

"Time to move! I don't think they know we're here yet, but they're on our trail. We've got half an hour at the most."

We quickly donned packs and herded together our companions. I directed Koba to lead them across the basin toward the cliff face, staying under the tree canopy, while I brushed old leaves over our campsite. A skilled tracker wouldn't be fooled, at least not for long, but it might slow them down. I scattered a few dead branches and trotted off to catch up with the others.

Koba and Corax had stopped within the edge of the forest; they talked and gestured toward the cliff.

"It won't be too hard," I said as I joined them. "It's not that steep and there are plenty of cracks and ledges. But we'll need to be careful getting around the rubble and loose slabs. That stuff is treacherous."

"Not that steep says the mountaineer," Corax muttered.

I caught myself on the verge of countering his banter; his sarcasm was infectious, even when ill-placed. Later, when our survival was assured, maybe then—if we had any energy left for it. I peeked around a tree and saw that the troops had completed their descent and approached the grove where we had camped. They still proceeded deliberately, without any sign of hurry. Once they entered the tree cover, they wouldn't be able to see the cliff. While they puzzled out the evidence of our camp, we could climb to safety.

As soon as the horsemen disappeared into the grove on the other side of the basin, we burst out of the trees and scrambled into the talus below the headwall. In the lead again, I picked the line of least resistance through the chaos of lithic debris. Every size of stone lay jammed together across the slope, from giant boulders to fist-sized blocks. Maneuvering through the jagged rocks required exacting foot placement; a twisted ankle would be disastrous. The goats leaped from boulder to boulder, looking back at us with curiosity as we crawled along. We had to lift the canids over a few spots where they couldn't jump. It was agonizingly slow. I kept looking back and forth between the woods and the slope ahead. Our pace made me frantic but trying to go faster increased the risk of injury, and injury would be a certain prelude to capture.

The animals seemed to have an understanding of the need for stealth and other than the human grunting, we worked our way through the obstacle course in silence. Now and then I heard the whinny of an idle horse from the other side of the basin. I imagined that the troops were inspecting the area around our campsite. Perhaps they had already sorted through my hasty camouflage and identified the combination of human, goat, and canid tracks. It could only enhance their predatory curiosity.

We emerged from the larger talus into a transition zone of pebbles and gravel scattered across the slabs at the base of the headwall. Even though it didn't provide the foot-trapping dangers of the talus, the scree was unstable and threatened to slide underfoot at every step. I envied the goats and their scrambling hooves. If they slipped, they leaped forward as if nothing happened.

With relief, I finally climbed over the worst of the scree and stood on bare granite. The rock was old and eroded, but clean enough to ascend by friction. Like a spider, I bent over and walked up the slab, hands on the rock in front of me while keeping my butt high to maximize the adherence between foot and rock. I stopped at a ledge and the goats bounced around me, happy to have human company on their preferred terrain. When it came to their turn, the canids whined. Corax crawled along behind Lykos, pushing him by the hindquarters. Yidi watched them for a minute before launching herself into a gallop and racing to my stance in her best imitation of a goat.

From the ledge, I led us to a vertical cleft in the slab. Formed like an open book, it was filled with gravel, but offered a safe route through the steepest section. Partway up this inside corner, I paused to look down to the woods a hundred yards below. The soldiers stood in a clump at the start of the talus, pointing up at us and gesturing. I counted again. Six of them. They tied their horses to the trees and started the ascent. I heard an excited cry: "Women and goats: we'll eat well tonight!" Scattered laughter chased the words across the rocks.

"Eat my shit!" yelled Corax, waving a fist.

Despite the bravado, we scrambled faster, abandoning caution. My foot slipped on the gravel, and I grabbed wildly at a handhold. Pain lanced my palm, but I held on. Levering myself to a secure stance, I noticed the blood trickling down my arm. An image flashed into my head of Koba brutalized by soldiers and I thought my heart would burst. We needed a plan. As soon as we got to the top, I'd send the others ahead while I picked off the soldiers one at a time with my bow. I saw no alternative other than killing them. If even one escaped, we'd soon have the whole squadron on our tail. So much for sneaking through the combat zone.

I climbed over the last bit of the cleft onto the top of the headwall, accompanied by the goats, who frisked around, oblivious to their position on the military menu. Corax came next, pushing Lykos ahead of him. Yidi, lean and graceful, jumped from hold to hold and turned to watch Koba as she joined us. Drenched in sweat and breathing hard, we stood together for a moment, studying each other. I saw a mixture of fear, pride, and love in their faces. I wanted to embrace them, but a cold hand squeezed my guts. Time for war.

"Okay. No discussion: you need to keep going. All of you. Head westward along the ridgeline, staying north of the crest like before. I'll catch up."

"I've heard that before," said Corax.

I pulled the bow and quiver out of my pack. "This is our best chance. Go!"

Koba looked at me with admiration. I absorbed what I could, figuring it might be the last I'd see of her. I glanced over the edge of the headwall. The soldiers had surmounted the talus and now stood on the scree slope, pausing to gauge the rest of the ascent. I turned back to my companions to shoo them on when, out of the corner of my eye, I saw the billy goat leap onto an exfoliated slab about twenty yards away. As soon as he stood on it, I heard a deep grinding noise. The slab started to move. Somehow, he'd managed to land on a fulcrum point that caused the slab to tilt, just slightly, but enough to set it in motion. The goat leaped off the slab as casually as he'd mounted it. Once the slab started to slide on the hard surface underneath, gliding on the gravel, there was no stopping it. The noise was horrendous, a hellish groaning of the earth. Koba and Corax, ignoring my directions, turned to watch as the slab picked up speed.

The rumbling and tearing of rock sounded like the whole headwall was falling apart. I stepped back from the edge, just in case. As the accelerating slab hit its first obstacle, a protruding quartz dike, the cliff itself shook like an earthquake. Rock dust blew out of cracks and several other slabs started to move. The soldiers below were frozen in place, transfixed by the noise and shaking. One of them turned to run and slipped on the gravel, tumbling head over heels into the broken talus where he came to rest and did not move. Despite his example, the others panicked and ran. Another one fell. Then the rockslide engulfed them like a tidal wave. The impact hit the talus with an explosion of volcanic noise. A brown cloud rose from the base of the cliff. A few pebbles still rattled down the slope, otherwise, an eerie silence pervaded the scene. I looked around at Koba and Corax, who stood still, mouths open and eyes wide. Cautiously, they put down their loads and walked back to see the outcome. I couldn't imagine any of the soldiers surviving all those tons of rock. As the dust settled, I saw that the slide had run into the trees, snapping over a dozen or more. I saw no sign of the horses, either, who must have been pounded to death along with their masters. A shame and I was sorry that they had such poor humans for companions.

"What in the name of blazes…" said Corax. "Did you do that?" He looked at me with awe.

I shook my head, still trembling from the shock of what happened. "Not I. It was our daring billy." I whistled and he trotted over to nuzzle my palm, licking at the dried blood. If he had any notion of what he'd done, he gave no sign of it.

We continued to stare blankly at the devastation below us. Koba put an arm around my shoulder. "Are you okay?"

"Too bad about the horses," I said.

"Yes. You're not responsible for this, you know that?"

I nodded, even though I didn't think she was right. Somehow, I must be responsible. At the very least, I brought the goat.

Corax gave the billy a hug. "A true hero! Deserves a laurel wreath, at the least. Though he'd probably just eat it. Anyway, not to put too fine a point on it, maybe we should move on? Just in case?"

"You're right," I said, snapping back to focus. "If the noise wasn't loud enough, then the dust cloud ought to draw the attention of the soldiers' camp. We're clear of pursuit for now. Let's make the best of it."

We shouldered our loads and headed to the west, dipping below the ridge crest for concealment. It was hard to predict where troops might appear next but being a silhouette would make us visible from either side. At least on the north side of the crest, we'd only be visible from the drainage below, where it was too steep and rough with brush for transporting *matériel,* and therefore unlikely to be occupied.

We were tired and hungry from the ascent of the cliff, but we agreed to get away from the area before resting. Fortunately, the ridge broadened, and we walked with ease on a meadowed terrace that paralleled the barren crest. The ridge declined gradually to a saddle, then angled up to a mounded summit about a league away. From there, perhaps we would be able to see far enough to the west to spot Koba's tower.

At the end of the saddle, we found a clump of alpine juniper dense enough to provide cover. We crawled under the bushes and collapsed on our packs. Corax pulled up his shirt so Lykos could nurse, and the sight inspired me to retrieve food and water from my pack. I passed around cheese, nuts, and the last of the wolf jerky from what seemed like years before. It had dried to the texture of leather, and it felt like chewing your shoes, but with enough gnawing, it softened to a digestible paste. We hadn't been eating enough, I thought, but given the journey, we were probably lucky to have eaten much at all. At least my leg felt okay and I was glad to be healed.

Blue skies and scattered cumulus clouds gave us confidence as we toiled up the slope toward the ridge terminus at the summit. Seeing the top and being there were two different things, though, and it seemed to take forever. At one point, looking back along the ridge, I saw a party of mounted men crossing over and traversing down toward the rockslide. They were too far away to count their numbers, which meant that they couldn't see us, either. I assumed they were soldiers; the high country had been flushed of peasants as far as I could tell. Normally, the shepherds would have already transferred their sheep, goats, and cattle, but I had seen no evidence of that.

I labored over the last ledges to the summit with the goats plodding behind. I imagined they were also tired of their packs. I dropped mine and helped them out of theirs. Free, I stood on the highest point and gazed over a broad swath of the world. On the far side of the mountain, two ridges split off, defining new courses for the gravity of water. Behind, I could see over an intervening ridge all the way back to the soldier camp. Everywhere I looked, ridges merged and divided, outlining basins and drainages. It was all simple enough if you were a bird, I supposed, soaring overhead. Or a floating dreamer. Down on the ground, it felt like a chaos of rock, heaved and folded into a frozen dance.

Corax, Koba, and the canids soon joined me. "Wow!" said Koba. "What a view! And look, isn't that the tower?"

[15]

I stared past Koba's finger as it pointed to the west. Projecting above a distant ridge, silhouetted by the setting sun, a rock spire drew the eye with its skyward thrust.

"That's your dream tower? Sure, seems about right from the map."

Corax looked into the west and groaned. "Shit, do we have to climb it?"

Koba giggled. "Only if you want to! Our goal is to enter a cave at the base."

"Remind me about the agenda," he continued, sounding tired and grumpy, "we crawl into the cave, resurrect a ten-thousand-year-old extinct mammoth, and, hmm, what? Ride it over land and sea to your place?"

"That would be great, wouldn't it?" she enthused, unaffected by the sarcasm.

"Listen," I said. "I think we should camp here for the night. The wind has slacked off, the weather looks good, and if anyone comes this way, we'll be able to see them first. There's enough grass for the goats and if you let me catch my breath, I'll hunt down a couple of ptarmigans for our four-pawed friends."

"Wow, what's that?" Koba exclaimed. This time her arm pointed overhead, into the violet sky. Sunlight reflected off the gray underwings and orange belly of a soaring bird so large it would dwarf an eagle.

"Lammergeier!" I answered. "A vulture big enough to snatch a pup." Corax looked worried. "Mostly they go for carrion," I added. Even though the bird was a thrilling sight, I found myself yawning in exhaustion. "You know, I'm just going to lay down for about ten minutes, then I'll go for a hunt."

I spread my cloak on a patch of grass, propped my head against the pack, and closed my eyes. Normally, I wasn't like this; I didn't take naps. Maybe I knew less about myself than I thought. Regardless, I didn't care enough to mull it over with the usual obsession. Instead, I just drifted away.

It was nearly dark when I awoke. The others sat quietly, eating. I heard the canids crunching on bones. "Shit," I announced. "I didn't mean to fall asleep."

"You needed it!" said Koba. "Yidi and I managed to hunt down some birds. Of course, they'd be delicious roasted, but we're just slicing thin strips and chewing them with cheese. Tastes better than it sounds!"

"Unsubstantiated opinion," said Corax.

I was embarrassed that I had failed at my self-appointed role as provider, but along with that, I felt a sense of relief that I didn't have to be the one to do all the slaughtering. The others were quite capable. It occurred to me that I had killed nothing all day. A strange thought for most people, no doubt.

"I'm going to make notches on my stick," I announced. "For each day without killing something."

At first, they both looked at me with concern, then Corax snorted. Koba scooted over, kissed the top of my head, and handed me some meat and cheese. I discovered that I was famished and glad for the bird's bloody flesh. While I slept, Corax had ground some of our barley between stones, rendering a fine-grained meal. Mixed with water and a little honey, it made a thin gruel that filled the remaining space in my guts.

After we ate, we snuggled up in an animal pile, humans in the middle with the others curled around. We stared into the sky and watched the stars reveal themselves while the last sunlight faded into the west. Koba, from the heart of our cluster, sang in her mother tongue, softly like a breeze, interrupted here and there by an "ooh!" when a meteor shot across the vault of night. Despite the tension of the day and our circumstances, I felt content. We were becoming a team, I thought. No, it was more than that. A family—with animals. But then we were all animals anyway, weren't we?

Another dream roused me from the depths of sleep. I woke smoothly, without the usual jerking or thrashing. Nonetheless, Koba was awake, staring at me. The shrinking moon rode high, once again favoring her eyes with silver accents. "Tell me," she whispered.

"Not much to tell. Just a single image, that's all that's left." I paused. "A woman with snakes for hair, like Medusa, only it wasn't Medusa, and they weren't snakes. More like… tentacles. When I stared at the face, I saw that it was my own. Awful, but deadly fascinating! Then I woke up. Not very subtle, eh?"

"Hmm," she said. "We simply must get to the sea. Maybe it's even more important than the mammoth."

"What? Why do you say that?"

"I don't know. An intuition. This kraken is calling hard for you, don't you think?"

"She's so far in my head that her limbs are pouring out of my skull. I'm starting to wonder who I am."

"You're the she-wolf. And maybe a sea-wolf as well. None of us are ever just one thing."

"I suppose not," I agreed.

"One thing I can assure you that I am not, is asleep," said Corax. "Time to stop babbling about sea and she-wolves and let this wolf mother get some beauty rest." He rolled over and threw an arm around Lykos.

Koba and I grinned. "Becoming a mother hasn't changed him, not really," I whispered.

"I heard that," he mumbled.

The next morning dawned through a light overcast, a welcome respite from the scorching high altitude sun. I tried to gently remove the head of the female goat from my chest and slide out of the pile, but she unfolded her knees and stood, ready for grazing. With the sun concealed behind the gray sky and the air dead still, the world seemed to have roused itself outside of time. I walked behind a boulder, peed, then scrambled to the top. Turning slowly around, I scanned the wild landscape. At least two ridges lay between us and Koba's tower. And that was only what I could see. Today we would descend the western ridge, traverse across a basin, and climb to a saddle over another ridge. The basin comprised an expanse of meadow and rock and offered an easy detour around the flanking mountain, but the idea of crossing the open ground made me nervous. I saw no troops ahead of us, but that guaranteed nothing. However, at the upper end of the basin, a band of pine trees spanned a large portion of our traverse. I aimed to take advantage of whatever cover it might provide.

We finished the raw meat from the evening, shouldered our loads, and set off down the ridge. The terrain required the usual attention to negotiate the endless meanders down and around outcrops, boulders, shifting rocks, and gravel. The goats made the rest of us look awkward with their sudden leaps and graceful prancing. The female showed extra roundness in her belly, but it didn't seem to slow her down. Of course, I'd emptied most of her load into the billy's saddlebags; I figured he was responsible for her condition and owed her that much. Whatever was left, I added to my pack.

With dirty faces and abraded clothing, we made our way down from the summit, looking like peasants blended to the stone and sky. Koba sang as we scrambled along, providing her latest interpretation of our progress through the land. She often found the perfect accompaniment to our movements, notes descending or rhythm shifting in time with a step or stretch.

Nearly two leagues of walking brought us to the low point of the ridge. The overcast made it hard to tell time, but it felt like early afternoon. By continuing up toward the summit, when we were level with the tree band, we could leave the ridge, angle down into the basin, and slip under the arbors. There was still no sign of troops, but I saw little reason to invite trouble by venturing into the open meadows.

Yidi growled, and I responded without looking. "Down!" We dropped to the ground, pulling the canids with us. The goats stood where they were and glared. I left them alone—they might pass for shaggy wild goats. I squirmed out of my pack and peeked over a boulder to survey the basin. A mounted patrol of around a dozen soldiers was crossing over a pass below the bald summit where we'd camped. Although half a league away, I worried that our courses would intersect. Certainly, if they saw us, they would give chase.

"Soldiers," I announced to the others, who still lay flat. "Let's move off the crest of the ridge and keep going. Hard to say where they're going, but there's no point in waiting to see if it's anywhere near here."

I donned my pack, hunched over, and with a goat under each arm, I shuffled down the northern side of the ridge. The others followed until we could all stand up and resume a normal pace. Normal? No, we forced the tempo. Anxiety pushed us along, despite the upward angle. After a quarter-hour, I asked the others to wait and crept back to the crest to check the soldiers' progress. They had reached the floor of the basin and were heading directly toward the woods.

"I'd hoped to cut off some climbing by traversing through that grove," I complained to the others when I got back.

"Well," said Koba, "maybe we'll just have to climb that mountain. I know Corax wants to!"

Corax looked at her with mock disgust, an expression which told me he'd grown quite fond of her. "Whatever," he said.

"We may have to," I agreed. "Though there are problems with that. Where the ridge blends into the mountain face, it gets steep. Not only tough going but we'd be visible. Our best option, though, for now, so let's push on."

Curiosity consumed me and after half an hour I signaled for another stop. While the others drank water, I crept back to the crest of the ridge, found a rock formation that provided cover, and peeked over. I looked directly down into the pine grove. The approaching patrol drew near the woods and I saw Duke Ganelon's standard flying on the leader's spear. The cavalry rode in a tight cluster, bouncing along with a casual air. Some of the men passed a bottle back and forth. I was surprised at that; it hardly seemed the behavior of veterans. As I evaluated the scene, I spotted more soldiers. But these were hidden in the trees, weapons drawn, waiting for the mounted patrol. An ambush. Ganelon's men reached the edge of the grove, pulled up, and dismounted. At that moment, the lurking archers stepped out of hiding and loosed a volley. I couldn't see every facet of the action, but several men and horses went down, screaming in pain. A battle cry rang out of the woods and echoed off the cliffs as a small host of infantry charged Ganelon's men, running with spears thrust forward. I spied the colors of King Blancandrin, then the two forces collided with ringing metal and dust.

I felt a tap on my leg and turned to see Koba and Corax crouched behind. "We heard the noise," she said.

"Warfare," I said. "In all its fucked-up glory. Take a peek if you want but be careful. I think this skirmish will soon be over and we don't want the victors looking for fresh targets."

We peered over the rock together. "Good God," whispered Corax.

Koba remained silent. No words could encompass the disgusting spectacle of men slaughtering each other. Five of Ganelon's soldiers remained standing, swords drawn, back-to-back in a tight circle of shields, surrounded by the crumpled bodies of horses and men, blood and death. A dozen Blancandrin warriors surrounded the survivors in a loose ring, shouting and gesturing with their weapons. The ring parted and two archers stepped forward, firing into the cluster, but the arrows clanged off the shields. I guessed that Blancandrin's forces hoped the others would surrender and everyone could avoid the messy finale. The attackers continued to shout and pound their spears on their shields, battering them with ferocity. It was a hideous sound, the strident noise of men and violence beating out the rhythms of state-sponsored carnage. Vague images floated into my head, images of burning houses, women running with children, horses trampling, and the smell of blood. I felt sick to my stomach. Suddenly, a hand stroked my back and the images faded into the recesses of memory. I looked at Koba, who offered a tight smile of comfort.

Blancandrin's troops could have swarmed the pathetic knot of survivors and finished them off, but not without sustaining losses. Nobody wanted the martyr's role, so they held them at siege while trying to scheme a resolution. They could, of course, simply wait them out. However, with victory in sight, that required patience and the day was wearing on. They tried another archery tactic, shooting arrows in a high arc to pierce the cluster from above. The calculated aim proved too challenging, and the arrows kept missing Ganelon's troops, once almost piercing one of their own men.

"I wonder when they'll think of the horses," I muttered.

"To overrun them, you mean?" asked Corax.

"Precisely."

Blancandrin's troops finally grew tired of yelling and shield-pounding. Instead, they switched to an onslaught of sharp insults. The beleaguered survivors seized these projectiles and hurled them back. Because of the quirk of sound channeling in the basin, we could hear every word. Occasionally, there was a hint of something clever, but most of it involved the predictable defamation of mothers and sisters. If a bolt of lightning removed all these men from the earth, I would not mourn.

When the war of words failed to break the stalemate, two of Blancandrin's soldiers rode out of the woods on enormous war horses. The surrounded troops groaned and tightened their formation. The horses charged, leaping over the fallen bodies, their riders wielding swords. The momentum of the heavy mounts drove them onto the spears of Ganelon's desperate men. As the horses reared in pain and were stabbed again, they crashed to the ground, crushing anyone underneath. The riders, hacking wildly in all directions, tried to leap from their steeds at the last second. One flew off and smacked into the cushion of a dead horse; the other fell under his collapsing mount and did not move. The ring of spear infantry rushed in and finished off the wounded.

We looked at each other, searching for sanity. Both Koba and Corax held their faces in the tight grimace of shock and despair. I hardly knew what I looked like; I just felt disgusted. All this over an imaginary boundary drawn on a map of mountains. If there was a point, it was hard to understand.

[16]

Locked in morbid fascination, we watched the aftermath of the battle. Yidi kept the goats out of sight on the other side of the ridge, and when Lykos slunk up to Corax and nosed his head into the philosopher's lap, Corax lulled him to sleep with pats. I still hoped to descend to the basin and cut through the trees toward the pass, even if we had to wait until dark. The overcast had lifted, and the afternoon shadows grew longer, so I figured that the victorious soldiers would soon loot their victims and ride off. They'd be keen to return to camp where they could display their prizes and brag about glory. On cue, they retrieved the horses hidden in the trees and started loading them with booty. They sifted through the various weapons, holding them up and turning them this way and that in the sunlight, discarding most but taking a few. They also pawed over the bodies and the saddlebags on the dead horses, stuffing their own pockets and bags. Laughter and jeering floated up to our perch, and I had to fight down the rage.

"I can understand why you don't want to do that mercenary thing anymore," Corax said.

"You can?" I said, surprised.

"Yes, this is shameful. You're a warrior, but you're not like those callous scum. When I first met you, I was intimidated. You were one scary woman. But since I've come to know you, you're not such a hardass. In truth, you're caring and, well, lovable."

I stared at him with an open mouth. From Corax, I'd never heard such sentiments. Yet there they were—I had a witness. "Uhh... thank you."

"Well said, Corax," added Koba. "She's much more lovable than she thinks she is."

I blushed from their compliments and let the heat trickle into my core; whatever kind of family this was becoming, I liked it.

Greed sated, Blancandrin's soldiers headed south across the basin, leading their over-burdened horses by the reins. We watched the procession of war spoils plod away, glad to see it go.

"Do your people also make war, Koba?" Corax asked.

"Rarely," she replied. "In the old times, we fought often. But things have changed. The elephants are against war, and they have taught us other ways to resolve such differences."

"What other ways?" he said.

"It depends on the nature of the conflict. Commonly, we assemble a council of matriarchs made up of an equal number from each of the parties in conflict. They convene and do not pause until they reach a consensus. It may take days, but usually, a few hours is enough. If the council cannot decide, sometimes a ritual combat of champions is staged. The combat is non-lethal, more or less, involving dancing, singing, and competitive poetry. Sometimes wrestling. Large representative crowds attend these contests. Fighting can break out between spectators, but usually, the contests are so much fun, and everyone is so exhausted by the festivities that at the end, people go home and forget about whatever made them mad."

"Sounds utopian," commented Corax, wrinkling his nose. "Pardon my skepticism, but I have a hard time imagining most groups of humans resolving differences that peacefully."

"The elephants make it work," said Koba. "They bring out the best in us, I think."

"And what about societies that don't cozy up to elephants? Surely, not everyone in your region lives like you."

"True. Most other people don't mess with us because our elephant/human alliance is very powerful. We're smart and we've got solid defenses. Still, some have ignored that and tried to make war. None during my time."

My curiosity was triggered. "Knowing you, there must be stories."

Koba shrugged. "Yes, there are stories. Later, I may sing you one, if you remind me. For now, let's just say the aggressive societies vanished."

"Vanished?" Corax and I said simultaneously.

"Poof," Koba affirmed, nodding her head and looking away. I had the impression she didn't want to talk about it.

"Time for us to vanish from here," I said, watching the last of Blancandrin's soldiers march over the far ridge.

Gathering our loads and animals, we worked our way down from the ridge crest into the basin, entering the pine grove but staying well away from the battleground. We stopped to refill our water containers at a stream flowing off the mountain, then pushed on around the flank, over the ridge, and into the next drainage.

"I'm glad you're guiding us," Koba said. "I think I'd be lost in the endless maze of ridges!"

"It's not so hard," I said, talking over my shoulder as we walked across a heather-covered slope. "Just focus on the peaks; everything flows from them. They're like giant starfish: they have ridges for fingers and the water courses down through the spaces between the digits. But travel through the mountains is never simple; you can't move in straight lines. It's always up and down and meandering along ridges and streams, in and around boulders, cliffs, and meadows. If you're fixed on a linear course, you'll never get there. The terrain teaches you patience."

"Much like life, eh?" noted Corax.

"Much," I agreed.

As the sun set, we made camp on a wide, grassy terrace. Above us soared the peak, a daunting fortress of vertical terrain. I was glad we'd been able to circumnavigate rather than climb over it. From this side, a descent appeared impossible. Beneath our perch, the mountain flank dropped into the valley in a giant's staircase of cliffs and steep meadows. Propped against a boulder, we tucked under our blankets and watched the silent shadows devour the land below.

I awoke in the middle of the night, as if on cue, with Koba's arm wrapped around my belly. She'd opened her wolfskin coat and her warm body pressed against my back. A month ago, my reaction would have been sexual. But now, I found something else in the intimacy, a simpler energy, the elemental attraction of bodies toward touch. Love in a less complicated form. Hardly ethereal, it was grounded in the physicality of our contact: her breath on my neck, the odor of dried sweat in her pores, the joy sparked by her sleepy fingers twitching on my abdomen. I had never felt this close to someone. I lay still as a mouse, not wanting to break the spell, wishing I could drown myself in the moment forever.

All too soon, I ceased luxuriating in the contact and only noticed that my arm tingled where it pressed against a rock under the ground cloth. I tried a small adjustment. As soon as I moved, she awoke, smiling her way out of sleep.

"Did you dream? I did," she said.

"Yes. The return of the tentacled Medusa. Only it wasn't me. At least, she had no human face. Instead, I saw the face of a wolf. She kissed me, all slurpy like they do. I opened my mouth and inhaled rich, animal odors. Then I woke."

"Ooh, your namesake! So now it's official! Did you like it, the kiss?"

"Yes, I did." I laughed. "But then I like the whole animal thing: the smells, the touch, the earthiness. Just who I am. Osana, apparently, in the flesh."

"Because you, Osana—I'm so excited that you've owned the name—you are an animal, too, like we all are! I get it. I dreamed I kissed someone, too, but I don't think it was you. I couldn't see who it was. The wolf?"

"An intermediary?"

"Yes. Something is bringing us closer together, don't you think? Can you feel it? And not just you and me. All of us."

"I feel it."

"I wish you had kissed me," came a sleepy rejoinder from Corax. "Either one of you."

"Are you lonely?" I asked.

"Not entirely," he said. "Not with this pup. But I've been thinking.... Now that I'm practically a woman, we could... you know. Do things. If there was any inclination for it, of course."

As he stammered out this confession, I could practically see the bloom in his cheeks, even in the darkness. It must have been difficult for him to admit such vulnerability, and I was touched by his trust. Koba held her breath, then let it out in a rush of air and sound, a soothing wave that settled over us.

"Well," I finally managed, "it's complicated, kissing. I don't only kiss women. I certainly had a mouthful of Dionysos during our last excursion, though of course, I didn't know it was him. But for me, it's not so much about *what* as it is about *who*. If you know what I mean."

"Sure, I get it. I know I'm not really a woman, or even exactly a man, either. A nothing, in truth. Plus, I'm ugly."

Koba clicked her tongue. "Oh Corax, you're not a category, you're a person! And a very fine one. Regardless of what sex you are, you're one hell of a mother—you've proved that!"

"You know," I added, "maybe you're still grieving over Diarmuid. As much as I like him, I'm beginning to think he doesn't deserve you. Why would he run off like that? I don't get it, not after all he went through to pull you out of the curse. And so what if you're not a woman or a man, not completely; that makes you special, a boundary walker, a transgressor, the person that goes back and forth and helps us understand life as a whole. My god, we need those people! And by no means are you ugly. Only the gods look like burnished statues. The rest of us carry our blemishes and deformities, inside and out. Regardless, it's all flesh."

He reached over Koba and patted my shoulder. "I don't believe a word of that fine speech but thank you."

"You're welcome. Now let's sleep if we can. Big day tomorrow, I can feel it." I had no idea what that meant. Lately, every day had been a big day.

[17]

The next morning, while squatting away from the others, I studied the land below my perch and saw a brown bear with two cubs playing in a meadow. The cubs ran up a grassy slope, tumbled down, and crashed into their mother, only to climb up and do it again. The mother stood in the same place, rooted to her job as a blocker. I felt a pang of regret. Although I had no desire to be a mother, I yearned for that kind of commitment.

We packed and negotiated the remaining terrace until it merged into a flanking ridge. The descending crest arced to a narrow pass and climbed to the next peak in the chain. Scrambling up ledges, I reached the crest of the ridge. I stared first at the imposing dome of bare rock, the ironically named Mountain of Flowers. Its walls of granite were worn smooth with the polish of time, sculpting it into a lithic breast that promised no milk. Below me, cliffs and slabs fell at least a thousand feet into another drainage, a scoop-shaped valley filled with dense forest. It was a giant's vista, dwarfing mortal ambition. Then I saw it. On the other side of the valley, far down the ridgeline, stood the rock tower, our destination.

When the others joined me, I pointed at the tower.

"Oh!" said Koba. "That's it!"

"And you know this from a dream?" asked Corax.

"Yes, that's exactly what it looked like!"

Corax shook his head. "Like I said before: as long as we don't have to climb it."

She hit him in the shoulder. "*We* don't have to do anything; I'm the one with the obligation."

"Don't mind me," Corax said quickly. "Just teasing. It's an honor to help you, if you call what I do *help*."

Koba beamed, "Of course it is!" She turned to me and delivered a hug. "Thank you, Osana, for bringing us here!"

"Don't forget that here is here, not over there, which is still a long way off. We'll have to descend into the valley and climb up the other side."

I estimated it would take most of the day to get to the tower. After an hour of climbing down the ridge, we found a safe descent into the valley. We dropped through outcrops and steep heather into a meadow along the main watercourse, a lively creek seeking its river destiny. The cascades tempted us with the promise of a bath in the tub-sized pools. We didn't bother to take off our packs, though, noticing the nearby trail with the tracks of horses. I saw where the well-worn path zigged and zagged above us to the pass. Another military supply route. Disappointed, we pushed on across the stream and started to ascend the far slope of the valley. A thousand yards above, the ridge was a daunting rock sawtooth, culminating two leagues away in the tower. There was little to be gained from climbing straight into that terrain, so I led us on a gradually ascending traverse. We were still in the open most of the time, but occasional patches of silver fir, birch, and pine provided enough concealment for rest. In a dense grove, we washed our stinky bodies at a feeder stream leaping through the moss, enduring the icy water long enough to rinse off at least one layer of grime.

As we climbed, I noticed the blooms of yellow gentian, a sign of limestone substrate. Outcrops confirmed this, and I welcomed the undulations of the weather-carved surfaces. They provided a pleasant change from the hard geometries of granite. And not that Koba needed any evidence to support her dream, but I knew that cave systems were common in limestone. With every step, we moved closer to whatever reality slept in the dream.

Yidi perked up at the sight of a hare, but our uphill toil discouraged any impulse to give chase. Instead, she stretched her neck and twitched her nose to inhale its essence.

"Look," said Corax, "Isn't that one of those lammerthings?"

I followed the direction of his arm and saw, high above, the motionless soar of the great vulture as it passed overhead. We stood still and watched it pass with a reverence due such a creature, turning to each other with smiles before resuming the trek.

We climbed higher and the vegetation dwindled in size; shrubs gave way to mat grass and delicate wildflowers like campion and maiden pink. Soon we would enter a realm completely dominated by rock, a world where every element met us with a hard surface. Already, the wind blasted the moisture from our flesh, and the sun flailed it into blisters. Desperate, we tied scarves over our heads for protection.

"Corax," I teased, "now you look like a woman, a peasant woman. If peasant women had beards, that is."

"Where I'm from, many do." Straight-faced, he turned away, knowing he'd gotten the best of me.

When I spotted a mounted caravan coming up the valley trail, even though we were a thousand feet above them, I called for us to stop until they passed. I saw no reason to advertise our presence. The goats, nonchalant as always, milled around munching the grass. Koba sat next to Yidi, curling her arm around the jackal's neck, and traded kisses. I watched them for a moment and thought of my dream. Lots of kissing in wolf families; it's just the way we are. Corax stretched out and let the hungry pup nurse. Meanwhile, out of habit, I scrutinized the caravan as best I could from the heights, cataloging numbers and types: maybe twenty pack horses, heavily loaded, led by a dozen mounted soldiers. Trailing along, four cows and a dog. Food and fuel for the war machine. I snorted in disgust. Koba looked at me with a mixture of curiosity and compassion, but I said nothing. Why bother? She'd heard it before.

When they were far enough away, I stood and hoisted my pack.

"End of idyll," I announced.

"Oh, look!" said Koba, pointing to the crags above us. I spun around to see five chamois leaping from ledge to ledge on the face of a cliff. They could have gone over or below this obstacle, but they had chosen the most difficult route.

"Intrepid creatures," I said, patting my goats. "And if it weren't for your packs, you'd be right up there with them, wouldn't you?"

We slogged along through the day until the sun dropped behind the ridge, cloaking us in welcome shadow. We were within a thousand yards of the tower. It dominated the surrounding rockscape, stabbing the sky like a weapon for murdering the gods. I couldn't take my eyes away from it as we drew closer. This led to repeated stumbling, and I finally threw down my pack and stared at the spire until the others caught up.

"We're close, but let's camp here and start fresh in the morning," I said.

Koba looked disappointed. "You know I want to go up there right this minute! But yes, that's sensible, let's stop."

That night, cold air slid down the rocks and overran our camp. We pulled on our wolfskins or whatever we had for coats and squirmed close together, summoning the available warmth from each curve of body. At this elevation, no matter how hot the daylight sun, everything froze at night and shady niches collected years of ice. On the crest of the ridge, there were bound to be snowfields. I didn't sleep well and awoke before dawn, in the wolfing hour. Koba, my trusty dream supervisor, stared at me. "Do tell," she urged.

"These things are getting weirder," I began, "but that probably doesn't surprise you. In the dream, I was right here, exactly where we're camped. I'm a little embarrassed to say that you and I were… kissing and stuff."

"Don't be embarrassed. It's all in there, isn't it, part of the unconscious? Desire, I mean."

"Yes, no avoiding it, is there?"

"Nor should you. But do continue."

"So, it was just the two of us, no one around, night, with a full moon that colored everything in silver. We were naked and wrapped close, resting in the embrace. I looked over your shoulder and saw tentacles slithering across the ground like snakes. I wanted to scream but we seemed paralyzed within our tangle. My eyes were the only thing I could move, and I used them to follow the tentacles back to the lower skirt of the tower. The whole spire looked like a sky kraken chewing on the ridge. Each tentacle moved with its own intelligence, though I'm not sure how I knew that. I needed to warn you not to look, but I couldn't do a thing. I almost fainted when the leading tentacle snaked over your head. It touched my shoulder, exactly on the spot where my tattoo begins. Instantly, the world went dark. I saw nothing. Instead, I was filled with the strangest sensation of expanding into the world, into a union with everything. Before I could understand what was happening, I woke up."

"Oh my!" she whispered. "Big Dream! You know... that kraken is stalking you with wolfy dedication."

"An interesting perspective."

I tried to get back to sleep but my head wouldn't allow it, so I slipped out of the bedding and abandoned our animal pile. A hint of gray in the east forecast the coming dawn, but my eyes were all for the tower, a dark silhouette against a field of stars. I walked to a boulder and sat; legs crossed. I stared at the spire, trying to imagine the sea beast squirming with life. I strained at my fantasy until the stars faded and the tower loomed overhead, a gray sentinel.

I drilled so far into my imagination that I lost all awareness of my surroundings. I only roused, cursing, when Koba waved a hand in front of my face. It was dawn.

"Captured, are you?" She asked.

I rubbed my eyes. "Fuck! It seems like it, doesn't it? I must be losing it."

"Or it could be that you're changing. You've been a warrior, but now you seem more like a... visionary? I wouldn't say that's a bad thing."

"Hmm. Maybe. But, old habits, you know?"

"I do. You're not the only one changing, though. We all are, even Yidi. I never saw her attach to another human as she has to you." She turned to stare at the tower. I followed her gaze to the base and its three-dimensional maze of buttresses, crags, clefts, and talus. "The cave should be up there, I think," she said. "Above that diamond-shaped snowfield. I get a strong feeling there."

"Well, let's wake the sleepy-heads and go look."

The rising sun lit the summit of the tower and illuminated it like a candle. I shivered at the sight and turned away. Anxiety yanked my guts and various muscles twitched. I needed action. I badgered Corax into ending his nursing session with Lykos so we could get going. He grumbled, as usual. I opened my mouth to cut him down but stopped when I felt a wet tongue on my hand. It was Yidi, slurping at my palm and staring up at me with big eyes. I forgot about Corax and my anxiety and kneeled, throwing my arms around the jackal. She continued licking me with the devotion of a true companion.

"She's getting better at stuff like that," observed Koba.

I nodded and felt the blood in my cheeks. In another second, I'd be crying again, so I focused on loading a small back-pack for our excursion to the tower.

"Let's pack up and leave our bags here, under some rocks. No reason to haul that stuff to the tower. We don't know what we'll find. For that matter, there's no need for the goats to come along, either. I think they'll be content to spend the day grazing."

"I'm not leaving Lykos," Corax said with a defiant edge.

"He probably wouldn't let you out of sight, anyway," I conceded.

For what it was worth, I whispered in the goats' ears that we would be back later and that they should stay close. The female nuzzled against my chest and the billy banged his head into my hip. Perhaps that indicated understanding; I was never sure with them.

We ate a hurried breakfast and started up through the talus above the meadow. Koba led, sniffing the air like a hound, searching for dream clues. Yidi followed behind, closely tailed by Lykos and Corax. I took the rear, toting our lamps, the oil flask, food, water, and my archery tackle. When I looked back at the goats, their heads were bent to the grass. I'm sure the billy was happy to spend a day without his saddlebags.

After about an hour of awkward scrambling through the talus, we arrived at the base of the diamond-shaped snowfield. The sun sat atop the eastern ridge, kindling the promise of another cloudless day. The light had yet to deliver any warmth and the snow was still hard from the night. We had our walking sticks, but when I tried to drive one into the frozen veneer, it bounced off.

"We could wait until the sun melts the surface enough to proceed, but that would be another hour or two," I said. "I suggest we continue up through the talus and hope we can traverse over the top of the snowfield. The snowfield is tempting, but we can't risk anyone slipping. Once you start to slide, you won't be able to stop until you hit rocks. Anyway, the higher we get in the talus, the longer the snow has been in the sun, so that works for us."

"I feel certain the cave is at the top of this snow," said Koba.

"So, we're not going to avoid it," said Corax.

"Maybe not," I agreed. "But let's gain some elevation on the rock and see what's next. If we have to, we'll just wait. By mid-morning, this will get mushy enough to kick steps. If I'd brought an adze, we could have chopped them well enough. Sorry, didn't think of it."

"That's okay, Osana," said Koba. "As you said, if nothing else, we'll wait."

The snowfield ran another thousand feet up the slope, so climbing straight through the rocks took us another couple of hours. We reached the base of the cliffs that flanked the tower, but we found no break in the snow. There was no way around it. However, by this time the sun had warmed the world and the edges of the snowfield dripped with trickles of water.

Waving her right arm, Koba pointed at a concavity near the base of the tower wall. "There," she said.

"There?" said Corax.

"I get what you mean," I agreed. "It looks like the angle drops back just before the wall, but from down here we can't see what's there. A place for your cave, perhaps."

"Ah," said Corax.

"I'd like to take over the lead from here, if you don't mind." No one did. "I'll kick steps as I go, and I'll make them close together. Your job is to follow in the steps. Keep your stick on the uphill side and jam it in before moving. If you slip, it should hold you." I did a test probe with my stick and watched it burrow into the snow almost half-a-foot. Enough to do the job. "If, for some reason, anyone starts to slide, don't let go of your stick no matter what. Instead, flip onto your stomach and drive the end of your stick into the snow like a brake, using the weight of your chest to push it down. Don't try a hard stop or it'll pull right out of your hands. You want to bring yourself to a gradual stop. Before the rocks. Oh, and don't wait too long to initiate the maneuver. The faster you're going, the less likely it'll work."

"You're kidding, right?" asked Corax.

"No, I'm not." I danced out a few feet onto the snow-field and threw myself down the slope. Both Corax and Koba shrieked, but I demonstrated the technique, which worked, as I hoped it would. I kicked steps over to the rocks and scrambled back up to them.

"Fucking gods don't do that again!" begged Corax. "But what about Lykos? And Yidi? They don't have sticks."

"They have something even better," I said. "Claws."

I worked my way out onto the slope. At each step, I used my boots to smash into the snow, stomping several times to make a big, level step. It was slow going, but we'd have a secure path. As predicted, the canids walked along without difficulty, sometimes using the steps, but sometimes making their own. Lykos clumsily fell over at one point and started to slide. Corax yelled in panic, but the wolf dug his claws into the snow and came to a quick halt. He then scampered back up to Corax, who praised his brilliance.

We ascended on a gradual traverse under the cliffs and up into the indentation seen by Koba. Nearing the crest of the snowfield, I saw the giant scoop in the cliff wall. Excited, I ran the last few yards, and there it was: the arched opening of a cave.

[18]

The entrance resembled the bell of a giant horn. It funneled into a circle of darkness, but even at that point, it was still big enough for an elephant or two. Tilting my head back, I strained to see beyond the lower walls of the tower. This close to the base there was no view of the summit. A bird shadow passed across the rock, gone before I could spot the outstretched wings. Below me, the valley opened to the sky, offering up the secrets of water-carved earth. No matter how small I felt in this place, it filled me with belonging.

"Holy shit," said Corax, wheezing up the last bit to join me. "It looks like the mouthpiece of the gods."

Koba followed close behind, breathing hard but with an even rhythm. I didn't know where she got her energy, but I could imagine her scaling the whole tower if she set her will to it. Yet she had no eyes for the heights, her gaze was locked on the cave entrance. She grabbed my hand and squeezed. "I can't believe we're here! Thank you, Osana!"

"And this is what you dreamed?" asked Corax, brow arched.

"Yes!" she affirmed.

The two canids, taking advantage of the halt, rolled in the snow and nipped at each other.

"It feels like we've traveled out of our world and into your dream," I said.

Corax wasn't going to let that pass. "Good grief, not the touchy-feely part again?"

I grinned at him. "We'll see what comes next. Even you may end up regurgitating your bone-blunt reality."

While we bantered, Koba walked to the opening of the cave. She looked like a mouse at the cathedral gate. Placing a palm against the polished limestone, she pressed lightly, her head cocked, and eyes closed as if listening. Corax and I rounded up the canids and joined her, careful not to disturb her concentration.

Without opening her eyes, she started to sing, softly at first, then letting her voice flow in an unrestrained cascade. The sound flew around the mouth of the cave, reverberating until she sang with her echoes. Low tones rumbled into extended strands that defied her need to breathe. Somehow, she seemed to be singing and breathing at the same time. Mixing in throaty growls, she swayed back and forth. Corax and I stared, feeling the music rolling off this young woman as she filled us with ancient intimacies of rock and the mountain. I was reminded of the songs I had heard from my combat teacher. For hours, we had practiced the acrobatics of hand-to-hand fighting, followed by hours of chanting. Always it had the same effect on me, raising chills along my skin. I wasn't much of a singer, but I was inspired and added my voice to Koba's. I felt like an angel, the way she folded my poor warbling within hers.

Maybe this went on for only a minute or two. Or it could have been longer. Finally, I stopped and Koba stopped, but the music kept going, echoing across the valley.

"Did I give us away?"

"I think if anyone heard that, it was so far outside their ken that they'd attribute it to magic or myth. Even if they wanted, it'd be hard to trace the source."

"That was beautiful," said Corax, eyes shining.

"The mountain's song," said Koba. "Rare, to hear such a thing. A blessing to sing it."

"And if you were hoping to wake a mammoth, that should do the trick," he said.

Koba stared into the cave and rocked on her feet. Her fingers twitched with eagerness. I didn't blame her; she'd traveled many leagues and waited patiently for this moment. Now we would find out the truth of her vision. I unshouldered my pack, took out the lamps, and filled them with olive oil. Shaped like palm-sized teapots, the lamps were cast from bronze. With a bit of linen stuffed in the spout, they could burn oil or animal fat, giving off the light of a large candle. I handed a lamp to Koba and one to Corax, feeling vaguely like a high priestess before the ritual. I repacked the oil and tucked my fire-starting kit in a pocket.

"No sense in lighting these till we need them," I said. "Koba, would you lead us into the mountain?"

She bowed and stepped toward the darkness with solemn grace. The rest of us followed in our customary single file. Lykos stayed as close to Corax as he could, tripping him several times. Corax didn't scold, though, and I admired his tolerance. I hesitated to point out that a true wolf mother would have nipped the pup more than once. Better to let him be his own kind of mother; I knew that much.

The passage narrowed down to a roughly circular shape about four yards in diameter. At first, enough light penetrated the tunnel for walking, though I could see that we'd soon need the lamps. When Koba stumbled over a stone, she asked for light. Using my flint, I sparked a twist of dried birch bark and lit the lamps. We walked on until the opening was a dot of light behind us. Then the passage took a turn and we moved into a realm of flickering shades, paced by our silhouettes dancing on the wall. I've never been fond of deep caves; the sensation of being enclosed always shortens my breath and tightens my nerves. Give me the vertigo of exposure any day.

Koba came to a stop, a free hand in the air in front of her like something was there. She moved the lamp up and down as if seeking a better angle of illumination.

"What is it?" I asked, coming up from the back of the line.

"There's something here. Like a wall, only I can't see it."

Extending my fingers, I felt a hard, cold surface. Yet there was nothing to see except a blackness, dark like the void of Chaos. Holding the lamp high in my right hand, I ran my free hand along the barrier as I walked across the tunnel. The barrier was uniform and polished like glass.

I looked at Corax. "This reminds me of the dark manifestations we saw with Mother Nyx. Whatever it is, it's blocked the passage."

Koba ran her palm over the surface and ventured a series of vocal tones. After several notes, she stopped and tossed her hand in frustration. "It has no voice. I'm not sure what that means; I've not seen the like. Everything in the world has a voice!"

Corax looked at each of us in turn, eyebrow raised. "Why don't you just use the door?"

"What in blazes are you talking about?"

"Right there, in the center. There's a door."

Both Koba and I raised our lamps and inspected the area he pointed out. I saw nothing.

"Right," I said, turning to face him. "Maybe, Master Hard and Fast Reality, you could explain yourself, because I don't see a damn door and I'm pretty sure Koba doesn't either."

"That's weird," he said. He stepped up to the surface and gestured with his arms. "It's this wide and this tall. It looks like a regular door, though it's mounted in a wall of polished material, maybe stone." He pawed at the area. "Funny, though. I can't seem to touch it. There's a sort of inset latch—I see it—but it eludes my touch. It's all just smooth."

"But you can see it, this door?"

"Yes!"

"I wonder why you can see it and we can't?"

"A crucial question, I'm sure," replied Corax. "You know, the kraken did something to my eyesight. I'm not sure I've completely understood what. Not only did it integrate the visual fragmentation and hallucinations, but now my eyes are keen as an eagle's."

"That's it!" said Koba. "Osana, put your lamp down and try touching the wall with your right hand!"

"Might as well—otherwise we've come a long way for nothing." If the kraken's influence gave Corax the ability to see the door, why not my own krakenized limb? Worth a try. I placed the lamp on the floor of the passage and touched the invisible wall.

"Pull up your sleeve!" Koba demanded.

I pulled my sleeve to the elbow and saw that my tattoo glowed with a bioluminescent blue. My skin tingled. I stared, fascinated, and I turned my arm to see the tattoo lit from within. Lifting my hand from the barrier, the light faded. I pushed my palm back against the wall, and it rekindled the glow, stronger than before. I looked at Koba, who grinned, then at Corax, who shook his head in disbelief.

"Okay," I said. "Where's this latch?"

Corax pointed to the spot. I slid my hand over the area; now I felt textures in the wall. There was a ridge like a jamb, then an indentation. Inserting three fingers behind a lever, I pulled. With a click, a door swung out, smooth on its hinges, and folded back against the wall. As soon as it moved, we could see the door, the wall, and the fixtures. Fashioned from marble and steel with otherworldly precision, it was unlike any architecture I'd seen.

"Who the hell built this?" I growled; I didn't know why the barrier made me angry, but it did. There was too much magic about it.

"And why?" Added Corax. We both looked at Koba.

She stepped back from the intensity of our demands and raised a palm. Her expression seemed almost guilty. "Sorry! I had no idea there was this much resistance! Whoa… why did I say that?"

"Resistance?" Corax wiggled his eyebrows. I just stood there; I didn't know what to say.

Koba fell quiet and withdrew into herself. After a long moment, her eyes opened wide, full of astonishment. "By all the gods of dirt and dogs, now I remember!"

"What? Remember what?"

"You see, after I first dreamed about the cave, I became obsessed. I badgered the elders until they told me to just go find it. No doubt, they wanted to calm me down; I can be a real nuisance. Anyway, while preparing for the journey, of course, I couldn't wait to get to the actual cave! I threw myself into lucid dream states to penetrate the mountain, or whatever remained in my psyche, recreating every image of the original dream, and pushing it, pushing it hard. I wanted to see the mammoth mother! I tried again and again, but each time something stopped me. Instead of continuing through the passage, I would freeze up and rewind back to waking. It was like I was blocking my own progress."

"Let me get this straight: are you saying that the barrier has something to do with *you*? Or you knew it was here? Or what are you saying, exactly?" A harshness crept into my voice, and I didn't want it there. Not with Koba. "Don't get me wrong, it wouldn't have mattered. I'd follow you anywhere. Or lead: whatever you want. But what does it mean?"

Koba absently petted Yidi, who rubbed against her leg. "I guess the barrier belongs to me. When I wasn't paying attention, I could have brought it into being. I mean, I don't know! It does feel familiar. There's a resonance... So yes, I'd say it's a construct of my psyche, manifest in the material world. Don't ask me how that works! What I'm trying to explain to myself is how I forgot all those lucid dream attempts. They were grueling!"

"Forgot? Repressed, more like it," said Corax. "You don't strike me as someone who accepts failure. Easier to bury it."

"That's true!" she said. "But I don't think repression is quite right. I forgot--entirely! If it was repression, it would be leaking out in all sorts of second-hand ways. But forgetting is at the heart of dreaming. Sometimes it's a sign of too much will. Certainly, I have been very willful in this whole pursuit.... I've wanted so much to bring home a great treasure for my people. Wanted too hard, perhaps. But, as Osana is showing me, the road to completion is not always direct."

"Osana?" Corax frowned.

"While I've been pursuing an obsessive vision of mammoths and mountains, the kraken is calling her to the sea—right now. We need to take her there. Whatever we find in this cave, our fates are joined to the ocean, I think. Maybe we didn't even need to come here."

"Maybe not," said Corax. "but you don't find anything if you don't follow the trail, even if you don't know where it's going. And though you'd be hard-pressed to find anyone more interested in analytical dialogue than myself, what about just going on and seeing what is here? There must be something of interest, or your psyche—assuming I believe your wild interpretation—wouldn't have walled it off. Or am I being too realistic?"

Koba laughed and I stepped back from the portal, gesturing to Corax to lead. He pushed his lamp into the opening, and I saw a continuation of the passage. No ghosts, no demons, only more of the same gloomy tunnel.

With Corax in front, we walked through the portal. I paused to jam a rock under the door, just in case. I wondered how much further we had to go into this lithic bowel system; I sensed the panic lurking in my guts. As soon as I noticed it, the anxiety expanded, feeding on my nerves. I wrestled it down with focused breathing, though I knew it wasn't gone. Without warning, Corax halted and spun to face us. His face twitched with excitement; clearly, he'd been thinking.

"Don't you see what this means?" exclaimed Corax.

"That we can go further into the darkest recesses of the mountain?" I asked.

"No, no, not that! This is a breakthrough for concrete phenomenology! Think about it: after the kraken enhanced my sight, I could see through the dross of the world, right down to the *eidos* itself. I could see the gods, not to mention Koba's neurotic door! But phenomenology isn't only about vision, it's also about touch. And here you are, enhanced with the kraken, a student of *Knowing Touch*, who is able to reach through the surface layers of the world and contact its essence! Even if it was merely Koba's psychic block, we resolved it through pure phenomenology. Do you understand the implications? Between us, we can influence how consciousness manifests in the world! I've got to start writing stuff down!"

"I'm sure that's a worthwhile endeavor," said Koba, "and you're welcome to park here and take notes, but I'm pushing on, looking for that mammoth. As you said, I'm following the trail that's in front of me."

Corax mumbled and stepped aside, but I could see that his mind was whirling around, charged with inspiration. I didn't blame him; something was happening. And that blasted kraken was at the heart of it, I was certain.

My tattoo had faded since we crossed the portal, yet it still retained a faint glow. I wouldn't mind if it stayed like that; no one else had radiant art embedded in their skin. I swung my arm and watched the arcing tracer of light. Meanwhile, Koba strode ahead, followed by a muttering Corax and the dutiful canids. I stopped playing and joined the procession of lamps.

Before long, I heard Koba's voice echoing down the passage. She sang in low tones, conjuring sensations of rumbling grief. I picked up my pace until I stood next to Corax. In the glimmering light of our lamps, we stared at Koba. She sat cross-legged in front of a giant mammal skeleton laying on its side. One of her hands rested on a curved tusk whose length was easily twice my height. The skeleton was intact, every bone in place except where they had collapsed as the connective tissue disintegrated. This, then, was the mammoth—or what was left. Both Yidi and Lykos circled the skeleton cautiously, sniffing. I had no idea what they smelled. Flesh would have been gone for millenniums; the only odors I detected were those of minerals and moisture.

While Koba rocked back and forth, singing her lumbering mammoth song, I looked around, holding my lamp high to illuminate the whole chamber. About ten yards in diameter, it had a domed ceiling. The only egress was the tunnel that brought us here. Stalactites were suspended from the ceiling near the far wall, forming stalagmites on the floor; some of them had merged into columns with undulating surface textures. Except for the skeleton, it was an empty sanctum. I didn't understand the scene at all. Why had the mammoth come here?

As I ruminated, the sound of Koba's voice tingled in my skin. Her song reverberated around the chamber and made it feel holier than any church or temple. I wondered if she was trying to sing the mammoth back to life. Only a god could do such a thing. Yet maybe she was, with her beauty, her glamours, her lively passions. Certainly, I had been fooled before. I shook my head and cursed myself for a fool. No divine explanations were necessary: she was a woman in the fullness of her power.

It appeared that Corax had moved on from his phenomenology project because he knelt and peered closely at the pile of mingled foot bones. His head hovered inches from the pile as he moved his lamp to illuminate the shadows. When he reached out to take one of the bones Koba stopped singing. "Please don't do that," she said.

He looked up with a start and withdrew his fingers. "Sorry," he muttered.

"The array is how it needs to be. The pieces have migrated past the end of life to this specific structure. What happens next is up to the slow hand of time. We can't interfere. Not even to collect a specimen."

I looked at Koba, surprised to hear her comments, which struck me as strange and even a little eerie. "Please explain," I asked.

She sat back with a sigh and Yidi trotted over to put her head in Koba's lap. "I don't know what I expected to find, exactly. That's one of the problems of working in the realm of dreams. It is real, in its own way, and entwined with the waking world. But the two realms are not the same and the correlations are never linear. Unfortunately, I'm vain enough to think that I can bounce back and forth and bring the two together. So, when my dear family members want an extinct genetic code, and I dream about a mammoth slumbering in a cave under a distant mountain, I assume that I can take my worldly body to that cave, sing the mammoth awake, and ride it home in triumph. That's my hubris. But enough of that. It's not my place to interfere with this creature's passage into the depths of time. Nor is it yours. On some level I knew this; that's probably why I blocked the passage. Now it's time to let go of the dream."

I walked to Koba and knelt behind her, wrapping my arms around her shoulders and pulling her to my chest. She dissolved into my embrace and started to cry. I remembered a lullaby of my grandmother's and hummed it softly as I stroked the bare skin of her arms. I noticed that Corax had slid away from the skeleton and rolled over on his side; Lykos had found his breast.

Usually, this activity sent Corax into a trance, but he looked at me with one brow raised and a gleam of query in his eye. I shook my head at him, and he nodded.

Koba sobbed and let me hold her, finally turning her head into my armpit so she could wipe her tears on my tunic. "Sorry," she said, with a guilty laugh. "I don't know why I did that."

"Because you knew I wouldn't mind one bit," I said.

"Holy shit," she said, "look at your tattoo!"

It glowed more intensely than before. Koba sat up and stroked my arm, her face full of wonder. "By the gods, maybe there's a way after all. Try touching the skeleton," she said. "There, on the tusk. I don't know why—call it a hunch. A message from the underworld to an errant daughter, yeah?" She giggled nervously.

After coming all this way, I'd try anything. I scooted over to the uppermost tusk, which was still fixed in the skull. Cautiously, as if it might hurt, I wrapped my right hand around the tip of the tusk. Cool and smooth in my grip, I admired the astonishing arc of ivory. Then my tattoo shifted from blue to green, the color of algae. I heard Koba's quick intake of breath while Corax exhaled "Fuck me." Lines of color appeared on the tusk above my hand, lines in motion, racing along the surface toward the skull, winding and wrapping themselves around the polished surface, interweaving patterns as they grew. When the lines converged at the skull, they bloomed into a green fuzz that spread rapidly over the bone. It looked like mold. Soon it covered the entire skeleton. I let go automatically when I felt the moist fuzz growing under my hand. The surface of the mold started to bubble and pop. The smell of fungus filled the chamber and within minutes, the bones were gone. Without a residue or remnant of its existence, the skeleton had dissolved into the essence of the world.

"What in the flame-licking fingers of Hades was that?" blurted Corax.

I slumped to the floor. "What a disaster! I'm so sorry; how could I know?"

"You couldn't know." Koba pinched her lower lip sideways between thumb and forefinger and worked it back and forth while she thought. "Obviously, there can be no revival or salvage of remains. However, I'm not displeased. Not at all. Look at your tattoo!"

It pulsed with a greenish light and the kraken design appeared to move on my arm. I held it up and peered at the intricate lines of the tattoo. It didn't feel any different.

"Is that freaking thing alive?" asked Corax.

"I don't know," I said.

"Well," said Koba, "she's alive."

"Yes, yes, of course. You know what I mean," Corax insisted.

Koba scrunched her nose at him. "I do know what you mean. But I repeat: she's alive. Therefore, the tattoo is alive."

Corax slapped his palm on the floor, startling Lykos, who stopped nursing and whined. "But does it have a life independent of Marianne... I mean Osana? That's what I mean!"

Koba repeated her lip-pinching gesture before speaking. "I'm going to say yes, but that's an intuition only."

I frowned at Koba. "So now I have the world's most amazing tattoo. But I feel terrible that we came all this way without finding that treasure for your people."

"Hmm," she said. "No matter; you've done what I asked you to do. At this point, there's nothing left for us here, though.

I think it's time to head for the ocean. The nearest port, where we can get a boat going south."

"But what about your elephants?"

"No one knows better than them how endeavors are not always successful. We'll cope. Plus, I'll be bringing back you two, a precious contribution in itself."

"Can I be a woman in your society?" asked Corax. "You know, wear dresses and jewelry—that sort of thing—without people losing their shit?"

I had to stifle an inclination to tease him, but Koba looked at him with a big, warm smile. "Oh yes. You might even be able to find a husband."

Corax's blush gave him the complexion of a bright apple. I tried, but I couldn't stifle a laugh. He took no offense and smiled at me. At that moment, his sweetness filled the chamber with its own radiance.

[19]

"From here," I said as I stood, ready to resume my role as guide, "if we stay high in the mountains and head west, we'll soon pass out of the duchy of Ganelon and into the Kingdom of the Tree, leaving behind this stupid war. Or so I hope; I doubt anyone else is foolish enough to join with Ganelon's grandiose ambitions. Once across the border, we can climb down from the mountains and eventually get to a river that flows west to the sea. A week of travel on the river will take us to Cathedral Port."

Corax nodded yet made no motion to part from his reattached orphan. But Koba was ready. She sprang to her feet, immediately joined by the alert Yidi. "The mountains are spectacular, but I'm ready to see the ocean!"

We gathered our lamps and left the chamber of the mammoth. When we came to the place of the barrier, it was gone without a trace, dissolved in the air like the skeleton. I anticipated a psychological commentary from Corax, but he said nothing. And what was there to say, anyway? It seemed obvious to me. Koba ignored the absence and cheerfully hummed as we walked through the dim passage and returned to the light of midday. At the entry, we paused, stunned in the brightness, blinking, and using our hands to shield our eyes until the world returned to its usual colors.

Taking giant steps, we strode on our heels down the now mushy snowfield and returned to our packs, but the goats were not to be seen. When I whistled, they peeked over the edge of a small outcrop, staring impassively at us as we dug food out of our packs and prepared to resume our trek. Yidi trotted up the hill to fetch them while we finished eating and tightening the loads. I took a long look at the tower, the spire of our endeavor. In the past, I might have cursed it. There was nothing to be gained from that. Instead, I let its soaring rock fill me with aspiration. Perhaps one day I would return and climb it.

I turned my gaze toward the valley. Columns of smoke rose from the forest in several pillars. "Military cooking fires, most likely," I said. "Must be time for lunch."

"Ah yes," said Corax. "The heroes need to eat. It takes a lot of nutrients to pillage and destroy. Wouldn't want them running out of energy before the killing is done."

"Exactly," I agreed. "The war machine consumes the earth; that seems to be the only reason for its existence. Anyway, let's stay well out of it by traversing high on this ridge until we can cross over into the next drainage."

Except for the labor of endless up and down, not much happened as we continued our alpine journey. Two ridges further to the west and we left behind the signs of war. We cooked our food again, enjoying the seared flesh and dripping fat of game, though it was the satisfying heft of cooked grain that we truly savored. I spooned in the plump barley and wondered what it would be like to forego meat altogether. Might not be so bad.

We reached the headwaters of a major tributary and started our descent into the broad, forested valley. I stopped at the edge of the last alpine meadow and turned to watch the group file down through the heather, following in my tracks. Just like a wolf family, I thought. We paced along together, we took care of one another, we even slept in a huddle. It didn't matter that we were different species, we were a family who chose to live like wolves.

I grinned at my companions as they joined me. I had plucked a few blossoms of maiden pink from the meadow, and I tucked them into everyone's hair, even the canids and the goats, although the goats ate them. Corax blushed with delight. Koba returned my favor, filling my braids with pinks and violets and yellow arnica. "As our guide," she said, "you should be adorned so that we can't lose sight of you."

Perhaps, when I was an infant at my mother's breast, I had felt this loved, but never in any existing memory. I studied these creatures who made up my family. We'd survived the ordeals of the mountains and the war, through our efforts and ample luck. Corax had grown darker, with a face burnt and cracked. I felt the same. Koba's brown skin remained a lustrous creamy brown, but her cheeks and lips also showed the desiccating effects of altitude. We'd quickly exhausted her supply of salves and now wore the results. Both Lykos and Yidi were lean and always hungry, yet their fur shined, and their energies never flagged. The goats, born to the mountains, showed no changes except for the burgeoning belly on the female. At that moment, I thought we were the most beautiful family an orphaned girl could hope to have, and I said a silent prayer of thanks to whatever fate brought us together. Of course, in the back of my mind, I wondered if it was fate at all.

It was a relief to leave the untampered sun and wind and walk under the canopies of beech, oak, pine, and holly, letting the shade caress us with a cool breeze. The trees here were abundant and the region was famous for them. Closer to the river, I knew we would find rafts of logs and barges of lumber heading to the port. If we could purchase a ride, instead of trudging our way to the sea, we might enjoy the pleasures of lazy sightseeing while drifting down the river.

A league into the woods, we picked up a peasant trail, which eventually brought us to a small inn. Built next to a thermal spring, it provided a healing retreat for folks willing to venture up from the towns below. We paid the fee to lodge for two nights, convinced that we would want an entire day of soaking. A vigorous old couple, Mathilde and Horace, owned the inn and agreed to house the goats in their barn. Showing true generosity, they let us rent a hut on the far side of the thermal pool and never said we couldn't keep the canids with us.

Our first business at the inn involved devouring a meal of pan-fried trout, potatoes and truffles cooked in goose fat, and, most glorious of all, bowls of fresh strawberries covered with cream. As we ate, we couldn't stop laughing and bestowing praises to the chef, the matriarch of the establishment. Wine was brought to the table repeatedly and highly touted by the owners, but mindful of Corax's history, we declined until they stopped offering it, slaking our thirst with mineral water. By the time we finished the feast, it was dark, and we were too exhausted to bathe. We walked slowly back to our cabin and fell asleep, scattered on the floor. Before long, Corax and Lykos snored in tandem.

When I awoke, it was so dark I could see nothing. Koba grabbed my shoulder. "Osana! Osana! It's okay! You're safe!"

"Ohhh…" was all I could manage. Koba embraced me, putting her hand behind my neck and pulling my head to her chest. Tears rolled out of my eyes; why, I had no idea. I could hear Koba's steady heartbeat, and it calmed my own. She stroked my back until I tingled. Half out of my mind and aroused, I reached around her to pull her torso firm against my own. Tilting my head back, I kissed her lips. Passion surged through me, and I felt wild, ready to tumble with her into the abyss. She placed her hands against my ears and firmly but gently pushed my head away.

"Let's not," I heard her whisper in the dark.

"I'm sorry," I said.

"No, it's okay. I wish I could give you what you desire. How can I deny you? After all, I do love you. But not quite like that."

"I understand. I don't know what possessed me. Well, yes, I do. I was running out of a dream, desperate to erase it, and there you were like a guardian angel. It was my selfishness, wanting to use you, take advantage of your kindness."

"Nonsense. Your impulse is natural. Don't expect me to blame you for it."

"Well, thank you for that. And for saying that you love me."

"You're a wonder. How could I not love you?" Her hand, cool to the touch, lightly caressed my forehead.

"Since I met you," I said, "I feel that I've been changing into someone else, like there's always been someone trapped inside who is finally emerging into her own life. I like this new person. She's not a killer, a murderer, a warrior, a thief, all those things I've been before. I'm not sure who the new person is, but I want to find out. I owe you for that. How could I not love *you*?"

"Pshaw," she said. "I'll take no credit. You're making the changes yourself. It's been a long time coming. And it won't be denied. You know, when we get to my home, I hope you stay with us always. Despite the differences in our family, we've learned to love each other. There are a lot of ways to do that."

"Yes, I have much to learn."

"And I have a strong intuition that you'll find someone to return your passion fully and openly. Oh yes…"

"What?" I asked, curious about her thoughts.

"It's tempting to want to set you up, but better to just let things happen on their own, don't you think?"

"I can't imagine wanting anyone else."

"You will. I'm sure of it. But what about your dream? You were crying and yelling; it was frightening. Admittedly, not enough to rouse our snoring philosopher."

"Oh god, sorry. I wish I could control it."

"No, no, you can't."

"Don't I know? Well… at first the dream seemed abstract; I floated calmly in black space. Then I realized that I was underwater and sinking. I needed to exhale, and I started to panic. My lungs were ready to explode when I felt the first tentacle, an exploratory touch on my abdomen. I twisted away and felt a second tentacle on my back. Suddenly, they clamped together, seizing me, and pulled me straight toward a kraken's mouth. Of course, it was a kraken. I shudder to recall its maw: a ring of pointed teeth behind a sharp beak, suitable for grinding flesh and bones. As I felt the teeth pierce my skull, I awoke. And thank you so much for waking me; I didn't want to experience the next part."

"No, I wouldn't either. So now the kraken has eaten you. Hold up your arm so we can see that tattoo of yours."

I did, but after glowing continuously since we left the mammoth cave, it was dark.

"Hmm," she said. "Guess it got what it wanted."

"Damn. I liked the glow."

We slept late, until the sun filtered through the trees to brighten the hut. Rolling out of the blankets, we agreed to get straight into the thermal bath. I looked intently at Koba, worried that there might be awkwardness after my advances in the night, but she seemed relaxed, humming and smiling as usual. She raised an eyebrow at me, as if she knew what I was thinking, so I mouthed a silent "thank you."

Corax was already in the pool, Lykos stretched out on the curb, dangling a paw so he could touch Corax's shoulder. The philosopher had shaved off his beard and the rest of his hair. It gave him a curious androgynous appearance.

"Look at you," I said. "Smooth as a roc's egg."

"Fuck this man thing. I've never really fit into that world, as you know. So, I'm going for it, removing the obvious masculine signs, trying to let the feminine out. I was hoping you two might help. You know, tips on clothes and such. If you don't mind." The blush on his newly naked cheeks burned brightly.

Koba and I exchanged glances. She giggled but quickly assured him. "You can count on me! We'll go shopping as soon as we can! I have extra clothes, but I'm not sure they'll flatter your figure."

I knew they wouldn't. Koba was a slender woman and although I wouldn't call Corax fat these days, he had a certain plumpness to him. I hoped he wasn't going to try to doll himself up into a hideous parody of a woman. We'd have to make sure that didn't happen. When I first met him, he wore flowing robes and jewelry. He could make that work.

"We'll help you find a look," I said carefully.

He beamed at us—no doubt relieved that we didn't scoff at him. I felt no need for that; like myself, he was rousing inner realities that had slumbered overlong.

We soaked on and off for the entire day. It was a small inn, and I was glad we had the place to ourselves; one of the rewards was plenty of attention from the owners. Shortly after we started our morning bath, they brought us robes and took away our clothes for washing. Somehow, they anticipated all our wants and needs. Mathilde or Horace would quietly appear beside the pool, holding a tray of fruit and drinks, smiling, offering a few pleasant observations before disappearing.

I remarked on this while sitting alongside the pool as Koba unraveled the remaining strands of my braids and brushed my hair.

"I paid them handsomely," she said. "We could probably stay forever." Her laugh tinkled like wind chimes.

"We are forever in your debt for this luxury," called Corax from the pool.

"Nonsense; the reverse is true," she said. "Now, my dear, should I do the same braids that you had before, or would you like something different?"

"Surprise me," I replied.

"Oh, a challenge! I'll try."

She hummed as she worked, then the humming slid into singing, and before long I realized she sang about our exploits in the mountains. Here and there she halted in mid-phrase and muttered to herself before resuming. Meanwhile, she yanked and tugged at my hair, working a different sort of magic. Hours seemed to go by, and I drifted into a daze of rumination. I let my eyes follow the curving lines of the kraken tattoo, something I'd done more times than I could remember. It always soothed me, putting me in a trance. Who did I want to be if I wasn't a warrior? I didn't know. It was a question I had ignored, though it had long lurked underneath my steel mask. Like most warriors, I'd assumed I would eventually die in combat. I wasn't afraid of that, not so much, but I was becoming interested in living. Love was good. Surrounded by love, I'd like that. But something else, too. A vocation. A philosopher, perhaps. Now there was a crazy idea, but as soon as the thought popped into my head, it took root. I burst out laughing.

"The verse wasn't *that* bad, was it?" asked Koba.

"Oh, I'm sure it was quite good. Sorry, I was lost in my head. Corax! I'm thinking of becoming a philosopher!"

During my reverie, he had crawled out of the pool and lay on a mat, nursing Lykos. "You have the head for it. Why not?"

His compliment surprised me. I was used to being met with his arguments, objections, and sarcasm, and I never thought he took me seriously. Of course, he was like that with everyone. Yet, I took it personally, thinking he saw me as a rescue machine and not much else. Perhaps I was wrong about him. Or her; we'd have to discuss the pronoun issue.

Koba finished my hair and handed me a mirror. I couldn't believe what I saw. I resembled an exotic princess. All I needed was a gown. She had formed two tight, dangling braids, one in front of each ear, fastened near the scalp with silver cuffs. The top of my head supported curved rows of thin, extremely tight braids that framed a larger braid, also cuffed, running along the median of my crown. There must have been two dozen braids in total down my back. Or they would have hung down my back, but she had bundled them into a high set ponytail. I had to move the mirror around to capture the artistry of the numerous details. I was dumbfounded. Even the goddesses of the inland sea never had such beautiful hair. That this was mine seemed miraculous.

"Do you like it?" she asked.

I said nothing, just turned, threw my arms around her, and hugged.

"I think she does," observed Corax. "And no wonder. If I had hair worth growing, I'd want the same."

After discussion with the others, I decided to trade the two goats to Mathilde and Horace in exchange for another day at the inn. Koba had plenty of funds, but the trade was an act of mercy. The goats would survive a lengthy ocean voyage, but they'd find little joy in the cramped quarters, and I felt certain they would miss their mountain meadows. With a kid to be born, they would want to teach it the ways of the crags. Our hosts were happy to take the goats, anticipating the milk. Mathilde assured me that the goats would run free, herded only by their gentle sheepdog.

During the extra day, I took the goats for a walk in the hills above the inn, romping with them, telling them how much I loved them, how much I appreciated what they had done for me, and explaining that the next part of my journey would hardly please them. I allowed myself to imagine that they understood, and maybe they did, because there was abundant nuzzling and licking of body parts. They enjoyed a game of *catch-the-braid*, where one would distract me while the other tried to nibble at one of the braid-locks hanging by my ears. An understandable temptation and I found it hard to resist myself, from time to time sticking a braid into my mouth to chew.

In clean clothes and a scrubbed body, I felt alive to the sensual world. When I wasn't romping with the goats, I gloried in the flower smells, the rich growth of summer, and the textures of everything around me. While the goats munched their way across a meadow, I lay down and released the pleasure of my skin, then fell asleep, only waking with the billy's tongue slurping across my mouth.

Reluctantly, we left the inn, promising Mathilde and Horace that we would return. We parted with hugs and kisses and a long-overdue sense of contentment. With one last farewell to the goats, we headed down the valley. When we arrived at the great river, a nearby town offered lodging and we continued to indulge in the benefits of civilization. The next morning, we purchased passage on a lumber barge headed to the sea. The captain let us rearrange some planks to make a shelter, and we covered it with a tarp to keep off rain and sun.

We idled with the current, occasionally poling through the shoals. A slow journey, but pleasant. As I had hoped, the King of the Tree had refused the calls to war, despite entreaties for alliance from both Ganelon and Blancandrin. The deckhands agreed, praising the good sense of their king. None of them expressed an interest in defining their borders in the alpine region, an area fit only for shepherds and outlaws, in their estimation. To myself, I hoped that their king could maintain this perspective, though history suggested otherwise. Kings and war were made for each other.

When I shared this thought with Corax, he agreed. "See," he said, "you've already started your career as a philosopher. And speaking of it, I don't recommend metaphysics. It's like a drug: alluring with its intricate pleasures, seductive in the notion that it will lead you to the core of all knowledge, but in the end, it's merely addictive. I suggest you specialize—and you will need a specialty—in ethics or politics. That's where the real work needs to be done."

I appreciated the sincerity of his advice. "Thank you. I will think on it. I don't know what I want to do, or even if I have anything to contribute."

"You do. I know you do. I expect you'll wield logic as accurately and sharply as your weapons. There's not much difference, really."

"You have a point!" said Koba, stifling a giggle. Corax and I groaned with feigned disgust. Inside, I felt great satisfaction at the ease of our company.

The barge stopped at every town to pick up and deliver small loads, but we finally made it, after a week, to the Cathedral Port. For some reason beyond my ken, the local God inspired architectural ambitions in his followers, and they had responded with a persistent dedication to construction. Corax pointed out that most gods had this effect on the faithful. The result in front of us was a town jammed with a variety of rather large churches. We admired their grandiosity as we wandered the streets searching for an inn that would lodge all of us, including Lykos and Yidi. People looked at the canids with wary curiosity and sometimes asked if that was a wolf or a fox, which we denied and called them dogs, pointing out that they carried packs and worked hard. No one doubted us enough to challenge the lie.

I lay down with the canids to nap in our room while Koba and Corax went shopping. When they returned, Corax had a bundle of clothes, including skirts, blouses, bangles, a necklace, and a purple silk cloak with a hood. We insisted that he show us, and fully attired, with the hood up, I thought he might pass for a woman after all. I wouldn't say he was a beauty, but he was round enough in the right places to pass. In a way, he reminded me of my old friend Isabeau, short and a little plump.

"You'll make a fine woman," I said. "Regardless of these unruly category questions—just a distraction, really—the clothes suit you."

"That's right!" agreed Koba. "Man/woman, elephant/human, jackal/wolf: these divisions can be counterproductive. We're all *becoming with* each other, whoever we were and whoever we're going to be, and love will reside in our connections, not our identities."

"Beautiful," I said. "Score one for the wordsmith!"

The next morning, we walked along the harbor quay to assess our chances of finding passage to the south. Many ships were moored or sat at anchor in the wide sweep of the river. The ocean lay a quarter of a league downstream, making the harbor a well protected stop for shipping commerce.

Canids in tow, we strolled the stone-crafted waterfront, casually inspecting our travel options. Men stared as we passed. Corax enjoyed the admiration though, to my eye, most of it was aimed at Koba. She wore her finest clothes, a dozen bangles on each arm, and newly rebraided hair woven into a complex bun. Her bare midriff rippled muscles between the curves of her torso; she looked like a goddess. If I built a cathedral, it would be to her.

"Wait," I said. "Isn't that Diarmuid?"

"What?! Where?" Corax ducked behind me and clung to my shirt while peering around my shoulder. "Oh no, you're right! What do I do?"

Diarmuid sat on a bench at the edge of the quay, in front of a gangplank attached to a small ship. He sipped from a cup and idly watched the promenade of commerce and tourists. His head revolved and he spotted us. I waved. Diarmuid stared, then slowly stood.

I pulled Corax from behind me and put my arm around him, pulling him to my side. "You're going to do what any civilized person would do. You're going to walk over and greet your friend. Now's the time to suck it up and be a woman."

As we approached, Diarmuid's smile grew larger with recognition. He grinned at me and flashed a curious eyebrow at Koba, but when Corax pulled back the hood of his cloak, Diarmuid rushed to him and picked him up in his enormous arms, twirling him with glee. Lykos, deprived of the constant contact with his nurse, barked and whined.

"Oh my, look at you," said Diarmuid as he set Corax down. "Is this the new you? I love it! And who is this?" He bent to his knees and extended his palm to Lykos, who took his time in sniffing before offering a reluctant lick. Corax crouched and hugged the wolf.

"This is my son," he announced proudly and with a defiant edge. "Lykos. He was an orphan and I adopted him. And he adopted me."

Diarmuid smooched Lykos on the nose and scratched behind his ears. "He is magnificent!" said Diarmuid. "And so are you, my dear, so are you." He kissed Corax hard, a kiss that might have gone on, except that Corax broke away, wailing and pounding his fists against Diarmuid's arms and shoulders.

"I thought I'd lost you forever, you fucker!"

Diarmuid wrapped Corax tightly in an embrace, crushing Lykos between them. "I said I'd be back, did I not? Admittedly, I was detained… I'm sorry."

Lykos squirmed out of the huddle, turned, and resolved the tension with his slobbery tongue. Three-way kisses led to laughter and tender strokes.

Hand-in-hand, Corax and Diarmuid stood and faced me. I probably looked like an idiot because my grin split the corners of my mouth. Diarmuid's eyes sparkled, and he started to speak but Corax interrupted. "Apology accepted, but we're not done with the subject. Meanwhile, let me introduce my dear friend Osana, who bears resemblance to someone you used to know."

"Yes," he teased as he extended his hand, "I seem to recall. Marianne or something, wasn't it?"

"Shut up, you fool." I leaped at him and wrapped him in a hug. When my lips brushed his ear, I whispered, "You'd better be nice to him."

He stepped back, surprised, and held me at arm's length. I thought I saw a glimmer of sadness in his eyes as he nodded.

Corax tugged Diarmuid's arm and turned him to face Koba, who had silently watched the reunion tempest. "Allow me to present a great visionary and wordsmith, Niokolo-Koba, and her stalwart companion, Yidi. Koba, this is Diarmuid, whom we might have mentioned once or twice, sometimes in a positive light."

Diarmuid took Koba's proffered hand in one of his while bending to reach the outstretched paw of Yidi with his other. "What extraordinary beauties," he said. "This one is a member of the canid family, no doubt," he nodded at Yidi, "but I'm damned if I know which branch."

"The jackal," said Koba. "I have heard much about you. This is well-met!"

"And no accident," said Diarmuid. "But let me introduce you to *my* new friend." He turned and extended an arm toward the ship moored to the quay. "This is my trusty *knarr*, which I have named *Cephalopod*. Scattered around town, I have a crew of ex-monks who can make this craft sing through the waves with a bard's grace. You'll meet them all in time because we're here to take you home."

Koba, Corax, and I exchanged glances. "We're going south," I said, mustering a firmness to stifle argument.

"Yes, that's what I meant," said Diarmuid.

I looked at him as if my eyes could drill out the truth. "Maybe you need to explain what you mean and why you're here. It's almost as if you expected us."

"I did. I've been moored here a fortnight, waiting. I heard rumors of the inland war and wondered if you had gotten tangled up in that. It's forced The Kraken Imaginary to bar the gates and shut down the training programs, the first time that's happened in ages. They've sealed themselves within the compound to wait out the tides of battle. Or so I heard via pigeon from François, who is one of the ones holed up. He said that the two of you were in the mountains as far as he knew.

"Anyway, when Fedelma and I returned to the Holy Isle, we descended back into the caverns. We stayed there for a long time, waiting for the kraken to return. Fedelma wanted more knowledge and she refused to surface without it. I thought it was obsessive, myself, and wondered if we would starve in the subterranean darkness. I didn't want to leave her to perish on her own, so I stayed, and we lived on seaweed and crustaceans from the underground bay. Eventually, the kraken came back to its lair. Just like that, one day there it was, floating quietly. Fedelma sang to it and coaxed it with her incomprehensible questions. I spent an undefined length of time attached to its tentacles as it fed me with strange chemicals. A lot of things happened that passed by like dreams. I don't how long we were down there, but when we emerged, I could sing the Language of the Deep."

"I'm jealous," I said.

"Yes, it's a great gift. It's certainly added a new dimension to sailing the ocean. Turns out, if you can understand the lingo, the open water is a bustling marketplace with commerce, music, and endless chatter. Also, I learned something else from the kraken. It made it clear to me that I needed to immediately obtain a ship and sail south to pick up a cargo. I had no mind to resist the command of a living god, so once we were back on the surface, I rounded up a small crew of like-minded acolytes among the dissident monks. They weren't all fanatics for Terminus, you know. We journeyed to the mainland and used Fedelma's apparently endless supply of money to purchase this *knarr*. And we were lucky to get it; she's a remarkable ship."

"Is Fedelma with you?" I asked.

"No, she went off on another mission. You know her; she's exhausting but apparently inexhaustible. We dropped her off at a vast megalithic site before heading south along the coast. I had no idea where we were supposed to go—just south. About three weeks ago, as we cruised far from shore, I heard a kraken singing. I leaned over the rail for a look when a tentacle slipped from the water and clamped on my arm. With it came a rush of information. Somehow, the kraken knew about your quest and knew that you would need help. Some of it is hard for me to understand. Something about a biochemical code? For tentacles?"

"Oh my god," gasped Koba. Hackles stiffened on my neck, and I felt the blood rush to my head. "It's her, it's Osana. Her dreams have been a conduit to the kraken!"

Amazed, I could only spew phrases in a tumbled staccato. "Not tentacles. Mammoth trunks. The code for mammoth trunks. For elephants. Elephants want better trunks."

"That's just it," said Diarmuid. "The kraken has a suggestion. It seeks an alliance with the wolf family—which I understood to mean you all, though I'm not sure where wolves and elephants converge—because it thinks a hybrid tentacle/trunk will better serve your needs. Apparently, the mammoth trunk is encoded in your tattoo, Marianne—I mean, Osana. Don't ask me how. The kraken is waiting for us in deep water. When we get there, it will make contact and pass additional code into the tattoo. With that accomplished, we'll sail south to your home, Koba. I'm assured that your people will be able to read the new code and benefit from it. I might have garbled some of that.

"By the way, M… Osana, I like your hair."

We all stared at Diarmuid with open mouths. Yidi sniffed at him and finally licked his hand.

"Tentacles!" said Koba. "Of course! Ingenious! More dexterous than trunks. Oh, the family will be pleased!"

[20]

We tagged along with Diarmuid as he traversed the town, seeking his crew in various establishments. We found them eating and drinking, as well as indulging in sinful pursuits usually considered out of bounds for monks. He sent them back to the *Cephalopod* to make her ready for departure in the morning. He wanted to oversee the preparations, but Corax and I insisted that he accompany us back to the inn for a full meal. He wasn't hard to convince. I was pleased to see that his reunion with Corax looked heartfelt and genuine.

Over a table loaded with plates of tender ham, artichokes in a sauce made from sheep's cheese, and cod cooked with peppers, tomatoes, and garlic, we feasted, cleansing our palates with chewy loaves of bread. We told each other the stories that needed telling, interrupting with impertinent questions and laughter. The innkeepers brought us course after course until we begged for an end to it. And then they served us fruit and local cider. Finally, it grew dark, and we made our way to bed. Corax splurged on a room for himself and Lykos, then asked Diarmuid to accompany him so he could show him something. Once the door closed, I doubt that Diarmuid emerged, but I had no way of knowing, because I collapsed into sleep under the weight of my belly.

The next morning was overcast with a light drizzle. The warm air hung still and heavy when we pushed away from the dock. The *knarr* carried two sets of oars, which propelled us downstream with the falling tide. I asked Diarmuid to put me to work but he proclaimed that the ship practically sailed itself. Still, I made him promise to recruit me if needed. Corax hung around Diarmuid, who manned the helm, and Lykos, as ever, curled at Corax's feet. The wolf had grown in our time together, fur shiny with the nutrients from Corax's milk, as improbable as that seemed. Well, he was a mammal, too.

Koba stood in the prow like a figurehead and devoured the breeze as the ship swept out of the river mouth and into the open water. I joined her and the loyal Yidi, casually putting my arm around her waist. She smiled at me, a wonderful, open-hearted smile, and she started to sing. Softly at first, a song of travel and the sea, then louder. The crew shipped oars, hoisted the sails on the single mast, and set the rigging. As they did so, they cocked their heads and listened to Koba, occasionally adding their voices to the wind-woven chant.

Eventually, Diarmuid signaled for quiet. With a deep voice, he launched a booming single tone across the water, then followed it with a rolling clatter of clicks and squeaks. It was eerie, reminding me of other times and places. Fedelma had sounded like that when she summoned the kraken in our time of desperation. It had come then, and so it came again. With no splash or breach, the giant squid slipped out of the depths, idly floating to the surface alongside the *Cephalopod*. Diarmuid motioned me to his side, and we leaned over the rail to get a better look at the formidable beast. If the ship was twenty yards in length, the kraken was longer by half. It raised one of its long feeder tentacles, waving the flat pad of its tip like the head of a viper. Diarmuid crackled and spit more sound, and the tentacle, with startling grace, drifted to me and draped itself over my right arm. As I felt the suction of its attachment, I sucked in my breath and stifled the fear that it would snatch me from the ship and stuff me in its maw as I had dreamed.

Resistance was pointless, of course, and as soon as I accepted the contact, a flood of calm coursed through my cells. I let go of my breath and welcomed the peace. I don't know how long the kraken maintained the contact, but without notice, it withdrew and sank into the sea. I watched it go, wishing that it hadn't, wondering when I might again be touched in such a way.

"By the prongs of Poseidon, look at your arm!" shouted Corax.

Originally, the tattoo had been a blackish color. In the mammoth cave, it had glowed first blue, then green with marine bioluminescence. Now it blazed in full color, a dramatic portrait in red, black, yellow, green, and blue. The colors glowed with crystalline radiance. I had become a palette of vibrant hue beyond the reach of any art I had ever seen.

I held my arm aloft and turned to the crew. They cheered; I don't know why, really, but it stirred my blood and pride. Koba's expression was golden, full of admiration and, I could see it plainly, love.

I turned to Diarmuid. "So, this is the code?"

"So she says. I have no reason to doubt it."

We turned south and navigated with the wind and the current. The rain continued, soaking us all, but no one seemed to care. We donned our cloaks and swayed with the rolling deck as we carved through the swells. Whatever lay ahead, I was ready for it.

THE END

AUTHOR BIO

The author lives with his dear wife in a creaky old house on the coast of Maine. He worked for thirty-five years as a psychotherapist specializing in family therapy and wilderness-based therapy. Before that he planted hundreds of thousands of trees in the industrial forest of the Pacific Northwest. During those years he lived off the grid, built log cabins, learned how to lay stone, and survived numerous exploits of mountaineering, rock climbing, and backcountry skiing. He is the author of two previous novels: *Rhizome* (2021) and *The Gorge of Despair*(2018), and a non-fiction work, *Mirror of Beasts: Episodes of a Reflected Ecology* (2013). Website: www.wrightjamesm.com

SOUND EFFECTS

For those interested in audio ambiance, especially concerning the kraken and its surroundings, composer Ben Stapp has released a beautiful, complex interpretation. Titled "The Imaginary Kraken," Stapp put together a powerhouse ensemble for this performance, including Stephen Haynes (cornet, flugelhorn, solo alto), Sam Newsome (soprano saxophone), Olivia De Prato (violin), Sara Schoenbeck (bassoon), Tyler J. Borden (cello), and Stapp (tuba). The music can be accessed through Stapp's Bandcamp page.

https://benstapp.bandcamp.com/album/mcsd-ch2-imaginary-kraken

Made in the USA
Las Vegas, NV
06 July 2022

51186607R00343